PERFECT SILENCE

Helen Fields studied law at the University of East Anglia, then went on to the Inns of Court School of Law in London. After completing her pupillage, she joined chambers in Middle Temple where she practised criminal and family law for thirteen years. After her second child was born, Helen left the Bar. Together with her husband David, she runs a film production company, acting as script writer and producer. The D.I. Callanach series is set in Scotland, where Helen feels most at one with the world. Helen and her husband now live in Los Angeles with their three children.

Helen loves Twitter but finds it completely addictive. She can be found at @Helen_Fields.

D0169395

By the same author

Perfect Remains
Perfect Prey
Perfect Death

HELEN FIELDS

PERFECT SILENCE

avon.

A division of HarperCollins*Publishers*
www.harpercollins.co.uk

Published by AVON
A division of HarperCollins*Publishers*
1 London Bridge Street,
London SE1 9GF

www.harpercollins.co.uk

A Paperback Original 2018

1

Copyright © Helen Fields 2018

Helen Fields asserts the moral right to
be identified as the author of this work

A catalogue record for this book is
available from the British Library

ISBN-13: 978-0-00-827517-4

This novel is entirely a work of fiction.
The names, characters and incidents portrayed in it are
the work of the author's imagination. Any resemblance to
actual persons, living or dead, events or localities is
entirely coincidental.

Set in Bembo by Palimpsest Book Production Limited,
Falkirk, Stirlingshire

Printed and bound in Great Britain by
CPI Group (UK) Ltd, Croydon CR0 4YY

All rights reserved. No part of this publication may be
reproduced, stored in a retrieval system, or transmitted,
in any form or by any means, electronic, mechanical,
photocopying, recording or otherwise, without the prior
permission of the publishers.

MIX
Paper from
responsible sources
FSC™ C007454

This book is produced from independently certified FSC™ paper
to ensure responsible forest management.

For more information visit: **www.harpercollins.co.uk/green**

Acknowledgements

When I told my editor, Helen Huthwaite, the initial idea for this book, the look on her face as I said, 'The murderer cuts the skin from their stomachs and makes dolls from it,' was all I needed to inspire me to get writing. Sometimes it only takes a single sentence. Since then, Helen has disappeared for a short while and produced beautiful, bouncing baby Rupert. So Helen, whilst I miss you, I guess I can forgive you in the circumstances (oh, and congratulations, he's just gorgeous). In her stead, Phoebe Morgan stepped in and had the unenviable task of providing structural notes and making sure the editing process ran smoothly. The more I write, the more I realise that most editors have to be diplomats above all else. Phoebe, thank you, both for the editing and for the careful handling.

Sabah Khan, I promised you this. Here goes . . . I will never, ever turn into some impossible diva who's a complete pain in the arse. Sabah, publicity perfectionist, you are always a step ahead. And, as ever, to the entire awesome and ever gorgeous Avon and HarperCollins teams who made this book with me: Rachel Faulkner-Willcocks, Molly Walker-Sharp, Alice Gordge, Victoria Oundjian, Katie Loughnane, Oli Malcolm,

Elke Desanghere, Hannah Welsh, Dominic Rigby, Anna Derkacz and Laura Daley. A special mention for the designer, Joseph Mills, at Black Sheep whose cover graphics are nothing short of stunning.

And to a few people whose support has meant a huge amount while I was writing this book. Cressida Mclaughlin, Twitter pal extraordinaire, you are one in a million. Fiona Sharp, champion of Durham and of books, you continue to throw your support behind so many writers. You are owed a debt of gratitude. To Ruth Chambers who went to Bloody Scotland with me last year, survived a potentially lethal situation and still came out laughing, I look at a map and wonder what might happen to us in any given corner of the world. To my mother – sorry I moved to California, and thanks for putting up with me whenever I venture back. To Andrea Gibson, first reader on this book (yet again), you are my heart's twin sister.

There are many, many more people to whom I owe thanks. To booksellers everywhere, but especially in Scotland, I owe you. To my new American friends who bought the books and offered me unconditional support right from the get-go. To my incredibly patient agent – Caroline Hardman – thank you for always being the voice of reason, amongst a long list of other attributes. Also Joanna Swainson and Thérèse Coen. Thank goodness for Hardman & Swainson.

And (the rest of you can skip this part) to David. Without you, this would all have been meaningless. Marry me. (Okay, we are married, but if we weren't, I'd ask you all over again.)

For Gabriel

When I look at you, I see the man you will become.
That man is kind and loyal, strong but gentle,
steadfast and principled.
He is a leader.
I am more proud than you could ever possibly know.

Chapter One

Zoey

Skin scraped stone. Gravel lodged in raw flesh. Still Zoey crawled.

Death was a ghoul in the dark, creeping up behind her one rasping footstep after another. Soon its freezing fingers would land on her shoulder. Then she would stop, but not until there was no blood left inside her. She was grateful for the pitch black of the autumn night. It meant she could not see the grotesque mess of her own body. What little strength remained in her upper arms deserted her. On her elbows, she dragged her body forward, hope still pulsing through her veins where plasma had once flowed.

Bad girl, she thought. The man had promised she would live if only she confessed. 'Bad girl,' Zoey whispered into the dirt. She did so want to survive.

Agony claimed her, planting her face down at the roadside, humbled by the devastating scale of it. Until that day, she had believed herself to be something of an expert on pain. There had been broken bones, a burst ear drum, a busted nose, but none of it had prepared her for how much torment the human body could withstand before death descended.

Picking her face up off the hard ground, she forced her unwilling right knee forward a few more inches. Someone would come, she thought. Soon, someone would come. But she'd been thinking that for days. Where were those movie-screen nick-of-time rescuers when you needed them?

Ripped from her normal life on a Sunday afternoon, it had been a week since her nightmare had begun. Time had transformed as if in a fairground mirror, bloating grotesquely with slowness as she waited pathetically for her imprisonment to end, and splintering into nothingness when the end – her end – was finally in sight.

Zoey had lain for days on a cold, hard table in low light. The cruel joke was that she had been kept fed and watered, relatively unharmed until the end. The sickness was that she had allowed herself to believe she might survive. Years of watching horror movies, of smugly knowing which victim would die and which would live, and still she had fallen into the age-old trap. She had allowed herself to believe what she was told in order to get through the next second, the next minute, the next hour without terror consuming her.

Zoey had a new perspective on fear. There was plenty she could teach the other women at the domestic abuse centre now, not that she would ever get the chance. A bolt of pain shot from her spine through to her stomach, as if her body had been pierced by a spear. The scream she let out sounded more animal than human as it bounced off the asphalt and echoed down the country road. No one was coming. With that thought came a new clarity. She hadn't been dumped at the roadside in the middle of the night to give her a chance for survival. This was her final punishment. It was her grand humbling.

Her decision wasn't hard to make.

Zoey put her face to the pillow of road and allowed one leg after the other to slide downwards until she was laid out flat. With the last of her strength she pushed herself onto her side, rolling further into the road, then gravity completed the manoeuvre onto her back, away from the trees at the verge. It didn't hurt. The good news – and the bad news, she supposed – was that all the pain had gone. All sense that her body had been torn in two had dissolved into the cool October air. If there was nothing else left, she could stare at the moon one last time. Complete dark. She wasn't within the boundaries of the city, then. No light spilled to dampen the shine of the stars. Scotland's skies were like nothing else on earth. Zoey might not have travelled much, but she never underestimated the blinding beauty of her homeland, never tired of the landscapes and architecture that had birthed endless folklore and song.

The stars had come out for her tonight. Perhaps they were doubled or trebled by the tears in her eyes, sparkling all the more through the brine, but it was a night sky to die for. She wasn't a bad girl, she thought. No point pretending any more.

'I'm good,' her lips mouthed, even if there was no sound left to escape them. Had there been enough blood in her muscles to have fuelled the movement, she would have smiled, too.

Happier times. There had been some. Early days when her mother had doted on her father, before her brother had left home. A day when her father had pretended it was their six-monthly trip to the dentist, only to take the family to a dog rescue centre. They had spent the afternoon cooing over every mutt before finding a scruffy little terrier forgotten in the last pen. They had called him Warrior, a sweet joke, although he had proved a fiercely faithful pet from that day on. Every day Zoey wondered if she would tire of walking, feeding and grooming him as she'd seen her friends grow bored of the neediness of animals they'd been given. Not so. Warrior had remained by her side from the age of five until she was twelve.

He had slept on her bed and quieted her crying when the big girl from over the road had bullied her every day for a month until her father had a quiet word with the girl's parents. Warrior had let her carry him around the house like a doll when she was sad. He sat on the doormat of their house Monday to Friday at half past three waiting for Zoey to walk in from school. It had always astounded her that dogs could tell the time. And Warrior had pressed his furry muzzle into her face as she'd cried when her father's car had been hit by a vehicle containing a man with more alcohol in his bloodstream than anyone had a right to. There had been no trip to the hospital, no long farewell, only a police officer at the door, solemn of face and softly spoken. Her mother had evaporated in grief.

Eighteen silent months later her stepfather had arrived. A year later her brother had celebrated his sixteenth birthday by signing up to join the army with their mother's consent. Zoey had hated her for it. She wondered if she would be able to find forgiveness with her last breath, but forgiveness required effort and concentration. It needed to be nourished by hope. There was none left where she was lying. Her brother's escape had been her entrapment. There was no barrier left between Zoey and her mother's new husband.

The fists her brother had tolerated until he could leave were turned to her. Her mother, a shard of broken china, said and did nothing. Perhaps she didn't care. Perhaps she was only grateful the blows did not touch her. The bruises were limited in their geography. Zoey's face remained untouched until the school summer holidays came around and then it was a free-for-all, the fear of prying teachers alleviated a while. Zoey had cried her tears into Warrior's warm fur, and shivered into his skinny but comforting frame in her bedroom at night. Until her stepfather had found the love she had for the hound too much joy for Zoey's life. He had declared himself allergic, and

4

the dog food too expensive, in spite of their large house and his good income. Letting out the odd, badly faked sneeze, he had said the dog must go.

That day had been etched in Zoey's memory like the scene from *The Wizard of Oz*, only Toto had not escaped from her stepfather's clutches to return to her. Warrior was pulled from her arms as she huddled on her bed, declaring that she would die if they took him.

'Stop making such a fuss,' her mother had said. Those five words had been a death sentence for whatever mother-daughter bond still fluttered like a fragile butterfly in the summer of Zoey's childhood. Her stepfather told her Warrior had gone to the dogs' home. He would go to a loving family better suited to him, he'd lectured. Zoey sat down that night and calculated how many days it was until her own sixteenth birthday, when she could flee as her brother had. Seven hundred and two. She had marked each one down in a notebook, ready to cross off with a red pencil as she waded through them.

What a waste of a life it had been, she thought. And the horrible truth right now was that if she could have even a tiny percentage of those bruise-filled, hate-inducing days back, she would take them with a grateful heart.

By seventeen she had been living with a college friend until the girl's mother had lost her job and couldn't feed or house Zoey any more. She had tried and failed to study and pass exams, but the constant moving between sofas was too exhausting. In the end she had given her mother one last try. Promises had been made. They were just as swiftly broken. Fists had flown once more.

At eighteen, Zoey had been wise enough to know when to cut her losses. She had walked out into the street to shout her opinion of her stepfather to the world, publicly enough that he wouldn't dare retaliate. Then she had taken herself and her plastic bag of clothes to a shelter she'd heard about. Sporting the bruises that were her passport inside the safe haven, she had settled down while she waited in the endless queue for social housing. Scars were examined. An offer to prosecute was made. Still Zoey couldn't be so cruel to her mother that she could put the man who kept a roof over her head in prison. Even if he deserved it a thousand times over.

The sky came closer as she stared at the moon. A gust of wind danced through the branches of the trees above her, scattering a sheet of golden leaves over her body. A many-legged creature skittered over her neck, but Zoey didn't mind. No point flinching now. In a while, all she would be was bug food. The road was long and straight, unadorned by regulatory white lines. She was in the countryside, then. The next car might not pass until morning. It would be an awful discovery for the poor driver, Zoey thought. Imagine starting Monday morning with such a monstrosity. That was if the car didn't run over her.

The last seven days of her life had begun with a mistake. How many times were children told not to get too close to a car asking for directions? She had been distracted, wondering what to cook for dinner as she made her way to the local supermarket in Sighthill. Zoey hadn't noticed the car following her, although she knew now that it had been. There had been no sixth sense as she'd cut through a car park between tenements. It hadn't occurred to her that the man who wanted to know how to get to the zoo might have a large knife up his sleeve, ready and waiting to poke into the side of her neck. Get into the car or bleed out in the parking lot, had been her options. She wished she'd chosen the latter in hindsight. It would all have come out the same in the end.

In the passenger seat, knife pointed into her chest, he had told her to put on handcuffs. Her hands had shaken so badly that she hadn't been able to close the locks until the fourth attempt. Just rape me, she'd thought. Just get whatever this is out of your system. Use me, then let me go. But let me live. Please let me live. I crossed so many days off in red pen. It's not fair for me to die now. The man had driven her further away, beyond the scope of roads she recognised as she lay across the rear seat. No bravery had been lacking. She'd slipped a foot under the door handle and tried to prise it open, only to find the child locks engaged. Dark windows at the rear of the vehicle had ruined her chances of waving for help. Even attempting to hit the man over the head with her bound hands had won her nothing but a contemptuous laugh and an elbow in her eye.

'Please don't kill me,' she'd said, as they'd finally pulled up into an overgrown driveway.

'I'm not going to,' he'd said. 'But you've been a bad girl.'

'What?' she'd asked, her mouth dry with fear and the shameful knowledge that her bladder had allowed its contents to run away, even while the rest of her couldn't.

'I need you to say it,' the man had said calmly. 'You've been a bad girl, haven't you?'

'You've got the wrong person,' Zoey had replied. 'I don't know who you think I am, but I'm not bad. I've never hurt anyone. If you let me go, I promise I won't say a word. I won't get you into trouble.'

'But you are a bad girl,' the man said. 'You're disrespectful. You're uncaring. You only ever think about yourself. Say it.'

'I'm not,' Zoey had cried, slinking away from him in the back seat. 'I'm not bad. You don't know me.'

At that, the man had climbed out of the front seat and opened the rear door. He was tall. His close-set eyes were such a dark shade of brown that Zoey couldn't discern pupils from irises. He smelled. As he leaned over her, grabbing a handful of hair to wrench her off the backseat, she caught the whiff of rotten matter.

'I'll do whatever you want. You can . . . you can have sex with me. I won't fight you. If you want me to be a bad girl for you then I can be. Okay? I can be whatever you want,' she had whispered, turning her face away as he pulled her to stand against him.

'You see? How many seconds did it take for you to show me exactly what you are? Say it to me,' he said.

'I'm a bad girl,' Zoey had complied, as he'd grabbed a handful of hair and marched her along the driveway towards a cluster of trees at the rear of the garden. The freedom with which he'd paraded her had signalled the end of hope. There could be no one around to notice what he was doing if he was so confident that they wouldn't be seen.

'Touching her is against the rules,' he had muttered as they walked. 'No touching. None at all.'

She had lifted her head to peer over the boundary bushes. Not a building in sight save for the one she was destined to enter. No one to hear her scream.

An owl hooted in the trees above her. Zoey had always loved owls. A snuffling sound came from the verge beyond her line of sight. It's Warrior, she thought. Warrior's coming to sit with me, and I'll be with Daddy again. Nothing to be scared of any more. The stars reflecting in her eyes went dark. Edinburgh's autumn was set to be long and cold.

Chapter Two

Detective Inspector Luc Callanach brought his car to a halt on the verge of Torduff Road. A pair of curious horses watched passively over a six-bar gate as blue flashing lights destroyed the early morning peace. Pulling a hoodie over his t-shirt, he checked the time. Five thirty in the morning. The crime scene investigators were in the process of erecting floodlights around the scene to make up for the lack of sunlight. The weak October rays wouldn't touch the ground until six thirty at the earliest. DCI Ava Turner pulled her car up behind his and climbed out in sports gear that had already seen a work out that morning.

'Do you never sleep?' he asked, as they fell into step together.

'Is it a French thing, using a question as a greeting? Because in Scotland we tend to say hello first. Surely you've been here long enough to know that by now. What do we know about the victim?' she replied, rubbing her hands together furiously.

'I haven't seen her yet,' he said, peeling off his gloves and handing them to Ava. 'Put those on, it's freezing out here. It's quite a long way up the lane. The route's long and narrow, heading south towards the reservoir, so the squad have sealed off a full mile section. Scenes of Crime are already getting started. I gather it's a single victim, young adult female.'

Ava showed a uniformed officer her identification as they ducked under yellow tape. 'The usual pathologist, Ailsa Lambert, is on leave at the moment, so who's looking after the body?' she asked.

'I am,' a man replied from behind them. 'Jonty Spurr. It's nice to finally meet you in person, DCI Turner.' He held out his hand, smiling. 'Luc, it's been a while. I would say it's good to see you again, but not under these circumstances.'

'Jonty,' Luc replied. 'What are you doing in Edinburgh?'

'Stepping in for Ailsa while she looks after her sister. Had a stroke, I gather. I have a good deputy in Aberdeen, but you're short-staffed here, so I'm on a temporary transfer. Shall we go and visit the young lady who's waiting for you?' he asked, handing them suits, boots and gloves. As they dressed, the forensics team erected an awning beneath the trees a few metres ahead of them, and the sound of a generator sent birds flying from the nearby woods. 'Sorry about that, seems incredibly loud out here,' Jonty said. 'The body is getting covered in leaves and water droplets, hence the tent. You'll need to keep your distance. There's a substantial area covered in blood and we don't want to disturb the trail. Have either of you had breakfast yet?'

'Only coffee,' Ava said. 'Why?'

'I've had two of my people lose their stomach contents so far this morning. We don't need any more distractions,' Jonty replied.

'We've both been doing this long enough to keep our lids on,' Ava said. 'But thanks for the warning.'

They trod slowly forward on the white matting path beneath the canvas roof, avoiding stepping to either side and contaminating whatever articles of evidence might be lying there. Dr Spurr went ahead of them and hunkered down next to a small mound that was covered by a forensics sheet. He lifted it slowly, as if trying not to wake a baby.

Callanach looked away. Ava covered her mouth with a hand. There were crime scenes, and then there was carnage. Whatever had happened to the young woman on the ground fell firmly into the latter category.

'Luc, call the station. Ask them if they have a young woman listed as missing in the last forty-eight hours. Just say between sixteen and twenty, long brown hair, red-brown dress. No other description for now,' Ava instructed Callanach.

'It's not,' Jonty said.

'Not what?' Callanach asked.

'It's not a coloured dress,' Jonty replied. He slid a gloved hand under the girl's left shoulder to raise her a few inches off the floor, exposing a small section of the dress behind her shoulder blade. The bright white patch of cotton glowed in the floodlights.

Ava took in a sharp breath. 'It's a white dress?' she muttered. 'How the fuck did she . . .'

Jonty answered the question by raising the hem up over the girl's thighs and abdomen. A massive section of skin had been cut from her stomach, the raw sections of flesh curling back where her body had begun to dry out. Blood was crusted over the whole of her lower half, washing down her legs and her bare feet.

'That's not all,' Jonty said. 'There's another equally large section of skin cut from her back. Her underwear was missing when we found her. I was preserving the scene for you to see it first-hand.' He stood up, covering the girl again as he pointed along the road in the opposite direction from which they'd come. 'She crawled several metres along the road. There are pieces of skin in the tarmac, which we believe came from her hands and knees. The bleeding increased as she crawled. We've

11

found two large wads of wound packing that must have dropped away from her, both completely blood-soaked. Whoever left her here gave medical assistance initially, then abandoned her to die where she almost certainly wouldn't have been found until it was too late.'

They stood silently, contemplating the scene for a few moments. A tractor could be heard starting up in the distance. The wind rushed noisily over the expansive reservoir to the south. It was a place of extraordinary beauty, just a few miles south of the Edinburgh City Bypass, and now it was home to a ghost.

'She was on her back,' Ava said. 'You think she collapsed from her knees and rolled?'

'No, she'd have stayed face up if she'd simply collapsed. There's not enough of a gradient for gravity to have moved her. I believe she stopped crawling and decided to rest. Or gave up hope. She'd have been delirious with blood loss and shock by then. Can I move the body now? I don't want it to degrade any further before I start the post-mortem,' Jonty said.

'One more look,' Ava said. 'You were right about the breakfast, Jonty. Every time I think my years in the force have hardened me, something new comes along.'

'Peace and justice. It's all we can do for them at this stage. I've some documents to sign. You can take another look but don't disturb her and stay on the mats, okay?' Jonty said.

Ava stepped forward to the girl and knelt down next to her, peeling the sheet back once more to reveal her face and arms. 'Her right arm's almost semi-circular on the ground. It's as if she was holding something,' Callanach said.

'It might have just fallen that way,' Ava said. She moved to the end of the body and lifted one foot. 'I can't see any injuries beneath the dried blood. No obvious bruising. I don't think she walked very far. She was dropped off close by.'

12

'It wasn't raining last night, and there'd have been no reason for the vehicle to have pulled onto the verge if there were no other cars around. We won't get tyre tracks,' Callanach said.

'Agreed. We don't know which way it was going so CCTV at the nearest junctions will be a needle in a haystack. There are a few houses dotted along the road, though,' Ava said. 'Get uniformed officers doing a house to house. Any vehicles seen or heard late at night. Ask if local landowners mind us searching their premises. Anyone who says no, do a background check.'

Jonty Spurr rejoined them, stripping off his gloves as a photographer stepped in to capture the scene before the body was prepared for transfer to the mortuary.

'Dr Spurr, any possibility this was an operation gone wrong? The cotton wool packing, the incisions. And dumping the body so publicly. Whoever did this wanted her to be found,' Ava said.

'It would have been obvious that the blood loss would have been beyond her capacity to recover from. There's no medical reason for what happened here. The wound packs might have been applied to simply keep her alive longer,' Jonty said.

'You're suggesting that treating the wounds was actually a way to prolong the agony?' Callanach asked.

'My remit is science, not speculation. It's a wonder she survived as long as she did. She was tough and brave. To have crawled at all, even just a few metres was, in the circumstances, remarkable,' Jonty said.

'How long since she died, do you think?' Ava asked him.

'Three to four hours. Apparently, she was found by a farm-hand who was on his way to let out some cattle further down the lane. I saw him talking to the first officers on the scene. Given that he's being treated for shock himself, I'd say he's nothing to do with it. The pathology aside, it took someone with a strong stomach to take a knife to this girl, then to turn her over and do it again. It's not like stabbing in anger. It takes

13

medically trained professionals a long time to prepare themselves to make major incisions.'

'A psychopath, then,' Ava said. 'Or someone completely inured to the extremes of violence and bloodshed.'

'Someone you shouldn't underestimate, I think I'd say,' Jonty confirmed. 'We're moving her now. I'll perform a post-mortem today but it'll take some time. Join me first thing tomorrow morning for some answers.'

They said their goodbyes. Luc and Ava stood watching as the corpse was moved from the ground into a body bag and onto a stretcher. The ground where the young woman had died was crimson in the centre and black at the edges. With the body removed, the trail she had crawled was more obvious.

'She didn't get very far at all,' Callanach said. 'My guess is that when she was left here, the perpetrator knew she wouldn't last much longer. I also think they drove away south west, towards the reservoir.'

'Why?' Ava asked.

'Because she started crawling towards Edinburgh. There's no way she'd have crawled in the same direction the vehicle went. You move away from your attackers as fast as you can. Gut instinct makes you go in the opposite direction to where they're going.'

'Do you think it was someone she knew?' Ava asked him.

'I'm not sure which would be more dangerous, having the capacity to do that to a total stranger or being able to look into the eyes of someone you know and cutting into them. It's like she was attacked by an animal. I've never seen that much missing skin,' he said. 'Let's walk down the road a bit, see if there's anything that's been missed.'

They walked quietly for a hundred yards, knowing each other's stride, finding some calm in the greenery. 'I hate this job,' Ava said.

'No, you don't,' Callanach responded, 'you just hate why it's necessary. You need to remind yourself that the decent people outnumber sick bastards like this one by the millions. If we weren't here, how many more bodies would end up mutilated at the side of the road?'

'Do you never think about going back to Lyon? I know what happened to you there was bad, but time has passed. You could rejoin Interpol, your name has been cleared. You can't tell me you haven't thought about it,' Ava said, turning around to stare back up the lane at the lights and the parade of white-clad personnel walking methodically to and fro.

'You never clear your name after a rape allegation,' Luc said. 'It's like trying to get ink out of a white shirt. I'm settled here now. I wouldn't go so far as to say that Scotland feels like home, but I'm comfortable. If we could just replace all of Edinburgh's fast food joints with delicatessens it would be better.'

'You're never going to forgive us for our food, are you?'

'If you expect me to accept atrocities such as haggis, porridge, and what I believe you call mince and tatties, then no.' Callanach's French accent accentuated the words as if they were exotic foreign diseases.

Ava smiled. 'This route becomes more track than road as it goes past the two reservoirs, but it's stony. The one time I wish the ground was soft, and we've had virtually no rain for a week. You're right. No fresh tyre marks. The vehicle will have her blood in it, though. We have to find the person who did this, and quickly, before they have a chance to destroy the evidence.'

'Which is what they'll be doing right now,' Callanach said. 'Let's get back to the station. I'll brief the squad while you sort out the resources we'll need.' His phone rang as they were turning around to go back. 'Yes, that's right. Get hold of next of kin. Ask for a photo first. We can't have anyone seeing this body if we're wrong about the identity. Thanks.' He rang off.

'A young woman was reported missing last Sunday who fits the general description. DC Tripp is chasing an up-to-date photo.'

'I didn't hear about that. Any reason why the missing person report wasn't widely circulated?' Ava asked.

'She was living in a domestic abuse shelter. Women come and go quite regularly. I guess sometimes they just get sick of the lack of privacy, or go back to their previous situations, and many don't want to be found. Police at the time took a statement from the shelter but there was no evidence of foul play, so they haven't done much about it since.'

'Did you get a name?' Ava asked.

'Zoey Cole. Eighteen years old. Caucasian, brown hair, hazel eyes. Sounds like our girl.'

'It does,' Ava said, picking up the pace as they walked. 'The question is, how did she come to be living in a women's shelter in the first place? Maybe whoever made Zoey scared enough to move there might have found out where she was and decided to pay her a visit.'

'I'd be surprised if this stems from domestic violence. It would be the most extreme evolution of offending I've ever seen,' Callanach said.

'People can suddenly erupt and reveal a completely hidden side to their nature. You only went on one date with Astrid and look what happened at the end of that. She was sufficiently fixated to accuse you of rape and to hurt herself dramatically to back it up. Can you imagine how much more obsessed and deranged she'd have been if you were in a relationship with her for six months, or two years? Human beings don't have any limits when they're broken. It's the damage you can't see on the surface that's the most dangerous.'

Chapter Three

The Major Investigation Team's incident room was empty. Detective Constable Christie Salter stood in the doorway, coffee cup in one hand, box of doughnuts in the other. One step forward would take her back into a world she'd left months earlier, when a hostage situation had gone terribly wrong and she'd been stabbed in the abdomen with a shard of broken pottery. Salter had lost her baby. Her sanity, too, for a short time, if she was completely honest. Coming back to work hadn't been a choice. If she'd spent one more minute at home, staring at the wallpaper and flicking through the TV channels, the damage to her mental health might have slid up the scale from temporary to irreparable.

'I hope they're all for me. I'm not sharing my trans fats with the rest of the greedy bastards when they get back,' DS Lively said behind her.

Salter smiled at the blank room she'd been facing, then made the effort to straighten her face before turning around.

'Sarge, you're such a lardy bugger anyway, I'm sure eating another twenty chocolate-iced custard-filled cakes won't make a dent. Knock yourself out.' She offered the box in his direction.

'Glad to see your wee holiday hasn't blunted your tongue. You recall that as your sergeant, you still have to make me coffee and shine my boots every morning,' Lively said, grabbing a week's worth of calories and taking a bite.

'The way I heard it, Max Tripp has taken his sergeant's exams and is waiting for the results. I'm guessing it's him I'll be making coffee for pretty soon. I'm sure you'll still have plenty of your usual goons willing to fetch and carry for you,' Salter grinned. 'Speaking of which, where are they all?'

'Got a call to a body found on the Torduff Road. They'll not be back for a few hours yet. Starting house to house enquiries, about now I reckon. DCI Turner and the underwear model I get to call sir are both down there,' Lively said, wiping his mouth with the back of his hand.

'You and DI Callanach still sharing the love, are you? I thought you might have got over your infatuation by now. Maybe I should get down there. If they're kicking off a new murder investigation, they'll need every pair of hands they can get.'

'I think they'll need backup here. You know how it gets. The phone'll start ringing off the hook with leads and enquiries. Pretty soon the whole place will be chaos. They've plenty of officers down there for now,' Lively said.

'That's ridiculous. We can get any number of people in here to answer the phones. I'll take a car from the pool. Traffic's not too bad this morning. It'll only take me . . .'

'Christie,' Lively said. 'It's a bad one. Young woman with her stomach messed up. I really don't think . . .'

'Stop,' Salter said. 'You'll call me Salter, just like you always did. And we don't talk about what happened. If I wanted to do that I'd have stayed at home with my family popping round twice a day to check on me. This is work. I need it. So don't patronise me and don't try to wrap me up. It's too late for that.'

The phone rang, sparing Lively a response. He picked up a pen and began scribbling details on a notepad, muttering a stream of affirmatives as he wrote.

'Give us ten minutes,' he said, before putting the receiver down. 'Get your coat then, Salter. We're off into town.'

Crichton's Close provided pedestrian access onto the Royal Mile and was a regular night stop for the homeless, courtesy of high walls at either side stopping the wind, and providing some shelter from the rain. As a no through route for traffic, it had the added bonus of excluding passing police vehicles. Only the drunks or unwitting tourists passed that way in the small hours. Unless you were looking for trouble. Lively and Salter took the car up Gentle's Entry and parked it in Bakehouse Close, walking the few metres round the corner to where uniformed police officers and paramedics were doing their best to persuade a man to get medical help.

'Who is he?' Lively asked an officer as they approached.

'Name's Mikey Parsons. Long-term homeless, known drug user. We see him fairly regularly on the beat. Never had any trouble with him except for public pissing, and then he moves on without getting nasty.'

'How's it going, Mr Parsons?' Salter asked, walking up to him.

The man swung round, trying to face her but missing by ninety degrees, staring instead at a poster for a gig that was hanging off the opposite wall. The whites of his eyes were an angry shade of red and his mouth was hanging open. Arms swinging at his sides, he swayed but remained standing. A paramedic took another step towards him with wipes, aiming for Mikey's left cheek. As he mopped the dried blood away, the three slashes on his cheek became clearer.

'That's just fuckin' great,' Lively muttered. 'We've got a deranged Zorro impersonator in the city.'

The top line of the Z ran from the bridge of his nose to the outer edge of his cheekbone, with the diagonal following down to the corner of his mouth and the final line reaching right back to his ear lobe.

'Lucky they didn't cut his neck,' the paramedic said. 'Mr Parsons, are you in any pain?' he asked loudly.

Parsons groaned. His face was sweaty in spite of the chill and he seemed oblivious to his wounds.

'What's he taken, do you think?' Salter asked.

'I'd put my money on Spice,' the paramedic said, sticking butterfly plasters every few millimetres along the slash to hold the sides together. 'We're seeing an epidemic of it at the moment. The accident and emergency room is stretched to capacity and it's freaking members of the public out seeing people standing in the middle of the street like zombies. The drug causes hallucinations and psychosis. Total oblivion like this is common. It can render the user completely incapable of normal communication. If Mr Parsons is still in there, he may well be in agony. No sure way of knowing.'

'Who notified you?' Lively asked.

'A shopkeeper walked past this morning, saw the blood, called it in. We didn't realise what had happened until we got a proper look at his face. He was trying to hide his head in a bin when we first arrived.'

'Well, it's not accidental,' Salter said. 'What do you think, Sarge? Row with his dealer, unpaid debt, or a fight gone wrong?'

Lively took out his phone and got a few close-up shots of the wound as the paramedic finished up, then added a few more of the general area for good measure.

'Not a fight,' Lively said. 'This is more of a branding. The lines have stayed pretty neatly on one side of his face and they're quite straight. It was planned. Any blood on the ground around here?' he shouted across to one of the uniformed officers.

'Over there, by the pile of bin bags,' came the response. 'We think that's Mikey's stuff.'

Salter and Lively walked across to the mound of stinking clothes and cardboard that constituted Mikey Parsons' home. An arrow of spattered blood decorated the external wall of a shop, a metre from the ground. Lively completed his portfolio of pictures with the images.

'If he'd been sitting down on the cardboard there, the spatters would have been level with his cheek,' Lively said. 'Given that he'd have been hard pressed to have rolled a joint with half his skin hanging off, I'm going to put my money on him being well and truly stoned before he was attacked.'

'You think someone just walked up to him while he was out of it, and decided to slash his face open?' Salter asked. 'Could it be another Spice user? If the drug causes psychosis, it's possible they looked at Mikey here but saw something completely different.'

'I strongly suspect that we'll never find out,' Lively said. 'Mr Parsons here doesn't seem to want to cooperate or go to the hospital, and he's sure as hell not going to be giving any coherent statement to us about it. Have you done all you can?' he asked the paramedics.

'Everything we can out here. Ideally we'd have taken him to the hospital to clean the wound, administer antibiotics and stitch him up properly, but he won't get in the ambulance and we're not going to try restraining him.'

'Fair enough,' Lively said. 'Salter, I hope you're not wearing your best frock. You and I are about to get Mr Parsons here into the back of the squad car. Could we borrow a couple of pairs of gloves?'

'Be my guest,' the paramedic replied, handing over scrunched-up rubbery balls to each of them. 'Good luck.'

They slipped the gloves on. Parsons remained in place, staring off into the distance, his mouth opening and closing as if trying unsuccessfully to speak. Salter went to one side of him and Lively took the other, guiding him slowly towards their car. It took some time to get him to fold his body into the right position to get in the rear seat, but eventually he was in. Salter closed the door and sighed.

'It's almost as if you planned this for me on my first morning back to put me off,' Salter said.

'Did it only take eight months for you to forget how glamorous and fun our job is?' Lively replied. 'I'm driving. You watch our guest.'

Salter checked out Mikey Parsons in the mirror. His head was bouncing up and down like a nodding dog with the movement of the car, and the white butterfly strips over his dark red wound resembled ghoulish Halloween face painting. He looked up suddenly, his pupils contracting as his eyes met Salter's.

'Hey, Mikey,' she said. 'Do you know where you are?'

He let out a long, whistling breath. The sourness from his mouth wafted through the vehicle. Fighting his seatbelt, Mikey threw himself forward to bash his head against the dividing screen at the rear of Lively's seat, then thrust backwards to slam the back of his skull into his headrest. Back and forwards he went, hammering his head harder each time.

'Stop the car,' Salter said. 'We've got to do something before he knocks himself out.'

'No, we're getting back to the station. If he's unconscious by then, we'll call an ambulance. I'm not touching him while he's like that and neither are you. We've no idea what he's capable of with that crap in his system. An officer got bitten last month during an arrest.'

'How much do you know about this Spice drug?' Salter asked.

'They market it as an alternative to cannabis, only it's

completely synthetic. Supposed to work like cannabinoids but the effects are more like LSD from what I've seen. Each brand is made using different chemicals so users don't really know what they're smoking.'

'Where are they getting it?' she asked, trying to ignore the thumping from the backseat.

'Everywhere. It's relatively cheap to produce, they package the stuff so that it looks professional, and it's less risky than trying to import heroin or cocaine. We won't get this stuff off the streets for a decade. Unless the anti-Zorro scares the crap out of users so badly, they stop.'

'Come on Sarge, don't go calling whoever did this the anti-Zorro. The press gets a whiff of that and it'll be everywhere.'

Mikey turned his head to the side for one last monumental smash against his headrest and split all the butterfly stitches open. Blood began to pour down his cheek in horror movie tears fashion, and Salter raised her eyebrows at Lively.

'Whoever's in charge of the carpool these days isn't going to like us very much,' she said.

They got him into the station fairly easily until the desk sergeant stopped them. 'You're not expecting me to process him, are you? He's straight for the hospital and you know it.'

'He's refused medical assistance, but he's drunk and incapable, needs a few hours in the cells. We've got to try to take a statement from him when he's slept it off,' Lively said.

'Stop the bleeding,' the desk sergeant said. 'Clean him up. If I'm satisfied, I'll book him in. Good to see you back, Salter,' he added.

Lively nodded at her. 'You go upstairs and report in with the boss. Someone should be back by now. Update the team with what we've got. I'll be up as soon as this mess is sorted. And have a cup of tea. That's enough for your first morning back.'

23

'Right you are, sir,' Salter said, heading for the stairs.

'Oh yeah, not arguing with me now. Let me do all the dirty work,' Lively mumbled.

'Stubborn and stupid are two different things, Sarge,' Salter grinned as she disappeared.

As soon as she entered the upper corridor, the buzz from the incident room electrified the air. Ava Turner appeared from the opposite end of the hallway and stopped, a smile spreading slowly across her face as Salter walked closer.

'Detective Constable Salter, good to have you back with MIT,' Ava said.

'Good to be back, ma'am,' Salter said. 'There's a murder, I gather.'

'Looks like it,' Ava said. 'I'm not warning you off any particular duties. You've been declared fit to return and that's good enough for me. Just communicate with me if you need anything. Agreed?'

'Agreed,' Salter said. 'And congratulations on the promotion ma'am, even if I am a few months late saying it.'

'I'm not sure congratulations is the right word. Feels more like a punishment most days. Where have you and DS Lively been this morning?'

'Someone slashed the letter Z into the face of a homeless drug addict. He was found this morning covered in blood. No witnesses, no leads. The victim's taken a drug – it's sufficiently strong that he's still unaware of what's happened to him. Lively's downstairs now booking him in as a drunk and incapable, in the hope that we'll be able to take a statement in a few hours.'

'Spice?' Ava asked.

'That's Lively's theory. Paramedics seemed to agree,' Salter said.

'The city's riddled with it,' Ava said. 'Let the drug squad know. If there's a new batch on the streets that's turning users violent, they ought to start checking it out.'

'Salter,' Callanach said, walking out of the incident room to join them. He hugged her and Salter blushed.

'Sir,' she said. 'Nice to see you again, but I'd better get going. I need to write up my notes, and DS Lively'll go off on one if there's no coffee ready when he comes up from the cells.' She hustled away into the kitchenette.

'Wow,' Ava said, turning to Callanach. 'Are you okay? That's the most emotional I've seen you since . . . ever, actually.'

'You're funny,' Callanach said. 'Should she be back so soon, though? After all she went through and the loss of the baby.'

'Give her time,' Ava said. 'I suspect she's pressing the bruise to see how much it hurts. Keep an eye on her. Let me know if you think there's a problem. Salter's a good detective. We need officers like her.'

DC Max Tripp poked his head out of the incident room and called to them. 'Ma'am, we've got some background on Zoey Cole and her stepfather, Christopher Myers. You're going to want to hear this straight away,' he said.

Chapter Four

Zoey Cole lay on a trolley beneath a sheet. Ava and Callanach stood silently, waiting for Jonty Spurr to join them. A worker from the domestic violence shelter had provided an up-to-date photo, and attended the previous evening to positively identify the body.

'Good morning to you both,' Jonty said, snapping on gloves as he entered. 'Public records have Zoey as eighteen years of age and I would concur with that. In addition, I spoke to the shelter worker who attended yesterday.' Jonty flicked through his notes. 'Here we are, a Miss Sandra Tilly. She explained that Zoey had complained of pain in her hands from badly reset finger fractures on her left hand. I found three old breaks, I suspect from two separate incidents in time. In addition, four healed rib fractures and a probable broken nose, although that one is always harder to be sure about.'

'Makes sense,' Ava said. 'Zoey was living at the shelter having left home. She claimed that her stepfather had been violent to her over a number of years. Mother was aware but did nothing to correct the situation.'

'There was never a police investigation?' Jonty asked.

'No. Zoey didn't want to press charges because her mother was still living there,' Ava said.

'MIT hasn't spoken to the stepfather or mother in person yet,' Callanach added. 'Uniforms went round yesterday and notified them of the death. That was before we had the full story. We wanted to get the facts from you before following up with a formal interview of the stepfather.'

'You may want to hold fire on that. I've been making my own enquiries overnight, but they've come up blank so far. Let me show you what we're dealing with.'

Jonty removed the sheet to reveal Zoey's naked body. The skin on her abdomen that had peeled back and lost its form had been laid back down and repositioned to reveal an outline.

'What the fuck?' Ava said, stepping closer to look directly down onto it.

'My exact words when I began laying the skin flat,' Jonty said.

Dried blood around the incision added a freakish outline to the miniature figure cut from Zoey's skin. A head shape had been taken from the area between her ribcages. Tiny arms spanned out to her sides and the legs extended down towards the top of Zoey's thighs.

'Was she pregnant?' Callanach asked. 'Is this supposed to represent a baby?'

'That was the first thing I checked when I identified the shape, but she wasn't pregnant at death, nor has she ever given birth. That doesn't exclude the possibility that she hadn't ever conceived and decided on a termination.'

'In which case we might be looking for a boyfriend. Someone who resented her decision,' Ava said. 'You said you were doing some research overnight, Jonty. What were you looking for?'

'Other similar cases. I found nothing, I'm pleased to say. In twenty-five years, I've not come across anything so outrageous.

27

Will you help me turn Zoey over, Luc?' Callanach stepped forward and assisted. 'It's exactly the same shape, cut out of the skin in her back. That would have been a more difficult procedure as the skin is tighter and there is less loose flesh.'

'Tell me she wasn't conscious when this was done,' Ava said.

'There's good and bad news on that front,' Jonty said, pointing at a few places along the cut line. 'I believe she was conscious, although the likelihood is that she would have passed out quickly from shock if she could see what was happening. You can see at these two points that an outline was drawn onto Zoey before the incisions were made. The ink is still just about visible although hard to make out.'

'What was the cut made with?' Callanach asked.

'A scalpel, medical grade. Easy to get hold of. We ran some tests on the skin around the edge of the incisions and have found substantial amounts of topical numbing cream. I think your murderer rubbed the cream into Zoey's abdomen and back over several days in advance of doing this to her.'

'They couldn't just have killed her first?' Ava asked.

'Not what they wanted, apparently,' Jonty said. 'There are also four injection sites. I've sent off tissue samples to the lab and confirmation will take a couple of days, but given the proximity to the incisions,' he pointed at tiny pin pricks at each shoulder and leg area of the cut-out shape, 'I'd say the surgeon – and I use that term as loosely as possible – injected Zoey with a local anaesthetic before starting. Both sides have the same marks.'

'Why bother?' Callanach asked. 'And before you say it, Jonty, I know that deduction is our remit, not yours. But if torture was the idea, surely there was no point alleviating the pain.'

'As a medic, the answer is simple. If Zoey had felt the full extent of the cuts, she'd have moved her body in a way which would have made cutting clean edges impossible. Also, she'd have died from shock, I think. Her heart wouldn't have coped. Her breathing would have suffered. The small amount of anaesthesia allowed her to live through the operation, and to make it easier to cut out the baby shape.'

'Then the killer packed her wounds and drove her somewhere public to die?' Callanach asked.

'That's where you take over,' Jonty said. 'The incisions were made not long before dumping her at the roadside. The wound packs wouldn't have stemmed the blood flow for long, and the loss of an area of skin that size would have killed her sooner or later whether infection had kicked in or not.'

'Where would the murderer have got the local anaesthetic from?' Ava asked.

'A contact in the medical profession. Theft from a hospital or GP surgery. Quite possibly from the internet. There are sites that specialise in providing medical supplies no questions asked, and this wouldn't normally be regarded as a high-risk item to sell. Tracing it will be almost impossible, which brings me to the gown she was wearing when she was found.'

'It wasn't a dress?' Ava asked.

'No. It was difficult to establish at first because of all the blood, but the opening is at the back, with three ties evenly spaced from the top down, which would have given easy access to her abdomen and back as necessary. No branding or label, and a very standard cheap cotton mix material, often found in clothing transported from China.'

'The chances of tracing its source?' Luc asked.

'Several thousand to one, I'd say,' Jonty replied.

Ava sighed. 'You said surgeon, but loosely. So is this a medical professional? What's your opinion on the surgical skills?' she asked.

'It's not butchery, but it's not anyone who's been trained. They made a poor job of lifting the skin away – all layers, epidermis, dermis and the subcutaneous fat. At one point the depth is one centimetre, but it thins out at the ends of the arms and legs to three millimetres. If you look closely you can see some hacking with the blade to lift the skin section out,' Jonty said, pointing.

'I'll take your word for that,' Ava said. 'What about the restraints? I can't see anything obvious.'

'That's because it was cleverly done. There's an area of skin worn off the ankles and wrists, between two and three inches wide with no knot mark. I'm assuming a binding was used to secure the limb against an immovable object like a pole. That would explain the lack of obvious bruising. A thinner binding would have chafed. Under a microscope you can see that the binding has left green fibres on Zoey's skin.'

'Her captor didn't find that out by chance,' said Callanach. 'Either they've done it before, practised, or they spent a long time researching. Any DNA or prints on the body?'

'Not that we've found,' Jonty said. 'Your murderer wore gloves. They probably washed her just prior to cutting the skin. Obviously the lower legs, arms and face had dirt, dust and foliage on them from crawling up the road, but nothing that will help identify her captor. There's only one other thing of note. A section of hair has been cut from Zoey's head. The roots are intact so it wasn't pulled out. It's not very much, but it does beg the question why.'

'A trophy?' Callanach asked.

'He's got plenty of those,' Ava said. 'The killer's already got her clothes, shoes, whatever jewellery she was wearing, possibly her handbag. Not to mention a large section of her skin. Is there anything else, Dr Spurr? I need to get back and speak to the superintendent.'

'Only that before she was cut, she was kept comfortable. Not injured in any way. She was hydrated and still had food in her stomach. Consciously kept alive and unharmed. No sexual assault as far as I can tell,' Jonty said. 'Good luck with this one. Whoever did this to Zoey . . .'

'Deserves to die,' Ava said. 'That's all there is to it, really. They'd better hope it's not me who finds them first.'

'I was going to say, is dangerous in the extreme, although I can't disagree with your sentiment, DCI Turner. There was no anger, no lack of control, no force used. It was seven days between this girl going missing and turning up again. That's a long time for her killer to be with her, to watch her plead and cry. Hard then to cut her and leave her to die.'

'That's what psychopaths do,' Callanach said.

'This is a psychopath with an especially strong stomach and an iron will.' Jonty stripped off his gloves and turned to go. 'Take your time.'

Callanach waited until the pathologist was gone before turning to Ava. 'Are you okay?' he asked. 'I've never heard you express the desire to kill anyone before.'

Ava peeled the sheet back from Zoey's face. 'Look at her,' she said. 'On the precipice between childhood and adulthood. She lived through violence, but had the strength to get out and seek help, even when her own mother failed to protect her. We know she doesn't have a criminal record, so in spite of her childhood she kept herself from spiralling downwards. Moving into the shelter should have been the start of a new chapter. She should have been safe. And the cruellest factor in it all was that Zoey was kept alive for a whole week, unhurt. She would have had hope. No matter how dismal it seemed, there would have been a part of her that thought she would go free. Having survived so much, surely it wasn't possible that she could die tied up and terrified. That's what she'd have been thinking.'

'You can't make it personal,' Callanach said. 'We have to take a step back and look at this dispassionately. The stepfather has to be the best bet.'

'It's a hell of a jump from domestic violence, however long-term, to this,' Ava said.

'Maybe Zoey had decided to prosecute. Maybe the stepfather hated that she'd left and couldn't handle it. The chances are that this was perpetrated by someone known to her,' Callanach said.

Ava pulled the sheet further down to reveal Zoey's abdomen. The layer of flesh below the missing skin shone greyish-pink in the bright electric lights.

'It's unreal,' Ava said. 'How do you start to conceive a torture so inhumane? Perhaps she did know the person who did this to her, and perhaps she didn't, but this was personal. Zoey was chosen. It can't be random because there's a purpose to it in her murderer's mind. Some twisted relevance.'

'Do you want me to get straight over to the stepfather's place now?' Callanach asked.

'Go to the shelter first,' Ava said. 'It sounds as if Sandra Tilly, who identified the body, knew a lot about what Zoey had been through. Get everything you can out of her to arm yourself with. When you interview the stepfather I don't want him to have any wiggle room at all. Speak to the other shelter residents. I want to know if she was still scared, if she thought she was being followed, or aware of any threat. Most of all, I want to know what sort of things the stepfather did to her. Then go through Zoey's personal items. Communications, diaries, an email address might help.'

'All right,' Luc said.

'Visit her stepfather, Christopher Myers, after that. Separate him from Zoey's mother during questioning, if you can. We've already got enough for a search of the house. I want it inspected from top to bottom, including any loft space and the garage,' Ava said.

'What about Zoey's mother?' Luc asked.

'I don't know what to expect from a woman who failed to protect her child against long-term violence. She ought to be grieving. Take it easy on her. I don't want any complaints jeopardising the investigation, but make sure she knows we have independent evidence about the violence. Perhaps suggest we might charge her with child cruelty,' Ava said.

'Wouldn't work without Zoey alive to make the case,' Callanach said.

'We know that, she doesn't. Scare the crap out of her off the record if you get the chance. She failed her daughter while she was alive. Perhaps now that Zoey's dead, her mother can finally be a half-decent parent and tell the truth.'

'You're telling me to break the rules?' Callanach asked.

Ava smiled tenderly at Zoey before covering her once more with the sheet. 'I'm asking you to do whatever it takes to find the bastard who did this. When you do, I intend to put them in a prison cell and keep them there until their last breath. Even then, justice won't have been done.'

Chapter Five

'Brought you a coffee, ma'am. I gather you've just got back from the mortuary. Thought you might need a pick-me-up.' DS Lively walked into Ava's office and deposited a steaming mug on her desk, closely followed by an unopened packet of rich tea biscuits. Ava inspected the gifts then studied Lively's face.

'For fuck's sake, Lively, tell me you haven't killed someone in police custody,' she said.

Lively managed to look offended for a few seconds before smiling. 'The job's making you cynical. Can't a lowly sergeant bring his chief inspector a hot drink without you assuming the worst?'

'We've worked together how long now?' Ava asked.

'I believe it's in the region of a decade, ma'am,' Lively said, sitting down.

'And in that time, how many hot drinks have you made me?' Ava continued.

'You're overthinking it, boss. What's the news on the girl you found out on Torduff?' he asked.

'Grim,' Ava said, ripping open the biscuits. 'Are you expecting me to share these, only you appear to have made yourself comfortable for no apparent reason.'

'No, they're all yours. I've been hiding them at the back of a drawer to stop the other thieving gits from nicking them.'

'That's enough. Tell me what you've done and how much shit you've got MIT in,' Ava demanded.

Lively reached over and plucked a biscuit from the packet. 'It's Detective Constable Salter. I'm worried about her,' he said, before stuffing the biscuit into his mouth whole.

'Has something happened, only I wasn't notified that there was an issue,' Ava said.

'Without wanting to sound like a paternalistic asshole, it's too soon. Christie shouldn't be back on duty yet.' He looked longingly at the coffee. Ava moved it beyond his reach before he began dunking.

'You got injured quite badly too, on a recent case. I seem to recall you being advised to get surgery on your left shoulder, not that you took any notice. When I questioned your decision to come back to work, you said you knew your own body better than anyone else.'

'This is different and you know it. You can't compare losing a baby to getting your arm into a fight with a crowbar,' Lively muttered.

'The doctor declared Salter fit for duty,' Ava said. 'I've spoken to her. She believes she's ready and I trust her judgment. What is it you know that no one else does?'

Lively brushed crumbs from his lap onto the floor, frowning.

'Come on, Sergeant, you came in here to say something to me. Get it over with.'

'Christie Salter nearly died in my arms, ma'am, on a kitchen floor after some sick fuck had taken her hostage and a dotty old woman misjudged her target and stabbed her. If the paramedics hadn't been on the scene, we'd have lost her. She was in surgery for hours. Her baby girl died in her womb. You can't tell me she's fit to be back out on the streets, not with the sort of crap we deal with every day.'

'Sergeant,' Ava said gently, 'you don't think that perhaps it would be a good idea for me to refer you for some counselling, given what you went through that day? DC Salter wasn't the only one who suffered a trauma. It must have been an appalling thing for you to have witnessed.'

'Would you fuck off! Oh shite – sorry, ma'am, I forgot who I was talking to,' he said.

'Forgiven. This isn't easy. I understand that the prospect of talking to someone about your emotions isn't natural for the more mature members of the force, but times have changed. There's nothing to be embarrassed about and no one need know except us,' Ava said.

'I don't need a bloody shrink. I need to make sure DC Salter's safe and right now, as her ranking officer, I'm not convinced she is,' he replied.

Ava held out the biscuits as a peace offering. Lively took a handful.

'All right. Your choice. But you can't make her feel as if she shouldn't be here, however well-intentioned you are. This is what she needs to help distract herself from her loss. You and I would both do the same in her position.'

'If you're keeping her in MIT, I want your word you'll keep Salter off the Torduff Road investigation. It's too much. I heard what a mess that poor girl's body was in.'

'I agree with you on that score. You picked up a face slashing, I understand. Probably a dead end case, but it needs investigating. I'm leaving it with you and Salter. I need every other body on Zoey Cole's murder, so don't expect help from anyone else. Wrap it up as quickly as possible, then I'll review DC Salter's suitability for another case. This stays between us, all right?'

Lively stood up, nodding, as Ava's office door opened.

'Sit your carbohydrate-endowed arse straight back down in that chair, Sergeant,' Detective Superintendent Overbeck said.

Lively crossed his arms and remained standing, but stayed where he was.

'Is there a problem, ma'am?' Ava asked her superior, who was looking stunning in a tight-fitting midnight blue suit and six-inch stilettos, with bright red nails. It was a wonder she could hold a pen or type, Ava thought, wondering if she was aware that all the police under her command called her the Evil Overlord out of her earshot, not entirely unjustly.

'When isn't there a frigging problem in your team, DCI Turner?' Overbeck said. 'I've just had the pleasure of being interviewed by some of those do-gooders who occasionally get to come in and visit the prisoners in their cells, just to check we're providing five-fucking-star care for Edinburgh's charming criminals.'

'I think the ones in our cells are usually called suspects, ma'am,' Lively smirked. 'Something about innocent until proven—'

'Sergeant, if you speak again before I ask you to, I will pour that steaming coffee on the desk all over your balls, get me?'

Lively winced and Ava did her best not to smirk. Lively was regularly insubordinate to her, and even more so to Luc Callanach. This was the first she'd seen him silenced by a superior officer and it was pleasing to watch.

'Am I to assume there was a slip in our usual standards?' Ava enquired.

'To be fair, only if you call having an incomprehensible man with half his frigging face hanging off, stuck in our cells instead of being in a hospital – or preferably still on the streets given how badly he was fouling up the custody area – a slip!' Overbeck hissed. 'Now,' she stood directly in front of Lively, 'as you were the arresting officer, you'd better have the shiniest, most watertight explanation for why this has happened to me on a day when I finally got my husband on a plane for a month-long golfing vacation and was looking forward to a serious amount of alone time without anyone pissing me off.'

'Gone somewhere nice, has he?' Lively grinned.

'Pass me your coffee, Turner,' Overbeck said, holding out her hand.

'Don't you dare, ma'am,' Lively said. 'That's the first cup of coffee I've ever made anyone in this police station. I don't want it wasted!'

'Sergeant, would you please answer DS Overbeck's question?' Ava said.

'Only if she says please.'

'Lively, you're going to get yourself fired.' Ava shot him an unmistakable look.

'Stay out of this, Detective Chief Inspector,' Overbeck said. 'I don't have any problem at all with your sergeant giving me a reason to fire him.'

'Lively,' Ava said, getting to her feet and glaring.

Lively tutted and gave in. 'He's a victim of crime, refused an ambulance but we need a statement from him. He's also homeless and a drug addict. We need to question him, and the only way to stop him from disappearing was to book him as drunk and incapable, and wait it out.'

'So you just made up the drunk charge?' Overbeck asked. 'Even though he actually wasn't?'

'That's right.' Lively smiled.

'So you've not only broken every procedure we have in terms of custodial care of the seriously injured, you've also reported a false charge against him.'

'Aye, that pretty much sums it up,' Lively said. 'Was there something else you wanted, or am I free to go and try to extract a statement from our guest?'

Overbeck stepped closer, her eyes level with Lively's, their bodies forming strange polar opposite silhouettes against the window, one stick thin and the other seriously paunchy. Ava held her breath while she waited for one or other of them to concede defeat.

'Get him out of my cells, out of this police station and preferably out of this city,' Overbeck said. 'Ensure not a single particle of shit is going to hit any proverbial fan, then either retire or make sure I never have cause to speak with you about this again. Do you understand, Detective Sergeant?'

'Yes, ma'am. Happy to oblige,' Lively said.

Callanach and Tripp parked around the corner from the domestic abuse shelter, then phoned ahead to have the back door opened up, the front door being used as little as possible to disguise the nature of the property from any save for those who needed to know. Most of the women inside were running or hiding. The police weren't always welcome visitors, either. Too many victims had been ignored, told there was insufficient evidence to prosecute, or just plain disbelieved. Modern policing was attempting to bridge the trust gap, but that was a long-term project. There were generations of failings to make up for, Callanach thought, as he rang a silent doorbell and looked into the security camera, holding up his identification for closer viewing. Tripp did the same. Eventually the door buzzed open and they stepped through into a vestibule. A woman appeared behind the glass of an internal door.

'Would you check that the outer door behind you is firmly locked, please?' she asked. Tripp did so. She unlocked the inner door and let them into a wide hallway. 'I'm Sandra Tilly, the deputy shelter manager. Would you mind coming into the kitchen to talk, only I don't want to disturb the women in the lounge.'

'Of course. I'm DI Luc Callanach,' he said. 'We don't want to disturb anyone unnecessarily but it would help if we could see Zoey's room. I know other officers have already been in there, but it's useful to get a better idea of who she was.'

They walked down the corridor and entered a functional room with cupboards marked only with numbers. 'They correspond with the bedroom numbers upstairs,' Sandra explained. 'The women who stay here often don't use their real names, although Zoey actually did. She said it was therapeutic for her to feel as if she'd stopped running. Other women use pseudonyms until they feel really safe with each other. If anyone ever does manage to break in, they won't find it easy to figure out which room they want. Zoey was in number four.'

'Do you mind if we have a look in her kitchen cupboard?' DC Tripp asked.

'Sure,' Sandra said, opening it. 'Have you arrested anyone yet?'

'Not yet,' Callanach said. 'Were you aware of anyone harassing Zoey, or trying to contact her? Any letters, emails, texts?'

'Nothing that I was aware of,' Sandra said. 'A lot of the women here choose to spend a period of time in the digital dark. They get rid of their old mobile numbers, change email addresses, shut down every form of social media. This shelter isn't for mild cases of abuse. We have limited places and it's expensive to run. As horrible as it sounds, we only house women or girls who have suffered long-term, major-impact abuse and who are judged to still be at risk and vulnerable.'

Tripp took out a few packets and tins, a couple of mugs and a cookbook. '*Healthy Eating for One*,' he read. 'Looks like Zoey was trying to take care of herself. No junk food in here. The tins are all vegetables rather than desserts. She was thinking about her long-term future.'

'How much did Zoey tell you about what she'd been through?' Callanach asked Sandra.

'She shared quite a lot in our group sessions. The girls have a daily meeting to share their experiences, when they feel ready. Zoey kept herself to herself when she first arrived, but gradually she started to talk to the others. She'd suffered violence and psychological abuse. Nothing sexual, at least not that she ever told us about.'

'Her stepfather?' Callanach checked.

'Yes,' Sandra said. 'Christopher Myers. He once broke her nose because she called him Christopher rather than Dad. Seems he couldn't bear to be reminded that anyone had ruled the family before him. Zoey had a brother, too, although she didn't talk about him much. Would you like to see her room now? I'm off duty in ten minutes and I can't leave you in the property.'

They followed Sandra upstairs, where she opened a door with two different keys to reveal an orderly bedroom with a chair, a chest of drawers and a matching wardrobe. A small en suite with a shower was behind a second door.

'The bed's made, all the clothes are away,' Callanach said to Tripp. 'Zoey didn't go anywhere in a panic and there's a suitcase under the bed. She wasn't running from any threat she was aware of and it looks as if she had every intention of returning.'

'And if she was aware of a threat, I'd guess she'd have reported it to someone here as a precaution. Not least to keep the other women safe,' said Tripp. 'So was this a random kidnapping and murder? Just an unfortunate coincidence that she crossed the path of an opportunistic killer?'

'Possibly, but the wounds inflicted have a personal meaning to whoever caused them. Come on. There's nothing else here, no laptop or mobile.' Callanach shut the drawers he'd opened. 'No letters or diary. I guess it's time to visit the stepfather.'

They walked back down the stairs to find Sandra waiting

41

for them with her coat on and keys in hand. She let them out and followed behind.

'Thanks for your help,' Callanach said.

'No problem. I'll just stay and lock up. Call if you need anything else,' Sandra replied.

Callanach and Tripp walked around the corner towards their unmarked car. 'Do we have Zoey's medical records yet?' Tripp asked.

'Still waiting. Hopefully we'll get them within the next couple of days.' Callanach stopped and sighed. 'I meant to ask Sandra for a copy of the CCTV footage from when Zoey last left the shelter. I'll go back. You start the car and put the stepfather's address into the SatNav.'

He turned around and made his way towards the shelter's back door. He was about to call out to Sandra when he saw a man approach her, kissing her at length before letting go. Sandra laughed, said something Callanach couldn't hear from that distance and kissed the man again.

The male shouldn't have been that close to the back door of the shelter, was Callanach's first thought. Even if he wasn't a threat, the women living there should be able to come and go without anyone seeing them. Judging by the intensity of the greeting, it looked like a new relationship. People rarely kissed for more than a couple of seconds after the first few months – not in public anyway. Keeping his footsteps light, Callanach walked in the shadow of the property's rear wall until he was close enough to Sandra to say her name quietly.

'Oh God, you made me jump,' she said. 'Did you forget something?'

'One last query. Hello.' He held out a hand to shake Sandra's boyfriend's. 'I'm Detective Inspector Callanach.'

'This is my boyfriend, Tyrone,' Sandra answered for him.

'Tyrone?' Callanach let the missing surname hang in the air between them.

'Tyrone Leigh,' the man muttered. 'Is there a problem?'

'DI Callanach's here about the incident,' Sandra explained to her boyfriend, before turning her attention back to Callanach. 'Tyrone knows because I asked him to drop me at the mortuary to identify Zoey's body.'

'Sandra shouldn't have had to do that,' Tyrone said. 'This job's tough enough already.'

'I agree,' Callanach said. 'It's a terrible thing to ask anyone to undertake, but unfortunately it was necessary. Did you ever meet Zoey?'

Sandra and Tyrone's eyes met briefly before he answered.

'We bumped into her once, in the supermarket up the road,' Sandra said. 'I was picking up dinner on the way home and Zoey happened to be in there.'

'Who else other than residents knows the address of the shelter?' Callanach asked. 'Have you told any of your friends or family, Mr Leigh?'

'Did I do something wrong?' Tyrone asked.

'Not at all. I'm just covering all bases. We need to know how Zoey was located by her attacker.'

'Seems pretty bloody obvious to me you should be arresting her stepfather,' Tyrone said.

Sandra glared at him. If looks were kicks, Tyrone would have been holding his shin, Callanach thought. He raised his eyebrows.

'I only told him because Zoey was a bit off with him in the supermarket, didn't want to shake his hand when he offered. I was just explaining that she'd had a rough time of it at home,' Sandra muttered, red-faced.

'I understand,' Callanach said. 'Probably best in future not to share any of your residents' details though, no matter what the circumstances. Could you let me have a copy of the security

43

CCTV showing the last time Zoey left the shelter? I'll send an officer to fetch it tomorrow. Thank you, Miss Tilly.'

Callanach took out his phone as he walked away and made a note of Tyrone Leigh's name, knowing that a row would be starting behind him.

Chapter Six

The Myers household was opposite the bowling club in Broxburn, its front windows affording a view of the river, with neighbouring properties adjoining on either side.

'This is nice,' Tripp said. 'Not quite what I was expecting.'

'Domestic violence doesn't only happen in tenements, Tripp,' Callanach said.

'I know that, it's just hard to understand why a man would provide for a family, with a pretty house in a good village, then ruin it all. What's the point?' Tripp asked.

'Control. It always boils down to that. Some people just need to feel powerful, and if this is their only way of achieving that, they don't care what the peripheral damage is. I asked PC Biddlecombe to phone ahead. They're expecting us.'

The door opened before they reached it and a short, thin woman opened it, clutching a handful of tissues. The paleness of her face and red eyes needed no explanation. Callanach studied her for signs of recent injury or older scarring, but saw none.

'Come in,' she said quietly. 'I'm Elsa Myers.'

Tripp and Callanach introduced themselves as they wiped

their shoes on the mat. Mrs Myers showed them into a pastel-shaded lounge. There were two photos on the mantelpiece, one of a young man in a soldier's uniform and one of Zoey in school uniform, looking shy as she smiled for the photographer.

'How old was your daughter in that photo?' Callanach asked.

'Fourteen,' her mother said. 'Please sit down. My husband's just coming to join us.'

She looked like Zoey, Callanach thought. There was a frailty about her that had to have preceded the news of her daughter's death. It looked as if the slightest breeze would bend her. Her wrists were almost skeletal beneath the white blouse she was wearing, and her cheekbones were harsh in her face.

'Where's Zoey's brother?' Callanach asked.

'Afghanistan,' Elsa replied. 'We hope he'll come back when we have a date for the funeral. Do you know when that's likely to be?'

'We can't release the body until we've made progress with the case, I'm afraid. I know that's terribly difficult to deal with but it's important that we get justice for Zoey, and that means preserving her body in case further investigations prove necessary. Have you spoken to your son about what happened?'

'That's not been possible. He's out on manoeuvres away from base. He'll be contacted as soon as practicable to let him know,' a man said from the doorway. Christopher Myers was well over six feet tall, with wavy brown hair and hazel eyes. He stepped forward, offering his hand. 'I'm Christopher. It's good of you to come out to speak with us. You must be Detective Inspector Callanach. Has my wife offered you a cup of tea?'

'That's all right, we don't need anything, thank you,' Callanach said, sitting back down as Christopher took a seat by his wife, wrapping a protective arm around her shoulders. She collapsed into him.

'So have you found something? Arrested someone?' Christopher asked.

'I'm afraid not, but it's early days. We are following up multiple lines of enquiry, however. That's why we're here. What we'd like to do is speak with each of you separately. I hope you don't mind. It's important that you recall events individually. Sometimes one person's recollections cloud another's, and we miss vital pieces of information.'

'Let me stop you there,' Christopher said. 'I know what this is about. It's no surprise. Zoey made a number of allegations against me when she lived here. To be honest, I was surprised the officers who came before didn't ask me about it.'

'We'd still like—' Tripp began.

'She claimed I was violent to her,' Christopher continued. 'I'm afraid Zoey suffered a terrible trauma when her father died. She was very emotionally reliant on him. When I arrived, she painted me as the wicked stepfather, and things only got worse during her teenage years.'

Elsa Myers nodded, tears forming in her eyes as she leaned her head on her husband's shoulder.

'Please don't mistake me,' said Christopher. 'Zoey was a precious, sweet, lovely girl and we both adored her, however hard that was at times. When she started self-harming we considered calling in outside help, but Elsa was worried that Zoey might end up institutionalised or taken away from us.' He wiped his eyes with a handkerchief before continuing. 'Perhaps if we had asked for help sooner, she'd still be alive.'

'When did you last speak to her or see her?' Tripp asked.

'When Zoey left here a few months ago, she had a sort of miniature breakdown, I guess you could call it. I think a friend had let her down and she took it out on us, screaming and shouting terrible things in the street before walking off, all of her possessions in a carrier bag, without even a coat. It was a dreadful day. I tried to stop her, but the law says she's an adult. What can you do?'

He looked tired, Callanach thought. Certainly Christopher hadn't shaved that morning, and perhaps not the previous day either. His shirt was ironed, though, and the house showed no sign of disruption. It was odd that there were no flowers or cards around the place from family and friends. Usually a couple of days after such a tragedy, the family home was unrecognisable.

'Have you had much support from friends and family?' he asked. 'Parents can sometimes feel swamped by the amount of cards and letters they receive, imagining they need to respond to them all. Flowers particularly . . .' He let the obvious question hang in the air.

'My wife's allergic . . .' Christopher Myers started to say.

'They're too morbid . . .' Elsa muttered at the same time. There was a moment of silence.

'We made the joint decision not to turn the place into any sort of shrine. It was too painful for my wife, and it seemed rather inappropriate given the lies Zoey had told about me.'

'I understand,' Callanach said, making brief eye contact with Tripp, who was busy making notes. 'Did you know where Zoey was living prior to her death?'

'With friends, we assumed,' Christopher said.

'Mrs Myers?' Callanach checked. Elsa shook her head. 'Zoey was in a domestic abuse shelter,' he continued. 'The allegations against you were quite detailed, Mr Myers, although Zoey declined to press charges. She had a number of unexplained fractures, old breaks that had healed over, but more than one would expect an eighteen-year-old to have suffered.'

Christopher Myers looked down at his wife. 'Tell them,' he said. 'They need to know how bad it was.'

'I don't know why she used to do it,' Zoey's mother

whispered. 'Whether she felt she didn't get enough attention, or that she was trying to punish me for remarrying. It started off small but got bigger. She would pinch herself, mark her body, deliberately bang into furniture to leave bruises up her arms. Once she even slammed her hand in a door. We suspected she'd broken several fingers but she refused to go to the hospital. By then I was too scared of how she'd react to insist.'

'Scared that she might be taken away?' Callanach checked.

'Or that they would believe her stories and Christopher would be arrested. What sort of choice is that? Lose your husband or your daughter. So I stayed silent.' Elsa let out a sudden sob. 'And now she's dead, and there's nothing I can do to protect her any more.'

Christopher rocked her in his arms, whispering soothing nothings into her hair and sniffing back his own tears.

'I'm sorry for your loss,' Callanach said. 'Does Zoey still have a bedroom here?'

'It's the guest room now,' Christopher said. 'We redecorated recently.'

'Do you mind if we take a look around?' Tripp asked.

'Help yourself. I'll stay here and look after my wife, if you don't mind,' Christopher replied.

Callanach and Tripp took the stairs quietly, Elsa's sobs fading as they reached the upper floor of the house and began opening doors. Two of the bedrooms were blank canvases, each with a double bed and standard furniture, ready for guests to arrive and make themselves comfortable. Only the main bedroom showed signs of life. Christopher and Elsa's room was warm and comfortable. A photo of them on their wedding day sat on Elsa's dressing table, next to a jewellery box and a hairbrush. The bed was neatly made and a small wooden cross hung above the headboard on the wall.

'Do you think it helps?' Tripp asked, looking at the cross.

'When you lose someone, but believe they've gone somewhere better?'

'I hope it helps them,' Callanach said. 'If it were me, I'd be wondering what sort of god could allow such an atrocity to happen in the first place.'

'What did you make of them?' Tripp whispered as he poked his head into the en suite bathroom.

'They seem to be genuinely grieving,' Callanach said. 'Substantial difference between Zoey and Christopher's versions of events though.'

'Zoey would have to have experienced serious mental health difficulties to have made up so many stories and maintained them for so long. Especially if she was breaking her own bones,' Tripp said.

'It's been done before,' Callanach said, wondering how much Tripp knew about his own history, and the woman who had inflicted dreadful injuries on herself to bolster her false rape accusation.

'Still, breaking her own fingers?' Tripp asked. 'Did Christopher's record show anything?'

'He's not on the police system,' Callanach said. 'Never convicted of so much as a traffic offence.'

'I can't see anything relevant up here. Officers checked the house when they visited to notify the mother of Zoey's death. They said both Elsa and Christopher seemed genuinely shocked, and they were given full access to the entire property at that stage,' Tripp said. 'The thing about the flowers was weird, though. His first instinct was to lie about it.'

'Embarrassment, perhaps, thinking how heartless it would seem to have thrown out the flowers and cards from well-wishers. Maybe they really couldn't bear to be reminded of it every minute of the day,' Callanach suggested.

'How could you forget, flowers or not? I wonder

if throwing it all out was Christopher's idea or Mrs Myers'?' Tripp replied.

'They'll present it as a united decision, whatever the truth of the matter. Let's go back down. I have a couple more questions then we can get back to the station. I'd like to confirm with the army about Zoey's brother, too,' Callanach said.

Back downstairs they found Elsa making a pot of tea and Christopher washing up. 'Best to keep busy, we've found,' Christopher said. 'If you let yourself sit and think about it for too long, you just can't get up again.'

'We understand,' Callanach said. 'For our records, as you're obviously related parties, could you tell us what you were doing last Sunday? We know where Zoey was until 11 a.m., then she went out and was noted as missing at 4 p.m.'

'We were at an autumn fete,' Elsa said, pouring milk into a teacup. 'A community event over at Kirknewton.'

'I'll write down the names of a few friends we were there with, plus there are photos. You know how it is these days. Everything's all over social media before you know it. We got there to help set up in the morning at about ten. I was running the bouncy castle.' Christopher gave a sad smile. 'Elsa was on the cake stall. It was a charity fundraiser. We were there all day. Got home about six in the evening.'

'And you didn't leave at any stage?' Tripp asked.

'Not at all. There was a bit of rain so we were huddled together under shelters for quite a lot of it. Didn't stop the children wanting to run around outside though,' Christopher said. 'Are you sure about that tea?'

'We'll be off, thanks. If you could just write down those names . . .'

'Of course.' Christopher busied himself with a sheet ripped off a notepad as Elsa poured tea for the two of them. When he handed his alibi list over, there were no fewer than a dozen names on it.

Callanach and Tripp made their way out of the front door.

'Is that your garage?' Callanach asked.

'It is. Feel free to go inside. Just pull it shut when you're finished,' Christopher said, shutting the front door.

Tripp pulled up the garage door. The floor had been recently brushed. No dirt or leaves remained. A few tools hung in neat rows and old kitchen cupboards had been rehung to house half-used tins of paint and essentials like WD40.

'This is the tidiest garage I've ever seen,' Tripp said.

'Check the cupboards.'

'Are we looking for anything in particular?'

'Green rope or string,' Callanach said. 'Blades, gloves, duct tape, needles. Anything you wouldn't want to see if you were kidnapped and woke up trapped in here.'

Chapter Seven

'Wait for me,' Ava said. 'I'm not making it that easy for you. If Overbeck's going to storm into my office and bollock you, I'm overseeing whatever steps you take to remedy it.'

'Don't sweat it, ma'am. If the Evil Overlord wants to use me as a whipping boy for a while, that's fine with me,' Lively said.

'And that's supposed to reassure me how . . .?' Ava asked.

'You're coming to the cells with me, are you then?' He ignored her question and responded with his own.

'I am, so no cutting corners. Write up a detailed statement afterwards, and so we're clear, you're to avoid sarcasm, aggression and all forms of fiction,' Ava said.

'I think you're being a bit harsh, to be honest,' Lively said, getting out his notebook which gave Ava a vague sense of hope that the proper processes might be complied with.

'Do you? I think I'm a goddamned angel,' Ava said. 'Come on then. Down to the cells.'

A few floors below, and a few locked doors into the heart of the building, Mikey Parsons' face was grim. Even Lively had the decency to let out a whistle of sick appreciation at the extent of the damage.

'How're you doing there, Mikey?' he asked.

'Hurts,' Parsons muttered.

'Aye, that was always going to happen when you could actually feel your face again. This here is Detective Chief Inspector Turner. She's come to ask you about what happened,' Lively said.

'Am I under arrest? Did I do something?' Parsons muttered, his speech slurred either from years of addiction or the wound across his cheek; it was hard to tell.

Ava unlocked his door and walked into the cell, leaning against the wall opposite the bed Parsons was laid out on. He didn't attempt to sit up.

'You're not under arrest, Mr Parsons. You're here for your own protection because you refused medical assistance and you were deemed too vulnerable to remain outside. Is there anything at all you can tell us about how you got that injury?'

Parsons raised a shaking hand to his face, investigating the extent of his injury. His fingertips came away bloody as he attempted to plaster the loose flaps of skin back down onto the structure of his cheeks.

'Don't remember anything,' Parsons said, turning his head away from her to stare at the wall.

'Perhaps the sergeant would get you a cup of tea,' Ava said. 'He's good at making hot drinks for people.'

'Oh, for crying out loud,' Lively said, scuffing his feet as he walked away. 'Give an inch and they take a bloody mile.'

Ava ignored him. 'Mr Parsons, whatever happened, you're in no trouble. I understand that drugs were involved, but I'm not interested in prosecuting individual users. Life is tough and you've got your reasons. What I want is to find the person who assaulted you. You could have died. Just because you're homeless doesn't mean you're worth less than anyone else. It's not okay to pretend this doesn't matter.'

'I'll heal,' Parsons said.

'If you don't get medical help, those scars will be more painful than they need to be and liable to infection. Would you mind if I took a closer look at the injury?' She crossed the cell to stand nearer to him.

Slowly, he rolled his head to the left for Ava to get a better understanding of the extent of the injuries. The slashes were clean, and there was no mistaking the fact that they had been designed to form a Z. This had been no chance encounter. The perpetrator had gone looking for a semi-conscious Spice user to mark. Edinburgh's so-called zombies were becoming a feature of city life, and apparently attracting the wrong kind of attention.

'It needs stitching. Not even glue will help with that and it's beyond our first-aid capabilities. Where did you buy the Spice, Mikey?' she asked.

'Traded it for half a bottle of vodka,' Mikey said. 'Don't remember who with.'

'Did you feel any pain when you were attacked?'

'Was asleep. Or unconscious. I had a dream there was something biting me. It wouldn't let go. I thought it was all just part of the trip. I woke up here. Do I get food?' he asked.

'I'll see what the custody sergeant can rustle up,' Ava said. 'I need you to give a statement, though. Someone else will write it out for you and you'll just have to sign it. Also, I'd like to take photos of your injury. Do you consent to that?'

'Am I under arrest?' Mikey asked again.

'No. As I said, you're not in any trouble.' Ava sighed. His brain was obviously still too addled to retain information. Taking her phone out of her pocket, she snapped a few photos.

He didn't seem to notice. Lively walked in with a polystyrene cup of lukewarm milky water.

'Sit up and get this down you, Mikey. It'll make you feel better,' he said. 'Does he remember anything at all?' he asked Ava.

'Not a thing. He dreamed some unspecified animal was biting him. Probably a similar dream to the one I'll be having about Overbeck tonight, thanks to you. Get a statement from him, just so there's something on record, then spend as long as it takes persuading him that he needs medical treatment. He doesn't walk out of here and back onto the streets without having that stitched up. I don't care how long it takes you, understand?'

'Can one of the uniforms not do that, ma'am? It sounds like rather a waste of MIT time.'

'Your mess, you clean it up,' she said. 'Do you have any idea if DI Callanach is back in the building?'

'Tripp just walked back in. I think the DI is in reception dealing with someone. Apparently he's looking for you, too. You and DI Callanach should probably stop asking after each other, truth be told. People will talk.'

'If I didn't need you to sort out this man's face, I'd fire you immediately,' Ava said, walking out.

'Promises, promises,' he muttered.

Callanach was exactly where Lively had said he would be, which was a surprise in itself. He had his back to Ava and was talking intensely to someone just out of sight. Whatever enquiry he was dealing with would have to wait, Ava decided.

'DI Callanach,' she said. 'Sorry to interrupt, but can I have a moment?'

He turned to face her, frowning. When she saw the woman behind him, she understood why. Ava had known Callanach was involved with someone, even if he'd been careful to keep his work and private life separate.

'Yes, ma'am,' Callanach said. 'Sorry,' he told the woman next to him. 'I'll call you later, okay?'

'No, finish your conversation, it's fine,' Ava said. 'I'll see you in my office when you're ready.'

The woman stepped forward, extending a hand. 'DCI Turner,' she said, her voice husky, with a Spanish accent. 'I'm Selina Vega. We met briefly at Luc's once before.'

Ava remembered. She tried not to look Selina up and down, but there was too much not to see. With long dark hair that gleamed auburn at its ends, melting brown eyes, and legs whose shape were not the least bit hidden by her tailored skirt, Ava figured Selina must be at least five foot nine. She suddenly felt short, underdressed and in need of a hair appointment.

'Selina's a registrar at the hospital,' Callanach explained as the two of them shook hands. 'We met when MIT was investigating a death a few months ago.'

'Of course, good to see you again,' Ava told her. 'I didn't mean to interrupt. This can wait a few minutes.' She withdrew her hand and stepped back.

'It's no problem,' Selina said. 'Luc has talked about you so much that I feel as if I know you already.'

'Oh,' Ava said. 'Well, that must have been very boring for you, so I apologise.'

'Hardly. It's obvious how much he admires you. I've been suggesting for months that we should all go out,' Selina said.

'Months? Wow, I didn't realise . . .' Ava's voice trailed away into nothing. 'Anyway, I've left DS Lively trying to change the mind of a man who's refusing medical assistance in spite of the fact that his face is hanging off, so I ought to get back and check on that.'

'I'll find you in a couple of minutes,' Luc said.

'No rush, honestly.' Ava smiled broadly at Selina. 'So glad we bumped into one another.'

'Can I help?' Selina asked. 'My specialisation is emergency medicine. Perhaps I could take a look at the injury and make an assessment. If he knows I'm a doctor rather than a police officer, he might be more inclined to take advice.'

'No,' Ava and Luc said simultaneously.

'That's not fair on you,' Ava said. 'You're off duty and I wouldn't want to impose. I've got it in hand.'

'It's no problem. I was going to wait until Luc had finished his shift anyway. I have a surprise for him,' she said, winking.

'You really don't want to spend the next hour in the cells,' Luc said. 'If it's necessary we'll call an ambulance.'

'Luc, you know I don't have an off switch. If there's a person in the cells who needs help, then it's my duty to step in.' She looked at Ava. 'Luc says he has another hour before he can get away. I'd rather fill my time usefully than sit here and do nothing. Besides, I'd like to get a look around backstage. Hopefully it'll be the only time I end up in a police cell.'

She laughed, and Ava noted how beautifully white her teeth were against the tan of her skin, which had somehow not lost any of its native Spanish glow in spite of the cooler Scottish climes. Selina was rolling up her sleeves before Ava could think up an excuse to dissuade her. Not that she wanted to dissuade her, she told herself. It was helpful. She had no idea why she felt suddenly territorial. What better compromise than for Mikey Parsons to have access to a doctor without going through the rigmarole of persuading him to get in an ambulance?

'Great, that's kind of you,' Ava said. 'I'll have the custody sergeant sign you in. Detective Sergeant Lively will stay with you to make sure you're safe, although the patient is very passive. He's a drug addict though, so help yourself to gloves. We keep a stock behind the desk.'

'Thanks,' Selina said. 'See you in an hour.' She leaned across to kiss Luc on the lips as she walked past him. Ava looked away until the doctor had disappeared into the space beyond the doors.

'She's really lovely,' Ava declared brightly to Luc.

'It's casual,' Luc said. 'But I guess it's easier seeing someone who understands shift work and why you're effectively on call all the time.'

'And you two have the European thing. That must be good for you. Not having to understand the Scottish accent, for a start. So how long have you been seeing each other now?'

'Weeks, in reality,' Luc said. 'Not that often either, given our work schedules. What was it you wanted to see me about?'

'Just a catch-up on Zoey Cole. We should talk in my office for confidentiality,' Ava said, waving her security pass in front of the electronic lock and pushing the door open.

'Sure,' Luc said.

'You want a coffee or anything?' she asked as they left the stairs and walked down the corridor.

'Um, no, I'm okay,' he said. 'Listen, I didn't ask Selina to come to the station. She was trying to surprise me. I'll make sure it doesn't happen again.'

'Don't be silly,' Ava said. 'I encourage my squad to invest time in their private lives. Happier homes make for happier officers, as far as I'm concerned.' She looked at him and cringed. 'God, I'm sorry, I don't know where that corporate sound bite came from. Listen, Luc, I'm glad you're involved with someone. I know how hard it's been for you, and Selina seems great. We absolutely should go out sometime. I could, I don't know, bring Natasha maybe.'

As they stepped into her office, Ava tried not to roll her eyes at her own suggestion. Going out for a foursome with Luc and the best-looking female he could have identified north of the border with her lesbian best friend as her plus-one wasn't exactly an ego boost. Somehow everyone on her squad seemed to have someone to go home to, or go out with, except her.

'I'm not sure Selina and Natasha would . . .' Luc said.

'You're just worried that Natasha would seduce her,' Ava said. 'You know how she is about women with legs that long. I'm not sure even a man as good looking as you would be able to compete with Natasha in full flirtation mode.'

'Are you okay?' Luc asked.

'Yes, of course, fine. Why?' Ava asked.

'You just paid me a compliment, that's all. Not that I'm complaining, but it's kind of unusual,' Luc said.

Ava adjusted some papers on her desk before answering. 'I think I'd call it a technical observation rather than a compliment,' she smiled. 'And don't expect another one. That's what your girlfriend's for, after all.'

'I'm not sure I'd call her my girlfriend,' Luc said. 'How is Natasha, by the way? I haven't seen her for ages.'

Professor Natasha Forge – Ava's best friend – disappeared and reappeared depending on the intensity of whatever fling she was in the middle of. Ava was used to it, but it still meant she suddenly got dropped without warning when a new woman appeared on the scene.

'Single,' Ava said. 'So I'm seeing more of her than usual. Right, any progress on Zoey Cole?'

'The stepfather has a watertight alibi and no previous convictions,' Callanach said. 'He was with about a hundred other people during the period when Zoey was abducted, and they're all sending us photos to prove it. The boyfriend of Sandra Tilly, who runs the shelter where Zoey was living, turns out to have previous for blackmail and threatening behaviour, though. I've asked for the files. His name is Tyrone Leigh.'

'Get an officer in the incident room to check it out for you,'

Ava said, 'then go and rescue Selina from the cells. She seemed keen to take you away to whatever surprise it is she's organised.'

'I'll stay if you need me,' Luc said. 'Selina can wait.'

'Don't be ridiculous,' Ava said. 'We'll have a briefing tomorrow morning to make sure the squad is up to speed. Have a good evening.'

'I will,' Luc said. 'Thanks, Ava.' He shut her office door as he left.

Ava sat down to write up her notes of the day, trying to banish the sensation that there were other things she was missing out on.

Chapter Eight

The news that another young woman had gone missing just three days after Zoey's body had been found was treated with quiet sadness in the incident room. Everyone on the squad had been prepared for the possibility, but that didn't make the announcement any easier to hear. Ava decided to handle the initial enquiry herself with Callanach. There was no point mobilising the full unit until they were certain what they were dealing with, but her guts were churning. There were coincidences and there were patterns, and the new missing person report felt much more like the latter.

Leith's mother and baby unit was housed in a grey building that had unmistakably been erected in the 1970s, featuring pebble-dashed walls to protect it from the sea to its north and the ensuing gales. Callanach met Ava in the car park, where she stood clutching the pre-noon necessity of two takeout coffees. She handed one over and began to walk towards the front door.

'Is this a hospital?' Callanach asked. 'I haven't been here before.'

'No, it's somewhere new mothers can look after their babies

with supervision if the court has concerns about the care they might provide. Better this than having the baby taken from them and adopted, but it's a last resort. The state provides medical care, rooms, food, guidance and prepares the mother for independent life,' Ava said. 'The baby's being seen by a doctor now.'

They entered the building through pale blue corridors that smelled of bleach and nappies, and were directed to a small room where a doctor was just buttoning up a Babygro.

'This little girl's fine,' the doctor said, stroking the baby's cheek. 'No marks on her, no signs of distress, her temperature is normal. I'd say the baby hasn't been touched. She is getting grouchy though, so I'll hand her over to a nurse for a feed.'

'Thank you,' Ava said. 'Still no word on the location of the baby's mother?'

'Not that I've heard,' the doctor replied, 'but you should speak to the unit director. He might have had an update.' The doctor left them and took the baby with her.

'How old is the missing mother?' Callanach asked.

'Nineteen,' Ava said. 'The pram was discovered a few roads away from here, left in an alleyway near a newsagent. No one saw who left it there. It was in a reasonably sheltered position out of the wind but a passer-by became concerned when she heard the baby crying.'

There was a knock at the door and a man walked in carrying a file and pushing an empty pram. 'I'm Arnold Jenkins,' he said. 'I manage the unit. Thank you for coming. This is the pram baby Tansy was found in. It belongs to the unit and it has an identification tag underneath, so we can be sure it's ours. I gather a search for Lorna Shaw is already underway?'

'Uniformed officers are checking CCTV footage and walking the streets in the area. Do you know what time Lorna left here?' Ava asked.

'Three hours ago. She was taking Tansy out for some fresh air, apparently, and wanted to top up her phone credit at the shop. Lorna had permission to take the baby with her. She'd agreed to be no more than sixty minutes. We were already concerned before the police notified us that the baby had been found,' Jenkins said.

'You don't think this is simply a case of a young woman under too much pressure who just ran away?' Callanach asked.

'Every report on her makes it clear that she was doing well. The baby is reaching all her milestones. We were helping Lorna apply for independent housing with a view to her moving out in a couple of months. All her supervisors say she's a doting mother. If it had been one of the other women here, then perhaps, but if Lorna was going to disappear she'd have taken her baby with her,' Jenkins replied. 'We're really very concerned. Lorna wouldn't have left her daughter out on a street. If she really had to run away, if there was something going on that we didn't know about, it would have made more sense to go to the shops alone and leave the baby safe here,' the director explained.

'Any violent former partners you're aware of?' Callanach asked.

'None specifically that Lorna ever talked about, although she had a hard life and kept less than desirable company. She had previously abused drugs, although she's clean now, and during her pregnancy she failed to keep medical appointments, which is why she ended up here,' Jenkins said.

'What about the baby's father?' Ava asked.

'Lorna slept with a number of different partners while she was using drugs. She's not sure of the father's identity and doesn't know the surnames of many of the men, so they can't be traced. Whoever the father is, he has no idea that he has a new daughter,' Jenkins said. 'Given the fact that Lorna was previously in contact with drug dealers, one possibility is that she bumped into someone she owed money to, or who felt there was an old score to settle, which is why we called you so promptly.'

'All right,' Ava said. 'We'll expand the resources and see if we can identify her last movements. I'll get the Police Scotland media liaison team on it. We'll put out a statement later today to see if any members of the public noticed anything. Do you have a recent photo of Lorna we could use, and details of the clothes she was wearing when she left here?'

'I'll go and sort that out for you now,' Jenkins said. 'Give me a few minutes.'

Ava waited until he'd closed the door. 'So that's not just one but two crimes linked to the drug users in the city. Who's to say whether or not Zoey had come into contact with some of the same people. The news will have spread around the city's drug community by now that Mikey Parsons' face was slashed. The small-time dealers who sometimes help when we need it won't be talking to the police. If Lorna's disappearance really is related to her previous drug use, there are hundreds of undesirables she might have crossed paths with.'

'Selina said Mikey's injury was atrocious,' Callanach said. 'Sharp blade, steady hand, clear intent. You think there's an anti-drug vigilante on the prowl?'

'I think we need a greater police presence on the streets until we get to the bottom of it. Lively described the Z on Mikey's face as something akin to a branding. I'm not quite sure what the shape cut out of Zoey's stomach is supposed to represent, but it may well have been born of the same sick imagination. It's all close-up blade work. Then there's the fact that Zoey's body was found the same day that Mikey's face was cut. I'm not sure which is worse – thinking there's one person out there capable of causing this much chaos alone, or the idea that perhaps there's more than one psychopath out to

65

maim and kill,' Ava said. 'I'll need to speak with Overbeck when we get back to the station. She won't want to agree the budget, but I can't see a choice. This needs to be a cross-division effort. The Major Investigation Team can follow the leads, but we can't be out there stopping all these incidents at once. Let's get Lorna's details then organise a briefing. We need to find that girl in the next twenty-four hours or baby Tansy might never be reunited with her mother.' Ava stood up and ran her hand down the soft, pale blanket in the pram. Its silky edge had been tucked in at the bottom to keep tiny toes warm. 'It's true about that baby smell. I always thought it was a ridiculous myth, but something makes me think of freshly baked bread and Christmas morning when I hold a small baby.' She untucked the blanket and held it up to her face, breathing in deeply and smiling into the fleecy material.

'I remember when the first of my close friends became a father,' Luc said. 'We all thought he was ruining his life, but the look on his face when he brought the baby to visit . . .'

'What the fuck?' Ava took half a step back from the pram, then leaned over it to look inside again. 'What is that?'

Luc peered over Ava's shoulder at a scrunched-up sheet that had been left in the bottom of the pram. The head of a doll peeked out, with strands of brown hair stuck roughly on, eyes drawn with pen onto the pale grey face, and a series of darting black stitches in an arc, as if her mouth had been sewn shut. Reaching into his jacket pocket, Luc took out a pack containing gloves and reached in to gently extract the doll from the pram.

'You don't think . . .' he said.

'Yes,' Ava replied, stepping away from the pram and pulling out her phone. 'I do think. Have you ever seen anything made from human skin before?'

'We can't be sure of that,' Luc said, holding the doll well away from his own body.

'Its hair is the same colour as Zoey's,' Ava said. 'And the doll is fractionally smaller than the cuts to Zoey's body, even to the naked eye, which would account for the margin needed to stitch it.'

Luc turned it over. The doll had been created by stitching two matching cut-out shapes together. A rag doll with crude arms and legs, no detail, no clothes fitted over it. The seams had been sewn with rough thread, the stitches pulling at the red-tinged seams.

Ava called for backup and a forensics team. Arnold Jenkins opened the door and stared at them. 'Stay there, Mr Jenkins,' Ava said. 'No one who has handled this pram since it was brought in leaves the unit. In fact, no one leaves at all until every person residing and working here has been spoken to by a police officer.'

Jenkins blanched. 'Has Lorna been found?' he stuttered. 'Is she dead?'

'Do you recognise this?' Callanach held up the doll. Jenkins wrinkled his face in disgust and shook his head. 'Lorna hasn't been found yet, but we do need to bring in a Scenes of Crime team to ensure that any evidence contained within the pram is preserved.'

Jenkins shut the door once more, his footsteps rapid as he disappeared up the corridor. Ava sat down, still clutching the baby blanket.

'This means that whoever took Zoey has Lorna,' Ava said. 'It was one week from Zoey's disappearance to her death. Lorna's abductor is a few hours ahead of us now. If we don't find her . . .'

'I know,' Luc said. 'What do you think the relevance of the doll is?'

'Something to love? Something to play with? It might be sexual, or even a sort of reverse trophy that the killer is presenting to us, rather than keeping for himself,' Ava suggested.

'You said him. I'm not necessarily disagreeing with you, but we don't know that yet,' Luc said.

'It's the most likely scenario. The victims are both young women. Men are statistically more likely to use cutting as a form of torture. I don't know, maybe he can't find a partner who'll give him a baby so he's creating his own quasi-offspring from their skin. God, that even sounds insane to me.'

'We've dealt with insane situations before,' Luc said.

'I've never seen a doll made from skin cut from the body of a young woman who was still alive when it happened,' Ava said, her voice less than steady. 'And I've never been more certain that the same is going to happen to another young woman who is already beyond our help.'

'The dolls are a calling card, then. An announcement of intent. Zoey's killer wants us to know what's in store for Lorna.'

Sirens followed by a knock at the door signalled the arrival of the SOCOs, who appeared white-suited and ready for action.

'I need a bag straight away,' Ava said. 'This doll and the pram need to be logged into evidence, then I'm taking the doll directly over to the mortuary. Somebody contact the pathologist and tell him we're on our way. I need him there, and I'll need access to Zoey Cole's body at the same time.'

'What about that?' One of the officers motioned towards the baby blanket that Ava had in her hand.

'Yes, this too,' Ava said. 'The pram needs a complete DNA, skin cell and foreign fibres check. Someone put their hand down inside the blanket and sheet, and tucked the doll out of sight at the baby's feet. We only found it by accident.'

Ava's hands were stripped with sticky tape to make sure she hadn't removed any crucial trace evidence from the pram, then she and Luc left the room. They found Arnold Jenkins, the unit director, in an office with four female staff members.

He introduced each in turn – a nurse, an administrator, a catering manager and one of the other residents. Each had handled the pram at some point, moving it or lifting the baby, and every one of them was tearful and shaken. Ava was glad they had no idea quite how bad the situation really was. Uniformed officers took over to record statements as Ava and Luc headed back towards the car park.

'You don't need to come to the mortuary with me,' Luc said. 'I can handle this alone.'

'I know,' Ava said. 'But I feel like I owe it to Zoey. We're taking part of her back. I know it sounds stupid, but I want to be there with her when we take this monstrosity in.'

'I understand,' Luc said. 'Sometimes it's personal.'

'It is,' Ava nodded. 'I can't even explain why. Dr Spurr, the temporary pathologist – you dealt with him before. Is he good? I mean as good as Ailsa, because if not I'm calling her back in. I need answers, and I'm not risking any mistakes.'

'Jonty Spurr is excellent,' Callanach said. 'Don't worry about that.'

They drove their cars in convoy to the city mortuary. Dr Spurr met them in the reception area, already gowned and gloved. Ava and Callanach suited up, handing the bagged doll to Jonty, who peered at it with undisguised revulsion.

Without exchanging a word, they filed into the autopsy suite, where Zoey was waiting for them, sheet pulled back to reveal her skinned abdomen. Jonty took the doll from the bag, laid it on a sterile tray and photographed every aspect of it, recording each measurement and dimension as he went. With immaculate care, and making sure he preserved the knotted parts of the thread, he opened the stitching and separated the two sections of material.

Holding the material up to the light, he turned it over and

around. 'That's human skin, without a doubt,' he said. 'I can clearly see the follicles, lines and pores.'

He walked slowly to Zoey, holding the front section of the doll by the ends of each arm. A sheet of plastic had been placed over Zoey's abdominal wound, and he placed the first section of skin flat over the top of it, smoothing out the parts that had been folded over at the edges. It almost perfectly filled the shape that had been stolen from Zoey's body.

'It's shrunk as it's dried out,' Jonty said, 'which accounts for the size difference, but you can see where there are tiny imperfections in the cuts. They match both the wound edges on Zoey's body and on the doll. There is no doubt at all that what you've found was made from Zoey's skin.'

'Thank you, Dr Spurr,' Ava said, talking a step forward and gripping Zoey's cold hand for a few moments. When she walked away, Luc could see tears in her eyes. She dumped her gloves in the bin and left.

'When Ava finds the person who did this, I think she might be serious about killing them,' Luc said.

'I believe you might be right,' Jonty said. 'You'd better just make sure you get there first.'

Chapter Nine

Lorna

True terror was exhausting. That sliver of knowledge was just one step on the steepest learning curve of her life. Twenty-four hours earlier, she had woken at 6.45 a.m. with her baby in a cot at her bedside, and wondered what to cook for breakfast. Now she knew how it felt to sleep strapped to a table in the dark, smelling dirt and rotting leaves. Lorna lifted her head, but the immobility of her arms and legs made it pointless. Through dirty, green-stained glass, a waning moon cast cold shadows. The blanket over her naked body was making her itch, but it kept off the insects that buzzed and flapped through the dark. Beneath her, the table stretched longer than her frame head to toe, and was a foot wider at either side, as if it had been taken from the dining room of some grand old house. What she couldn't believe was that she had slept. How was it possible to fear for your life and still fall into dreamless sleep? Lorna remembered crying. Being made to eat and drink. Screaming uselessly for as long as her voice held out. Then nothing. At some point she had simply burned out.

Beyond the creaking walls of her prison, she could hear the rustle of leaves and the movement of branches in the wind. It was a cruel parody of the few holidays she had enjoyed as a child, before drugs had reduced her mother to a silent, shadowy creature. They had borrowed a tent and trekked out with friends or family to sleep in a field and toast marshmallows for a night or two in the summer. It had been all her mother could ever afford, and it was uncomfortable – usually freezing cold – but Lorna had loved it. So much adventure could be found just by stepping beyond the walls of their tiny flat, even if they did have to pee behind trees and wash in a cold stream each morning.

Pins and needles prickled her skin from inactivity as she flexed her legs. With ankles tied fast to the table legs, the best she could do was slowly clench then relax each muscle to get some blood flowing. Her breasts throbbed. It was two in the morning then. Like a farmyard cockerel, baby Tansy awoke hungry at the same time each night. This would have been the moment when Lorna would have plucked the baby gently from her cot, quickly enough so that the crying didn't wake the other mothers who were grabbing precious hours of sleep, and held her to a breast. Tansy's warm snuffling as she grabbed Lorna's hair would have been worth the lack of rest. For a moment, she could actually smell her baby. Milk, talcum powder, a fresh Babygro after her bath, and the slight acidity of a nappy as yet unchanged after six hours' wear. Lorna was determined not to cry for her. If she started crying, then it was as good as an admission that she would never hold her girl again. And she would. She would escape, get help, and find her way back to the mother and baby unit. If she could get clean of drugs and persuade a judge not to take her baby from her, then she could do this. The bastard who had abducted her had no idea what he was up against.

Tansy – her pride and joy – had also been her Achilles heel. The man had seemed harmless enough, following her through the lanes from the unit to the shops, whistling and texting on his phone. As he'd got nearer to her, he'd said a cheery good morning, stopping to peer into the pram and exclaim at the bonniness of the wee girl. Lorna had been delighted. No matter how many times she heard it, a compliment about the baby was affirmation that finally she had done something right. Her first selfless act, she often thought. She had given life to another human, and giving up her vices for the baby had made it even sweeter.

There had been bad times before that. Smoking the odd joint at school had matured into taking the occasional ecstasy tablet at a party. Those ecstasy tablets had introduced her to cocaine, and that had seemed so grown up and glamorous, and God knew it really did make you feel good. But there were bigger highs out there. More explosive ups and more mellow downs, with nothing in between but floating and colours and warmth. She had taken heroin for the first time while she was coming down from crack. It had seemed almost harmless, just smoking it. She had never taken a drug that had controlled her, and she managed to convince herself for a few ignorant weeks that heroin wouldn't either. Her mother had done nothing about it. After all, it was her boyfriend who had sold her the crack in the first place, and one of his colleagues who had promoted her into the narcotics big league. Addiction was swift, and a casual modern-day tragedy had followed. Drugs were expensive. Her need for them ruled her world and rendered her unfit for work. The lack of money had been met with suggestions that she could offer her body to her dealers and others for cash, favours and freebies. And the need to forget that she was effectively prostituting herself had required ever-increasing doses of drugs. Then she had fallen pregnant. It was give up the drugs or give up the baby. There were no other options. Lorna wished the decision had been easier than it was.

She would have been more proud of herself if she could claim a revelation, and a magical new start. Fortunately for her, the lure of motherhood and the sense of a growing bond with the wriggling, churning thing inside her won out. Methadone was easier than cold turkey, and not getting screwed every night to pay for her drugs was a positive blessing. Tansy had literally saved her life.

Which was why, when the happy, whistling man had held a knife to the baby's throat as they'd walked together down a side street, she hadn't had to think twice about saving her baby's life in return. She had climbed into his vehicle, followed his instructions to clip on handcuffs and watched as he pushed the pram into the nearest alleyway to await a kind passer-by who would figure out that something was wrong. Lorna stared up at the moon. Her baby was safe. The man hadn't wanted Tansy. Someone would have found her and returned her to the unit where she was now being looked after. The bargain had not been unfair. Looking back, she wondered why she hadn't screamed and run, protested and fought him. The truth was that she would have done anything – anything at all – to have secured her baby's safety, and heroics had been just another risk. Seeing the blade pressed into the chubby flesh beneath her baby's face had been enough to drain the fight from her. It had been enough to make her realise that whatever was coming – rape, mutilation, death – was preferable to the prospect of living with the memory of her baby dying in her arms.

Lorna tugged a few more times at the restraints around her wrists. There wasn't even enough movement to try scraping the twine against the edge of the table beneath her. She would wait. That was all there was to it. If nothing else, she could be grateful that she'd remained unhurt throughout the process of being kidnapped. Her early decision to remain compliant had meant that not so much as a fist had been raised. No one had responded to her screams and her kidnapper hadn't bothered silencing her. Wherever she was, it wasn't in the middle of civilisation. Having blindfolded her and led her over a gravel path, twigs brushing her face, he had opened a door and pushed her into an outbuilding.

'Take your clothes off, then lie on the table on your back,' the man had directed her.

Lorna had the perverse benefit of being unafraid of rape. Men had used her body in ways she tried not to think about any more. One more wasn't going to add to her nightmares. If that was the worst of it, then she would celebrate. If the sick fuck wanted to tie her up first, and keep her in the cold outdoors for a while, then she could take that, too. She would keep her nerve and stay strong. Come hell or high-water, she would be reunited with her baby. Lorna slept again.

When she awoke it was fully daylight. The additional hours of cold had left her muscles cramping hard. She started at her toes, tightening and loosening her muscles until there was no more she could do for relief. When the door opened, she had almost convinced herself that the man wasn't coming back for her, and that she would die of hunger and thirst in the middle of nowhere. She knew better than to speak first. Better to wait and see what he wanted from her.

'You have to eat and drink,' he said, pushing a mouldy pillow beneath her head to prop her up enough that the cup of milk he held to her lips didn't spill. He was patient as she sipped. No drops ran down her chin. When she'd finished, he took a chunk of bread from a plate. Ripping off small sections, he held them to her mouth and watched as she chewed and swallowed. He said nothing, staring at her face as she pretended not to notice. Eventually it was all gone.

'My name's Lorna,' she said quietly.

'I know,' the man replied as he took the plate and cup away.

'I'm a bit cold,' Lorna said. 'Could I have another blanket, please?'

'The cold's good for your skin,' he said. 'I have something else here for that, too.'

She raised her head from the pillow and watched him pull a bottle from beneath his coat. Spilling a dollop of cream onto his palm, he slipped his hand beneath the blanket. She waited for it. Better over sooner rather than later she thought, waiting for the violation. His hand found her stomach and began smearing on the cold gloop. Lorna shivered but knew better than to complain.

'What's it for?' Lorna asked.

'Just following orders,' he replied, spreading the liquid down over her abdomen to the tops of her thighs. He pulled his hand out and squirted more onto his palm. This time he ran his hand under her back, lifting her a little with his free hand, beginning in the middle of her back and rubbing it in until his hand was dry.

'Whose orders?' Lorna asked, making sure her voice was low and compliant. So far he wasn't showing any signs of aggression and she wanted to keep it that way.

'You're a bad girl,' he said, slowly pulling the blanket down from her neck to reveal her nakedness beneath.

This was it, then, Lorna thought. This was what he wanted. No point being shy. She might only get one opportunity to get out.

'I can be bad for you, if that's what you want,' Lorna said. 'You can keep me tied up, or let me go. I won't run. I know what men like. Let me show you.'

His face seized into a scowl, and for a second Lorna saw the snarl of teeth.

'You see?' he said. 'You're not even bothering to pretend. At least you don't lie about it. Perhaps that's better. Even here, on your back, all trussed up, you still want it, don't you?' He leaned down to breathe hot words into her ear. 'Whores always want it. They never stop. Does it itch? Does it burn? It will. You'll always be a bad girl while you're alive.'

Lorna froze. The misjudgment sat heavy in her stomach like a mountain of cold pasta. She thought fast.

'I was just scared,' she said. 'I was saying what I thought you wanted to hear. I'm not like that, really. I have a young baby – you saw her – and I love her so much. I'm a good mother. I take proper care of her.'

'Are you married to her father?' the man asked. 'Has the baby been baptised? Do you even know who the father is?'

A sob caught in the back of Lorna's throat.

'How many men did you have to fornicate with before one of their seeds took in your filthy belly?' he asked.

'It wasn't like that,' Lorna said, fighting the rising sense of panic that was drawing a black veil over everything around her. 'I had a difficult life. Things went wrong. I made some bad choices but I've made it all better. If you let me go, I can go back to my baby. I can be good for her. I'll be good for her forever.'

'You're a bad girl,' the man said, holding a quivering hand over her pubic hair. 'A bad girl who let anyone and everyone into this.' He slapped down hard and Lorna cried out, still raw from the stitching after labour.

'Please don't,' she sobbed. 'Please don't hurt me. I want to see my daughter again.'

'Do you not think she deserves better than you, slut?' he asked, pulling the belt from his trousers, red in the face and panting.

'I know she does,' Lorna cried out. 'I know she does and I try so hard every day to be the best I can. I'm begging you, let me go back to my baby.'

'I'm going to let you go back to her,' he said. 'When this is over, I'll take you back. When you're clean. When you're saved.'

Lorna saw the truth in his eyes. Her bravado had been pointless. She knew what hatred looked like. It was the black full stop in each of a man's eyes. Once again, she filled the air with the desolation of her screams.

Chapter Ten

Callanach handed Dr Spurr a bottle of Oban single malt and sighed. 'Don't you ever wish you'd chosen a different career, Jonty?'

'The dead would miss me, I fear. It takes a number of years to properly understand how to strike up a conversation with them. It's the last thing my trainees learn. These are not just bodies; they are untold stories,' the pathologist said. 'Thanks for the whisky. What's the occasion?'

'You're away from home and I thought you could use the comfort. This isn't the easiest case. And . . . I'm worried about Ava. I know she can handle herself, but she's taking it particularly hard. I'd like to move the investigation forward as quickly as I can. Is there anything more you can tell me about the doll?'

'Quite a lot, actually,' Jonty said. 'Come through. I was in the process of writing up my report, so I'll take you through it as I go.'

They walked into the lab, pulling on gloves. 'Regarding the other young woman who's been taken, Jonty, we've made no progress overnight. You've seen more of these cases than me, and I worked enough of them with Interpol. How long do you think she has? Zoey Cole survived a week.'

'The relentlessly ticking clock. I always hear it as the number of heartbeats we have left until we die. If it's good news you're after, you've come to the wrong man. I appreciate the single malt, although I think we might want to drink it together. The doll has provided additional information, none of which favours Lorna's situation.' He pointed towards a tray where various piles of materials had been left accessible. Both skin sections from the doll were laid out flat. Next to that was a mound of cut-up cloth. Finally there were two clear evidence bags. Callanach could see hair in the first, but nothing in the second. 'I spent yesterday conducting tests on the skin sections after you left. It has a strange texture, so much so that I broke the golden rule and handled part of it without my gloves on. That was the only way I could be sure, but the skin feels hardened. A medicated ointment had been applied to encourage the skin to thicken. It's used for people who have various conditions and it would have made cutting the skin easier, and less prone to tearing.'

'That's quite some level of preparation,' Callanach said.

'Which indicates that the kidnapper knew exactly what he or she had in mind well before taking Zoey. It took research and care. Not only that, but they knew that Zoey would need to be kept restrained for a minimum amount of time, requiring a place where she couldn't be discovered easily or accidentally.'

'Now they have Lorna, too.' Callanach crossed his arms. 'You think she's headed for the same treatment. That means we have just six days to find her.'

'Five days, given that it's nearly 5.30 p.m. now. And there's more,' Jonty said. 'This pile of cut-up rags was used to stuff the doll. It's cotton and contains a clothing label. Here.' He picked up a bag, inside which Callanach could see a small, silky label proclaiming a high street brand name and that the item had been a size 8.

'The killer cut up some of Zoey's clothes to stuff the doll with?' Callanach asked.

'I'm certain of it. We're testing for skin cells and DNA, but it makes sense. There are strips from a shirt and what is probably underwear. The shirt strips match the description of the clothes Zoey was wearing when she left the shelter,' Jonty said.

'What's in the other bags?' Callanach asked.

'This one,' Jonty held up a bag containing blunt snippets of brown hair, 'is hair from Zoey's head. We've matched it up with a section where you can see recent cuts. It was stuck onto the doll's head very crudely with superglue, a standard brand available from any supermarket, but it wasn't very effective. The doll's skin wasn't a good surface – too many oils and the medicated cream prevented the hair from really bonding. Much of the hair had fallen off into the pram.'

Callanach took another look at the skin sections, taking a closer look at the side where a face had been drawn. 'The eyes drawn on here are the same colour as Zoey's, and the mouth is small with thin lips, even with these weird vertical stitches over them,' he said. 'The killer literally tried to recreate her, right down to the details.'

'Hence the second bag,' Jonty said. 'In here are a few eyelashes, pulled out from Zoey while she was still alive. The injuries were too minute to have been spotted until the doll pointed us in the right direction, but under a microscope it's possible to see the redness on Zoey's eyelids where the lashes were plucked.'

'How many?' Callanach asked.

'Maybe a dozen from each eye, hard to be specific, and not all were stuck onto the doll,' Jonty said. 'Again, they didn't bond well.'

'Perhaps the killer gave up halfway through, or ran out of time,' Callanach said.

'That's a fair theory. It's meticulous work and that level of skill isn't on show here. Have you ever seen items made from human skin before, Luc?' Jonty asked.

'I haven't,' Callanach said, 'although I've read about it.'

'It's labour intensive, expert work. Human skin is hard to fashion. Various monsters throughout history became quite adept at it, but this is a clumsy recreation. Let me show you the stitches. I have close-up photographs on my computer.'

In Jonty's office, they sat next to each other in front of a computer screen. The images resembled a child's crude attempt at patchwork.

'The knots are quite basic. In places the cotton thread has been pulled too tight and has split the fine edges of the skin. The stitches are irregular and change direction,' Jonty said.

'It's like a work in progress,' Callanach said. 'A carefully thought out idea, highly symbolic, but which was poorly executed.'

'Exactly,' Jonty said. 'But now your killer holds another young woman.'

'You think the first doll was disappointing, but that it's a learning curve?' Callanach asked.

'It doesn't feel like a one-off to me,' Jonty said. 'The killer worked too hard at it. So much effort for a single pay-off. Then there's this.' He picked up a flat plastic folder from his desk. 'There was a message rolled up to form a tiny scroll, right in the centre of the stuffing. I found it minutes before you arrived. I was just processing it.'

Callanach picked up the folder and read aloud the words that were on the long strip of paper contained within. '"If there is anyone who curses his father or his mother, he shall surely be put to death; he has cursed his father or his mother, his blood-guiltiness is upon him." Oh fuck, Jonty, this sounds like a crusade.'

'Unfortunately, I agree. I was just looking up where it comes from, if you'll forgive me crossing into your discipline. The quote is from Leviticus, chapter twenty, verse nine. There are other references here to disrespectful children being put to death. It's proper fire-and-brimstone, Old Testament stuff.'

'It's someone who's aware of Zoey's problems with her stepfather then,' Callanach said.

'Not the stepfather himself?' Jonty asked.

'He didn't abduct her – we know that for sure. He has a watertight alibi. Spent the day at a community fete, photos and all. Zoey's mother seems genuinely upset, even though Zoey had left home and wasn't in contact with them.'

'Were other family members aware of the allegations?' Jonty asked.

'There's a brother in the army, but we've had confirmation that he was away on manoeuvres and hasn't been back in the UK for eighteen months. Plenty of other people were aware of the allegations against Christopher Myers, though. Zoey had contacted social workers, staff at the shelter and friends she stayed with at times. The police were even called in at one stage to encourage her to prosecute. She declined. If we consider everyone who knows what Zoey had alleged to be a suspect, it'll make a long list. What about the paper it's written on?'

'It's a section of paper cut with scissors to the shape of the quote, probably from an A4 sheet originally, no watermark on it. Looks very standard. I hope that's not your best lead,' the pathologist replied.

'Bloodguiltiness,' Callanach read. 'Who the hell uses language like that these days?'

'You'll have to check which version of the Bible it's from,' Jonty said. 'I didn't get that far in my research.'

'I'll need the paper transferred to a handwriting expert. Have you tested for fingerprints and DNA yet?' Callanach asked.

'I can't see any fingerprints, and other tests are underway, but referring this to a forensic handwriting analyst will be a waste of your time, I fear. Look at this.' Jonty brought up a photo of the writing, grossly enlarged. Callanach sat down next to him again. 'Every same letter – you see these letter f's – is exactly the same. Not just the shape and style, but the precise measurements. However, each letter has a small break before the next one. The script is cursive in style but not properly joined. It's all too regular.'

'They used a bloody stencil,' Callanach said.

'Your swearing sounds much more authentically Scots these days,' Jonty said. 'But I'm afraid you're correct about the stencil. You can probably source it on the internet. The font should be copyrighted.'

'But it means that it'll bear no resemblance to the killer's normal writing. Not the pressure points or the strokes, none of it. Clever,' Callanach said.

'Clever, well organised, dedicated, passionate. Unfortunately the word obsessive is the one that's been in my mind.'

'It needs to be kept quiet, Jonty. I know you won't say a word, but anyone on the staff here who knows about this . . .'

'No one knows yet, and only those with access to my report need find out. It'll be harder to control it at your end.'

'Can I sign this out of your evidence log and transfer it to our custody at the station?' Callanach asked. 'Ava will want to see it straight away.'

'You can. Would you join me this evening to open the bottle you so kindly brought?'

'I can't tonight, Jonty. I'm seeing someone, when work allows. If I leave the office at all tonight, that's where I'm going.'

'Glad to hear it,' Jonty said. 'I thought for sure you'd be headed back to France after the first case we did together. I'm pleased to see you've decided to give Scotland more of a chance.'

Callanach smiled at him. 'It was touch and go,' he said. 'Call me when you get the other test results in? Straight away, day or night.'

Back at the station, Callanach went immediately to Ava's office. She was wading through a mountain of paperwork, frowning at numbers.

'Sorry to interrupt. I'm just back from the pathologist. Zoey's murderer sent us a message.' He explained what Jonty had shown him. Ava was on her feet before he'd finished, checking her watch.

'Eight o'clock. The superintendent might just still be here. Come with me. I need Overbeck to sign off on the extra funding we're going to need.'

Together they went up the additional flight of stairs to Detective Superintendent's Overbeck's office, neither of them saying a word. Overbeck's reaction to them asking for more money was always the same. Keep it below budget. Finish it yesterday.

As Ava knocked on Overbeck's door, it opened. Lively's face appeared from within.

'Ma'am,' he said to Ava.

'What have you done now, Lively?' Ava asked. 'You need to learn to watch your mouth. I don't want any members of my squad in trouble at the moment. Get everyone together for a briefing. DI Callanach and I will be down in five minutes.'

Lively gave a small nod, didn't even bother insulting Callanach, and made for the stairs.

'What do you need, DCI Turner?' Overbeck called through the open door.

'Is there an issue with DS Lively?' Ava asked.

'Nothing that a period of suspension and a diet wouldn't cure,' Overbeck snarled. 'I see you brought DI Looks Over Substance with you. This doesn't bode well.'

Ava carried on in spite of Overbeck's jibe at Callanach. She'd never liked him, but then she'd never liked anyone, as far as Ava was aware. 'Zoey Cole's killer is a religious extremist, or at the very least is using that as an excuse to kill. He or she left us a note inside the doll that was found in the pram with Lorna Shaw's baby. There's also the possibility that the Mikey Parsons assault is linked. It's all twisted vigilante behaviour – cleaning up the city, exacting retribution for poor life choices or whatever the offender is telling himself. I'm also concerned that this may turn out to be a serial killer, and I believe it's going to get even nastier.'

'Three, Detective Chief Inspector. That's the magic number. You wait until you have three linked dead bodies before you get to use the S-word.' She sighed. 'You're here for me to lift the overtime limit, extend your funding and give you a uniformed squad as backup, right?' Ava didn't bother to answer. Overbeck checked her watch and flicked through a couple of pieces of paper on her desk. 'Fine. Off you go then. I'll see to the paperwork for the funding. Keep me updated and phone me next time you need something. It's quicker than taking the stairs.'

Ava risked a look at Callanach, who was staring open-mouthed at Overbeck.

'Thank you, ma'am,' Ava said. 'We'll need to say something to the press, but I'd like to keep quiet about the doll for now.'

'Agreed. Work out a statement with the media team. You can put my name on the bottom of it if that keeps the communications pressure off you during the investigation.'

'I will, thank you,' Ava said.

'I don't want the number three to be reached. You understand that, right? Edinburgh has had enough death to last it a while. See to it that the funding I'm extending is an effective pre-emptive strike, Turner.'

'Yes, ma'am. I understand,' Ava said. 'I'll do my best.'

'I know you will,' Overbeck said.

Ava and Callanach walked slowly out of the office without speaking. They were on the stairs down to the next floor when they both stopped at the same time.

'What just happened?' Callanach asked.

'I have no idea,' Ava said. 'But honestly, at the moment, I don't care. We need extra officers working with MIT if we're going to stand any chance of finding Lorna Shaw in time. I'm sure there'll be a price to pay later, and I, for one, plan on staying out of Overbeck's way until she's back to her normal foul-mouthed self.'

'Maybe she's really changed,' Callanach said.

'Maybe a prince on a white horse is about to ride through the station, throw me on the back of his trusty steed and whisk me away to a world where birds land on my hand and sing to me, and I never have to see another dead body again,' Ava said.

'Ma'am,' Salter called up the stairs to them. 'We've got another slashing victim in the city centre. Worse than before. The paramedics called us. They're not sure the victim will make it. The sergeant and I are going straight to the hospital. Everyone else is waiting for you in the briefing room.'

'All right, Salter,' Ava called back, raising her eyebrows at Callanach. 'Then again, maybe not.'

Chapter Eleven

The Meadows recreation area in the city, due west of Arthur's Seat, provided a vast green space for city dwellers' use, with long paths to jog or walk, tree cover providing shade for summer picnics and tennis courts for the more adventurous.

'Were you always told not to walk through the Meadows at night?' Salter asked Lively as they parked the car and headed for the area where the victim, now lying in a hospital bed, had been found.

'You're joking. If I'd been attacked and killed, my parents might have got a few quid from the local rag for the story. They'd have been delighted,' Lively laughed.

'Don't joke about it,' Salter said. 'No parent wants to lose a child.'

Lively's footsteps stalled. 'Christie, I'm sorry, that was stupid of me, I didn't mean . . .'

'I know you didn't,' Salter said. 'I just think about what happened more when we're at crime scenes like this. Somehow it seems worse when the victims are homeless or prostitutes. Imagine dying and thinking no one really cares.'

'That's what we're here for,' Lively said. 'We pick up the

pieces and make sure justice is served, even for people the rest of society has dumped. We're the last-ditch family, or something like that.'

'I suppose so.' Salter smiled. 'That's a good way of looking at it. Right. The victim, Paddy Yates, will lose his left eye, the surgeon said. The nerves on the side of his mouth aren't expected to recover either.'

'How long until he'll be out of surgery and able to talk to us?' Lively asked.

'Tomorrow lunchtime before they'll let us in the same room as him,' Salter said. 'Not that it'll do any good. The paramedics I spoke to found an empty Spice packet in Paddy's pocket. He was completely incomprehensible but still on his feet. It's amazing how Spice users stay upright with all the crap they've got in their systems.'

'Aye, should call them Weebles, not zombies,' Lively said. Salted looked at him blankly. 'Never mind, girl, you've to be a certain age to remember that one.'

The tennis courts were a stone's throw from the children's play area. Huddled at the base of the climbing equipment was a bundle of cardboard boxes, a shopping trolley, and bin bags overflowing with clothes and tatty old sleeping bags.

'How're we doing over here?' Lively called out cheerily as he approached.

'Fuckin' polis,' was the response.

'Did any of you happen to witness the incident?' Lively continued unabashed. 'Only there's a man having his face stitched back together as we speak, and he's not the first. We'd be grateful for any help you can give us.'

'Like you'll fuckin' do anything about it,' one of them muttered.

'Got any money?' another asked.

Salter looked across the park at a nearby row of cafes. Most were closed, but one was catering for the evening student crowd and still serving hot food. 'Tell you what. See if you can remember anything that might help, and I'll buy each of you a hot meal, waitress service and all. Your choice of coffee or tea, but no booze.'

A general muttering followed, then one of the huddle of men spoke up.

'Paddy had taken that zombie shit. He'd been standing up, just staring, away with the fairies for about two hours. Stupid prick. Couldnae even speak his own name by that point.' The man drew a bottle of unidentified clear liquid from his sleeve and took a long swig. The odour Salter caught from it was more reminiscent of a hardware store than an off-licence. 'Then he started walking round in circles, all the way round the edge of the playground. Must have done twenty laps. Walked into that bin over there every friggin' time. Could we have the cash instead of the meal?'

'No, you cheeky git, you can't,' Salter said. 'Did you actually see Paddy get attacked?'

'We heard it,' another of the men said. 'Sounded like someone had cut his balls off. I never heard a man scream like that in my life, poor bastard. Didn't make him run or nothing though. He just staggered out from behind those trees looking like someone had run his face through a shredder. I nearly puked.'

'You must have checked around to see what had happened,' Salter said. There was a shuffling between the men and a long pause. 'Come on,' Salter said. 'You saw something. Now really isn't the time to get huffy about sharing information with the police.'

'Give it to her, Stonk,' one of the men said, elbowing his companion sharply in the ribs.

'Fuck's sake,' the one known as Stonk replied. 'Give me a

minute.' He got slowly to his feet and began the painful process of lifting one layer of clothing after another, checking through endless pockets and cursing intermittently when he came up empty. 'Where did I put the wee bastard?' he muttered to himself.

'What exactly is it you're looking for?' Salter asked.

'The key,' he said, letting the vowel sound extend as he gleefully presented it, dangling from his fingertips.

Salter watched DS Lively drift across the play area to a small copse of trees, where uniformed officers were pointing at something on the ground. His timing wasn't coincidental. Now that Stonk had actually produced what might prove to be relevant information, Salter would have to take a formal statement from him, and that meant spending at least an hour writing it out, checking it through with him and sitting in the vicinity of fumes that would haunt her clothing until they next made it through the wash. She sighed.

'All right. Where did you get the key and why is it relevant to the attack on Paddy?'

'We saw three blokes running away. One of them dropped it,' Stonk said. 'I went over to pick it up.'

'How far away were they from you?' Salter asked.

'They were taking off down that path, just to the right of the trees, where your man is now,' said another, pointing.

Salter stared and tried to estimate the distance. It was at least thirty metres away. 'Are you telling me you saw an object this small fall from a man's pocket as he was running in the semi-dark? Forgive me, but that seems unlikely.' There was a lack of reply and an uncomfortable ducking of Stonk's head into his multiple hoods. 'I see,' Salter said, the picture clearer as she imagined how the scene must have played out. 'Paddy screams, you all listen to see what's happening and then you hear the joyful sound of metal falling onto the concrete. How quickly did you manage to get up to see if it was a coin that had been dropped?'

'That's not nice,' Stonk said. 'I'm helping you.'

'And I appreciate it, but an accurate picture would be more helpful than the one you're giving me. So you didn't actually see it fall then, you just heard a metal object hit the floor and this was what you found?'

'Aye, maybe,' Stonk said. 'But it was in the right place at the right time. That's got to count for something.'

Salter rubbed a tired hand over her eyes. 'You three stay here,' she said. 'I'll need a statement from each of you. Do you want dinner before that or after?' Predictably, there was a chorus response in favour of before. She called a uniformed officer over to stand guard so that none of her witnesses could disappear before she returned from the cafe with their food, not that they were likely to get difficult until after their bellies were full. Still, a deal was a deal.

'Sarge,' she shouted, holding out a gloved hand for Stonk to give her the key. She walked over to find Lively staring at a patch of ground that even in the dark she could see was crimson.

'They cut deep this time, much deeper than with Mikey Parsons. That's a lot of blood right there,' Lively said.

'Apparently three men ran from the scene. This was picked up afterwards, over here, and it was heard hitting the floor at the same time as the men ran. It needs logging as evidence.' She dropped it into a bag that Lively produced from his pocket.

'Could have been from anyone,' Lively said. 'They might just have kicked it when they ran.'

'I know, but it's enough that I've to buy them all dinner,' Salter said.

'Right you are. I'll have one of the uniforms go and start taking statements. Bloody mess this is. Two attacks days apart, same Z mark on the face. What sort of animal does that to a bunch of men already down on their luck?'

'The sort that don't want to run any risk at all of a victim fighting back or being able to identify them,' Salter said. 'Cowards.' She wandered off towards the lights of the cafe, hands shoved deep into her pockets, head down.

Ava inspected the key. 'How good are the descriptions they gave of the men running away?' she asked Lively and Salter.

'Three figures that looked male, all wearing dark clothing with hoods up. Can't accurately state height. Average weights, not obese, too tall to be young kids. Didn't see any faces. That's the best we can do,' Lively replied.

'And the witnesses themselves? If one is very poor and ten is perfect, how are we rating their reliability in terms of them being made to look absolutely ridiculous by a defence lawyer?' Ava asked.

'It really depends if you regard being drunk, potentially stoned and possibly with some mental health issues as affecting credibility,' Lively said.

'It's a one, ma'am,' Salter added.

'Great,' Ava replied. 'Prognosis for this victim?'

'He'll live. Lost a lot of blood though. Might easily have died from shock alone. We phoned the hospital when we got back. He's out of surgery but has lost an eye. They say his vital signs indicated severe amounts of drugs in his system, so to be frank, he'll be sod-all use in terms of identifying his attackers,' Lively said.

'Right, let's process the key for prints, DNA and any useful fibres. It has a tiny fob on it. Have you checked that out yet?' She peered closer at the key, turning the bag over in her hands.

'Not yet. We came straight to see you,' Salter said. 'Quite a large area of the Meadows had to be sealed off and by the time we left there were journalists grilling the officers at the cordon. It seemed likely you'd need an update as a priority.'

Ava hit the space bar of her computer and brought the screen to life. '"Pro Libertate".' She squinted to read from the fob, typing the words into a search engine. 'Blue and white quarters, with a unicorn.' She hit the enter button and waited. Seconds later a website appeared, displaying photos of happy young men and women under a decorative banner across the top of the screen, and the legend 'Scotland's future leaders, educated here today' written in bold script below the words 'The Leverhulme School, Edinburgh'.

'That's an independent school not far from the city centre,' Ava said. 'Its pupils must use the Meadows as a thoroughfare into the city. What we have here is probably a locker key.' She turned to Salter. 'What was your impression of the witness who produced it?'

'He was reluctant to hand it over at first, but when he did I got no sense that he was lying, ma'am,' Salter said. 'Although I had offered them a hot meal if they gave me anything concrete to go on,' she added slowly, her tone acknowledging the fact that such inducements were likely to produce results just for the sake of the food.

'Feels like a hiding to nothing, but we can't leave it without checking it out. Lively, get the key through forensics so we can take it to the school and follow it up. We'll need a public appeal for witnesses in the Meadows at the relevant time, anyone who might have seen three men leaving the area quickly. You handle that, Salter. I also want to pursue a line of enquiry to see if we can link Lorna Shaw with either Mikey Parsons or the latest slashing victim, Paddy Yates. Same dealers, same drugs, known common associates or hangouts, anything at all. Concentrate on Lorna first, then double-check all the same information for Zoey, just in case they ever crossed paths. We now have three victims who've been on the wrong end of a blade, and one more still missing. I want to know what the common factor is.'

Lively seemed to be having a problem with his neck, tipping his head with increasing jerkiness in Salter's direction. Finally Ava realised what he was doing. 'How are you holding up, DC Salter? I'm happy to accommodate you coordinating in the incident room if the crime scenes are proving difficult for you.'

'They're not, ma'am, and whilst I appreciate the sergeant's concern, I'd prefer it if he'd stop trying to send messages behind my back. With respect, it makes him look like a complete prat.'

'I agree with you on that score, Constable.' Ava smiled. 'Although he means well. Just take it a week at a time, and make sure you come to me if you feel you're being coddled. Agreed?'

'Agreed,' Salter said.

'You can go, Constable. I'd like the appeal for information to go out while it's still fresh in people's minds. If we don't get a lead soon we're going to have to set up an undercover operation. I won't leave the city's homeless population to get butchered with no one out there to protect them, but uniforms aren't the answer. More importantly, if we can find whoever's assaulting the city's drug addicts, it might just lead us to Lorna Shaw.'

Salter and Lively turned and moved towards Ava's office door.

'Not you, Sergeant,' Ava added, waiting until Salter had left before continuing. 'DS Lively, you'll have noticed that we're busy at the moment. We have one dead young woman, two badly injured vulnerable members of our community and a missing mother whose baby needs her. Is there any particular reason you appear to be choosing this week to pick fights with the Detective Superintendent?'

'To be fair, ma'am, no one needs to pick a fight with the Evil Overlord. She just seems to have taken a shine to me. What can I say?'

'That was more than enough, so let me issue a very clear order. Stay out of her way. Don't break any more rules. Do not add to my to-do list, and sort this case out immediately so that I have every pair of boots back out there looking for Lorna Shaw. The only response I require is confirmation that you have heard me and understood.'

'Yes, ma'am,' Lively said, managing by some miracle not to smirk.

'Good. Now get on with it,' Ava said.

Lively walked towards the door, stopping as he held it a few inches open. 'You're more like her than you realise sometimes, ma'am.'

Ava stared at him. 'Leave now, Lively, before I make a phone call that will deprive you of that hard-earned pension you're waiting to collect.'

Lively smiled, shook his head and did as he'd been told. Ava didn't need to threaten to fire him. She was pretty sure Overbeck already had that in hand.

Chapter Twelve

The mother and baby unit was eerily quiet, as if even the babies appreciated the direness of the situation and weren't bothering their mothers. An effort had been made to make the place homely, but there was no mistaking its institutional feel. Cheap prints hung limply on the walls. The kitchen was functional more than welcoming. Each bed was the same, with unadorned white duvet covers. It was far from inhospitable, but it certainly wasn't where any girl dreamed of ending up, Callanach thought, and it wasn't somewhere you'd want to stay very long. Much like Zoey's domestic abuse shelter, it was a stepping stone rather than a destination.

Tripp and Callanach had spent the morning interviewing the residents, asking the same questions of each of them. Had Lorna Shaw seemed scared? Had she confided anything out of the ordinary? Did she have any reason for running away? The answer from each new mother to every enquiry was the same. No, on all counts. Lorna loved her baby. Regular voluntary blood and hair samples showed that she was both alcohol and drug free. She had kept every appointment. Lorna had even begun talking about returning to education part-time when her baby was a little older. She had plans – that was the message Callanach took from the interviewees. Motherhood had given her hope.

Presented with her files, Tripp had begun the task of cross-referencing each person involved in Lorna's care with Zoey's. More names came up in both girls' files than they had been expecting.

'That's not unusual,' the unit director told them. 'We share resources with all the government-funded institutions in the city. The advisers travel around and see the women where they live, so those women don't have to go into public places. For the women living at the shelter, it avoids them potentially bumping into someone who might be violent or want to silence them. For the residents of our unit, it also means they steer clear of old haunts where drugs might be passed over, or the temptation to go to a pub might be too strong, or unhelpful acquaintances might be remade. There will be benefits advisers, housing consultants, medical professionals, even lawyers who have come into contact with both women. All of them would have been vetted, of course, and there will be a record of each occasion on which they came into contact with either of the young women.'

'We'll need to take these files back to the police station,' Callanach told him. 'We have to cross-reference and find those people who worked with both women.'

'Of course,' the director agreed. 'May I ask . . . We've kept Lorna's baby here for now. We're able to provide care for her in a familiar environment, and the last thing we want to do is suggest that the situation is hopeless . . . but I suppose I'm asking if you are any further forward in terms of locating Lorna. Sooner or later I will have to make longer-term plans for Tansy.'

'I understand,' Callanach said. 'Early this morning, uniformed officers identified CCTV footage of someone pushing the pram into the lane where it was found, but it's black and white, very grainy, and it was raining at the time. We have no clear facial features to help us identify her kidnapper, but it is believed to be a tall male. The CCTV clip only lasts a few seconds before the man goes round a corner. We have no vehicular details. I need to ask you to keep that confidential for now. A press release will follow shortly.'

The director nodded. 'I'll see you out,' he said. 'Is your instinct that Lorna's kidnapping is random – that she was simply unlucky – or that someone chose her for a reason, Detective Inspector?' he asked as they walked quietly through the corridors. 'We're obviously concerned about the safety of the other mothers here.'

Callanach glanced across at Tripp. It was the question that had been on all their minds since Lorna had been taken, and the answer was becoming increasingly obvious. 'We don't believe it's a coincidence,' Callanach said, his French accent all the more pronounced when he was speaking quietly. 'I'm afraid it seems as if Lorna was targeted. There are too many similarities between her situation and Zoey's. Also, if the kidnapper wanted any random girl of Lorna's age, it would have been much easier to take someone who wasn't pushing a pram. There have also been two other attacks in the city in the same timeframe, with drug users being targeted for some vigilante treatment. It's possible that all the crimes are linked, but we don't yet know how or why.'

'I see. Thank you for being so open with me. You evidently have your hands rather full at the moment.' The director paused outside a room in which a nurse could be seen feeding a baby as she chatted to another woman who was busy filling out a chart. 'Poor little thing,' the director said. 'Life is so cruel. Tansy had a mother who was shaping up to be the sort of parent she

99

really needed. Imagine growing up never knowing where your mother was, if she was dead or alive even.'

'That's Lorna's daughter?' Tripp asked, wandering into the room.

The nurse giving the feed smiled at him. 'It is,' she said. 'Would you like to feed her?'

'Oh no, I've never held a baby,' Tripp said. 'I'd be terrified I might drop her.'

'I'll do it,' Callanach said. He sat down in the chair next to the nurse and held his arms across his chest for the baby to be placed safely into. Supporting her head, he held the bottle at an angle, feeling the baby wriggle then settle as she began to feed again. 'She's smaller than I'd imagined,' he said. 'Is this okay?'

'That's absolutely fine,' the nurse said. 'Do you have children of your own?'

'No,' Luc replied quietly, stroking the baby's face with his free thumb as she sucked.

'Well, you should,' the nurse said. 'Just look at you.'

Luc concentrated on the tiny face beneath him and tried not to wonder if he would ever have children. In his twenties he'd have sworn that a family wasn't on his horizon. Now, in his mid-thirties, it was a more pressing consideration, complicated by the fact that his body was showing no signs of recovering from the post-traumatic stress disorder that had rendered him impotent after the rape allegation. His body softened into the cushions behind him as the baby lost interest in the bottle, her eyes starting to close as her fingers squeezed and relaxed around his thumb. She fought sleep for another minute as Tripp, the nurse and the administrator watched silently, then snuffled into a contented rest.

'She'll need winding,' the nurse whispered. 'Why don't you let me take her now?'

'Is there any news on Lorna?' the administrator asked while Callanach gently transferred the baby to the nurse.

'Nothing yet,' Tripp whispered. 'We're working round the clock, trying to trace her last movements.'

'I can't believe it,' the administrator said. 'It's so unfair, really. She was such a troubled girl when she first came to our attention, and now when she's finally getting herself straightened out and making progress, this happens. It just seems cruel.'

Callanach stood up, noting the baby smell that lingered on his clothes. 'We're going to do whatever it takes to find her,' he said.

'I'll keep her in my prayers,' the nurse said, putting Tansy over her shoulder and gently patting her on the back. 'Do call if we can help at all. There's someone on duty here twenty-four hours a day. Tansy needs her mummy back, don't you, sweetheart?'

'You're a natural at that, sir,' Tripp said as he and Callanach got into the car to head back towards the city centre.

'End of conversation,' Callanach said, taking out his note book and turning to the page with Tyrone Leigh's details. 'I've got the full file on Sandra Tilly's boyfriend. Not the sort of person you'd want in a relationship with a woman who runs a domestic abuse shelter.'

'Previous for blackmail, you said, sir,' Tripp replied, as he stopped at traffic lights. 'What were the circumstances?'

'He found out that a next-door neighbour was sleeping with her boss. Apparently a car was appearing at her house during the working day and he got curious. When she couldn't pay what he was asking, the woman had no choice but to turn to the police for help.'

'Are we going to his home address?' Tripp asked.

'No, he works at a hardware store. I think he'll feel more

compelled to get rid of us with straight answers here than on his home turf. Pull over,' Callanach said. They walked into a cavernous store that was piping various announcements regarding that day's deals across the air. The manager spent a few minutes trying to persuade them to see Tyrone out of work hours, then got called away to resolve a pricing problem. The deputy manager had no problem summoning Tyrone immediately.

'You can't come to where I work,' was Tyrone's opening gambit.

'You're a potential witness, Mr Leigh,' Callanach said. 'Does it really matter where we ask to talk to you?'

'You know fucking well how this is going to look to my boss,' Tyrone said.

'Ah now, see, you want to watch your language,' Tripp said mildly. 'Bad language is what people use when they're feeling defensive. Would you be feeling defensive for any reason at the moment?'

'I don't have to take this shit,' Leigh said, pulling his head up and squaring his shoulders. 'I've done nothing.'

'You've done things before,' Callanach said. 'Does your girlfriend, Sandra, know you once blackmailed a woman? I'm guessing not, given her job.'

'And threatening behaviour,' Tripp added. 'Was that the same victim, or someone completely different?'

'Keep your voice down,' Leigh said. 'We need to go into the car park if you want to discuss this.'

Callanach glanced around at the patchy green walls of the staff room and picked up a grubby mug from the sink. 'I think here is fine,' he said. 'Presumably you declared your convictions when you got this job, so it shouldn't come as any surprise to your employer.'

'Wanker,' Leigh said.

Callanach ignored the half-hearted insult. Tyrone Leigh had

already lost the fight. 'You bumped into Zoey in a supermarket once, and you knew about her stepfather. What else?'

'Nothing,' Tyrone moaned. 'I've done nothing wrong.'

'You didn't like that she was offhand with you when you met her,' Callanach said. 'So much so that your girlfriend had to explain Zoey's personal circumstances. Do you always get that annoyed when people aren't as friendly as you'd like them to be?'

'She was always snooty. It wasn't just then.' Callanach crossed his arms and waited for Tyrone's brain to catch up with his mouth. 'Sod it,' Tyrone said after a pause.

'Tell us about the other times you saw her,' Tripp said.

'It was only ever coming in and out the back door of the shelter. Sandra and I both work shifts, so I pick her up when I can. I used to hear Zoey outside the back door on her phone sometimes.'

'You mean you waited out of view and listened,' said Tripp. 'I'm guessing Zoey would have made those calls elsewhere if she knew she was being overheard.'

Callanach looked him up and down. Tyrone Leigh was a meathead. He'd have thought Sandra Tilly would have figured that out for herself, given her career choice, but then there was no accounting for attraction. Leigh was big, burly and stupid. Too stupid to withstand more than a couple of minutes of questioning without giving information away. Not at all within the profile boundaries of the kidnapper they were looking for.

'Tell me about the conversations you overheard,' Callanach said. 'How did Zoey seem?'

'Same as all of them,' Tyrone said. 'Scared. Stressed. Fed up with living in the shelter. None of them are grateful, not really. Maybe for the first week or so, then it's all about how soon they can get a flat and how little space they've got. Don't know how Sandra puts up with them.'

'Think carefully,' Callanach said. 'I want details. Did you hear her say any names on the phone? Did she talk about anyone in particular? Did she have any plans for the future?'

'I once heard her talking about her brother,' Tyrone said. 'She'd been trying to get in touch with him, but he hadn't seemed bothered about calling her back. She was angry about that. Said she'd left the address of the shelter for him and all – that's a straightforward breaking of the rules. I don't know who she was talking to. Other calls were to mates, making plans to see them.'

'Do you know someone called Lorna Shaw?' Tripp asked him.

'Is she the girl who's gone missing?' Leigh asked, his voice going up a notch, hands in the air. 'Aw no – no, you don't. You're not making out I had anything to do with that one. I never even heard that girl's name before it was on the news. What's she got to do with Zoey anyway?'

'Have you come across a man called Mikey Parsons?' Callanach asked.

'Now I've really got no fucking clue what you're talking about,' Tyrone huffed.

'Or Paddy Yates? Both men have had their faces cut open in the last few days,' Tripp said.

'That's fucking great, that is. So this is just find a sucker and pin every bit of shit you can on him, is it? No, I don't know either of them and I think I want a lawyer, if you don't mind.'

Callanach motioned to Tripp that they could wrap it up and took a step towards Tyrone. 'Mr Leigh,' he said, 'we'll leave you in peace now. But if you hang around at the back of the shelter any more, I'll find a reason to arrest you. If you listen to those women's conversations when they don't know you're there, I'll make sure your boss knows all about your criminal history. And if you don't tell your girlfriend about the blackmail and the threatening behaviour in the next forty-eight hours, I intend to make sure she has all the information necessary to make an educated decision about whether or not she should continue to be in a relationship with you. Is any part of that unclear?'

'Froggie bastard,' Tyrone said, pushing his face towards Callanach's but keeping his feet where they were. Callanach noted the false threat and smiled.

'I think you have some paint pots to stack,' he said. Tyrone held his stance, scrunching up his mouth in protest but unable to come up with a sufficiently good comeback to risk the consequences. Eventually he stepped away, turning his head and spitting on the floor as he went back into the store.

Callanach's heart sank as he watched him disappear. He had proved to be just another dead end. Lorna Shaw was out there somewhere, waiting to be rescued, and they still had absolutely no idea how to find her.

Chapter Thirteen

Leverhulme School was housed in one of Edinburgh's most impressive privately owned buildings, at the end of Millerfield Place, and resembled a grand old hotel more than an educational establishment. Parents had the option to send their boys there for the day or the whole term, depending on their views of boarding. The school catered for eleven- to eighteen-year-olds, and the air was almost tangibly thick with hormones. Ava stared at the deep red brick facade and the ornate chimneys, knowing the beauty of the outside would be matched by the pomposity of the souls inhabiting the place. Day fees alone were in excess of forty thousand pounds a year. Boarders could pay double that. Her own boarding school days had been spent avoiding the bitchier girls and being unavailable to befriend the really dull ones. Ava had sought normality in the midst of entitlement and oestrogen. Escaping to university had been the most liberating experience of her life.

'Did you have to forcibly send Salter home or did she go willingly?' Ava asked DS Lively.

'I didn't tell her I was doing any more work on the case tonight,' Lively replied. 'And she looked grateful to be going.

Whether Christie wants to admit it or not, she gets tired faster than before.'

'I imagine the scarring from the wounds – both internal and external – is painful. She'll have lost fitness and muscle as well. Keep an eye on her hours,' Ava said. 'So the headmaster agreed to let us in then? Not to doubt you, but . . .'

'Ma'am, would I lie to you, then turn up at the door of one of Edinburgh's finest schools – or so it says on their website – and demand entry unannounced?'

'Yes,' Ava said, walking towards a pair of wooden doors above which the school motto was carved in Latin. The right-hand door opened as they neared it.

'Detective Chief Inspector, please do come in. I'm the headmaster, Anthony McGowan.' The man extended his hand. It rested limply in Ava's when she grasped it. She tried not to shudder.

'I'm Ava Turner, and this is Detective Sergeant Lively,' Ava said, hoping her sergeant wasn't pulling faces behind her at the overblown grandeur of the entrance hall. Gilt work enhanced the beams and matching fireplaces adorned each end of the hall. Oil paintings the size of hockey goals hung on the walls, depicting famous battles, and leather furniture that might have sat around for centuries tempered the formality of it all. Ava's heart sank. The phrase treading on eggshells was going to be such an understatement when they explained their purpose in visiting the school that she might as well have broken down the front door.

'Nice place you've got here,' Lively said, crossing the hall to rub his hands in front of one of the roaring fires, which really weren't necessary.

'Thank you,' the headmaster replied. 'We feel very privileged to occupy such a historic house. Would you like some tea while we chat?'

'Actually, Mr McGowan, we're here to identify the owner of this key,' Ava said, pulling the plastic bag from her pocket and holding it aloft. 'Its owner might have witnessed a crime and we're keen to talk to them. Do you know where it might have come from? It's on a Leverhulme School fob.'

The headmaster's face indicated that the marked key fobs might not be used in the future.

'Ah, that would involve you going into the student areas, I'm afraid, and that is a slightly complicated procedure. Do you have any paperwork with you that would facilitate such an activity?' Mr McGowan asked, his voice professionally sugary in spite of the turn in the conversation.

'It's just a lost key,' Ava said. 'It's late in the evening. I'm sure all your students are tucked up in their dorms so there's no risk that we'll come into contact with any of them. Of course, we expect a member of your staff to remain with us for the duration of our visit. We're not intending to take any liberties.'

The headmaster cleared his throat and took a deep breath, nostrils flaring dramatically. 'I hope this doesn't sound more heavy-handed than I intend it to, but I am extremely well acquainted with some of Police Scotland's most senior figures. I'm not sure they would be very impressed to hear that an officer had requested access without the legal steps being taken.'

'We don't need to take any legal steps, if you consent to us being on the premises,' Lively said.

'From the school's perspective, it's more discreet,' Ava said. 'No paperwork, filing of grounds, court hearings, publicity. This way, we come in, we look, we leave. If we find nothing of relevance, it's as if we were never here.'

The headmaster made a small sound in his throat that might have been a suppressed expletive. He sighed. 'I can allow you thirty minutes, then I must insist on locking the doors for the night. What you're holding is a key to a student day locker, for those pupils who do not board with us. There's no number on it, so that the locker cannot be accessed if the key is dropped and picked up by someone other than the rightful owner. I'll show you to the corridor.'

They followed him in single file, Ava first, then Lively. Somehow, making conversation seemed taboo as they walked. The corridors sported wooden panelling and paintings of former masters, which became photographs as they reached a new section of building. Grand glass cases of sports trophies gleamed and their footsteps echoed on the oak flooring. Ava felt as if she had gone back in time. So many British public schools were like this; it was a wonder they hadn't all failed with centuries of inbreeding.

'Here you are,' the headmaster said, presenting a row of metal cabinets. He looked at his watch. 'There's no spare staff member to supervise you, and I myself have work to do, but I'm sure Edinburgh's finest can be trusted.' Ava recognised his intonation as question and statement in equal measure, and opted for silence in response. 'You have thirty minutes, then I shall return to fetch you. Should you find that the key opens a locker, please do not touch or disturb any of the contents. I will be able to tell you the name of the student to whom the locker is allocated, and we'll take the matter from there.' He stalked off in the direction from which they'd come, leaving Lively staring with crossed arms and raised eyebrows at Ava.

'Not a word, Sergeant,' Ava cautioned him. 'There's nothing you can be thinking that I haven't thought myself.'

'Were you thinking how ironic it is that this school uses a historic Scots clan motto meaning freedom when it embodies almost everything William Wallace stood against?'

Ava paused in the process of shedding her coat and turned to look at Lively. 'I'm going to have to give you that one. That hadn't occurred to me. Do I owe you an apology for failing to have spotted your hidden philosophical depths and historical expertise?'

'Not really. I was actually thinking what a complete bawbag the headmaster is, but I got your attention with the clever stuff, did I not?' He grinned.

'God help me,' Ava muttered. 'Three hundred lockers. Let's start at the far end. I'll try fifty, then you try fifty. Come on.'

She took the key from the plastic bag, holding it in gloved hands as she inserted it into one locker after another. Sometimes it went into the locker but wouldn't turn, or else it wouldn't go in at all. Four times it got stuck and they wasted precious minutes jiggling it back out. They were at locker number 278 and losing faith that it would fit one at all when the key slid happily home and turned silently in its lock.

'Careful not to disturb anything inside,' Ava said. 'At this point, we really should have permission to search.'

'I'm looking, not touching,' Lively said. 'Cigarettes, phone charger, sunglasses, scarf . . .' He checked up and down the corridor before reaching in a hand and lifting up a textbook. 'Condoms at the back. Unopened, although you have to admire the constant optimism of teenage boys. A few photos. Nothing groundbreaking.'

Footsteps echoed from a distance. Ava and Lively backed away from the open locker and waited for the headmaster to reach them. He appeared carrying a clipboard.

'I see you've had some success,' he said. 'May I have the locker number?'

'278,' Ava said.

'That'll be one of our sixth formers. The lockers are allocated in order from lowest years to highest.' He ran one finger down a sheet of paper. 'Plunkett, Leo. He's been with us for several years.'

'Do you have his home address?' Lively asked.

'Is that really necessary?' the headmaster asked.

'He may be a witness in a very serious assault case which is not a one-off occurrence. We need to speak with Leo tonight. If he has information that might avoid further attacks, we'd like to get it sooner rather than later.'

Fifteen minutes later, they were knocking on the cherry-red front door of a Heriot Row house that stood an impressive five storeys high. Outside, a Maserati sat like a lifestyle price tag. After several minutes, a man opened the front door with a face like thunder.

'Mr Plunkett, I'm Detective Chief Inspector Ava Turner. I apologise for calling on you in the evening, but I'm afraid it's important that we speak with your son, Leo.'

'It's late,' Mr Plunkett said.

'We wouldn't ask if it weren't both urgent and important,' Ava said.

'Dad?' a voice queried from further inside the house.

'Leo, go into my study,' Mr Plunkett ordered. The boy walked briefly into view as he crossed the hallway behind his father. Ava estimated Leo Plunkett to be five foot eleven and of medium build. The headmaster had told them Leo was seventeen. It was a difficult age for boys, she assumed. The combination of a man's body and a teenager's immaturity could be toxic and confusing.

'What's this about?' Mr Plunkett asked.

'An assault in the city. We just have a couple of questions for your son, in case he saw anything.' Ava didn't wait to be asked anything else, walking past the father into the study, where Leo was perched on a sofa, texting. As she introduced herself, Lively and Mr Plunkett followed her in.

'Leo, have you lost your locker key recently?' she asked.

He nodded slowly. 'Yeah, actually. No idea where, though. It must have fallen out of my pocket somewhere. I've been meaning to ask for a replacement from the office, but the reality is that I rarely use my locker these days. There's nothing much in it.'

'Number 278, is it?' Lively asked.

Leo Plunkett stared at him as if he had crawled out from under a large and unsightly working-class rock. 'Is there a problem?' he asked.

'Have you been in the Meadows recently?' Ava asked, keeping her voice light.

'I go through the Meadows most days, both during the week and at weekends. Is that where my key was found? Makes sense. I probably dropped it while I was taking my phone out of my pocket. How sweet of you both to come round and return it.' Ava watched the corners of the boy's mouth curl, and fought the urge to put him in his place. She had grown up with boys like Leo Plunkett. Her parents had assumed she would marry the sort of man the Leverhulme School produced. Luckily, she had decided to attach herself to her career rather than a member of the opposite sex.

'When were you last in the Meadows?' Ava asked.

'Where's this going?' the boy's father interjected.

Ava ignored him. 'Yesterday?'

'I must have passed through at lunchtime,' Leo said. He yawned and stretched. 'Are we done? I have a fitting for a new suit in the morning before physics, and I don't want to miss it.'

'Your key was found in the area where a man was attacked,' Ava continued, 'at about the same time as the attack. What were your movements after school yesterday until the evening?'

'That sounds like more than just a witness question,' Mr Plunkett said. 'Leo, you don't have to answer that.'

'It's fine, don't fuss.' Leo turned his attention fully onto Ava, keeping his eyes focused on hers and speaking slowly. 'I finished school. I walked home. I'd also been through the Meadows at lunchtime, around 1 p.m. I had no idea there had been an incident. I do hope no one important has been hurt.' He smiled. Ava's mouth went dry as she maintained eye contact with him. Most teenagers would look away, she thought. This boy had a confidence born of a sense of entitlement, and from a lifetime of never being told he was just flesh and blood like everyone else on the planet. Somewhere deep inside Leo Plunkett was the certain knowledge that his cells were comprised of finer atoms. He would learn, Ava thought.

'The attack was on a homeless man, Paddy Yates,' Lively said. 'Would you know anything about it, by any chance?'

'Homelessness? Not really,' Leo joked, his eyes still locked on Ava's.

'This is ridiculous,' Plunkett senior chipped in. 'You claimed this was an urgent matter. There must be hundreds of attacks on homeless people across the country every week. How dare you disturb us and question my son like this? You're going to have to leave now.'

'Just before we go, I don't suppose you ever met a girl called Zoey Cole?'

'I'm afraid not,' Leo smiled. 'Much as I'd like to have been able to help you.'

'Or Lorna Shaw?' Ava continued.

'What on earth is the relevance of this now?' Leo's father growled.

'It's an ongoing situation. We're asking anyone we come into contact with at present. Lorna's missing. There's a nationwide attempt to locate her. As Leo goes through the Meadows regularly, it's possible he might have bumped into her there.'

'Is she another homeless drug addict then?' Leo asked politely, raising his eyes with smug innocence.

'She's another victim,' Ava said, keeping her tone equally polite.

Leo stood up and offered Ava his hand. 'It was lovely to meet you, DCI Turner. Was he very badly hurt, your Mr Yates?'

'He was, actually,' Ava said. 'It's nice of you to show concern.'

'I'm only sorry I can't help with your enquiries,' Leo said.

His father sighed from the doorway. Ava extracted her hand and left the house, with Lively close behind her. The front door closed with an ill-disguised slam.

'Lovely family,' Lively said as he did his coat up. 'No doubt the boy will be a politician one day. He has all the hallmarks of a fine member of society.'

'If you're waiting for me to tell you that he's very young and you shouldn't judge him, or that you shouldn't hold the sins of the father against the son, I won't. My impression of Leo is that he's a complete idiot. However, being utterly dislikeable and having a motive to carve up someone's face are two different things. Leo's key could have landed on that path in any number of ways.'

Lively walked ahead of her towards the car. 'Aye,' he said, as he went. 'Then again, it's just possible that little fucker thought it'd be funny to maim one of the proletariat. You looked into his eyes. Tell me you didn't feel it too.'

Ava couldn't.

Chapter Fourteen

'Try this,' Natasha said, grabbing a free food sample from a vendor and thrusting it towards Ava's mouth.

'Wow, how much garlic?' Ava asked. 'Seriously, I have to work tomorrow. I'm going to be breathing fumes all over everyone.'

'It's your own fault. I've been asking you to come to the food festival with me all week. It's not my fault you left it until nearly closing time on the final day. Why are you suddenly free to see me, anyway?' Natasha asked, taking a samosa off another plate and nibbling it as they walked.

'I knew I wouldn't be able to sleep tonight. Too much in my head. What's your excuse? Presumably there's no insatiable woman waiting in your bed tonight,' Ava said, handing over a ten-pound note and getting passed a couple of pints of beer in return. She handed one to Natasha.

'I'm sworn off relationships for the next six months,' Natasha said. 'It's all too much like hard work. As I get older, I seem to have a lower boredom threshold. Did you know the stands here have said they'll stay open tonight until either all the food is gone or until everyone's gone home? Isn't it fabulous?'

They wandered up the Royal Mile – cordoned off for pedestrians only, Ava was pleased to note – eating as they went and trying not to spill their beer. She should have gone straight home to bed, but it would only have proved frustrating. Sleep didn't come easily when there were active cases on her desk. She was only allowing herself downtime because procedure was in place to prevent police officers from staying on duty for more than a set number of hours. She could clock in again at 7 a.m. and not before. Spending time with her best friend since childhood at least gave her brain the opportunity to think about something other than missing women and slashed faces for a while. Natasha was irrepressible, and Ava didn't see her often enough. Linking her arm through her friend's, she pointed out a cheese stand across the street.

'Luc would love this,' Ava said, pulling Natasha in the direction of a mountain of shades of cream and orange.

'Looks like he does,' Natasha said. 'Luc!'

Luc turned his head to see who was calling his name. Natasha dashed forward to give him a warm hug.

'Hey, you,' Natasha said. 'Where the hell have you been hiding? Every time I tell Ava we should go out together, she goes on about how busy you are with cases. I thought it was just an excuse to keep me all to herself – unless you've been avoiding me.'

'I wouldn't dare,' Luc smiled. 'I think Ava's just worried that if I have any fun it'll distract me from my caseload.'

'She's the one who's no fun,' Natasha complained. 'It took actual threats for me to get her out this evening, and even then she couldn't make herself available until thirty minutes ago. Where is she?'

Ava concentrated on the conversation she was having with the cheese vendor, comparing a few different products and being shown bottles of wine that were supposed to be complementary. Natasha took her by the hand and pulled her in Luc's direction.

'I didn't know you were coming here this evening,' Callanach said.

'Neither did I. You remember how persuasive Natasha can be though,' said Ava, grinning.

Selina appeared at Callanach's side, clutching a baguette, wine and paper-wrapped parcels.

'Natasha,' Callanach said. 'This is Selina Vega.'

'Hi,' Selina said, holding out a hand to shake Natasha's. 'Good to meet you. Luc's talked about you before. Such a shame we haven't been able to agree a date for us all to go out together yet.'

'I guess our jobs are just too unpredictable,' Ava said. 'Anyway, you guys are having an evening out. We won't keep you.'

'That's a shame. There are still plenty of stalls open. We could get a drink together now,' Selina said.

'I was just heading home actually,' Ava said. 'I'm on enforced time off, so I really should use some of it to sleep.'

'We should put something in the diary, though,' Natasha said. 'Surely we can find a weekend soon for a meal?'

'Tell me about it. I've been trying to get Luc to agree to a weekend away to do some scuba diving. You'd think I was asking him to donate a kidney!' Selina laughed.

'It's difficult, never knowing what's going to come up at work. I feel bad committing myself to something and then having to cancel,' Luc said quietly.

'Of course you should get away for a weekend,' Ava said. 'There's nothing MIT can't handle without you for forty-eight hours. You have to prioritise your social life. It's important to get some balance. Let me know the dates and I'll make sure I've got cover for you.' She checked her watch. 'It's nearly 1 a.m.

Sorry, Natasha, but even food can't keep me awake any longer. We should go.'

They said their goodbyes to Luc and Selina, and went their separate ways. Ava began counting in her head.

'I'll pay your mortgage for the next year if you tell me that woman is bisexual,' Natasha said.

'Nine,' Ava said.

'Is that a code for something I'm not aware of?' Natasha asked.

'That's the number of seconds you managed to wait before talking about her.' Ava grinned. 'And I get it, she's gorgeous. She's also a doctor, Spanish and seems genuinely nice. I'm afraid I have no information about her sexual preferences though.'

'Forget it. I didn't get any vibes. Given how hard she was clutching Luc's tricep, I'm guessing she's firmly in the hetero team. What a waste. Did you see her legs?'

'Believe it or not, I wasn't looking. You coming back to mine for coffee?'

'I thought you needed some sleep,' Natasha said.

'Don't think I'll get any, to be honest. I just wanted to let those two get on with their evening without feeling obliged to chat to us,' Ava said. 'Let's find a cab.'

'That's it?' Natasha asked.

'What's it?' Ava replied.

'That's the only reason you refused a chance to go for a drink with a good friend of yours and his new girlfriend?' Natasha persisted.

'I'm also his boss now, so it's kind of awkward. We haven't really socialised since my promotion. I feel as if I need to give him some space from me, too. It's hard maintaining authority at work and then confiding in each other when we're off duty.'

'Wow,' Natasha said, stopping in her tracks. 'Did you just hear yourself? I'd be genuinely worried about you if that wasn't obviously such a massive lie.'

Ava turned in the street, hands on hips, glaring. 'That's ridiculous. Why would I be lying? You have no idea what it's like trying to care for the people in my command at the same time as having to maintain discipline. I can't be all things at once. There has to be a line somewhere.'

'Even with Luc?' Natasha asked.

'Especially with Luc,' Ava said.

Natasha smiled. 'Now that was an honest answer, at least. So do you like Selina?'

'I haven't spent more than a few seconds with her, to be honest. She and Luc are obviously well suited though. They have the European thing and the outdoor sports thing in common.'

'And the being crazy good-looking thing. I for one wouldn't mind having her legs wrapped around me,' Natasha said.

'Please can we not make this about sex?'

'One of us should think about it every now and then. When did you last get any?'

'Natasha, give it up. My life is complicated. I'm just not designed for relationships,' Ava said.

'So have a fling. It doesn't have to be long term. You need a bit of fun in your life. None of those dead bodies is going to keep you warm at night,' Natasha said.

'That's disrespectful, Tasha. I'm in the middle of a murder case like nothing you can imagine and another girl is missing. Fuck, why do I let myself get drawn into this with you?' Ava picked up the pace, marching away down the Royal Mile, looking for a cab.

'Okay, okay. I'm sorry. I was making a point and I did it badly. Ava, would you stop? I care about you,' Natasha said, jogging to overtake Ava and stand in her path. 'I know you better than anyone and I can see you're lonely. Who do you talk to when your day is shit? Who holds you when the pain of the work you do gets too much? You're only human, and you have a breaking point. Luc's got your back, and I know how much he cares about you. You can't tell me it's wrong to socialise with the person who best understands how hard your life is.'

'Luc needs to get on with his own life. He needs a relationship that allows him to stop thinking about work for a while and lets him heal. God knows he went through enough in France. He deserves some fun. Why would he want to spend his free time with me? The only thing we have in common is the police.' She stepped forward, smiling tenderly, enveloping Natasha in a long, hard hug. 'I know you love me, Natasha. I know you'd do anything for me. You keep me sane. But I don't need to be in a relationship, and I don't need saving from anything.'

'Ava,' Natasha whispered.

'Don't,' Ava said. 'We shouldn't talk about this any more. I don't see you often enough as it is. Let's just . . .'

'No,' Natasha said, tapping her shoulder. 'Look.'

Ava turned slowly, already drawing her right elbow back, tensed ready to punch. Natasha was rigid in her arms, staring over her shoulder.

'Don't be scared,' Ava told Natasha. 'They can't hurt anyone except themselves, and it's too late to stop them doing that tonight.'

In the mouth of Brown's Close stood two women and one man. They were swaying on their feet, eyes wide and bloodshot from lack of blinking. One of the females was making a gargling sound at the back of her throat and the other was plucking listlessly at something that didn't exist in front of her chest. The man, older than the women, was hanging his head as if he were dangling from some unseen noose that had snapped his neck.

'Can they even hear us?' Natasha asked.

'Not really,' Ava said, walking forward, pulling rubber gloves from her pocket and snapping them on.

'How do you always have those in your pocket? Are you never off duty?' Natasha asked.

'Never,' Ava said, walking to the nearest female and explaining that she was a police officer, for the record. She began sliding deft fingers in and out of the girl's pockets.

'What are you looking for?' Natasha asked.

'More drugs. Weapons. I can't leave people in this state in public if there's a possibility they'll hurt themselves or anyone else. Here we go,' she said, pulling out a small paper packet with the silhouette of a marijuana leaf on the front. Gold lettering declared the contents as 'Premium Spice. 100% Pure.'

'So that's what Spice does,' Natasha said. 'I've heard the students talking about it on campus, but we don't seem to have a big problem with it at the University.'

'It's the first time I've seen users high on it,' Ava replied. 'That's one of the problems with spending more time at my desk than on the street. It's horrible, and it's everywhere. These people are completely vulnerable. Anything could happen to them right now and they'd be completely unaware.'

'It's a huge rape risk, particularly for the girls,' Natasha said. 'Shouldn't we get them off the street? Can you arrest them or something?'

'No,' Ava said. 'But I agree, the risk they're taking using this stuff is unquantifiable. We're lucky we've only had two attacks so far.'

'What attacks?' Natasha asked.

'Sorry, give me a second, would you?' Ava said, dialling a number into her phone and talking to the control room as

Natasha stared into the blank faces of the drug users. 'Okay, I've got a patrol unit on its way. I'll have them stationed here to make sure nothing happens to any of them tonight.'

'Just how widespread is this?' Natasha asked.

'It's a bigger problem than you'd imagine. Spice is cheap. It's marketed as the equivalent of a strong type of weed, but the effects are more like heroin. You can buy it from any drug dealer, as the courts aren't yet handing out high enough sentences to put people off.' She walked over to the male and patted him down, pulling out a flick knife that was concealed in the waistband of his trousers. 'He'll have to do without this,' Ava said, taking an evidence bag from her handbag and tucking the knife inside.

'I don't get it,' Natasha said. 'In the philosophy department at the Uni we have a lot of students who dabble in drugs, but they want to be present for the experience. Apart from weed, they pretty much stick to ecstasy and cocaine if they can afford it. This looks like committing temporary suicide.'

A police car drew up next to them and Ava walked over to give instructions.

'Come on,' she said. 'There's a cab waiting for us that the control room organised. I think I've had enough for one evening.'

They walked along until the cabbie flashed his headlights at them, then climbed into the welcome warmth.

'Let me ask you something from a philosophical perspective,' Ava said. 'Why would one person brand another?'

'You mean literally, physically branding? Because the proper connotation of that denotes permanency.'

'Literally, physically, and yes, permanently,' Ava replied.

'Okay. Start with ownership in practical terms. You can retrieve your goods if they go missing – cows, sheep, pigs—'

'People. Why would you brand another human?' Ava asked.

'God, I hate these conversations,' Natasha muttered, glancing sideways at Ava's face. 'Fine, take prostitution as an example. There's growing evidence that some gangs who run prostitution rings have their women tattooed. You establish ownership, you can count your chattels, they can't run off without being known for what they are. You can instruct other people to find them for you. But there's a level to it that runs deeper. It's about power and control, the destruction of liberty. The owner is empowered when the slave is disempowered. Branding is demeaning. It's an insult. At its most base level, it's a humiliation.'

'And the psychology of the sort of person who would want to do that?'

'Depends on what they're setting out to achieve, but I'd say you're looking at someone egotistical and self-entitled. The sort of person who believes in hierarchy. Someone who feels that they can categorise other people, sort them into types. They would also be someone who liked control and who didn't enjoy being disobeyed.'

'Someone self-righteous?'

'Quite possibly,' Natasha agreed.

'Thank you,' Ava said, thinking about Zoey and Lorna, Mikey Parsons and Paddy Yates, and all the people who might have felt entitled to categorise them and judge them.

'I shouldn't have lectured you earlier,' Natasha said. 'How you do what you do, every day, is beyond me.'

'It's just a job; you get used to it. You're not exactly unimpressive yourself, youngest head of department at Edinburgh University,' she said. 'And you're a fine one to talk about not having a relationship. How many have you been in over the last few years?'

'I've lost count.' Natasha laughed. 'Maybe we average one another out. How about I cook dinner one night next week? We could invite Luc and Selina, drink too much wine and be silly. I won't even set you up on any secret dates – promise.'

'Maybe just us,' Ava said.

'How about just the two of us and Luc?' Natasha said. 'I don't really feel like encouraging this Selina thing. It feels strangely as if she's treading on your toes.'

'Hardly,' Ava said.

'I know,' Natasha replied, directing the driver to pull over at her address. 'I just can't help feeling a bit sad that you two didn't have a certain conversation before you were promoted. Seems like a wasted opportunity.'

'Natasha, what are you talking about?'

'Thanks,' Natasha said to the driver, pushing a twenty into his hands. 'Get my friend home safely now.' She climbed out of the car, waving and laughing as she disappeared up her driveway.

Chapter Fifteen

Arriving at Lorna's mother's house on Pennywell Medway at 8.30 a.m. was probably a mistake, Callanach thought. It seemed unlikely that Mrs Shaw would open the door to them so early, let alone be feeling communicative, but the investigation had run out of leads. All they could do was retrace the investigative steps and see what, if anything, uniformed officers might have missed when they'd first spoken with Lorna's mother. Her father was unidentified, although a stream of stepfather figures had moved in and out throughout her life, according to the information Lorna had given the nurses at the mother and baby unit.

Callanach climbed out of the car, taking a long look at the area. The wind off the sea to the north had left rough rendering the only long-term decorative option. The 1960s tenements and terraces looked desolate and anonymous. A woman in a dressing gown and slippers screeched at three scruffy children as she walked them to school, lugging a mountain of bags. A postman plodded from door to door, an expression of hopeless-ness heavy on his face. No one wanted the sort of news he was delivering. Too many mouths to feed and not enough cash:

the landscape and architecture told the story without the need for words.

Callanach let Tripp knock, standing far enough back that he could tell if any curtains twitched. He wasn't prepared to be given the runaround. Lorna – wherever she was – was in grave danger. He was surprised her mother hadn't bashed in the police station door to get answers before now.

'What the fuck?' a man shouted, poking his head out from an upper window.

'Good morning,' Tripp said. 'Sorry to bother you so early. I did phone yesterday to say we'd be coming to speak with Ms Shaw. Is she in?'

'She's asleep,' the man said.

'Could you wake her up, perhaps?' Tripp suggested.

'Could you sod off, perhaps?' the man responded.

Callanach stepped forward to get a better look at the irate male. His irises were pinpricks, his skin greasy with an oily sheen and his hands shaking as he held on to the windowsill. 'Thirty seconds. You open the door and talk to us or this conversation turns into a drug raid. And don't give me any shit about needing a warrant. You're all the evidence I need.'

'Fuck you,' the man said.

'Tripp, kick the door in,' Callanach ordered.

'I'm frigging opening it, ya cunt,' the man replied. His head disappeared from the window. Seconds later the door swung open. 'She's coming. Just let her get some clothes on.'

More likely Lorna's mother was either flushing or hiding their stash of drugs, Callanach thought. They walked directly into the lounge. One half offered bare concrete as flooring, the other was covered in a rug that looked as if rodents had feasted on it. The bottom inches of the windowpanes glowed an unhealthy green. Callanach wondered just how many contaminants were floating in the air, before deciding he preferred not to know. One glance at the sofa was all it took to persuade him to remain standing. Tripp's face confirmed that the detective constable had reached the same conclusion.

Several minutes later, a hunched figure plodded down the stairs. Callanach was reminded how much he hated drugs. If you could trace a user from the point at which they'd never touched class As to their point of no return, it would be like seeing the evolution-of-man graphic in reverse. The literal destruction of the body. The killing of brain cells until simple communication became difficult. The prehistoric stereotype of dirty, limp hair; skin that perfectly illustrated the death of nutrition. He felt a welling up of pity for Lorna Shaw's mother who, in all probability, would end her life as the wrecked straggle of skin and bone that she now was. Successful rehab was about as likely as banning deep-fried food in that part of the city.

'I've gave my statement. What d'ya want now?' Lorna's mother asked.

'We believe Lorna's in real danger,' Callanach said. 'There was a doll found in the pram. It originated from another crime scene. Inside it was a scroll of paper with a Bible quote on it. Has anyone tried to convert Lorna, or offered help that she rejected?'

'I explained to your lot before. She's run away. I told her not to wreck her life being a mother at her age. Look what it did tae me. I knew she wouldnae stick at it. She's no' been taken. She's away and probably better for it.'

'The mother and baby unit are really pleased with Lorna's progress,' Tripp said. 'She and the baby were doing well. Had you visited?'

'Do you see a car outside?' she responded, sniffing before wiping her nose with her sleeve.

'Ms Shaw, the religious message?' Callanach reminded her. 'It was quite judgmental in tone. We're keen to contact anyone you think might have disapproved of Lorna's lifestyle.'

'Aye, well, there's not much sign of God around here – unless he's taking the fuckin' piss,' the boyfriend said. 'Who cares what Lorna got up to, anyway? S'up to her. I reckon she saw sense. Baby's better off without her anyways.'

'The baby is currently being cared for in the unit, but they'll have to place her in foster care if Lorna can't be found. It might help if you could contact the unit and suggest a family member who could help,' Tripp said.

'Why should we help raise someone else's kid?' the boyfriend said.

'Ms Shaw, this is your granddaughter,' Tripp said gently.

'We've got other stuff to look after,' the boyfriend said, taking a step towards Lorna's mother and putting a hand on her arm. 'You think we just sit round here all day? There's no time for a baby.'

'She'll come back,' Lorna's mother said. 'Couple of weeks. She probably just needed a quick fix. They don't let you have nothin' at all in them places. Give it two or three more days. You'll see.'

Callanach saw the disbelief in her eyes as she spoke. Lorna's mother was persuading herself, not them. Tripp was wasting his time. Even if Lorna's mother stepped up, there was no way the baby was going to be released into her care and she knew it. The prospect of what was actually happening to her daughter drifted away more effectively with enough pills or powder.

'Perhaps we should speak with Ms Shaw alone,' Tripp said.

'Perhaps you should get the fuck out of our place,' the boyfriend said, lifting a hand to point into Tripp's face, revealing a knife in the waistband of his trousers as his shirt rose.

Callanach stepped between them, raising both hands and shaking his head.

'We didn't come here for any trouble. All we want is to find

Lorna,' he said, keeping his eyes on the boyfriend's hands, ready to disable him if he went for the knife. 'We'll be out of here in a minute. Ms Shaw, when did you last speak with Lorna?'

'A few weeks ago,' she mumbled.

'What was that about?' Callanach asked.

'I just needed, you know, to see how she was doing,' she replied, but there were tears in her eyes as she answered.

Callanach's first thought was that she had called to see if Lorna had any spare cash. It was unkind, but realistic. Lorna's mother was too far gone to worry about anything except her next high.

'Have you ever come across either Mikey Parsons or Paddy Yates? They're both drug users in the city,' Tripp said.

'What the fuck're you implying?' the boyfriend said, squaring up to Tripp.

'I'm asking if you've met either of them, or if Lorna might have met either of them. It's a relatively small city,' Tripp replied mildly, keeping his body language neutral.

'We don't know any goddamn drug dealers, do we babe?' he snarled.

'Don't know any,' Lorna's mother echoed, wringing her hands together.

'Time's up,' the boyfriend said. 'That fucking girl's caused nothing but problems. She can't even disappear without leaving a load of shit behind her.'

'We're going,' Callanach said. 'If you remember anything, or if anyone contacts you about Lorna, please give us a call.'

Her mother responded with an incomprehensible murmur. The boyfriend just laughed. Callanach and Tripp retreated to the car.

'Should we not do something, sir?' Tripp asked.

'About the drug situation in there, you mean?'

Tripp nodded.

'There's nothing we can do. The boyfriend had a knife, but knock any door round here and half the residents will have a weapon within grabbing distance. Drug-raid the entire community and we'll just take away their supply until they can afford another fix. Substantial amounts of crime will probably be committed in order to help them afford that next fix. This is what poverty does, Max. It's corrosive. Unless you can fix the problem, it's unwise to judge the symptoms.'

'What if next time they're high, he uses the knife on Lorna's mother?' Tripp asked.

'The next time they're high will be about ten minutes from now, and Lorna's mother is just as likely to grab that knife and use it on her boyfriend. It's no wonder Lorna ended up in the mother and baby unit. The only surprising thing is that she was doing so well they were going to let her keep the baby. It must have taken a monumental effort to get off the drugs when her mother was a user too. Come on. I need to let DCI Turner know we've hit another brick wall.'

Ava waited all afternoon to get five minutes with Detective Superintendent Overbeck, and then she was warned by the super's assistant to expect no more than a few seconds. She gritted her teeth and went in.

'Ma'am,' Ava said, nodding at her superior.

Overbeck was surrounded by piles of paperwork and looking uncharacteristically imperfect. Her usually immaculate nail varnish was chipped on one hand and a few greys were showing through at her roots. Not good timing, then, Ava thought. Not that there ever was a good time when reporting to Overbeck. On most occasions it was like trying to step over a sleeping tiger without getting your leg bitten off.

'Go,' Overbeck said.

Ava turned to look at the door.

'I don't mean go away. Just tell me what it is you need as quickly as possible. What am I, surrounded by idiots?' Overbeck asked as she screwed up a sheet of paper and slammed it into the wastebasket.

'We're no closer to locating Lorna Shaw,' Ava began. She paused, waiting for Overbeck's inevitable tirade. The super-intendent circled a hand in the air. 'DI Callanach went to reinterview her mother today. There were no new leads. I'd like to make further enquiries, however, in the facial slashing cases. A key dropped at the second crime scene indicates that a student from the Leverhulme School might have been in the area and witnessed something, or possibly even have been involved.'

Overbeck peered over the mound of files. 'Leverhulme?'

'Yes, ma'am. DS Lively and I attended there yesterday evening and identified the relevant locker. It belongs to a student called Leo Plunkett. We spoke to him at his home and I got the impression he knew more than he was telling us. I'd like to pursue the line of enquiry at the school.'

Overbeck sat upright in her chair and glared at Ava. 'You got the impression he knew more than he was telling you,' she repeated.

'That's correct,' Ava said.

'Some specifics as to how you reached your conclusion might be useful,' Overbeck said, taking off her reading glasses and studying Ava's face.

'Leo was smirking, cocky. He asked how bad the victim's injuries were. I didn't think he was as surprised by our visit as he should have been, and he had a story already prepared about the lost key, as if he knew he might have to explain it.'

'So to summarise, this Plunkett boy was able to answer your questions comprehensively. He engaged with you and showed an interest in the victim. Oh, and he was displaying all the signs of being an overconfident, privileged teenager.'

'I just feel as if there's more below the surface . . .'

'For Christ's sake, woman, you want to go rampaging through the most expensive school in Edinburgh based on a dropped locker key? What did the boy say about the key, exactly?' Overbeck snapped.

'That he goes through the Meadows regularly and was aware that he'd dropped it at some stage. He's been meaning to request a replacement.'

'And you think he's lying because?'

'Intuition, ma'am,' Ava said.

Overbeck stood up. At five foot ten the effect was dramatic, enhanced by ridiculous heels and a stick-thin figure.

'DCI Turner, describe in as few words as possible the witnesses who drew your attention to this key.'

'Homeless, alcoholic, possible drug users, poor lighting,' Ava said. 'Ma'am, I know what the limitations are here, but if you'd seen Leo Plunkett answering my questions last night . . .'

'Not one more word. Your instincts count for nothing. Go into that school again and there will be hell to pay. Leo Plunkett's father owns the tech company that provides most of Edinburgh's governmental IT backup. Every parent with a child at that school is connected in a way that you, of all people, should understand, given your family background. There will be a living wall of lawyers around this place before you can apologise. None of our jobs will be safe if you piss off that many people at once, and on what basis? On the word of a bunch of drunks who may or may not have seen something, and all because a teenager had the temerity to fucking smirk at you? Jesus wept, is that really the best you've got?' She was at fever pitch. It was all Ava could do not to cover her ears. Overbeck took a deep breath in and blew it out at the ceiling. 'So in summary,' she continued softly, 'you do not have my permission to continue making enquiries with the school. You can place undercover officers on the streets. You can use all the CCTV facilities the city has to offer. You could even try good old-fashioned police work, taking statements, photofits, the usual. But you don't go near that school. Do you hear me?'

'Yes, ma'am,' Ava said.

Overbeck smiled. 'Good chat,' she said. 'Now get the fuck out of my office and don't ever make me yell like that again.'

Ava went, all too aware that the cessation of yelling was only temporary, and that the next time it would be substantially louder.

Chapter Sixteen

'Jonty,' Callanach said, transferring his mobile to his left hand and picking up a takeaway coffee from the counter with his right. 'What's the news?'

'We identified a substance that was widespread across Zoey's abdomen and back, mixed in with the chemical designed to thicken the skin. It's all over the doll, too. It's a topical anaesthetic but quite high grade. It's often used on the backs of children's hands at the hospital before the nurse inserts a cannula, or for nervous patients with low pain thresholds who don't like injections. The amount we've identified across the skin indicates that it was being spread over the victim for a few days repeatedly before the incisions were made.'

'So how much pain would Zoey have felt as her skin was cut?' Callanach asked quietly, leaving the coffee shop to dive into a street doorway. There were some conversations that no one beyond their scope of work should have to listen to. Quite often, he wished he didn't have to ask the questions, either.

'The initial incisions would have been relatively painless, I think, but lower in the skin, when the layer of the dermis was pulled away, that would have been excruciating. There were, however, some traces of an opioid painkiller found in her system. It seems likely she was given Valium prior to the operation being performed, which would explain why the cuts were so precise and clean,' Jonty replied.

Callanach took a sip of coffee as he thought about it. 'I don't get it,' he said. 'If the aim was to torture, why administer Valium and anaesthetise the skin?'

'Add to that the impressive wound packing, which is commonly available in bulk from online pharmacies. It seems the killer didn't want death to be immediate. Zoey was always going to die from her wounds. It was inevitable and would have been obvious to whoever did this, but they worked hard to keep her alive for a while,' Jonty said. 'Wherever you are, it sounds chaotic.'

'On my way to the mother and baby unit. Ava's there and we need to regroup and agree next steps. I just stopped to grab a coffee. What's your assessment of Zoey's death, Jonty, knowing what you know now?'

'If anything, it's the lack of rage that's so disturbing. Criminals who work with human skin are specialised and obsessive. Sociopathic to the point of zero emotion. It's as if all human functioning is void. Almost every normal human emotion is pretended,' Jonty replied. His voice was hushed and lacking its usual buoyancy.

'And the prospects for Lorna?' Callanach asked.

'You don't need me to quantify that, Luc. You knew the answer the second you saw the doll in her baby's pram.'

Back at the mother and baby unit, Callanach paused in the corridor, taking a step backwards out of sight, knowing he shouldn't watch but unwilling to break the moment between Ava and the baby. Tansy was snuffling against Ava's chest, doing her best to clutch the bottle Ava was holding for her. Ava was walking as she fed her, rocking her slightly and humming. Callanach wished he could freeze time. He'd never seen Ava smile like that before. She was the most practical woman he knew, almost incapable of self-pity, tough without sacrificing gentleness. She always spoke her mind. He'd never considered what she was giving up to pursue her career in Police Scotland – not that she would have considered it a compromise. The work she did was everything to her. Yet here she was, looking blissful and at peace. She would hate it if she could hear his thoughts, he knew, laced as they were with centuries old, inbuilt misogyny, but he couldn't help feeling a surge of alpha male protectiveness towards her as she held the tiny, motherless creature.

A nurse entered the room from a different doorway, handing over a muslin cloth for Ava to wipe the baby's chin.

'Has there been any response to my query about fostering?' Ava asked her.

'The unit director is speaking to the social workers,' the nurse responded. Callanach took a step further back into the corridor. 'It's a long and technical process, with a lot of safety checks, but police officers already have enhanced security clearance, which should speed things up.'

'So it's just a question of putting in the application?' Ava asked.

'Yes,' the nurse said. 'We would make sure the matter was handled swiftly from our end to make sure the baby gets a good home as soon as possible. She really can't stay here much longer.'

'I'll get on it,' Ava said. She put Tansy over her shoulder and began to gently rub then pat her back.

Callanach wished he hadn't listened in. It was clear breach of trust, one he couldn't possibly admit, and yet he wanted to talk to Ava about her enquiry. He entered the room at a brisk pace, taking her by surprise.

'Hi,' he said. 'I was told I'd find you here. I need to update you on a couple of things.'

'Of course,' Ava said. 'Here you go,' she muttered, handing the baby back to the nurse with a wistful glance. 'Shall we go outside? There's a courtyard for the mums to take the babies out for air, but it catches some autumn sun and it's private enough.'

No one else was braving the oncoming wintry edge to the air. They huddled together on a bench and looked into the watery blue above. There weren't many few clear days left until cloud took control of the horizon, but the season was milder than normal. Ava shut her eyes.

'You're not here because there's been progress,' she said. 'You'd have phoned me for that.'

'Lorna's wallet, believed to have been in her pocket when she went to the shops, was found at a roadside. Looks as if it was thrown out of a car window, perhaps by Lorna herself if she was forced into a vehicle. A street cleaner picked it up and handed it in at five this morning. Her photo ID was in it with a picture of the baby. No doubt at all that it's hers.'

'So all hope that she had some sort of breakdown and decided to run away is gone,' Ava said.

'It has,' Callanach said. 'That's what her mother was clinging on to, between drug binges. She's convinced herself that her daughter was never up to the task of parenting and wanted out.'

'Still no leads on any possible vehicle used in the kidnapping?' Ava asked.

'No. It was a busy day on the roads. There was no CCTV in the immediate area where the baby was left. We suspect the road was carefully checked for exactly that reason. Jonty phoned with the forensic results this morning. Anaesthetic was applied to Zoey's skin and a strong painkiller was given to her before the cutting began. So why did the killer let her go? What was the point in allowing the body to be found? It just increases the chance of being captured.'

Ava bent her neck right then left, rubbing the knots out with one hand. Callanach heard the clicks as she moved and wondered if she'd spent the whole night at her desk.

'Okay,' she said. 'I abduct Zoey. I've prepared a space to keep her restrained. It has to be soundproof or with no neighbours who might overhear, as I'm going to feed her regularly and I don't want her to scream and create interest in what I'm doing.'

'And you've got supplies in advance. Plenty of wound padding, scalpel blades, prescription-only painkillers,' Callanach said.

'So I know what I'm intending to do. The doll is the motivation. Why not just deliver the doll somewhere it will be publicly found? DNA tests would soon link it to a missing person. Why keep Zoey alive in the meantime? Surely killing her before taking the skin would have made the whole thing easier,' Ava responded.

'There's a lot of extra effort involved in keeping Zoey alive, so it must fulfil a purpose. It has meaning for the killer, those last few hours or minutes he gives her,' Callanach said.

'So I pack her wounds. She's dying, but I put her in my vehicle, with all the additional risk that involves. Her DNA will be everywhere, probably visible blood. If I'm stopped for any reason, there'll be no hiding it. Then I leave her at the roadside to be found later, possibly even run over in the dark, like I'm throwing trash out of my car window. The girl's the trash. It's a public statement.'

'So is the killer waiting for more of the details to break in the news?' Callanach said.

'It's a lot of trouble to go to with no payback, and the self-righteousness is in keeping with the message inside the doll,' Ava said.

'But the doll's a different thing,' Callanach said. 'It feels even more personal. There are any number of ways the killer could have sent that same message, and yet he or she chose to create a morbid imitation of a child's toy.'

'True,' Ava said. 'The killer could have stencilled directly onto Zoey's skin if they just wanted to leave their mark.'

'So there are two elements. One, Zoey's body was left for shock value – there was no possibility of us keeping it out of the news. Two, the doll. That's for the killer. A reference only they truly understand,' Callanach said. He paused, looking at the dark circles beneath Ava's eyes, wondering when she'd last eaten. 'Lorna's almost out of time.'

'I know,' Ava said. 'Waiting for a body to appear is the single worst part of policing. You think there'll always be leads, that you'll be proactive every time. No one tells you it's the waiting that will haunt you when you look back on the cases you've done. Those hours when you're sure you missed something, and you end up sitting around until the next trip to the mortuary. I can't bring myself to think about what that girl's going through right now.'

Callanach reached out and put his hands over Ava's, more for his own sake than hers. A year earlier, human contact would have been the last thing he wanted. Then he'd resettled in Edinburgh, Ava had befriended him, and he'd slowly regained his faith in people. She wrapped the ends of her fingers around his, staring into the distance.

'What about the slashings? Where do they fit into this picture?' he asked.

'I don't know. At first it all felt linked. Now I'm not so sure that wasn't just wishful thinking – solve one case, solve them both. Running up to someone so high they can't even feel their face and leaving a gash in it, however brutal, is a far cry from being able to ignore the desperate pleas of a young woman who knows she's staring death in the face. The slashings feel more like an act of cowardice. What's being done to these young women is nothing short of pure evil.'

Callanach's mobile rang. He answered it with his free hand, murmuring into the phone. 'Hey, Selina. I'm with Ava, talking through a case.'

He paused as Selina spoke. Ava slipped her hand out of his and walked to the other side of the courtyard, picking the last stubborn summer flower from a bush and inspecting its petals. Callanach watched her as Selina talked.

'I can't tonight, I'm afraid. I'll be working all evening,' he said.

Ava took her own mobile from her pocket and began checking her text messages.

'No, don't bother bringing me food,' Callanach said. 'Someone from the squad will organise a takeaway, but thanks. Listen, I'll call you tomorrow evening, okay?' He rang off.

'You don't need to do that,' Ava said. 'There's no point in you staying at the station half the night. We've got nothing to go on. If anything new comes in, I can call you at home.'

'What about you?' Callanach asked. 'How many hours have you spent in your own bed this week?'

'There's not much point me lying there awake,' Ava replied. Alone, a small voice corrected her. There's not much point in lying there alone. 'Staying at your desk comes with the promotion at times like these. Plus, you have someone to go home to.'

'It's only casual. No more than a friendship, really,' Callanach said.

'Isn't that how all relationships start?' Ava asked. She checked her watch. 'I have to get back to the station. I'm briefing a unit to go out on the streets and watch the city's Spice users, see if we can't catch whoever's targeting them in action. Needle in a haystack, but it's more than I'm achieving on Lorna's behalf. What about you?'

'We're filming a reconstruction of Lorna's disappearance this afternoon,' Callanach said. 'Salter and Tripp are organising it now that we've found her wallet, too. Gives us firmer geography. It'll be aired as soon as it's edited. Hopefully it'll jog some memories. What'll happen to the baby, do you think?'

'I'm still hoping against the odds that she'll end up seeing her mother again,' Ava said.

'In reality?' Callanach asked, knowing he was prying, too curious about the question he'd overheard Ava ask earlier to be able to stop himself.

'She'll be found a new home. A foster carer until the situation is clearer, then adoption. It won't be hard to find someone to love her,' Ava said. 'Tansy's beautiful.'

Callanach stood up. 'Do you never think about having children?' he asked.

'Because I'm a woman, and it's what I should be thinking about at this age?' Ava asked.

'Actually because you're kind and loving, and have more to offer a child than most people,' Callanach said.

'I'm not sure I'm up to the task,' she said. 'Police work turns you into an emotional sieve. You start off with so much hope and good intention. Little by little it runs out of you and you're left with only the hard bits of yourself. Some days I think I'd like motherhood, though. Being able to do one single job well for just one other person, but the years keep rolling by, and the weeks disappear into case files. I'm in my mid thirties. I can't keep the food in my fridge in date, Luc. How the hell am I supposed to nurture a long-term relationship, let alone become a parent?' She shook her head. 'That's enough of that. Good luck with the filming. Let's hope it makes a difference.'

She left the courtyard, calling to a nurse as she walked back into the unit. Callanach waited until she'd disappeared before exiting. He hadn't really thought about the issue of his impotence in terms of anything but the loss of sex before. He was amazed that he hadn't considered the longer term. It was only seeing Ava with the baby and hearing her talk about parenthood that had suddenly changed his perception of his problem. Unless he could conquer his post-traumatic stress disorder and function as a man again, there would be no fatherhood for him. No seeing his wife hold their baby for the first time. No latenight feeds while the rest of the world slept quietly. No teaching a child to ride a bike or to swim, no helping with homework or worrying when they were late home. Wherever Lorna was right now, she would be thinking the same thoughts about her daughter's future and the milestones she would miss, he thought, only her baby wasn't some distant dream. She was flesh and blood, and she needed a parent. No wonder Ava had been making enquiries about fostering her. He left, unable to resist checking on Tansy one more time, just as Lorna was being given the pills that would dull her final pain.

Chapter Seventeen

The inevitable call came in the small hours. It was 3 a.m. when the phone on Callanach's desk began to ring, at exactly the same moment as Ava picked up the landline on her desk. Four minutes later, MIT had mobilised its squad from their homes, and Scenes of Crime officers were leaping from their beds and running for the vans that would transport everything needed to do all they could for Lorna Shaw. Too little, too late, Callanach knew, as he walked to his car, wondering who would phone the mother and baby unit, and if Tansy was sleeping soundly in her cot or crying for the mother who would never return to hold her.

Bankhead Avenue was west of the city centre and at the top of the Sighthill area. That was the killer's stamping ground, then. Not all that far from where Zoey's body had been found. Not far at all from where Zoey had actually gone missing. The road itself was industrial, a departure from the deserted, rural stretch where Zoey had crawled her last. So much more of a risk, Callanach thought, as he drove there. What luck they'd had avoiding press interest at the first crime scene had been more than made up for by the startling presence of cameras in

143

Bankhead. Whoever had found Lorna's body had made more than the one phone call by the look of it. Callanach could see outside broadcast vans, and a few newspaper reporters he recognised. If the site wasn't sealed off quickly there would be helicopters, too. He could only hope that no one had been callous enough to have snapped any pictures with their mobile while waiting for the police to arrive.

Ducking the crime scene tape, he flashed his ID badge and went to suit up. Ava was in the process of snapping gloves on.

'How did the press get here so fast?' he asked her.

'Social bloody media. No pictures, thank God. There's a lot to process, so it's only the two of us allowed to see the body in situ. Jonty is on his way. They're erecting a canopy, as the Met Office says rain is imminent, and to ward off any eyes in the sky,' Ava said.

'Is it definitely Lorna?' Callanach asked.

'Scenes of Crime officers have compared her face to our photo. It's a positive match, not that there was ever any doubt.'

They walked together in silence the thirty metres up the hill to the body. Street lighting cast an orange hue over the area and illuminated the fine mist that hung at the tops of nearby trees. There was a good view down into the valley and across the large non-residential buildings that lined the road. At the top, approaching a bend, a large area of white sheeting had been laid over a central mass. Sporadic photographic flashes brightened the air, and from below the scene echoes of shouted questions from press to police officers could be heard. Callanach and Ava blanked them out. This was Lorna's time. The SOCOs stepped back to allow them access to the corpse as Dr Spurr arrived from the opposite direction carrying a camera and thermometer. Carefully peeling back the protective sheeting, they revealed Lorna's face.

If Zoey had chosen to stop and allow death to steal her,

Lorna had fought it with every ounce of strength she had left. Her mouth was open as if mid howl. Hands scrunched into tight fists, she seemed to have fallen to her side as she crawled along the middle of the road. Flared nostrils indicated the struggle to take in air at the end, the blood loss depriving her brain of oxygen. Deep markings on her wrists edged in purple bruises showed the level of restraint that had been necessary to keep her still. Part of her hair had been roughly clipped away. Her eyes were sunken and dull. She might have been fed enough to keep her alive for the last week, but it hadn't been enough to keep her healthy and properly hydrated. Perhaps she'd refused nourishment, but Ava thought it unlikely. Lorna had a reason to survive. She'd have known that keeping up her strength was the sensible option.

Ava sighed, saying nothing as she pulled the sheet further down to reveal a bloodied, once-white hospital gown clinging wetly to the young woman's body. Jonty took over, peeling the sticky blackening material away from Lorna's abdomen millimetre by millimetre to reveal what Ava had been dreading.

Medical packing fell from the wound, revealing a perfect doll shape. They didn't need to roll her over to know the same damage had been done to her back. The amount of blood and debris on Lorna's clothes and along the road was evidence enough. She was slightly shorter than Zoey, and skinny in spite of having recently given birth. As a result, the doll cut-out appeared even larger on her body, leaving arrows of skin pointing into the centre of the wound. Jonty took a tape measure from his pocket and held it against the wound, first length then widthways.

'The measurements are precise in every detail,' he said. 'The distance from the arms to the sides, the split of the legs. The killer has used a template. There's no question that it's the same person as inflicted the wounds on Zoey.'

Callanach stood up and looked at the trail of body fluids Lorna had left from the pavement to the centre of the road. 'Lorna was trying to make sure she was found,' he said. 'If she'd stayed on the pavement in the dark, a passing vehicle might not have spotted her. She took a huge risk trying to survive.'

'Why here?' Ava asked, joining him in staring down the road as Jonty continued his work. 'The killer might easily have been seen. It's an industrial area. Stopping a vehicle along this road late at night could have attracted attention.'

'Let's walk up the road a bit,' Callanach said. They moved past the body to a bend in the road where a turning facilitated access to a college. Down a lane forking to the right, surrounded by high metal fences, was the recycling centre.

'Her killer was dropping off the rubbish at the dump,' Ava said, plunging her hands deep into her coat pockets. 'It's the ultimate insult. Lorna's just a piece of trash to this person.'

'Why not drop her right at the gate then? The attacker stopped short of their mark,' Callanach said, as Ava gave up on her pockets and began furiously huffing warm breath onto her fingertips. 'Do you ever remember to keep gloves in your car? Your hands turn blue every time we're at a crime scene.'

'I always lose them. Government ownership of the recycling site means there's security,' Ava said, pointing into the air. A CCTV camera pointed at the gates. 'This can be a dangerous area, and some of the metal loads dropped are high value. The attacker wasn't going to risk getting their licence plate caught on camera.'

'Which means the driver knew in advance where the camera was. They've recced the area, probably at roughly the same time of night as they dropped Lorna off tonight, to figure out how much traffic they were likely to encounter,' Callanach said.

Jonty joined them, stripping off his gloves and shoving them into a bag. 'She's been dead about an hour and a half. There would have been a period before that when she was unconscious, but even so, her killer took a risk that she would be found and give details away that could lead to arrest. He or she must have been confident before they left her that she was close to death.'

'Have you noticed anything substantially different to Zoey's body?' Ava asked.

'The marks on her ankles, like those on her wrists, are much more pronounced, and the surrounding bruising extends further along her limbs. I suspect she fought harder. A greater amount of her hair has been cut off, and there's an empty piercing hole in her left nostril with a scratch, which suggests the jewellery was recently and forcibly removed.'

'It'll be on the doll,' Callanach said. No one disagreed with him. 'Do you think she was drugged to kill the pain, like Zoey was?'

'I won't know until I've got tox samples back, but logic dictates that she was given pain relief. Without it, I doubt she'd have been able to crawl even the short distance that she did. She'd simply have passed out where she was dumped from the vehicle and bled out right there,' Jonty said.

'So he wanted to get her here alive,' Ava said, looking back down the road to where the press had blockaded the area. 'He packed the wound well enough to stop her from bleeding to death in the place where he cut her. So what's his maximum journey time before she dies in his vehicle? That must have been factored into the calculation. The killer wasn't driving from the Borders, or down from Aberdeen. Lorna would have died en route. What's your best guess, Dr Spurr?' she asked.

'The killer's sticking to the west side of the city,' the pathologist said. 'I doubt he wants to run the risk of getting stuck at numerous traffic lights or roundabouts. It would have to be reasonably local. Just the act of getting her in and out of the vehicle would increase the bleeding. It's the length of a piece of string, and not particularly scientific, but I'd say the killer wouldn't have risked driving for more than fifteen minutes.'

'Fifteen minutes driving radius from here, then – call it twenty for a margin of error. We need to draw a circle around this point and figure out the distance,' Ava said. 'That's better than nothing.'

'We also have fingermarks,' Jonty said, 'which is new. Zoey was remarkably unharmed, given the horrific nature of her death.'

'Show me,' Ava said.

They walked back to the body. A white gazebo now created a ceiling over Lorna's corpse, and electric lighting brought fresh vigour to the blackening blood, giving texture to the clots over her wound, revealing the detail of the exposed muscles and vessels. Lorna's remaining skin had paled into a waxy pallor. Jonty donned a fresh pair of gloves and pointed to the top of Lorna's left arm. On the inner skin, just below the armpit, was an oval print a little over an inch long, black in the centre and red around the edges. A slim line of yellow highlighted the outer edge of the mark. Turning her arm to show the outer section more clearly, it was possible to make out two further marks, each slightly shorter than the one on the inside of her arm.

Callanach snapped a glove onto his right hand and knelt as close as he could get to Lorna's body without disturbing it, reaching out to put his fingers over the top of the marks.

'It's a left hand,' he said.

Jonty leaned down to get a better view of the overlay of Callanach's fingers against the bruises. 'The bruising is slightly larger than your fingers. I'd say the hand that caused the bruises is most probably male. Slightly larger hands than yours, Detective Inspector, which makes it likely he is also slightly taller than you.'

'He's over six foot one then,' Callanach said. 'Which accounts for the ease with which he seems to have been able to physically dominate both Zoey and Lorna.'

'If that's where his left hand was, then where was his right?' Ava asked, angling one of the lights so that it shone across Lorna's torso with minimal shadow.

Jonty got onto his knees, turning Lorna's right arm around to check the skin for discoloration. 'Nothing here,' he said. Tipping Lorna's head back he inspected the underside of her jaw. 'Ah, yes, got them.' He pointed to the soft area where her neck met the underside of her jaw. 'Easy to miss and less obvious because the pressure was applied to very pliable tissue but there are marks either side of her lower jaw. It would have made it difficult to breathe, and Lorna would have felt ill from the oxygen deprivation. She might even have passed out. I'll have to let you know what internal damage was done after the full post-mortem, but there are no broken blood vessels in her eyes. A serious attempt at strangulation would have caused petechial haemorrhaging. This looks more like an effort to restrain, frighten or silence her.'

'When she was first taken?' Ava suggested. 'Perhaps getting her into the car?'

'I'd say more recently than that. There is a rim of yellow around the bruising, but still central blackness. Two days ago, maybe three. Some event occurred while Lorna was restrained that Zoey escaped,' Jonty said.

'If she was tied on her back, it would have been awkward for him to have his left hand on her arm, with his fingers in those positions, and his right at her neck,' Callanach said.

'Not if he was on top of her at the time,' Ava muttered. 'Dr Spurr, I want Lorna checked for signs of sexual assault as a priority. I appreciate that you've been called out in the middle of the night, but do you think you could start examining her tonight?'

149

'Of course,' Jonty said. 'I won't be getting back to sleep in any event. Might as well put the insomnia to good use.' He disappeared in the direction of the Scenes of Crime van to oversee the processing of the body as Ava and Luc wandered to the roadside, overlooking the dip in the valley below.

A scattering of lights shone from the windows of early risers. Thousands more residents were still asleep, blissfully unaware of the tragedy unfolding just streets away. The morning news would be full of it, though, and the panic would start to spread. A second body. A man preying on vulnerable young women. It was every despicable cliché in the book.

'We're going to have to handle the press now,' Callanach said. 'One body could have been a deranged boyfriend or an impromptu attack, but this is organised. It'll be international news within the hour.'

'I don't care about the press,' Ava said. 'Get the media office to put out a brief statement. No one from MIT is to comment. I only care about one thing.'

'The doll,' Callanach finished for her.

'And which young woman it's going to be exchanged for this time.'

As Ava took her car keys from her pocket and made her way back to her car, the final stitches were being pulled into place. A new doll was ready to find a home.

Chapter Eighteen

Callanach, Tripp, Lively and Salter stared at the screen in the incident room, watching as the young actress tasked with playing Lorna Shaw could be seen pushing a pram towards a distant row of shops. She paused as a car pulled up. The driver lowered his window and called out to her. She left the pram and walked across to speak with the driver.

Salter tutted.

'Something wrong?' Callanach asked.

'I don't believe she'd do that,' Salter said. 'It's not natural. Your hands would be glued to the handle of the pram. You don't just walk away and leave it in the middle of the pavement, even if you're only moving a couple of feet.'

'He had to get her to the vehicle, though,' Tripp said. 'He didn't drag her there in daylight.'

'I understand that, but the reconstruction goes against everything we know about Lorna. She's had a troubled past, fought to get away from the dealers who got her addicted and misused her to pay for drugs. I reckon she's the last person who'd walk up to a car window. If anything, she'd have been even more protective of the baby. After all, she'd spent the last few months knowing little Tansy would be taken away if she put a foot wrong,' Salter said.

'All right,' Callanach said. 'Let's suppose he parked close by and approached her on foot.'

'That would be less threatening. The question is how he managed to persuade Lorna to get into the car, and then pushed the pram into the alleyway to be found later,' Salter said.

'Or he had a knife to Lorna's back and they pushed the pram together, then he put her in his car,' Lively said.

'Still doesn't feel right. Lorna's streetwise. She'd have known that once she was inside the vehicle, there was a chance she'd never see her baby again. I'd have sooner risked a stab wound and screamed blue murder than have got in that car, thinking I might never see my child again,' Salter said. There was a long silence, the loss of Salter's own baby hanging in the air. 'So that's it?' she said. 'You're all going to go quiet whenever I say the word baby from now on?'

'You're right. I'm sorry,' Callanach said. 'It doesn't fit with what we know about Lorna.'

'Aren't we making assumptions?' Tripp said. 'What if there's more than one person involved? It would make sense. One of them gets Lorna into the car, the other pushes the pram into the alleyway.'

'You know the statistics on cooperative killers,' Ava said from the doorway. 'And the cutting is particularly specific, designed to fit to one person's vision. Killers working closely with other people make up fewer than 0.1 per cent of cases globally.'

Callanach pulled a chair across from another table and moved his own back to allow Ava to join them. She sat down.

'Unless she knew her abductor,' Lively said. 'Perhaps she'd called a dealer for a quick pick-me-up, or was meeting up to pay off an old debt. Any number of scenarios are possible.'

'Taken on their own, they are,' Salter said. 'But not following on from Zoey's death. Perhaps Lorna did have some debts and know some dangerous people, but it's a far cry from there to dumping a body with a doll shape cut from the skin.'

PC Biddlecombe appeared at the door, looking flushed. 'Ma'am,' she said to Ava. 'I was told you'd want to see these straight away. Sorry.' She walked in and dumped a stack of newspapers on the desk before scurrying back out.

'Let's see what the damage is,' Ava said, unfolding the first front page. Half the space was a photograph of the crime scene, showing the gazebo and lights with white-suited workers at all angles. Ava and Callanach were standing at the roadside, huddled together. Blue lights strobed from emergency vehicles, and the crime scene tape fluttered out of focus in the foreground. It couldn't have been more dramatic if the photographer had staged the scene themselves.

'Oh shite,' Lively said, spreading the pages of a different paper out in the middle of the desk. 'The Babydoll Killer. Fuck me. How do those bastards come up with this stuff?'

'We've been airtight about the details of this,' Ava said. 'How the hell did the press get hold of that headline?'

'Who's with Lorna's parents?' Ava asked.

'Family liaison officers are there now,' Callanach said. 'Although I doubt they'll be there long. I suspect Lorna's mother will be looking for some form of chemical escapism shortly.'

'Well, they'll have to be given all the details now,' Ava said. 'I was hoping to wait until Jonty had done a full autopsy so I could at least confirm that Lorna had been given pain relief. I can't have them finding this out from the papers, though. Tripp, get in touch with the officers who are there. They'll have to break this as gently as they can. And I want to know who leaked the doll details.'

'It'll be impossible to pin it on anyone,' Lively said. 'Between

Zoey's and Lorna's crime scenes, processing and enquiries, there have been hundreds of officers and civilians involved. It was never going to stay a secret for long.'

'But the Babydoll Killer?' Ava said. 'It makes Zoey and Lorna's deaths sound like some sort of semi-consensual sex game gone wrong, for Christ's sake.'

'I agree, but at least it's memorable and creepy,' Callanach said. 'Hopefully it'll raise awareness among other young women. We should turn the press coverage to our advantage. Let's make it harder for the killer to take another victim, see if the details jog someone's memory about a bizarre online conversation or a neighbour behaving strangely.'

'All right,' Ava said. 'But I'm not having a free-for-all. Salter, organise a press conference for later this morning. I'll give a statement myself and issue a request for witnesses to step forward. Just keep the moron whose byline this is out of my sight, or I'll give them more than just a few more inches for their column. Tripp, get Jonty Spurr on the phone for me right now. Lively, what's the update on the undercover officers we sent out last night into the city centre?'

'They've all reported in and gone off duty to rest. Nothing to report. Uniformed officer patrols were increased too and asked to speak with any homeless people they saw. The agitation from the slashings seems to have been short-lived. There's a perception that risk is part of the lifestyle. You won't find any of them knocking down your door demanding to know what action's being taken to keep them safe.'

'Yeah, well, speaking of knocking down my door, the superintendent's being less than helpful about following up with the Leverhulme School. She'd rather we found someone less affluent to blame than chase actual evidence,' Ava said.

'Maybe she's right, ma'am. Not that I want to agree with the Evil Overbitch, but we'll never get a case into court based on the ramblings of some drunk guys who only gave statements because we bought them a hot meal,' Lively said.

'For fuck's sake, I must be going insane. Did you actually just agree with the brass?' Ava asked him.

'Ma'am, I've got the pathologist on the line,' Tripp said, moving a phone to the centre of the table. Ava pushed the speaker button and motioned for them all to quieten down.

'Dr Spurr, this is DCI Turner. I have squad members from MIT listening in. Can you update us with regards to the findings from Lorna's body?'

'I can indeed,' Jonty said. 'The same thick string was used to tie her limbs as with Zoey, wrapped repeatedly round ankles and wrists, leaving green fibres in the grazes. The finger and thumb marks identified at the scene had some depth under the neck tissue. A considerable amount of force would have been used, although none of the neck structure was seriously damaged. It appears that the force was probably exerted for a short period of time.'

He paused.

'And?' Ava said.

'And it appears likely that the fingermarks were occasioned during a different sort of attack. Lorna was raped. The violation produced severe bruising around her genitals. I double-checked my findings with regard to Zoey and I'm absolutely sure she suffered no sexual assault. Lorna's assailant used a condom. We've confirmed the presence of the relevant chemicals and lubricants internally. Externally, her body had been thoroughly washed with a detergent to get rid of DNA from skin cells as well as any fingerprints, which is strange, really, given what we found internally.'

'Go on,' Ava said.

'We have a pubic hair. They're often found internally after a rape, even when a condom has been used. Force, friction, the condom itself causes rubbing, hairs loosen. I wouldn't be surprised by it at all, only it's so at odds with the effort made to clean the rest of the body of any evidence.'

There was an eruption of noise, hands banging on the desk and spontaneous outbursts from the double-edged victory. It was a breakthrough, albeit at a terrible cost to Lorna.

'Okay, settle down,' Ava said. 'We've got his DNA, that's what matters. I need results on that ASAP, Dr Spurr. I don't care what other work gets queued to push it to the front, and I'll authorise whatever overtime is incurred at the lab,' Ava said.

'It's already underway. Top priority. I'm hoping to have a DNA profile for you within forty-eight hours,' Jonty replied. 'We're hoping that's the breakthrough, unless she was having sexual relations with anyone else.'

'Unlikely with her living at the mother and baby unit, especially having recently given birth,' Callanach said.

'Hard to see how the psychology of a rapist fits with the Bible quote inside the first doll,' Tripp commented.

'Perhaps he lost control,' Callanach said. 'Still, it's a major escalation from Zoey.'

'But then he switched back into meticulous mode,' Ava said. 'He cleaned up, made a good job of it, packed the wound and got Lorna into his vehicle.'

'You were saying Lorna's body had been washed with a detergent. How come there are still fibres from the rope around her wrists, then?' Callanach asked.

'There was detergent found over the top of the wounds, but the remaining fibres were microscopic and had become caught in the irritated skin. The killer would have had to excise the top of the wound to ensure there were no traces left, but certainly he attempted to free the body of debris,' Jonty explained.

'Dr Spurr, how do the skin incisions compare to the ones found on Zoey?'

'If anything they're cleaner, more consistent in terms of depth. Made with a steadier hand, I'd say, but then the killer had the benefit of practising on Zoey. This time, he would have had a better understanding of how much pressure to apply, how to handle the curves, how to separate the skin from the underlying tissue. Other than that, the hospital gown, the substance applied to the skin and the anaesthetic injection sites are all identical.'

'So the picture I'm getting is of a man who lost control enough to rape forcefully, leaving bruising and fingermarks and being careless about internal evidence, but who then performed the remainder of his chosen tasks with extraordinary skill, back on form,' Ava said. 'He has a complex, layered personality, and he's unpredictable.'

'We need to keep the rape quiet,' Callanach said. 'Keep the public on a need-to-know basis only. That way, if anyone admits the offences, we won't waste time investigating the fakes.'

'Lorna's mother can do without any more details getting into the press, too,' Ava said. 'Thank you, Dr Spurr, we'll be in touch. DI Callanach, you're with me for the press conference. Everyone else, get the squad in for a briefing and make sure we have enough people to answer the phones. There'll be no stopping the calls once we appeal for information.'

The press room was full to capacity and noisier than Ava had ever heard it. She'd changed her shirt but not bothered with uniform. There was too much to do already without wasting time on dress code. She tapped her microphone impatiently and the room came to order. Callanach watched her survey the room. The relationship between police and press was difficult at the best of times. Symbiotic to an extent, they needed one another. Then an incident of insensitive sensationalism would leave a sour taste, and communication would break down for a while. Just like it had right now, Callanach thought.

'This morning we were called to a report of a body found in a road,' Ava began. 'You have all been provided with a summary sheet giving the logistics of the incident, so I won't repeat them. Lorna Shaw had been missing for a week. Prior to that, the body of Zoey Cole had been found in similar circumstances. Both girls were wounded. Sections of skin were removed from their abdomens and lower backs. We are asking the public to consider where they were at the times either girl went missing or was dropped off. It is clear that a vehicle was involved on each occasion. We do not as yet have any details about that vehicle or vehicles. If anyone recognises either Lorna or Zoey and saw them getting into a vehicle or on the street on the day they went missing, we would like you to contact us to help fill in the details of each timeline. Zoey and Lorna's killer must have somewhere private he kept them. After the girls were hurt, he would have had substantial amounts of blood on his clothing and would have needed to clean up.'

Ava paused, looking up to identify the nearest television camera, looking directly into the lens before continuing. 'If your husband, boyfriend, brother or son has been behaving strangely over the last two weeks, and you believe they might be involved, please do contact us. It will be easy for us to exclude them from our enquiries with the forensic evidence already available. If you know of anyone who has expressed a desire to hurt young women in such a way, whether you have made contact in person or on the internet, please come forward. We're not interested in anyone except the man who killed Zoey and Lorna. You do not need to worry about your own internet searches. However, if any person is found to have withheld information that is later uncovered, you might be prosecuted for assisting the offender. There is a crime line number and full details are also available online. Thank you for your—'

'What's the Babydoll Killer doing with the actual dolls,

Detective Chief Inspector?' a man halfway back stood up and shouted.

Ava took a deep breath. 'All questions should be submitted in writing through the media team.'

'Are the dolls being used for some sort of cult purpose?' another reporter shouted.

Callanach motioned for the door to be opened so that he and Ava could leave.

'Has the Babydoll Killer left Lorna's doll anywhere yet? Do you expect to find it soon? Are there photos available of the Zoey doll?'

Ava halted and turned back round to face the crowd. 'Who asked that question?' she said.

'Me,' a journalist said, pointing a microphone in Ava's direction.

'You want to know if we have a photograph of Zoey's skin available for you to broadcast or publish, is that right?'

The journalist began to falter. Callanach was surprised the man wasn't sprinting for the door given the ice in Ava's voice. 'Um, yes, it's a relevant part of the story . . .'

'You want to profit from the pain Zoey experienced, is that right?' Ava asked.

'These are victims of crime,' the man responded. 'It's in the public interest to inform . . .'

'Let me stop you right there,' Ava said. 'You're going to tell me that the public needs to know what's happened. Then you're going to extend your argument to using publicity to help ensure that there are no further victims. I can assist you with all of that.'

Part of Callanach wanted to tell the journalist to run and not look back, but he didn't. Watching Ava in action was too mesmerising.

'You want to sell copy or get viewers. I get it. You need the advertising revenue to pay your staff, which means you have to get the best story from the most intriguing angle. What you don't have to do is turn this tragedy into some ghoulish spectacle. You don't need to profit from the deaths of two innocent young women. Anyone with your resources and intelligence should be able to find a means of reporting this story without delighting in the horror of it. You should be more than capable of persuading the public that they need to be vigilant without resorting to showing the skin a young woman has lost. And you should know better, much better, than to use the phrase "public interest" to justify giving nicknames to evil. You should know better than to dig into every last dark corner to satisfy the sick desire for revelling in misery.'

Callanach counted to three before the camera flashes erupted, blinding Ava, who simply stood glaring furiously into the crowd. No one else asked for pictures of the skin doll. A red line had been drawn. No member of the press would be brave enough, or foolish enough, to tread over it that day. But the damage had been done. The publicity circus had raised its curtain and the audience were in their seats.

The killer was finally getting the attention they wanted.

Chapter Nineteen

The remainder of the day had passed as predicted. The phone lines in the incident room were awash with callers who had no useful information, but who sought reassurance or wanted to offer condolences. Officers were chasing a few leads, but more out of good form than because there was any realistic substance to them. Callanach had put his head round Ava's door at 8 p.m., offering to fetch her food. She'd sent him home – ever the good boss. He, like her, hadn't slept for too many hours. Exhausted detectives were no use to anyone. There was a skeleton crew downstairs taking the few calls that were still dribbling in. Ava was a floor up, enjoying the quiet, taking the time to do more research. Nothing she read was making her feel any better.

Leviticus chapter twenty, from where the note in Zoey's skin doll was taken, was a lesson from God on how to punish a variety of sins. The majority of the punishments resulted in death, some of which were specified to be by burning. A lucky few sinners were simply to be cast out from their community, but most of the guilty were going to end up in the ground. It didn't make for happy reading.

Ava took a sip of coffee that had gone cold half an hour ago and winced at the bitterness. The truth was that she was angry at herself. She'd lost her temper in the press conference. It wasn't acceptable at her rank and there would be consequences, but once she saw red there was no stopping her. It had been her weakness since her teenage years. One look at Callanach's face before she'd let rip at the journalists had told her she was past the point of no return. He had been bracing himself. To his credit, he hadn't jumped in and tried to stop her. He knew her well enough to understand that such an attempt would have been futile. When the debacle had come to an abrupt halt, he'd simply walked by her side to her office, delivered a coffee to her desk and given her some space while he briefed the MIT squad and the uniformed units drafted in to assist.

Her eyes began to close as she waded through a pile of paperwork. The clock told her it was one in the morning, although it felt later. She couldn't even figure out how long it had been since she'd last slept. The one comfortable chair in her office suddenly looked overwhelmingly appealing. Kicking off her shoes, Ava moved to the armchair and curled her legs into her chest, turning her face into the cushions and hoping her phone would allow her a couple of hours of peace. All she needed was a nap.

Jolting wake, Ava assumed she'd been dreaming. There had been a scream, scraping furniture. Something breaking. She'd seen Lorna's face, then she'd come to, gasping as she opened her eyes, clutching the arms of the chair and lurching forward. Then there was a second scream. This time Ava knew it was real. The noise had come from the floor above. It was 3 a.m. There shouldn't be anyone on the upper floors. Moving swiftly to her desk, Ava grabbed a can of pepper spray. Taking the stairs to the upper floor two at a time, she ran, pausing at the top fire doors to listen again. For twenty seconds there was nothing, then a woman's voice, gasping, sounding desperate.

'Please,' the voice said, begging, strangulated.

Ava slipped into the nearest office, picking up the phone to the station's front desk below. 'Violent incident, third floor, possible hostage. DCI Turner already engaged. Send backup,' she said.

She ran, her heart pounding, towards the door at the end of the corridor, pepper spray held out in front. It wasn't that difficult to get into the police station. Wait until someone else was walking through a door, catch it as it was closing, flash a fake ID if needed. It had been done before, and there were plenty of people with a reason to hate police officers, even before stretching the imagination to anything like terrorism. She had one shot, though, and that was the element of surprise.

Taking a deep breath, she kicked the door and burst in. 'Police! Hands up, don't move—'

'Turner, what the fuck do you think you're doing?' Overbeck shouted.

'Balls, ma'am, it's three in the morning . . .' Lively growled.

Ava covered her face, turning to the door as other feet began pounding along the corridor towards them.

'Situation under control,' Ava shouted, slamming the door shut before the officers racing to assist her could see inside the office. 'Misunderstanding. No danger. Stand down,' she yelled through the wood.

'With respect, DCI Turner, protocol is that you need to open the door so we can ensure you're not being held hostage,' an officer shouted from beyond Superintendent Overbeck's office door.

'Get them the hell out of here,' Overbeck whispered, buttoning her blouse and pushing past DS Lively, who was desperately trying to pull up his trousers.

163

Ava let her head fall against the door, screwing her eyes up tight and wishing she could unsee her detective sergeant furiously bashing against the semi-naked superintendent's body, bent over the desk. She took a deep breath, quelled her nausea and shouted out again.

'One minute.' She turned around to Overbeck and Lively. 'Lively, get behind the desk out of sight right now. Ma'am, sit down and say nothing.'

Overbeck tutted but did as she was told. Lively grinned as he squashed his bulk into the space beneath the desk. Ava opened the door, and left it wide enough that the backup team could see all corners of the room.

'Entirely my mistake. I thought I heard an incident, but it turns out it was the detective superintendent engaged in a heated telephone conversation. I panicked. Too many days without sleep, I guess. Sorry everyone. You can go back to whatever you were doing.'

There was a ripple of laughter at Ava's expense and some good-natured muttering as the six men and women walked back down the corridor. Stepping through the doorway, Ava made to pull Overbeck's office door closed behind her as she exited.

'No you don't, Turner,' Overbeck said. 'Get back in here.'

'Actually, I'm going to my office,' Ava said, 'and I'm going to pour myself a massive fucking drink.'

'Not if you know what's good for you. We're going to sort this out right now.'

Ava raised her eyes to the ceiling, biting down hard on her bottom lip, before whirling round and storming back into Overbeck's office, slamming the door behind her. 'You know what, ma'am, you lost the moral high ground a couple of minutes ago, so you can stop talking to me as if I'm a schoolgirl.'

'I don't see what all the fuss is about,' Lively said. 'Can you

164

not turn a blind eye, Chief Inspector? We're consenting adults, after all.'

'I wish I had been blind for a few seconds back there. Sadly, the sight of you naked is now going to be burned into my brain for the rest of my days. That's before I start to consider just what a hypocrite you are, after everything you've said . . .' Ava ranted.

'Now, you're not allowed to get personal, ma'am,' Lively said. 'The superintendent and I—'

'Lively, get the fuck out of my office,' Overbeck commanded. 'And go straight home. I don't think DCI Turner wants to bump into you again for a while.'

'Ever,' Ava added.

Lively picked up his coat from where he'd draped it over the back of a chair. 'Women,' he muttered as he left.

Ava waited until she heard the stairway door at the far end of the corridor slam behind him.

'He's been in a relationship for more than twenty years. Did you ever stop to think about that? And it may be none of my business, but you're married, too. Do those relationships not matter to either of you?' Ava asked.

'You have no right lecturing me. I'm still your superior officer,' Overbeck said.

'Lively is my detective sergeant, and he is not supposed to be engaged in an extra-marital relationship with a superior which might impact on his work, specifically undermining my working relationship with him, so I have every right to ask about this. I need my team balanced and focused. That does not include having their home lives wrecked because you got bored and fancied a bit of rough!' Ava shouted.

'How dare you!' Overbeck responded.

'You want to know how I dare? I dare because I woke to a scream and was concerned that an officer was being attacked.

Instead I find some grotesque scene from a soft porn flick being played out above my head.'

'Not that,' Overbeck said, walking to within inches of Ava's face. 'How dare you call DS Lively a bit of rough! He's intelligent, loyal and one of the few people in this goddamn building not scared to stand up to me.'

'Don't turn this around. I wasn't calling Lively rough from my perspective, but he hardly fits into your high society landscape, does he? I've never heard you say a good word about him,' Ava replied.

'Life isn't always as simple as you make it out it to be, Ava. For the record, both our relationships have gone the way most do when you're married to a police officer. It might last a year, or twenty, but sooner or later the long hours, the stress and the carnage we can never unsee gets too much. My husband left me, DCI Turner. Apologies for not explaining that to you. Lively's partner refuses to talk about his work. Not one word. She's banned the subject from the house. Kind of tricky when he's dedicated his life to the service, don't you think?'

She stepped away, reaching for a cupboard and taking out a bottle of cognac and two glasses. She poured an inch into each glass before handing one to Ava, who downed the contents.

'I'm sorry,' Ava said.

'Oh, cut the crap,' Overbeck replied. 'Tell me what you want.'

'What?' Ava spluttered.

'There'll be a price. There always is. You stay silent, and I do what? Guarantee a recommendation for your next promotion? Let you have your pick for the open detective inspector position? Name it. The only caveat is that you don't go after Lively. He doesn't need disciplinary proceedings at this stage of his career.'

'You know, you really should try to see the world in a more positive light,' Ava said. 'I won't go after Lively. Not because you've told me not to, but because he's a bloody good policeman and I need him on my squad. And believe me, he's capable of finding disciplinary trouble without my help. More to the point, I don't want anything. Do I wish I hadn't walked in on you? You bet I bloody do. But this will be the last you'll hear of it. I don't want to ever think about it, or be reminded of it, again. I want nothing from you in return. Not everything in life is about negotiation and prices, Superintendent. Certainly not when two people apparently care about one another.' She set her glass down gently on Overbeck's desk.

'I'd rather pay my debts,' Overbeck said. 'It's very simple. You keep quiet and I'll make sure I repay you.'

'Honestly, I'd prefer that you didn't,' Ava said. 'Now if you don't mind, ma'am, I think I'll go home. I could use a shower.' She made her way to the door.

'Turner,' Overbeck said. 'It wouldn't do you any harm either – a relationship. Don't think you're beyond needing human contact. You're cutting yourself off. The loneliness catches up with you in the end. Take my advice. A flawed relationship is better than none at all.'

'You're going to give me relationship advice after this?' Ava laughed. 'Good God, and there was me thinking tonight couldn't get any more bizarre.' She stepped out and closed Overbeck's door behind her.

Ava took the stairs two at a time, feeling grimy and angry, more from Overbeck's suggestion that she might want a favour in return for silence than from what she had witnessed. Worse than that was the sting of Overbeck's advice. Ava didn't need a relationship to be happy. She was busy and fulfilled. It was true that police officers made bad partners. What was the point of starting something that was inevitably going to go wrong in the end anyway? She took her keys from her desk, trying not to think about the spectacle of Lively and Overbeck having sex. Trying to ignore the fact that it seemed as if everyone else in the world was having sex, except her.

Chapter Twenty

The film ended and Selina moved her head sleepily against Callanach's neck.

'Can you stay?' she asked.

'I'd better get back to my apartment. I have to be at the station early,' he replied.

'You're not far from the city centre here,' she said. 'You've got your mobile with you. They'll find you if they need you.'

'I know,' he said. 'But I won't sleep properly here. I'm just used to my own place. It's going to be a tough day again tomorrow. I don't want to keep you awake all night if I'm restless.'

'I was hoping we wouldn't get much sleep,' Selina said, smiling up at him and running a hand lightly down his chest.

Callanach took her hand in his, kissed her wrist then moved away to stand up. 'I really can't,' he said. 'Although I appreciate the offer more than you know.'

Selina stayed in her seat, stretching out her long legs and propping her head on her hand. 'Luc, we've been seeing each other a couple of months now and you haven't stayed over once. If I can state the obvious, you haven't tried to get me into bed either. I'm getting all the signals, but it never leads anywhere. Can we at least talk about it?'

'It's late,' he said. 'There's a conversation to be had, I agree, but could it wait until the weekend?'

'By the weekend, there'll be another crisis at work or I'll be putting in a double shift and we won't see each other. I'm a patient woman, Luc, and I like you. A lot, actually. I also have no desire to jump straight into bed with every man I date, but I'm starting to think that maybe you're not interested in me the same way I am in you.'

'It's not that,' Luc said. 'Honestly, it's complicated. I told you at the start that I didn't think I was ready for anything intimate. Perhaps this was a mistake. I'm sorry, Selina. We've drifted into a relationship I know I can't have. I should go.'

Selina stood up, taking hold of him by the arm as he picked up his coat. 'Luc, no. That's not where I wanted this to go. If you need more time, I can wait. If I'm doing something wrong, I'd rather you told me now than letting this ruin everything. I didn't want to push you. It would be good to know if you're attracted to me or not. Sometimes it seems as if there's a wall between us.' She took her hand off his arm and smiled. 'Whatever it is, I'd rather you just told me. Even if things don't work out between us. I'm your friend if nothing else.'

She sat down again, passive, unpushy. Callanach had known the conversation was coming. You could muddle through a few weeks of a new relationship with coffee and the odd meal, but then there was kissing. Hellos and goodbyes in public or an arm slung casually around another person's shoulders did no harm. But then there had been meals at Selina's flat, evenings spent relaxing after long hikes, and late arrivals home from nights out. He had always been able to use work as an excuse before now. But Selina was right. She had been patient with him and she was owed more. Even if she decided not to see him again, he felt the weight of responsibility for having drawn her into beginning something that he couldn't see through.

'You know about the rape allegation,' he said, sitting down at the far end of the couch. 'When it all finished, it became clear that I was suffering from post-traumatic stress disorder. Even after the court entered a not guilty verdict, once Astrid had decided not to give evidence against me, the process left me devastated. Not being believed. Leaving Interpol under a cloud. At times, questioning my own sanity when Astrid produced medical evidence about her injuries.'

'It must have been appalling for you,' Selina said. 'Of course it impacted on you psychologically. How could it not?'

'It was more than just psychological. My health suffered. I wasn't seeing anyone when I was first arrested for the rape charge, and there was no possibility of getting close to anyone while I was awaiting trial, so I didn't realise for a long time just how badly I'd been affected. For months I couldn't sleep properly. I didn't want to eat, I stopped exercising, all the usual stuff. I was facing the prospect of a long jail sentence with the lifetime label of sex offender. At one point, although I'm sure I'd never have gone through with it, I contemplated suicide.'

'Did you seek help at the time?' Selina asked.

'No. I hid myself away and pretended it wasn't happening. When your own lawyer is telling you things don't look good and that perhaps you should enter a plea and hope for a shorter sentence, it really doesn't feel as if there's much point in going on. A therapist would only have told me what I already knew – that I had to wait for the outcome of the trial, for resolution of one sort or another, so that I could move forward. At that stage I had no idea quite how long term the devastation to my life would be.'

'I understand,' Selina said. 'And I know you must find it hard to trust women now. I get that the prospect of putting your faith in someone must seem daunting. You have to take it one day at a time. I'm sorry if I've been pressuring you . . .'

'It's not that,' Callanach said. 'As much as I resented having to move to Scotland at first, I've come to feel at home here. I have no desire to spend the rest of my life alone. For what it's worth, I already trust you. I know you're nothing like Astrid.'

'I can find you a counsellor here, a good one. There are some specialist PTSD psychologists around who'll help get you through this. The fact that you're able to talk to me about it now is a good sign,' Selina said.

'Selina, it's no good. Rehashing the whole thing with a psychologist is the last thing I want.'

'But you have to try to move forward. Giving in to this can't be the answer . . .'

'I'm impotent,' he said.

Selina was silent for a few seconds. 'That's why you haven't wanted to stay,' she said finally.

'Exactly. It's also a difficult conversation to have with a person you're dating. I shouldn't have kept it from you for so long. It wasn't fair and I'm sorry. This can't work. I hope you can forgive me for dragging you into a hopeless situation,' he said.

'Well, what have you tried? Viagra might be a means of starting things again.'

'I've been there and I really didn't enjoy it. Getting a fake reaction from my body isn't what I want. It's knowing that my body doesn't respond that's the worst of it. Using chemicals to enable myself to have sex is almost worse than not having it at all.'

'Have you . . . tried many times?'

'A couple,' Luc said. 'Disastrously. None that I want to talk about, to be honest.'

'And is there nothing that gets you interested? Maybe thinking too hard about it is wrong. Just getting a little bit drunk, relaxing, taking your time.'

'Drunk, sober, high, asleep, nothing will make any difference. I get no reaction at all. All I can think about are the things Astrid claimed I did to her. I know it's just fear, and I know where it's coming from. If I have sex, will I be accused of rape again? It's very basic psychology, no different than a child being scared to go into the garden because they were stung by a wasp, but it's so ingrained in me now that I can't see a path to recovery.'

'That's the PTSD talking,' Selina said. 'It might be slow progress but that doesn't mean you shouldn't bother trying. What's the worst that can happen? If there's no reaction to sexual stimuli at the moment, you're at zero. Any recovery at all would be an improvement, even if it's gradual or partial.'

'Spoken like a true doctor,' Luc said.

Selina smiled. 'I'm sorry. I just put my diagnose–plan–treat head on. Sometimes it's easier to think of problems that way. Disassociate yourself from it a bit. How about a three-pronged attack? Feel free to accept or reject any of this as you see fit.'

'I'm listening,' Luc said.

'I'll put together some recommendations for psychologists who have experience in treating sexual disorders. I won't talk to any of them, or take it any further than that. Then, if and when you feel ready to talk about it with a professional, you'll have some options.'

'Okay,' Luc said. 'That sounds sensible.'

'And I'll investigate other medical solutions, just because more information is always better than less. I'll exclude oral medication as you've tried that and you weren't happy with it,' she said. 'I won't attempt to persuade you about any of it. You can ask me about the options if you feel like exploring them.'

'That's fine,' Luc said. 'What's the third part?'

'Okay, well the third part is where I stop being a doctor and I'm just your girlfriend again.'

'I think I prefer that approach,' Luc said.

'Me too,' Selina replied, standing up and undoing the buttons on her shirt.

'I appreciate what you're doing, but I really don't think another failed attempt is going to do my ego much good,' Luc said softly.

'Oh, this isn't for you,' Selina said, peeling off her shirt to reveal a midnight blue lace bra. 'We've been seeing each other nearly three months. Do you have any idea how frustrating it is, dating the best-looking man you've ever seen, complete with six-pack and French accent, then going to bed alone at the end of every date?' Luc shook his head. 'Well, I'll tell you. Most of the time I've felt as if I might explode from wanting you.' She undid her zip, pushing her jeans to the floor. 'So what I think is this. Your body might not be firing on all cylinders just yet, but mine definitely is. Let's forget about trying to have intercourse and be more inventive. I have no problem with devoting a couple of hours exclusively to my sexual pleasure, if you don't. And just maybe, perhaps not now but at some point, you'll be able to forget what you went through for a few seconds and get that spark back. Because there's nothing wrong with you physically. Certainly not from where I'm standing. You do seem to be wearing substantially more clothes than me though, and I think we should remedy that pretty quickly.' She began to unbutton his shirt. 'It can be our project. I'm going to make my body available to you any time you need some therapy. As long as it doesn't get too frustrating for you, I'm happy for you to give me any amount of pleasure.'

'That's very magnanimous of you,' Luc laughed.

'I know,' Selina replied. 'How are you with bras, only mine seems to still be on, for some reason.'

'That's a particular skill of mine,' Luc said, reaching around her back and unhooking it.

'Good to know,' she replied, standing up in front of where he was sitting. 'But I still seem to be wearing one last item. Shall we see if you can find a way to help me out of those, too?'

Luc did as she requested, then stood up, picking her up in his arms and carrying her through to the bedroom. He had no complaints. Selina was beautiful. In his previous life in Lyon, she was exactly the sort of woman he'd loved spending time with – passionate, intelligent, fun and sporty. And she was right: just because he couldn't experience sexual fulfilment didn't mean he had to stop engaging in it with her. He was good at it. He understood women's bodies, what to say, how to touch, the timing and psychology of it. None of those skills had been lost or even reduced by what he'd been through.

He was lucky. He'd found himself dating a woman he could talk to about what he was experiencing and who had been able to respond in a calm, open manner. She had even been honest about her own needs and desires, which he found refreshing and attractive. But still, as they lay together, exploring their bodies, familiarising himself with her likes and dislikes, he couldn't help wondering if this was all there would ever be. If he would ever be able to have sex again.

Chapter Twenty-One

There was a storm raging to match Ava's mood as Natasha knocked on her office door and entered.

'Hey,' Ava said. 'I thought the front desk had made a mistake when they said you were here. Have you ever been to the station before?'

'Only once before, to give a statement when you were . . . Let's not talk about that again. It still gives me the chills,' Natasha said. 'Otherwise, getting arrested is on my bucket list, but I think I'll do it somewhere you're not in charge. Seems like cheating if my best friend can bail me out.' She looked around. 'I love what you obviously haven't done with the place. Very authentic, and strangely reminiscent of an ancient BBC police drama.'

'Sit down,' Ava said. 'I'd get you coffee, only . . .'

'Too busy. I know. I saw your press conference yesterday. I'm sorry about Zoey and Lorna. I wanted to talk to you about it.'

'You don't have to worry about me. I know I went off on one with that reporter, and I should have controlled myself better, but I'm doing all right,' Ava reassured her.

'Actually, it wasn't that,' Natasha said. 'I'm probably being paranoid but there's a student I can't get hold of at the University. She's in her third year, studying modern languages, and she missed a meeting we were supposed to have last night.'

'You're head of the philosophy department, Natasha. I don't understand.'

'I'm sure I'm overreacting, but I run a help group. We're more there to listen than anything else. If I tell you this, it's in confidence. I know you'll be careful but the information I have is very sensitive. Most of the students who talk to us come on a first-name basis only, but obviously I see some of them around and I know who they are anyway.'

'Sure,' Ava said. 'But if this girl's a degree student, I really can't see that she matches the profile for the sort of young woman the killer is targeting.'

'It depends how much he knows about Kate. The help group I run is very specific. We don't even have funding yet. It's too controversial. There are a few of us involved – some academic staff, counsellors, doctors. Have you heard of the websites that set up young people, predominantly women, with so-called sugar daddies?'

'I saw a news report about it a while ago. It's not something I've come into contact with professionally though,' Ava said.

'Well, whoever saw that little marketplace opportunity is making serious inroads into the student population. Student debt is at an all-time high. Some non-Scottish students pay full tuition fees, so they're particularly vulnerable. Even with loans, who wants to start their twenties owing several thousand pounds? So the websites offer to hook you up with a wealthy older person. They might buy you clothes, pay your car insurance, help with your rent, but the websites pretend you're not obliged to do anything in return,' Natasha said.

'Except there's no such thing as something for nothing.' Ava picked up a pen and began to take notes. 'What's your part in all this?'

'We're just there as a sounding board, really. The girls who're doing this don't want it on their medical records, so they're not asking the right questions about contraception, sexually transmitted diseases, you name it. Some of them are finding themselves trapped. What the site doesn't publicise is that once you're in this, it's hard to get out. A couple of our girls have found themselves under pressure to continue bad relationships or do things they don't feel comfortable with. The older men have rather an "I've paid for you, now you're mine" attitude. There have been threats to do with social media shaming, even contacting the girls' parents.'

'So it's just prostitution without the street corners,' Ava said.

'It's complex because it's being sold to these young people as exercising their right to choose, a control-your-own-body scenario, but they're doing it to avoid financial problems or restrictions. We offer medical advice with no questions asked. We tell them what their legal options are if they're scared. We talk about issues like never having their photo taken, always using a false name, never letting a so-called sugar daddy pick them up from their home address, and basic safety, like carrying rape alarms. Very few of them listen until it's too late. Same old story.'

'How does your student – Kate – fit into this picture?' Ava asked.

'She'd been using a website – SugarPa, I think – but she was struggling with the emotional backlash of sleeping with older men. There'd been an incident where a man had bought her what amounted to a fast food dinner and thought he was entitled to sex. When she refused he became verbally abusive, used every derogatory term he could to describe her as a sex worker, then grabbed her, intimately, and she had to fight him off. Since then she'd carried on using the site, which just goes to show the desperation that's being taken advantage of, but she was traumatised. She's been meeting me once a week to talk it through and so I could keep an eye on her safety. Last night was the first session she's missed and she's not answering her phone. I checked with her faculty. She didn't attend any lectures or seminars there today, and she's not in the student halls. I knocked her door and got no response.'

'I understand it's out of character and that you're concerned, but you know what I'm going to say, right?' Ava asked.

'Yup. She could be with a client. She could have decided enough was enough and gone home. It's possible that she got a boyfriend and decided to stay at his house for a few days. In any event, I'm not giving you enough to open a missing person report. Does that sum it up?'

'Maybe we should swap jobs,' Ava said.

'Not for all the tea in China. You'd terrify every member of my faculty and persuade all the students to swap discipline to something more real world,' Natasha said. 'Seriously, Ava, Kate would have phoned me or texted. She has my number and she knows I'll be worried.'

'I believe you, and I'll do what I can to help, but with two young women dead and the press all over it, every female teenager who doesn't get home on time is currently being reported as missing. Let me take some details. Full name and age?' Ava asked.

'Kate Bailey. Nineteen. Five foot six and pretty. I can pull her photo from the student database if you need it,' Natasha said.

'If it becomes necessary, that would be great,' Ava said. 'Does she drive?'

'I don't know if she has a licence or not, but she doesn't have a car at the Uni that I know of. Is there nothing you can do? Kate's vulnerable, Ava. She would never have gone through that bloody website if she hadn't been.'

Ava looked at her watch. 'All right. I have a meeting in an hour, but after that we'll go to her halls and check it out. Will security open her room if I have my ID and you vouch for me?'

'I'll make sure they do. Thanks, Ava. I'm sorry to call in a favour.'

'You're not calling in a favour, you idiot. You're concerned about a potential missing person. Calling in a favour is making me listen to you singing the same song a hundred times when you're drunk.'

'That was the Proclaimers. Everyone sings that song over and over again when they're pissed,' Natasha said. 'Honestly, sometimes it's as if you're not Scottish at all.'

The halls offered a variety of student accommodation, some shared rooms, some singles. The majority were occupied by first-year students but a few were taken by second or third years. Kate's room was on the third floor, at the end of the corridor. It was quiet when they arrived. The communal kitchen, Ava noted, was remarkably clean and tidy. In her university days there was an atmosphere of constant chaos. Natasha caught the look of disbelief on her face.

'It's a females-only floor,' Natasha said. 'Not that it's always the case that the males of the species are messy and disorganised, but . . .'

'A young woman who chose to live on a female-only floor decided to make money through a sugar daddy website? Couldn't she just get bar work?' Ava asked.

'On minimum wage, when she has to study? That's the problem with this sort of camouflaged prostitution. It's fast, immediate. There's no tax and it's based on socialising. That's how they sell it, anyway. Personally, I'd like to see the people who run these sites jailed for pimping. They're making money out of membership fees. It shouldn't be legal.'

'You won't get any argument from me,' Ava said. A security guard wandered down the hall towards them, whistling as he unlocked the door with only the briefest glance at Ava's ID.

'Does he know you?' she asked Natasha after the guard had walked away.

'No, but I phoned ahead to say I'd be here with you,' Natasha replied. 'All the external doors work with electronic keys, so it's a safe building.'

'Unless some helpful outgoing student holds the door for you,' Ava said.

Kate's room was tidy. It consisted of a bedroom area with an en suite, in which there was a shower, sink and toilet. The bedroom had a built-in wardrobe, a single bed, bookshelves and a desk. No matter where you went in the world, student rooms were all the same, Ava thought. A stuffed dog was flopped across her pillow, and photos of friends and parents were pinned to a board on the wall. A phone charger snaked unattached from a power socket and her laptop sat, lid open, on the desk.

Ava ran one finger over the touchpad. The screen sprang to life, offering a woodland scene with a lake in the foreground. There was no request for a password to be entered.

'Kate's still logged in,' Ava said. 'She really should have better security than this.'

'Can you get into her emails?' Natasha asked.

'I didn't think you'd want me to,' Ava said. 'Didn't you once write a paper on the police overstepping their powers?'

'I'm not suggesting we actually read any of her emails. I'd just like to see when she last sent an email or replied to one. If it was in the last couple of hours then we know she's okay.'

Ava moved the cursor down to the bottom of the screen and clicked on the email icon.

'Her email is password protected, which is slightly reassuring, but it means I can't see when she was last active. What was the name of the website you said she was using?'

'SugarPa.'

Ava typed again. 'Got it, and Kate's got the password auto-filled. Let's see.' She clicked and scrolled down as Natasha bent over her shoulder to look. 'How do the girls tolerate it? These men are mostly old enough to be their fathers. Some would pass more convincingly as their grandfathers. A month's rent doesn't seem enough to let these leeches touch them.'

'Desperate situations breed desperate solutions. Some of these young women take the view that if they sleep with a guy they hook up with in a nightclub, they might as well throw in a couple of older men and get something in return.'

'Her "dating history" is here,' Ava said. 'How's that for a euphemism? There's a messaging system for them to make arrangements, too.' As Ava clicked on the dating history time-line, a picture popped up of a young woman dressed in a tight white t-shirt and shorts. She was smiling sweetly at the camera, her long blonde hair shining like silk, loose over her shoulders. Ava experienced a moment of nausea. It wasn't hard to imagine their rapist-cum-murderer seeing that particular photograph and becoming fixated. 'Can you confirm that this is Kate?' she asked.

'It is,' Natasha confirmed.

'You're right. She is pretty. Judging by the amount of messages she's received, she was popular on this website. Here, this is her last message thread.'

A new window opened on the screen and Ava scanned the communication.

'She did have a meeting yesterday,' Natasha said.

'With a new man,' Ava noted. 'He gave her instructions on how to recognise him. Carrying a red umbrella. No description of his physical appearance though.'

'Can you get into his profile?'

'Here you go. It says he's forty-two years old, unmarried, likes going to the gym, works in the travel industry. Looking for someone to spoil, apparently. The photo's blurred though. How many years do you think he knocked off his real age?'

'I'm guessing the average on this website is a decade,' Natasha said. 'That photo's useless.'

'It could be one he just found on the internet and copied, so I wouldn't rely on it anyway. We do have an answer though. She went to meet someone yesterday and took her phone with her. Left the laptop here. It's possible she decided to stay the night at his and he offered to take her out somewhere today.'

'Perhaps,' Natasha said. 'I do feel a bit better knowing this was set up through SugarPa. They must have some sort of vetting facility. Members have to pay a monthly fee, so there'll be a record of who she was meeting. I'm sorry, Ava. I wasted your time.'

'You didn't, and I'm glad there's no indication that Kate was panicked when she left here. The room hasn't been disturbed by anyone.'

'She could still have let me know she was going to miss our meeting,' Natasha said. 'And it's not like her to miss lectures. Her whole rationale for using the SugarPa site was to save some money and ensure she could afford her education. She wants to be a journalist.'

'Could she not ask her parents for additional support, rather than use SugarPa?'

'No,' Natasha said. 'Her father's ill, although Kate didn't want to discuss it in detail with me. Her mother is providing twenty-four-hour care. All I know is they live in Durham. Most of the students we help struggle to talk about their home lives. I think part of it is knowing how much their parents would hate it if they knew what they were doing for money.'

'Understandable. I think at this stage, where there's no evidence that anything's definitely wrong, the best you can do is ascertain who her closest friends are and approach them carefully to see if anyone's heard from her. Leave my number with them in case they have any relevant information. You'll have to make up an excuse, but that won't be difficult.'

'Okay,' Natasha said. 'You can't trace her phone, can you?'

'I'd need an official investigation in progress to do that, which would mean notifying her next of kin, if for no other reason than to check she hasn't gone home to Durham.'

'Don't do that. Kate would never forgive me,' Natasha said. 'I'll find out who she was friendly with. Her personal tutor should be able to help with that.'

'I'll check she hasn't been admitted to a hospital, or even arrested. Can you email me the photo of Kate the university has on file? I'll circulate it with the city's beat officers immediately so we're actively on the lookout for her tonight. I'll phone you if anything turns up and in the meantime you keep trying her mobile number. If Kate's still not been in contact first thing tomorrow morning, we'll make a decision about moving this forward.' Ava walked to Kate's bed and turned back a corner of the duvet to form a neat triangle.

'Thank you,' Natasha said. 'I feel better already.'

'No problem,' Ava said, giving her friend a reassuring smile and hoping it was convincing. Natasha might feel better, but she didn't. As certain as she had initially been that Kate's disappearance was just another misunderstanding among the hundreds that Police Scotland were currently sifting through, being in the student's empty room had given her the creeps.

That was just tiredness and paranoia, Ava told herself. There was no evidence at all of foul play. Not yet, her brain autocorrected her. Just not yet. Natasha closed the website and shut the lid on Kate's computer.

Chapter Twenty-Two

When the call had come for Ava to attend a crime scene, she'd been fighting one of those dreams that pulled you deeper and deeper into its weirdness, inducing panic as she tried to find someone but had forgotten who it was. The shrill ringtone had saved her, leaving her panting breathlessly into the receiver. If the control room officer had noticed anything strange about her demeanour, he had been either too sensible or too professional to comment.

Ten minutes later a patrol car picked her up, dropping her some minutes later in George Street. All Ava knew was that Dr Jonty Spurr had asked for her personally and that the road was cordoned off from traffic and pedestrians. She had asked only one question on her way to the scene.

'Is it a young woman?'

'It is,' the officer driving her had confirmed. 'That's all I know, I'm afraid.'

Kate Bailey, Ava thought. Natasha's instincts had been right. Somehow, Ava had felt it too, as they'd looked through Kate's room and nosed into the details of her private life, secreted in the impersonal container of her laptop.

The pathologist was taking photos when she arrived. The multi-storey nature of the buildings in the street had necessitated the erection of a tent to spare local people from trauma, and to spare the dead young woman from prying eyes. At the top of the road, a bus was stationed outside a hotel. There were police officers everywhere, keeping concerned citizens inside their apartments and keeping the area clean for the Scenes of Crime officers. It was a busy month for the SOCOs, Ava thought absently, ducking under the crime scene tape to get closer to the manic activity beneath the awning. A couple of pedestrians were deeply engaged in describing events to the officers who were taking statements. One was gesticulating angrily, another was crying, shaking, arms wrapped around himself. Ava felt for them. Witnesses were often the forgotten victims at crime scenes, pumped for information then moved along so that the investigation could progress. No one intended it, but priorities had to be made. Ava called a police officer over, handing him a bundle of notes.

'I don't care how you organise it, but get those witnesses hot drinks and make sure taxis are standing by to take them wherever they need to go.'

'All of them, ma'am? Only there's another bunch of them under the access to that hotel.' The officer pointed to a bridge structure set into the buildings.

Ava sighed. Little chance of stopping so many people from giving the press all the gory details when so many witnesses were involved. 'Yes, all of them,' Ava said. 'And ask the hotel to open its lobby so the witnesses can be spoken to inside rather than on the street. They'll be cold from shock.'

Jonty Spurr was packing away his camera as she went to speak with him.

'What happened?' she asked.

'The victim was in the road and got hit by the bus,' Jonty

said. 'I'm afraid her body is in a dreadful mess. It's a difficult scene to process.'

Another body dumped in the road. Ava sighed as she zipped up a protective suit. Perhaps if she'd listened to Natasha, gone looking for Kate earlier, she could have saved this life. Anything might have been possible. SugarPa might have given them the identity of the man Kate had met. They could have traced her mobile signal. How many hours of the search had she lost by following procedure rather than instinct? Now they had a body to document, rather than a young woman to return home safely to her parents.

'All right. Let me see,' she told Jonty, standing on a mat placed near the corpse so that her feet would not disturb other evidence left on the road.

He peeled back the body bag. The damage was overwhelming. Her face was unrecognisable, completely distorted by the impact. No part of her had been left unbloodied. Her limbs were a shattered mess. She looked, Ava thought, like a burst balloon. As a forensics officer moved away, unblocking the beams from a light, a small portion of her hair became visible, fluttering as the wind picked up. It was red, not as a result of the carnage, but from a dye. Almost purple, she noted, bending down.

'This isn't Kate,' Ava murmured.

'Kate who?' Jonty asked.

'I was expecting . . . Never mind. You said this girl had been hit by a bus. If this is a road traffic accident, why did you ask for me?'

'Sorry, I assumed you'd been properly briefed. Let me show you what I found when I was doing a preliminary assessment of the body.' Jonty knelt next to the girl and lifted her head gently to reveal the left side of her face. It was dented, and already blackening, but he pulled out a tiny, fierce torch and shone it on the area where her cheek had once been. 'It's hard to make out with the subsequent trauma from the vehicle impact, but you can see here.' He pointed with the torch to the top of her now-flattened nose. 'Follow the line right to her cheekbone, then down diagonally to her mouth and back across to the edge of her jaw.'

The Z became clear as Dr Spurr pointed out the cruelly deep laceration. 'Has this just happened?' she breathed.

'The cuts are very fresh. I haven't been able to piece together a timeline yet, as I've been concentrating on managing the area. The bus driver is giving a statement as we speak. He might be of more use to you.'

Ava straightened up, the world spinning as she got to her full height and made her way along the street towards the driver. Why had she been so sure it was Kate? She'd reassured Natasha that some perfectly plausible explanation for the girl's absence would present itself, but deep down she'd been certain she'd missed something. Now another girl lay dead. The bodies would be starting to back up at the mortuary. None could be released until their case was closed.

'Excuse me, I'm Detective Chief Inspector Turner with the Major Investigation Team. I appreciate you're in the middle of explaining the events to this officer but I wonder if you could just run through it now for me.' The bus driver was the man who had appeared agitated and distressed when Ava had arrived. He nodded his head, cleared his throat and wiped tears from his face.

'The girl came out of nowhere,' the driver said. 'I was on my normal route, going slowly, as I'd just dropped another passenger off. Then this shape sort of whirled off the pavement, spinning, still upright. I knew she hadn't seen me but she was already screaming anyway. I was braking by the time I hit her, but it wasn't enough. I had maybe a second, perhaps two, to respond. She was right in my windscreen, full in my face. I don't know how I'll ever stop seeing it.'

His body was shaking as he spoke. Ava took him by the arm and led him to the edge of the pavement to sit down.

'This man needs to see the paramedics now,' she told the officer who'd been taking his statement. 'There are other witnesses you can talk to. Notify the bus company to come and remove the vehicle, although it'll need to be kept untouched and available for forensic evaluation.' She leaned down to the bus driver. 'We're going to get you some help. The officer will call any family member or friend who you might like to be with you.'

A commotion taking place at the front door of a hotel a few buildings down distracted her. The officer she'd tasked with finding a warm place for the witnesses stood, hands on hips, while a woman ranted at him.

'What's the problem?' Ava called as she walked towards them.

'The problem is that this is a four-star establishment. It's guests only at this time of night. With the best will in the world, the people you're asking to bring in are hardly the sort of people we'd welcome as clients and they . . .' The woman lowered her voice by several degrees. 'Frankly, they smell, and I wouldn't be surprised if they didn't have infestations.'

'I'm curious about your understanding of the phrase "With the best will in the world",' Ava said. 'It strikes me that there's very little goodwill here. These people' – Ava motioned towards the group who were huddled a few metres away – 'have just witnessed a very traumatic event. A young woman is dead. I need somewhere warm and safe to ensure that I can establish the facts quickly and easily. We're not asking for catering and no one will make any noise that might disturb your guests.'

'The last time I checked, the police didn't have the right to simply barge into private premises and demand the free use of space. Perhaps I should notify the media of your supercilious attitude,' she said.

'Feel free to do that,' Ava said. 'But Edinburgh is a city built on a tradition of kindness and dignity. You might find you don't come out of this portrayed as the victim.'

The hotel night manager fumed quietly, looking around to see who, if anyone, was witnessing the debate.

'I'll need you out of here an hour from now,' she hissed at Ava. 'And you need to limit yourselves to the front chairs. No wandering around and absolutely no one is to go near the lifts.'

'Thank you,' Ava said. 'That's extremely generous of you. We'll make sure your hotel is left untainted.'

Ava waved the group into the warm foyer, where they took chairs gratefully. The hotel manager produced three jugs of water with paper cups. No doubt, Ava thought, she would feel more comfortable throwing them away once they'd been used, rather than washing real crockery for her guests to touch later. The homeless really were despised. Perhaps not always openly, but the sense that they carried diseases, were unclean and unsafe, had pervaded every level of society. They were the nation's underclass. No wonder they made such easy targets. It wasn't simply that the homeless went unseen. It was that no one actually wanted to see them.

She sat down next to a man who was sipping water and staring around at the large modern art sculptures in the lobby as if his world had turned upside down.

'Can you tell me what happened?' she asked.

'Didnae see a thing,' he muttered.

'It was dark and it must have happened very quickly,' Ava said. 'Do you know the woman who died?'

He stared at his shoes. Ava waited. Her years on the beat had taught her nothing if not to be patient.

'Mellie,' he said eventually.

'Mellie. Is that short for Melanie?' she asked.

'Don't know,' he said. 'What's it matter?'

'We'd like to be able to find her family,' Ava said softly. 'Was Mellie attacked?'

'Ask the others. One of 'em was wi' her,' he said.

'Thank you. Do you have anywhere safe to sleep tonight?' Ava asked.

'Do I look like a fuckin' landowner?' he asked, sharpening up and meeting her eyes for the first time.

'I'll arrange a place at a hostel if you want it. You shouldn't sleep on the street tonight,' Ava said.

She moved to another woman, who was busy reorganising various articles between different bags. Ava introduced herself and waited until she had the woman's attention.

'Do you know Mellie's last name?' Ava asked.

'Dunno. She wasn't around much. I think she's got a bloke somewhere,' the woman said.

'So she's not homeless?' Ava asked.

'Nah, comes out when he kicks her out. Gets a fix. Goes home when she runs out of money or it gets too cold. Are we going to get fed here?'

'Not here, but I'll sort something out,' Ava said. 'Did you see what happened?'

'What's the point? It's happened to two others before her and the police have done nothing.'

'Are you talking about the other attacks?' Ava asked. 'Did you see who hurt her?'

'I'm saying nothing. She got hit by a bus, in case you couldn't tell. I'm not going to court for no one. If there's no hot food here, I'm leaving.' She picked up a multitude of carrier bags and bundled her way through the door.

'Wait,' Ava said. 'I'm arranging for all of you to get a place in a hostel tonight. Fully paid for, and I'll make sure you all get a hot meal, too. Give me five minutes to arrange it and I'll have an officer escort you all safely there.'

Back inside, Ava called the other uniformed officers over. 'Any joy getting them to talk?'

'No, ma'am,' a sergeant answered. 'Can't say I blame them. The only time they have any contact with us is when they're being moved on. There's not much trust there, to be honest.'

'Right. There's an officer undercover in the homeless community at the moment. His name's Detective Sergeant Pax Graham. Have the incident room contact him – he's got a mobile with him. I want rooms booked for all these people at a shelter straight away. Just ensure that DS Graham is in that same shelter before we get there. Hold everyone here until then. Get some takeaway food for them if there's going to be a delay. Say we'll pay for two nights at the shelter, whatever you have to do. I need Graham to get whatever information he can out of them about what they saw tonight. If they think he's on their side, they might just open up to him.'

The officers got organising as Ava located Dr Spurr again.

'The deceased is known as Mellie, no surname as yet. The bus driver said she spun into the road. He reckons she was still on her feet when his bus hit her. Does that correspond with the injuries you've seen?' she asked.

'It does. There's been a massive trauma event which has left direct impact wounds from her head to her feet. She'd have been facing the bus when it hit her. The bus then skidded slightly to the left and her body was thrown off to the right. We're lucky she didn't go under the bus, or the damage to her body might have been so bad that it could have proved impossible to isolate the injuries to her face.'

'How soon will you be able to tell me if she'd taken any drugs?'

'Forty-eight hours to be definite, and that's rushing the tox screen through. Did the witnesses not help you with that?' Jonty asked.

'I don't think they're feeling inclined to discuss drug use or anything else with the police,' Ava said. 'Did Mellie have any identifying documents on her? A wallet or mobile?'

'There was some cash in her jeans pocket and a door key in her jacket. No mobile, but there was a photo in the rear pocket of her jeans of a young woman holding a baby.'

'Could I see it please?' Ava asked. Jonty called over an officer who produced the photo for them.

'Could the deceased be the woman in this photo?' Ava asked.

'Entirely possible. Her hair's the same colour. To be honest with you, I'm struggling to establish a good estimate of her age at the moment. If you can't ID her, it might be that I can only give you an age from her bones and teeth after a full post-mortem.'

'There's a number on the door behind them,' Ava said, squinting. '26a. Must be a flat.'

'You're not going to find her from that,' Jonty said.

'Maybe not, but there's an electricity pylon almost in the back garden. That should reduce the search. I'll get a team on it straight away. One of the witnesses thinks the woman was in a relationship. The least we can do is notify her family.'

'Ma'am,' a uniformed officer interrupted. 'The food and the hostel. I'm not sure how we pay for that.'

'Here,' Ava said, getting out her wallet and handing over a credit card. 'Use this.'

'Unless Police Scotland has changed its way of operating beyond recognition, I'd say that was your personal credit card,' Jonty said as the officer walked away. 'I'm not sure you're going to be able to reclaim that on expenses.'

'I don't intend to try,' Ava said. 'Days like these, it feels as if nothing we do will ever be enough to protect the vulnerable.'

'You're only one woman, Ava,' Jonty said. 'Don't be so hard on yourself.'

'Hard on myself? People are being butchered in the streets. The homeless population is scared. They feel as if we're doing nothing for them and I don't blame them. Where's the public outcry? Where's the press interest? At what point did we decide that some lives mattered more than others? I just don't know where it stops, Jonty. When all the homeless people in the city have been branded? Or is it all the drug users? What about the alcoholics? Because that would take a while.'

'You're doing all you can,' Jonty told her gently.

'I've been doing nothing at all,' she said, 'but I'm going to. This stops tonight.'

Ava stripped off her white suit, dropping it into a bin as she walked away. Hard on herself? She didn't think so. There were victims waiting for justice, and if they had a voice, she was pretty certain they would tell her she wasn't doing nearly enough to keep the innocent safe.

Chapter Twenty-Three

Ava's office armchair seemed to be getting more use than her bed. She awoke there at 7 a.m., her neck sore from sleeping at an angle, her feet cold and numb. Her clothes felt sticky where she had sweated against the leather of the chair for the four hours she'd spent there. It was no good. She would have to go home, shower and change into fresh clothes. If she was fast, she could be back for 8 a.m. in time to prepare for a squad briefing at 9 a.m.

For once the weekday traffic did not hinder her, even through the rabbit runs amongst the city's old buildings and down the one-way streets. Ava rarely failed to appreciate Edinburgh's architectural beauty, but today she had eyes only for her watch. Throwing on jeans and a white shirt, she raced back towards the station. When her mobile rang, she let it go to voicemail. Five more minutes and she'd be parking. It rang again as soon as she pulled the car to a halt.

'Natasha,' she said, glancing at caller ID. 'Are you okay?'

'Kate's still not answering my calls,' her friend replied. 'I know what you're going to say. It's not quite 9 a.m. and if she'd gone away to stay with a friend for a couple of days, she might not get back until later . . .'

'Okay,' Ava said, trying to squash the resurrection of the dread she'd felt the previous night while winging her way towards the George Street crime scene. 'Does Kate have lectures today?'

'No, it's her library day. I made some enquiries yesterday in her halls and with her faculty, and they gave me a couple of names of friends. No one's heard from her.'

'You still shouldn't start panicking. Have you been to Kate's room this morning and knocked for her?' Ava asked.

'Do you think I'd be phoning you this frantically if I hadn't even bothered doing that?' Natasha responded. 'I'm sorry, Ava. I don't mean to take it out on you. It's just that these girls can be subjected to serious violence, not to mention rape. I know we established that she'd been meeting a client, but the fact that she hasn't been seen since then doesn't feel right to me at all.'

Ava walked up the stairs to her office, motioning for Tripp and Salter, who were huddling in the kitchenette, to join her. 'All right. It's been long enough now, but we have to follow procedure. Technically this is a simple missing person enquiry at the moment, so I'll have to keep my involvement brief. There was another incident in the city last night and I need to focus on that. We'll check her room again, and if there's no sign that she's been back, I'll get a uniformed squad to take over. How does that sound?'

'That sounds great. And really, I'm sorry. I know how busy you are right now. See you there.'

'What's happening, ma'am?' Tripp asked.

'A student has stopped turning up for lectures and isn't answering her phone. Whilst normally I'd say that was standard student behaviour, this girl went on what you could loosely call a date through a sugar daddy website.'

'Prostitution,' Salter said.

'Exactly, only Kate Bailey hasn't been seen or heard from

since. Tripp, my notes to brief the squad are on my laptop on my desk, in a folder with today's date on it. Salter, you come with me. If anyone wants us, we'll be back in the station in one hour. Ask Lively to take the lead organising a meeting with our undercover officer on the Spice woundings. It'll have to be at the safe house later this morning.'

'Very good,' Tripp said.

'Right, Salter, you drive. It's exactly 9 a.m. now. Clock's ticking,' Ava said.

This time the student halls were busy with young people shouting to one another, hurrying down corridors bumping backpacks, playing music and texting.

Ava smiled to Natasha as they arrived on Kate Bailey's corridor. 'Would you go back and do it all again, if you could?'

'In a heartbeat. I had the best sex of my life at university. Oh, to live in a world where adults managed to reach their middle years without developing hang-ups and chips on their shoulders. It was all so exciting. The world was waiting for you, and you were so certain nothing bad could happen.' They stared at Kate's door as Salter came up behind them, chatting with the security guard.

'Professor Natasha Forge, meet Detective Constable Christie Salter,' Ava said, as the guard opened Kate's door. Salter nodded a polite acknowledgment, snapping on gloves as she walked inside.

'Nothing's moved,' Ava said. 'And the bed hasn't been slept in. The corner of the duvet is folded back exactly as I left it yesterday.'

'Does her phone ring when you call it?' Salter asked Natasha.

'It did yesterday morning, but it doesn't now. I assume her battery has run out of charge.'

'That would explain it,' Salter said, looking at Ava.

Sliding the wardrobe door across, Ava searched through the rack of clothes. 'To your knowledge, does Kate have more than one winter coat?'

'I've only ever seen her in a dark green parka,' Natasha said. 'Sometimes if it isn't cold she'll just turn up in a jumper with a scarf.'

'Then her winter coat is here,' Ava commented.

'Which means that perhaps she wasn't planning on staying out very long,' Salter said.

'If she was going away for a few days, she'd have taken it,' Natasha said. 'Ava, I have a bad feeling about this. I know that's what everyone who reports a missing person must say, but . . .'

'Get back into the SugarPa website,' Ava instructed Natasha. 'Make some notes about the profile of the man Kate was supposed to meet. We'll have to contact the company behind the site as soon as we get back to the station and see if they'll volunteer his details. We'll find her, Natasha. I promise.'

Salter wandered into the corridor, knocking on doors as she went. Ava could hear her talking quietly to a few of the other students, asking if any of them had seen Kate or heard from her.

'Not for a couple of days,' a girl's voice came clearly and loudly. 'And I wish she'd come back because she left some beef on in her slow cooker. I unplugged it eventually, but it's stunk the place out and now it's just sitting there rotting. It's disgusting. People shouldn't just go off and forget stuff like that.'

Natasha turned ashen. Ava put an arm around her shoulders as they stared at the laptop screen together.

'Here it is,' Natasha said, clicking open the messages and scrolling over the name of the man with whom Kate had been making plans. 'John White.' She clicked and they waited for a new screen to appear. A small circle wheeled uselessly beneath the cursor for twenty seconds before a new pop-up box declared that the member had left the service. 'That can't be right.' She clicked several more times. 'Ava, we have to do something. Where the hell is she?'

Natasha stood sharply, upending the chair. Ava reached forward and took her by the hands. 'Listen to me. There's still no evidence that anything bad has happened. Maybe she had a difficult experience with this man and took the first train home to Durham. You said yourself she'd had problems before. Perhaps she didn't even bother coming back to pack a bag if she has spare clothes at her parents' house.'

Natasha took a few deep breaths. 'Right,' she said. 'Okay, fine. So we call her parents.'

Salter came back in. 'Nothing. No one I've spoken to has seen her. A couple of the girls here tried to call her about the slow cooker causing a problem in the kitchen but there was no reply. The girl in the next room is on the same course as Kate and confirms that she's missed her classes for the last couple of days.'

'Salter, pack up her laptop. Let's see what the cyber team can get off it. We'll need a good photo of Kate – there was one on the SugarPa website. Natasha, I'll need her mobile number and the details to contact her parents.' Ava walked into the en suite, pulling a plastic bag from her pocket and returning with a hairbrush inside it. 'For a DNA profile, just in case we need it. Better to be fully prepared. If we end up with any suspects it'll ensure we know as quickly as possible if Kate's been in a vehicle or at their house.'

'Her fingerprints?' Salter asked.

'Will be all over the laptop. Have it processed as soon as we're back at the station before sending it to the cyber unit. Let's go. We've done all we can here.' Ava left the room first. Natasha stood fighting tears in the centre of the room. Salter took her gently by the arm and led her out into the corridor and down the stairs to the exit.

There was a rush of students from behind them as they moved towards the doors, each trying to get their hands into a series of pigeonholes, pulling out envelopes and boxes which they ripped open as they made for the outer doors. Ava and Natasha went ahead. Salter turned back, looking along the top row of alphabetically arranged pigeonholes and locating Kate's. She reached up, grabbing the items stacked within. Two standard letter envelopes and a package were there. She flicked through them. The return address in Durham made one likely to be a letter from her parents. That saved one avenue of investigation. Another was a mass-mailing offer for a credit card that Kate could no doubt ill afford. The package was large and soft, lined with bubble wrap. Clothes, Salter thought. Probably the result of some online shopping. If the sales receipt was dated it might help with the precise timeline. Having not yet shed her gloves, she slipped a nail under the seal and ripped along, opening it up to check the contents.

Christie Salter produced a strangled noise from deep in the back of her throat, then closed her eyes momentarily, sighing deeply. As she pulled herself together, the hallway filled with students advancing towards their postal pigeonholes.

'Everyone, stop right where you are,' Salter said. 'No one touches anything. I need you all to exit the area.'

'You can't stop us from—' the first voice whined.

'Yes, I can. I'm an officer with Police Scotland. You need to either go back to your rooms or leave the building. This area will be closed off for a few hours.' She turned to stare out of the double doors to the street. 'Ma'am,' she called, to no response. 'Ma'am!' she shouted, louder.

Ava opened the exterior door to look back into the corridor. 'Problem?' she asked.

'And then some,' Salter replied.

★ ★ ★

Ten minutes later the area was sealed off. University security supervised students entering and exiting the building via a fire door. Callanach turned up with Tripp while Ava comforted Natasha beyond the crime scene perimeter.

'Where is it?' Callanach asked.

Leaving Natasha with DC Salter, Ava accompanied him to the officer who was labelling the exhibits. He opened the envelope gently, lifting its contents with gloved hands to avoid contaminating it with his own DNA.

This doll was a more accomplished finished article than the first. The stitching was smaller and neater, with no discernible tears. The eyes had been coloured in a good match for the brown of Lorna's. Hair had been more artfully and permanently glued to the doll's head. Where the nose would have been, a tiny gold stud pierced the skin, gleaming under the harsh electric light.

'They must have changed the type of glue they used this time,' Callanach noted. 'There are virtually no strands loose in the envelope.'

'The mouth is different on this one,' Ava said. 'The downward stitches are more deliberate, thicker. It looks as if a different thread was used. We'll have to open it up soon and see if there's another note inside.'

'Agreed. Who found the doll?' Callanach asked.

'Salter. I've been trying to keep her out of this investigation. I wasn't sure how she'd handle it, but she seemed calmer than I felt. Natasha is a mess. She knows the missing girl and I think she's feeling responsible for what's happened to her.'

'Leave Salter here with Natasha and the forensics team. You and I can take the doll directly to Jonty. He can confirm if it's a match to Lorna. Once he's taken all the photos and measurements, we can ask him to open it up.'

'Fine,' Ava said, slipping the doll back inside the evidence bag, pausing as it was halfway inside. 'This one's much more lifelike, don't you think? Whoever made it did a good job of capturing the shape of Lorna's eyes.' She ran a gloved thumb down the soft skin from which the doll was made. 'You know, this is one of the most inhumane things I've ever witnessed. Most of the people we deal with, I can get a handle on their psychology. Their rage, jealousy, insecurity, whatever drives them. But this? It's completely alien to me.'

Callanach took the package from her and slid the doll back down inside, resealing it. 'We have to go,' he said. 'The sooner we start getting answers, the better chance we have of finding Kate alive.'

'I've already wasted twenty-four hours,' Ava said. 'If I'd just trusted Natasha's instincts when she came to me yesterday . . . There's so much I could have done in that time.'

'You can't undo what's done, and you couldn't have known what had happened to Kate. If we'd raced off investigating every missing person report we've had in the last day, we'd have exhausted every officer in Police Scotland. There has to be more than an empty bed to believe a criminal event has occurred. You followed procedure. Focus on now. Tripp has Kate's laptop and is taking it to the cyber investigation unit himself. We've got people waiting to attempt to trace the emails, and the procurator fiscal is ready to apply to the court for SugarPa's confidential member information. You did the best you could with the information available to you yesterday.' He took a half step forward and gripped Ava's hand. 'We can still find her, Ava. She's not dead yet.'

'You can't know that for sure,' Ava said quietly.

'I know that Kate being alive is the most likely scenario. A pattern is emerging and we have no reason to believe he'll deviate from it. Thinking about the things you could have done will only slow you down. Don't give him an advantage he doesn't deserve,' he said, reaching out gently and running the tips of his fingers down the back of her thumb, wishing he could rub the chill from her hands. They always seemed to be in the middle of a crowd these days. Six months ago there had been plenty of evenings when it was just the two of them. He wondered what had changed. Selina, he remembered guiltily. And before that Ava had been seeing Joe for a while. Their evenings laughing in the back row of an empty late-night cinema screening had ground to a halt in the midst of other relationships. And Selina was trying so hard to make things work. Almost too hard. Being with Ava, though, had always been effortless.

'Thank you, Luc,' she whispered. 'At some point you should probably remind me that I'm supposed to be the one with the answers.' She smiled at him, visibly pulling herself together. 'Right, let's go. Jonty will be waiting.'

As they drove through the city's ancient streets towards Cowgate and the City Mortuary, Kate awoke on a table in the dark. It would be another four days until she returned to the city.

Chapter Twenty-Four

'"Then when lust has conceived, it gives birth to sin; and when sin is accomplished, it brings forth death",' Ava read from the tiny scroll hidden within the stuffing of the doll.

'It's a reference to baby Tansy, literally a birth arising from the killer's perception of Lorna's sinful life,' Callanach said. 'Apparently it's from James, chapter one, verse fifteen. Whoever is doing this believes they have some divine right of judgment over these young women.'

'It's not the first time,' Jonty said. 'The Yorkshire Ripper claimed he'd heard the voice of God telling him to murder his victims. Ed Gein was brought up in a strict religious household. He's another killer who used the skin of his victims, although I don't believe there were any dolls involved.'

'Ed Gein?' Ava asked. 'Did the police ever establish his motivation?'

'He had something of a mother obsession. It's likely he was brought up being told all women were wicked and sinful. He dug some of the bodies up for their skin, others he killed. When police finally raided his home they found a vast array of items made from human skin. Seat covers, a belt of women's nipples, a wastebasket, a corset. It was never established exactly how many women he'd murdered, but the bodies taken from the graveyard were largely females who bore some resemblance to his mother,' Jonty responded.

'So it was personal to him, deeply meaningful,' Callanach said.

'Undoubtedly. Gein was devastated by his mother's death. There was some suspicion he'd killed his brother, perhaps to have his mother to himself. In the end, Gein was declared legally insane and spent the remainder of his life in institutions, where he eventually died.'

'So the doll might be a representation. It could be that the killer lost a baby they cared about, perhaps a brother or sister, even. Or perhaps it represents their own abusive childhood, the loss of that early innocence,' Ava said. 'The skin thing is what throws me though. What's behind it?'

'The theory is that it's the feel of it. With Ed Gein, I believe, when his mother died he wanted to carry on feeling close to her, literally still feeling her skin. Most people grow up holding their mother's hand, sitting on her lap, being cuddled. We may never think about it consciously, but the feel of our mother's skin is the first thing we learn from birth. As investigators we spend a lot of time considering the way things look. I'm acutely aware of how different organs smell when I'm performing a post-mortem. Sound is often a particular focus in witness state-ments – a scream, or a thump, or a vehicle's engine. We often ignore touch and yet it defines our relationships. Deprive a human of it and they'll find a means to fill the gap. Self-hugging is often seen with psychiatric patients. For whoever is creating the skin dolls, the texture, the feel of them, is likely to be a tremendous motivation.'

Ava and Callanach stared at him. 'Is that what you spend your spare time doing, Jonty? Reading about bizarre horrors from criminal history?' Callanach asked. 'Not that I don't appreciate it, but . . .'

'All part and parcel of the job, sadly. It's no different than recognising a pattern in types of assaults. Understanding what motivates a killer often fills in missing information that then helps me identify the process that's led to a death. Please don't get worried about me. My downtime reading tends towards the romantic rather than crime.' He smiled. 'Now, on to this latest monstrosity.' He carefully separated the skin doll into its front and rear sections and overlaid the front part onto Lorna's abdomen, a sterile sheet between them. 'There's no doubt the skin's from Lorna,' he said. 'Look, there's a tiny nick to the right of the head where it looks as if the original incision was begun. We'll send a sample of the skin for DNA testing to confirm, but I'm as sure as I can be.'

'How long until we get news on the DNA from the pubic hair?' Ava asked.

'We successfully obtained a DNA profile from the hair, but no match has been found on the police database,' Jonty said. 'We're double-checking, but it doesn't look hopeful at all.'

'A rapist and killer who's never been arrested before?' Ava said. 'You don't just switch from model citizen to psychopath like that.'

'No, but he might never have been caught before. That's the problem. Send the DNA profile over to Interpol as well, Jonty,' Callanach said. 'It may be that the offender isn't from the UK, or hasn't been convicted of a crime here yet.'

'I'll get it sorted as soon as we're done here,' Jonty said.

'Do you have the first doll here? I'd like to compare the two,' Ava asked.

Jonty went to a refrigerated cabinet and took out a sealed tray, placing the two dolls next to one another for inspection, but careful to ensure they didn't quite touch, to avoid cross-contamination of the evidence.

'It's the mouth that's really changed. On the Zoey doll it was haphazard. Just a few stitches where the mouth should be. With Lorna's doll, the killer has gone to much more effort. The lips are drawn on with considerable care, then the stitches run over the top. Each stitch is individual – you can see each has its own knot. The dolls are silent.'

'Because the girls have been silenced?' Callanach said.

'Or because the killer didn't like what they were saying. To stop them screaming, or begging for their lives. I don't know. There are so many possibilities,' Ava said, glancing at her watch. 'Damn, I need to be elsewhere. Jonty, what can you tell me about the bus death? We still don't have a full name for the victim, I'm afraid.'

'I managed to isolate the knife wound from the bus impact damage. I won't show you unless there's a need. You've more than enough to deal with today. There's a wound in the eye directly above the upper horizontal slash, which would have been enough to wake a drug user from even the deepest fugue. There's no drug that could have blocked out that level of pain save for medical anaesthesia. I suspect that the person wielding the blade was clumsy and caught the eye. It's also possible that the effects of the drugs were wearing off and the woman felt the damage to her face, jolting as she panicked, and that's when the eye injury was incurred.'

'Or the attacker was bored with inflicting the same injury and decided to increase the damage to see what would happen,' Ava said.

'Maybe. The additional wound ran upwards from the lower eyelid to the eyebrow, cutting the surface of the eye. Sorry, I know that's a dreadful thought. Even I had trouble comprehending the amount of pain it would have caused. It would explain how a victim might end up wheeling around out of control into the path of an oncoming bus. Her vision would have been completely compromised on that side immediately, and she'd have been aware of nothing but the undoubted agony of it,' Jonty said.

'So it's a murder,' Callanach said. 'If the wounding to the face caused her death, recklessly, that's enough for intent.'

'It's enough for a trial. At the very least we'll get a verdict of culpable homicide,' Ava said. 'Superintendent Overbeck and I are overdue another conversation about it. Not right now, though. Dr Spurr, thank you. Will you call my mobile if you find anything else? Luc and I are due on a train to Durham in a couple of hours. DC Tripp is holding the fort in the incident room if you need assistance from there.'

'You've a lot on your shoulders,' Jonty said as he returned Lorna's body to its chilled enclosure. 'Three open murder cases now, and another young woman missing. Make sure you get some rest. My patients may be dead, but I can still recognise the symptoms of exhaustion in the living.'

Chapter Twenty-Five

The safe house amounted to a dingy two-bed apartment above a barber's shop in Bread Street. Many of the surrounding storefronts declared that units were to rent, the tourists not straying that far from the city centre. Traffic largely went through rather than stopping there, keeping the doorway relatively free from prying eyes. It served a variety of purposes for Police Scotland, and was a regular haunt for the undercover officers who were concerned that they might have been compromised, avoiding returning to a home address. Ava and Callanach did what they could to scruffy their clothes and make their visit appear in keeping with the property, grabbing a carrier bag of food shopping from a nearby supermarket before venturing inside.

Lively opened the door, wearing a massive, tatty jumper and jeans that should have seen a bin years earlier. Ava couldn't meet his eyes. She hadn't been in the same room with him since she'd caught him and the superintendent in flagrante delicto. She might never be able to touch the super's desk again, she thought, as Callanach and Lively exchanged greetings.

'Is the undercover officer here?' Ava asked.

'He's taking a shower,' Lively said. 'Needed one, too. He stank the place out when he arrived. I know undercover officers are specially trained, but I think this might have been taking things a step far.'

'At least he's got an excuse,' Ava replied. 'More than you can say about your jumper.'

'Ach, now you're being personal, ma'am. There's no cause for that,' Lively said.

'I think we'll save that argument for a better time. Get him out of the shower, would you? I need to debrief then go. We're running late as it is.'

'Sorry, I thought you'd prefer to be able to get close to me without gagging,' said a deep voice from the doorway between the sitting room and one of the bedrooms. A man walked out with what appeared to be a tea towel wrapped around his waist, hand outstretched. He was at least six foot four, the width of his shoulders best suited to a rugby scrum, more mountain than man. His dirty blonde hair hung in multiple rough plaits that straggled below his shoulders. Ava did her best to keep her eyes on his face as she shook his hand.

'DS Pax Graham,' he said. 'You must be DCI Turner. I don't get to meet many people outside my unit. Comes with the territory when you're undercover. I've heard a lot about you though.'

'For fuck's sake, man, could you not have got dressed before coming out?' Lively blurted.

It had been Callanach's policy to agree with Lively as rarely as possible since the detective sergeant had made his early days with Police Scotland a constant piss-taking festival, but right then he agreed with him wholeheartedly. Ava, on the other hand, didn't seem the least bit fazed.

'I'm going to have to put the same clothes on again. If you don't mind, that's not really the sort of lasting impression I want to make. I can hardly enter the building looking like I've been

211

living rough for a month and leave ready for a party, can I?' Graham said.

'Not a problem, although frankly I've had enough of seeing police officers naked for a while,' Ava retorted. Lively didn't so much as blink. 'Perhaps we should sit down before you lose the tea towel, DS Graham.'

'Someone's been watching a bit too much *Outlander*,' Lively muttered as they organised themselves.

Ava took a seat on an old wooden chair, which rocked beneath her. Callanach and Lively remained standing as Graham took the couch, sprawling his legs out before him, entirely comfortable with his lack of clothing, it seemed.

'Take me through last night,' Ava said.

'The witnesses arrived well fed, and happier for it, although they were tired by the time the hostel was finally sorted. They wanted their beds, to be honest, but the offer to share a bottle of whisky persuaded them to stay a while. Your victim's name is Melanie but they couldn't give me a surname. A couple of glasses in and they were more than willing to talk. They might have been stony-faced to you, but the Spice assaults are getting a lot of publicity on the streets. The group of them were sheltering in an archway on George Street when it happened, keeping well back from the road so they weren't spotted and moved on. Melanie had been with them earlier in the evening, then she disappeared for a while to score whatever drugs she could afford.'

'Did they think it was Spice?' Ava asked.

'Quite possibly, but none of the witnesses were with her when she bought it or took it,' he said. 'From what I could piece together, Mel was back on George Street and walking in a daze towards them when she was attacked.'

'By how many people?' Lively asked.

'Different version from each witness, varying between two,

three and four, although none of them is particularly reliable and I doubt they were sober. They were all clear that the attackers were hooded, though. They approached Mel directly. No one heard them say anything, then there was a scream and Mel ended up flailing into the road.'

'Did no one see the knife?' Ava asked.

'It was too dark, even with the lights from the George Street premises. Street lighting causes the sort of shadows that makes it hard to see clearly, and these folk haven't been to an optician for a few years. One of them described what looked like a tussle surrounding Mel. As she went into the road, the attackers ran west then disappeared down a side street. By that time, all hell had broken loose with the bus and no one paid them any more attention. One witness heard something after the bus hit, though. Apparently one of the people running away shouted, "You fucking cretin."'

'At who?' Ava asked.

'I'd guess at their fellow attackers. No one mentioned anyone else being out on the street,' Graham said.

'Cretin,' Ava shouted. 'Not exactly street language.'

'That it's not,' DS Graham said. 'The regular homeless community is scared now – even the ones who don't take drugs. It's starting to feel like a campaign.'

'Maybe they should try confiding in the police rather than us having to go to these lengths to get information out of them,' Lively said.

'Maybe you should try living on no money and sleeping where drunks piss on them of a Friday night after work, then judge,' Graham said, grinning at Lively.

Ava didn't bother to intervene. Lively could stick up for himself, and it was about time he met someone of his own rank who was willing to answer him back.

'Is that it?' Ava asked.

'They all want an extra night at the shelter paid for as they got there so late this morning,' Graham said.

'That's fine. Lively, you organise that. The hostel should already have my credit card details,' Ava said.

Graham nodded at her. 'They said you treated them kindly. I'm grateful to you for it. It's not often I hear positive feedback from people in their situation.'

Ava stood up and Graham followed suit. 'Are you willing to go back out there?' Ava asked. 'I gather from the incident room you're due a night off, but at the moment . . .'

'I wouldn't think twice about it, ma'am,' Graham said. 'Don't worry about me. I don't tire easily.'

'Good. DI Callanach and I are on our way to Durham. We have a young woman missing at the moment, believed to be in imminent danger. DS Lively will give you my mobile number. If you hear or find anything else of relevance, phone me immediately, whatever the hour. DS Lively is in charge of this investigation in my absence.'

'Is there no other detective inspector available in your absence?' Graham asked.

'MIT is currently shortlisting to appoint a new one,' Ava said. 'I appreciate your help on this.'

'And I'd appreciate it if you'd get some clothes on while I see the DCI out,' Lively said.

'Sure.' Graham smiled. 'I was just enjoying the feeling of being clean and wrapped in fewer than a dozen layers for ten minutes. Good to finally meet you, ma'am, having heard so much about you.'

Lively glared as DS Graham went back into the bedroom. 'Honest to God, is Police Scotland taking recruits from a casting agency these days? First you' – he nodded in Callanach's direction – 'and now Highlander there, although I suspect those abs are spray-painted on.'

'I'm too busy for the jokes today, Sergeant, and I may never be in the mood for them again from you. Get back to the station and coordinate the squad so that we have a five-man team on Melanie's murder. Use the photo we found on the body to cross-reference the house number with pylons in close proximity to residences, and locate her family. Somebody somewhere is waiting for the poor woman to get home. And update Overbeck on the case status. She won't be pleased.'

'I could phone her from the car en route to Waverley station,' Callanach suggested.

'No, that's okay. Lively can do it. Overbeck seems to like him.' Ava glared. 'Can't imagine why.'

Chapter Twenty-Six

The train journey from Edinburgh to Durham took only an hour and forty-five minutes, but to Ava it felt like forever. Making the call in person was an absolute necessity in the circumstances, and Luc had insisted on accompanying her. Even so, she couldn't stop checking her watch.

They sat in the first-class carriage for the additional quiet and space, taking and sending texts and emails every few minutes. Eventually Ava sighed and set her phone down.

'You okay?' Callanach asked.

'Not really,' Ava said. 'Jonty's right. I'm exhausted. It's not helping my ability to be insightful about either case at the moment.'

'What's going on with DS Lively? You were both acting strangely. Who has he pissed off this time?'

'No one, sadly,' Ava said. 'Complaints about him, I can handle. This is . . . never mind. It'll burn out. I have a bigger issue to deal with – the hooded attackers who ran away from Melanie and shouted the word cretin. I appreciate that language isn't exclusive between social classes, but it's one of those words I can just imagine the boys from my school days using. It's

216

demeaning and yet it makes you – or you think it makes you – sound clever. If this was our usual bunch of drunks or gang members, they'd have used any number of colourful obscenities – but cretin?'

'You have a theory?' Callanach asked.

'Lively and I traced a key that was found at the site of the second attack. A witness thought they heard something metallic fall as the men ran away. It's from a locker at possibly the most prestigious private school in Edinburgh. It could have been a coincidence. The witness could have been mistaken, and yet when we went and spoke to the boy whose locker it was, he seemed prepared for us. Smug, even. Perhaps I was imagining it.'

'But now you have another witness who heard a form of speech that fits the same suspect,' Callanach said.

'Which is no more evidence than saying a witness talking extensively about wine and cheese must be French,' Ava said. 'Overbeck has already warned me off.'

'When did that ever stop you?' Callanach asked.

'Never, only this time I'm reaching and she knows it. I'm not even close to having reasonable cause to interview, ask for a search warrant to look for a weapon or seize clothing to check for blood spatters. With Kate missing on top of that, it feels like I have to prioritise.'

Callanach stared out of the window for a few minutes before speaking again. 'I know I'm going to regret asking this, but you said something to Lively about having seen enough police officers naked . . . I forget the exact words. Did I miss something?'

'Annual Police Scotland rugby tournament,' Ava replied smoothly. 'All the players end up off their faces and thinking it's clever to strip off. They usually end up in their own cells overnight while they come to their senses.'

'Is that right?' Callanach asked, staring at her as she busied herself checking emails on her mobile.

By the time they reached Mr and Mrs Bailey's house, the afternoon was leaking light. A local police officer was waiting for them in the road, briefed to offer ongoing support after they left. Ava knocked on the door. It took several minutes for a woman to open up. Mrs Bailey was prematurely grey, with bags under her eyes and clothes that needed changing. They offered their IDs, introducing themselves.

'Can we come in, please, Mrs Bailey? It's about Kate.'

Mrs Bailey's face transformed. That look. The instant knowledge and denial that was world-changing, so often tempered with good manners and patience.

'We don't have a lounge. We had to convert it into a downstairs bedroom for my husband. He has chronic rheumatoid arthritis that has caused lung disease.' She kept her voice low. 'I'd prefer it if we spoke away from him.'

'Of course,' Ava said. 'Would your kitchen be a good place?'

Mrs Bailey walked into the hallway and pulled a door shut before motioning them into the small kitchen. 'Before you start, I need to know. Is Kate . . .'

'She's missing and hasn't been seen for two days,' Ava said. 'There's no reason to believe she is dead at the present time, but we think possibly your daughter has been kidnapped.'

Mrs Bailey sank into a chair, banging her elbows heavily onto the kitchen table. Ava looked around as she gave Kate's mother time to recover from the shock. The kitchen was small but clean. A dish with the remnants of something savoury sat beside the sink, with a spoon in it. Kate's father had to be very weak indeed if he was being fed. No wonder Kate hadn't felt able to ask for financial assistance from them.

'What makes you think she's been kidnapped?' Mrs Bailey

asked quietly. 'Surely she might just be with friends? Sometimes she does long shifts with her job and then I don't hear from her for a few days. Has there been a ransom note?'

Callanach sat down at the kitchen table and gently took Mrs Bailey's hand in his own. 'When did Kate last contact you?' he asked.

'Three days ago. Just a quick call to say she was all right. She got an A on her last assignment and wanted me to tell her dad. He's so proud of her.'

The tears began in earnest. Ava could almost have timed it. There was often a three or four minute delay from when you arrived at a front door to deliver bad news to when the horror of it broke through the trauma. She handed over the tissues she'd had ready in her pocket.

'Would you mind putting the kettle on and making Mrs Bailey a cup of tea?' Ava asked the uniformed officer.

'We're doing all we can to find Kate,' Ava said. 'But I'm afraid we need to explain the full reason for our visit. The person we think is holding her has likely been responsible for the kidnapping of two other young women. I'm sorry to have to break this to you, but it's important you don't hear it from the media first.'

'What other girls? Did you find them? Did you get them back?' Mrs Bailey sobbed.

'I'm afraid not,' Ava replied. 'We didn't locate them in time. The other girls are the two whose bodies were found in Edinburgh over the last fortnight.' Ava looked to Callanach. He was ready to catch Mrs Bailey if she fainted. Ava didn't continue offering information immediately. She'd just delivered what amounted to a death sentence on this woman's daughter. Nothing Mrs Bailey was told for the next few minutes would sink in or be of value. Sometimes you had to remain silent and know these were the moments you would despise your career choice, but that they were also the reason you chose the job in the first place. Giving the bad news. Trying to stop what was happening before you had to deliver the same bad news to any other parents.

Mrs Bailey bolted for the sink, vomiting, shrieking, then vomiting again. Ava held the woman's shoulders gently as she spat, rinsed her mouth in the tap and then doubled over, howling.

'My baby girl,' she cried. 'He's got my baby. Please stop him. My little Katie.'

Ava didn't speak. There were no words for the terror a parent felt when a child was taken. Soothing noises and promises were a pathetic drop in the ocean of fear. Better just to lend a body to hold on to during those first horrendous moments.

Callanach disappeared into the corridor. He was checking on Mr Bailey, Ava thought, making sure he hadn't been disturbed. He slipped back into the kitchen, mouthing that all was okay. Not for long, Ava thought. Sooner or later Mr Bailey would have to be told just how dire the situation was.

'Why did he choose Kate?' Mrs Bailey asked when she could speak again.

Ava gritted her teeth. This would be the final blow, and it was one she wasn't sure Kate's mother could take at the moment.

Callanach interrupted. 'You said Kate worked long shifts with her job? What was it she did, Mrs Bailey?'

'She worked in a restaurant a few evenings a week, waitressing. The tips were good, she said, so she could afford to help us out. I didn't want to take it, but she insisted. Was it someone from there? A customer? Or another member of staff? Do you know how to find him?'

'We're working on the theory that Kate's abductor first came into contact with her through her work,' Callanach said. 'And we're checking everybody out. We don't know where he is at present but we hope some information on Kate's laptop will help us find him.' Ava opened her mouth to speak but Callanach shook his head. 'That's as much as we're certain about for now. We're going to keep you updated though, all the time. Your local police force will make sure they talk you through every step and relay information as we get it. You can also use them to contact us with questions.'

'How do you know it's the same man who hurt those other girls? You can't know for sure . . .'

'He left an item, something personal to the last victim, in Kate's pigeonhole,' Ava said. 'It's what he did the first time, too.'

'What did he do to those other girls?' Mrs Bailey asked. 'I want to know. Did he rape them? Torture them? How did they die?'

Ava looked her directly in the eyes and spoke quietly but deliberately. 'One girl was raped, the other was not. They were each held for a week before he inflicted wounds to their abdomen and their back. The blood loss caused their deaths. There is some media coverage which is speculative, not entirely accurate and which won't help you. I know you'll want to look, it's only natural. For your own sake, I'm going to urge you not to. Let us answer your questions instead. Local police will stay here on a shift pattern twenty-four hours a day if that's what you want, until we can resolve the situation.'

'Or until you find her body,' Mrs Bailey snarled.

Ava didn't answer. She wouldn't lie, however tempting it was.

'Bloody Edinburgh!' Mrs Bailey shouted. 'I wanted her to stay here, go to Durham University. But her father studied in Edinburgh and all she ever wanted was to be like him. They love each other so much. When he became ill, it broke her heart. This is going to kill him.' She broke down again, her momentary flash of anger dissolved in a new wave of grief. 'I'm going to lose them both. I'm going to lose them both.'

The uniformed officer took over, taking Mrs Bailey by the shoulders and returning her to the kitchen chair, where she sat rocking back and forth.

'We have a specially trained counsellor coming over,' the officer said, 'and my sergeant's joining me soon. I know you have to leave.'

Ava knelt next to Mrs Bailey's chair. 'We won't rest until we've done all we can to find her. Don't lose hope yet. Are you caring for your husband all by yourself?'

Mrs Bailey nodded. 'We get by,' she said. 'If we want extra nursing care, we have to pay for it. There's just no money left over at the end of the month. When my husband was diagnosed, he had to stop working. His benefits just about cover the mortgage.' She stopped there. It wasn't necessary to explain that there was little money left for anything else. 'Kate sends what she can, of course.' She looked up suddenly. 'She's such a very good girl.'

They left quietly, wondering how the news would be broken to Mr Bailey, wishing he could be left oblivious, but he had a right to be informed. They should have a doctor there when they did it, Ava thought, texting that instruction back to the uniformed officer they'd left with Mrs Bailey as the taxi transported them to the train station. Twenty minutes later they were headed back towards Edinburgh, soothed by the rocking of the train.

'Lively says they've identified the bus crash victim,' Callanach said, reading from his phone. 'Melanie Long, aged thirty-three. Officers are with her partner now. They've one child, a boy aged five, but he lives with his grandparents.'

'MIT delivering one bereavement notice and one kidnap notice to different parties on the same day. That has to be a record,' Ava said bitterly, staring out of the window.

'Lively's also notified Overbeck that the facial assaults have been upgraded to a murder enquiry. She's pulling some more bodies in to bolster MIT while we handle the two cases. Sounds like the detective sergeant's doing a good job,' he commented.

'I bet he is,' Ava said. 'I'm sorry. Ignore me. It's so tiring, watching other people's pain, unable to help.'

'That and the fact that you haven't slept for days. You should close your eyes a while.'

'I can't. It's not comfortable enough, and I should call Natasha. She'll be in such a state by now.'

'Natasha can wait. You need to rest if you're going to focus on either case. Jonty told you the same. You're going to burn out, Ava. It was the right thing for us to go and see the Baileys in person, but you know neither of us will see our homes for a few days after this. Put your head on my shoulder if you like. I'll keep an eye on messages between here and the city, and I promise to wake you if there's anything you should see.'

'I'm not sure I should be falling asleep on my detective inspector's shoulder.' She smiled. 'Seems to me that might be a breach of protocol.'

'Then pretend I'm nothing other than a friend for the next hour. No rules against that,' he said.

'I appreciate the offer but I'm not sure I'll be able to sleep anyway,' she murmured, closing her eyes and keeping her head upright for another five minutes, before sinking slowly down to rest it on Callanach's shoulder.

He brushed a long brown curl away from her face, thinking how young Ava looked when she was sleeping. He only ever saw her alert, often tense. Whilst she kept her team upbeat, even when she wasn't feeling it herself, he rarely saw her with her defences down. It was such an intimate thing, having someone sleep against you. He could feel the rhythm of her breathing, the warmth from her skin. He shifted slightly to leave her head at a better angle and she smiled briefly, finding some happier place in her dreams. When Selina slept at his house, it was as if she was still awake, constantly moving and shifting, the energy she had unable to find peace. Ava was more like a child. Wilful and brilliant whilst awake, trusting and serene in slumber. It was unfair to compare them, he thought, guilt rendering him uncomfortable. Selina wanted nothing more than to make him happy in every way, and she was determined to succeed. Ava had never tried to be anything other than herself, whether that made Luc happy or not. Perhaps when you were just friends with a member of the opposite sex, it was easier to be yourself. No pretence, no complications. He forced his gaze off Ava's face and back to his mobile, reading incoming emails and making sure nothing was missed. Keeping his mind off his personal life.

Ava awoke an hour later, as they were drawing into Waverley station. A minute later, her phone began to ring.

'Ma'am,' Tripp said. 'We have CCTV footage of Kate meeting a man in a shopping centre. Professor Forge has confirmed that it's her.'

Chapter Twenty-Seven

'SugarPa won't give us any information at all,' Tripp said, striding along the corridor to keep up with Ava. 'We've sent an email request and followed it up with phone calls.'

'Did they say why they wouldn't cooperate?' Ava asked.

'They say we have no proof that the man she met through their website is holding her or that he is the same person who left the item in her pigeonhole. Technically they're right.'

'Get a court order,' Ava snapped. 'I want a lawyer in my office in the next hour preparing the paperwork. If they won't comply, I'll get a judge to force them.'

'Actually, it's more complicated than that,' Tripp said.

Ava stood still. 'Tell me.'

'The company who owns and runs the SugarPa website is based in Spain. In order to save costs, their servers have been outsourced to another company, situated in Russia. That means we have to deal with Scottish law, European Union law and potentially Russian law as well. Even if we could get through to the Spanish company, forcing the Russians to provide information might prove . . .'

'Impossible,' Ava said. 'It'll prove impossible, and it's going to

take too long to get results. Kate has four days left, in all likelihood, before she's beyond saving. What did we get off her
laptop?'

'Just the normal front-end stuff. We got into all of Kate's
previous conversations, which is how we came to check out the
shopping mall. They were incredibly good about reviewing
their CCTV, which is why we got a hit so quickly. The footage
is in colour and the man Kate met was at the corner they'd
agreed, carrying a red umbrella as per his suggestion.'

'Great,' Ava said. 'Does his image match the one he used for
his profile photo on SugarPa?'

'The profile photo was taken down when he cancelled his
membership. It's one of the pieces of information we're
trying to get from the website, but Natasha mentioned that the
photo wasn't helpful in any event,' Tripp said. 'The man on
the CCTV footage was wearing a hat, an old-fashioned one,
like a trilby, pulled down low over his eyes. We can see that
he has dark hair, fairly standard length from the back view. He
was also wearing thick-rimmed glasses and had a scarf around
his neck that covered the lower section of his chin. He's tall,
but he was wearing a long overcoat so we can't make out
much more of his figure. The tech team are trying to enhance
the images now.'

'Get the footage ready for viewing in the incident room
straight away, and gather whoever is still in the building. We
need to expand our search based on what we have. I'll be there
in five minutes. I just need to speak with DI Callanach first.'

Ava ran to Callanach's office, knocking as she walked in.

'I need a favour,' she said. 'Your friend, the hacker who helped
with a previous investigation.'

'Ben Paulson,' Callanach said.

'That's right. Ben. Is he still in Edinburgh?' Ava asked.

'I'm pretty sure he is, although we haven't talked for a while.

He's working for himself now but I don't think he's gone back to the USA,' Callanach said.

'Good. I want him to hack into the SugarPa website for me. I need all the information available on John White, the man Kate Bailey met at the shopping centre. The name will prove to be a pseudonym, but there should be an email address, IP address, credit card details. SugarPa won't play ball and it'll take more time than we have to get through the legal red tape.'

'You know, Ben was a suspect in a serious case led by your former fiancé. He has very little love for the police, and now we're asking him to break the law on our behalf. He might be wary,' Callanach said.

'I'll go with you and beg him if I have to, and I'll pay whatever it takes. I'll even give him a signed confession that I blackmailed him to force him to break the law for me. It's the only conceivable way I can get this information, Luc. Ben Paulson helped you before and it saved a woman's life. I can't think of anyone better qualified to help us now.'

'All right,' Callanach said. 'I'll make the call, but he'll want to see me alone and in person. Ben doesn't discuss work over the phone.'

'That's fine. We're about to start a briefing on the CCTV footage. You handle this. Check in with me once you've spoken to him. I'll be in my office.'

The team was already gathered in the incident room. Tripp turned the lights off as a huge screen, split into four quarters, showed different angles in a covered shopping mall. The strip lighting was unhelpful, but the cameras weren't bad. The man first walked into shot from an exterior door, moving directly to the corner of a toy store, where he waited, keeping his head down.

'He should be looking around for her,' Tripp said. 'Suggests he was aware of the cameras. Why risk meeting in a place where he knew they'd be filmed?'

'It's a calculated risk,' Salter said. 'It's probable that many of the students making money through SugarPa don't tell anyone what they're up to. He had no way of knowing she'd confided in a counselling service. Likewise, that she'd left her password plugged into the website on her laptop. He deletes his profile, disappears, chances are no one would ever trace the time or place they were due to meet.'

'It's still a risk though. There are plenty of places he could have suggested they meet up that have no CCTV coverage at all.'

'I think he chose it to reassure Kate, to stop her from getting spooked,' Ava said. 'It's clever. Let's meet in a busy, public place, guaranteed to have CCTV cameras. Better still, let's meet outside a toyshop. Brilliant subliminal messaging. It says, I'm a child-friendly person. I know where the toyshop is. I am non-threatening and unafraid to be seen.'

Ava un-paused the footage until Kate came into view from the opposite direction, walking straight up to the male and pointing at the red umbrella. They exchanged a few words then turned back in the direction of the exterior door through which the man had come, exiting together.

'Perfect. He minimised the view we got of him but seemed harmless enough for Kate to leave the safe area straight away. Tripp, get me the best lip reader you can find. I want to know what he said to her, if he has any speech impediments, an accent if they can tell, mannerisms, the works.'

'Got it,' Tripp said.

'Salter, get the maths done from the scale of the outside markings on the shop window. We know the angle of the camera, so we should be able to figure out his height to a precise measurement. How are interviews going with the people working in the other stores nearby?'

'A couple of people confirm noticing him but not paying any real attention,' a uniformed officer said. 'It's been cold and wet, so people in hats and scarves going into the shopping centre from the outside are two a penny. No one has been able to give us any additional facial details and no one heard him speak. We are tracing another potential witness who seemed to take an interest in the male, although she moved on quickly when approached by a shop assistant.'

'I don't understand. What woman?' Ava asked.

'There's a women's clothes shop on the opposite side to the toy store, two units down, called Night and Day.' All heads turned to the screen again to search for the shop. 'Its usual customers are aged between eighteen and late twenties, lots of students. The woman in question was standing between a couple of racks of clothes for several minutes, not moving or browsing, staring out of the front window from behind the mannequins. The shop assistant originally thought she might be a shoplifter as she was behaving oddly, then became concerned that something might be wrong. When she approached her, the woman made an excuse and left the shop. The assistant remembers the male at the corner of the toyshop, because she automatically looked to see what the woman had been staring at and noticed a man holding a red umbrella. As soon as the woman left, she was asked to help another customer and thought no more about it until we started interviewing staff in the vicinity,' the officer said.

'Jealous partner, maybe, who'd caught on to the fact that her husband or boyfriend was using SugarPa?' Tripp asked.

'Quite possibly, especially if she was staying out of sight of the male, which means that if we find the woman, we can identify the man,' Ava said. 'Contact the security staff at the mall. They need to review their CCTV again for all clips of that woman, particularly which exterior entrance or exit she used, then see if we have further cameras that can follow her to a vehicle or bus stop in the city. Any joy with exterior cameras for the male?'

'None,' Tripp said. 'He chose a route where he wouldn't be seen by cameras, so presumably he used side streets, potentially going into premises such as pubs that have a front and rear entrance to make it hard to follow.'

'So let's stick with the information we have.' Ava rewound the footage by a few seconds and played it again. 'We've got a good, recent image of Kate where she was last known to have been. We can release that image with this male in shot. Even if we can't identify the woman in the clothes store, if that's his wife she might just respond to publicity. Kate is wearing jeans, black boots, a green jumper and a scarf. She's carrying a small black handbag. We should also have officers looking for those items on the streets to see if any of them have been dumped in alleyways or public bins.' She paused the footage. 'Look,' she said, pointing at the male in the last visible frame. 'He's hidden the umbrella underneath his coat before leaving the shopping centre. He had no intention of using it outside, even though it was still raining. You can see through the external doors. That means he didn't want to be noticed carrying it on the streets.'

'Far too memorable,' Lively said. 'Which means there's no doubt he was up to no good.'

'So we're proceeding on the assumption that the man Kate Bailey met still has her, and that he killed both Zoey and Lorna. The pubic hair gave us DNA, so we can exclude other suspects easily and quickly, but he's not on the police national database, which means his fingerprints will prove useless too. Anyone got anything else?' Ava asked.

'Nothing helpful,' Salter said. 'We interviewed the security staff at the halls where Kate lives. The package was left outside overnight, found by a security guard and put in her pigeonhole in the morning. The guard assumed Kate had dropped it by mistake. Given it had Kate's full name, room number and hall on it, it was easy to return it to her.'

'Was that information available on Kate's SugarPa page, or given in her conversations with the man she met?' Ava asked. There was a rustling as notes were checked, and the consensus in the room was negative. 'No. So either he was stalking her for some time, which would have been difficult – he'd have been noticed in the halls and I think someone would have come forward to tell us by now – or he got the information directly from the source.'

'You think he managed to get those details out of Kate once he'd taken her, and left the doll there after that?' Lively asked.

'I do,' Ava said. 'It's the simplest solution. He's having to achieve a lot in a short space of time, which means he's organised rather than chaotic, meticulous rather than compulsive.'

'So he has a reasonably high IQ, given that he's avoiding obvious methods of tracking him. We're looking for a man capable of multitasking with a high level of self-control,' Tripp said.

'Although it slipped with Lorna. He raped her, but he didn't rape Zoey. That means something changed for him between taking the two women,' Ava said. 'One last thing before you all leave. The fact that Kate was working for SugarPa is highly confidential. You can release general pictures and descriptions to the press and public, but not that. Understood?'

'Can we ask why, ma'am?' another uniformed officer asked. 'Should we not make it public to warn other young women arranging dates through the website that they're putting themselves in danger?'

'That's a fair point,' Ava said, 'and I'll handle it. But Kate's parents don't know how she was making money and I don't want them to find out. Kate was using SugarPa to support her parents because of her father's illness. They're going through enough. I'm not sure they'd survive this additional piece of information.'

They disbanded, with men and women rushing to various tasks, as Ava took out her mobile to text Callanach.

'If he'll help, I need him to do one more thing. Copy
the data then kill the site. Leave no one else at risk.
Delete this text.'

She walked into her office to find DS Pax Graham waiting for her in jeans and a t-shirt, looking relaxed in her armchair.

'Detective Sergeant, I hadn't expected to see you again so soon,' Ava said. 'Is there new information?'

'Forgive me for coming into your office without invitation, ma'am, but I try to stay out of the corridors and common areas in case any suspects are brought through or the press are allowed in for a briefing. Being undercover means my life is very restricted.'

'I understand,' Ava said. 'It's a sacrifice. I appreciate it.'

'You've been to see your missing girl's parents, I gather.' Ava nodded. 'I don't envy you that. I think I'd sooner have delivered news of an actual death than tell parents that their daughter is still alive in the hands of a psychopath. Do you have any solid leads?'

'We're getting there, though not as fast as I'd like, sadly. Tell me you're here to deliver better news.'

'I have a theory,' he replied. 'Something the witnesses said, although it didn't register with me at the time, or perhaps I processed it wrongly. As Melanie was attacked, but just before she got hit by the bus, the witnesses described a flash of light. At the time, I assumed it was the bus headlights, perhaps as he swerved to avoid her. After we talked I went back to the scene and looked at the angles and windows. From where our witnesses were sitting, deep under the archway, but facing towards the bus, the bus swerved away from them. It wouldn't have caused a flash. If anything there would have been a sudden reduction of light. The flash must have come towards them, but there was no one else there except for the attackers. No other vehicle, and all the buildings are in a straight line. If someone had suddenly switched on a light, it would have shone down onto the street, not in the direction of the witnesses.'

'A torch?' Ava asked.

'I'm thinking something more noticeable. What if one of the attackers decided to take a photo as Melanie's face was cut?'

Ava perched on the edge of her desk. 'As a trophy?'

'Maybe to gloat over later.'

'Or perhaps it was so dark they were going to miss seeing the effects of what they'd done. A photo means they could go home and get a good look at it later.'

'Pointless without the flash on. They'd have got nothing,' Graham said. 'It's a theory. Not much good to you without suspects though. DS Lively suggested you had someone in your sights for it.'

'It's a shot in the dark,' Ava said. 'A bit like the photo you think the attackers took. I've already been warned off by my detective superintendent.'

'But if they shared the photo, messaged it, copied it onto a computer, there'll be a trail. Even if they think they've deleted it from their phones, it might still be retrievable at this stage. You'd need a court order to seize the phones or to get into their communications data. Worth trying, I'd say.'

'All right, I'll consider it. Thanks for bringing it to me. Are you going back out onto the street?' Ava asked.

'No, I've got some paperwork to catch up on. Lively has my mobile number if you need me. I'm happy to help out if I can. Oh, nearly forgot. I left a Caesar salad and a sandwich on your desk. Wasn't sure what you like, so it's nothing very exciting. Seems to me, you probably haven't eaten in a while.'

Ava stared at the brown paper bag on her desk. Plastic cutlery was balanced on top, next to a bottle of sparkling water. She'd thought that food was last thing she wanted, but her stomach told her differently.

'That was thoughtful. I owe you a favour,' she said.

'Not at all. I'm from Thurso, ma'am. We never leave a woman feeling in our debt.' He left. Ava sat behind her desk, taking the salad from the paper bag and digging into it. However much guilt she felt about Kate Bailey's capture, she still had to eat. And if she had to face Overbeck for yet another row, she was going to need all the energy she could find.

Chapter Twenty-Eight

'You haven't had your hair cut since I last saw you then,' Callanach said as he hugged Ben Paulson hard and slapped him on the back. They walked through the doors into The Inn on the Mile, where South Bridge met the High Street, and headed for the bar. 'Beer or something stronger?'

'I'll settle for beer. Judging by the tone of the message you left me, I'll be spending the rest of my evening working,' Paulson said, his Californian twang turning heads. 'Just reassure me that helping you this time won't end up with me in the cells waiting to be bailed out again.'

'As I recall, what put you in the cells last time was the fact that you'd hacked into a financial institution, and moved money from the staff bonus account to various charities,' said Callanach, smiling.

'Hey, you have to put the word "allegedly" in front of that. They never proved a thing. Shall we sit?'

They took their drinks to a booth where they sipped for a couple of minutes, watching the mixture of locals drinking wine or whisky, and a tourist hen weekend sampling the bar's infamous cocktails as they flirted with the staff. The Inn was warm and comfortable, and Callanach had discovered they served the best fish and chips he'd ever tasted. Not a meal the Frenchman in him would have admitted becoming addicted to, but Scotland was all the better for comfort food.

'I'm surprised you're still here, to be honest,' Callanach said. 'Once the last investigation was over I figured you'd be headed back to the sunshine. What made you stay?'

'Usual story. There's a girl. She campaigns for a human rights group. I tried to persuade her to come back to the States with me but she's lochs and kilts through and through. Much as I'm craving the sunshine, I just couldn't leave.'

'You sound hooked. Have you introduced this girl to Lance for approval yet?'

Lance Proudfoot, a local journalist, had befriended Luc and Ben during an earlier investigation, and taken a paternalistic interest in both their lives ever since. The only problem was his uncanny knack of landing right where the worst of the action was. Callanach still hadn't forgiven himself for the dreadful injuries Lance had received during an operation that went wrong a few months earlier.

'I have, as a matter of fact. They were unbearable together – started talking so fast I couldn't decipher the accents any more. By the time we left, Lance was convinced I wasn't good enough for her. Scots blood and all that. He said he hadn't seen you for a while.' Ben raised questioning eyebrows over the rim of his pint glass as he drank.

'Not enough hours in the day,' Callanach replied.

'Really? Only I heard there was some rather attractive Spanish doctor on the scene.'

'No one can keep secrets from Lance. Is he recovered yet?'

'Don't worry about that. He told us the story three times in as many hours and he's wearing the scars like war wounds,' Ben said. 'So come on, you've just checked your watch for the second time since we arrived. I've seen the news. Go on, ask me the favour – or do I have to guess?'

'We could probably get a warrant eventually, but it'll take too long. There's a girl missing. I won't go into the details, but she's in the hands of someone likely to hurt her very badly and very soon. We believe he contacted her through a website called SugarPa and they went on a date. She hasn't been seen since.'

'SugarPa won't play ball voluntarily?'

'Not a chance,' Callanach said. 'They're citing privacy and data issues. That's what happens when your members are paying to take young women out to – and I quote – spoil them, no strings attached. Except for the fact that there are plenty of strings attached.'

'Complexities?' Ben asked.

'Servers are in Russia. Member who has the hostage undoubtedly used a false name. We have their last communication but he's no longer an active member and has erased his profile. I've already emailed you the details. We need anything that might help trace him. Email, credit card, phone number. All his communications history. Can you do it?'

'I can try,' Ben said. 'But if the company was making enough money, they'll have invested in a good security system. After a couple of high-profile dating websites got hacked, everyone built up their walls. Nothing puts off members like your wife reading your name in a tabloid. How much danger is the girl in?'

'You know the other two bodies found in the last fortnight?'

'Shit.' Ben whistled. 'How much time?'

'Running on empty,' Callanach said. 'Sorry if you had plans.'

'That's okay. I'm freelancing. I'll sleep when I've finished. Is there anything else I should know about the case? Sometimes it's the details that make the trail easier to follow. What's different about this guy than all the other sickos you guys come up against?'

'There are religious overtones. Real Old Testament stuff about sin, punishment and retribution. We're not sure yet if this is some sort of extremism or just an excuse to torture vulnerable young women. I'd tend towards the latter. All we have so far are Bible verses linked to each victim.'

'Okay, I'll bear it in mind. As good as it was to see you, I'm guessing you'd rather I was at home getting started,' Ben said, finishing his beer and pushing the empty bottle into the middle of the table.

'Ava wants you to know that she's not expecting you to do this for free. She'll pay the going rate. It's just that we can't make it official,' Callanach said, standing up.

'Ah, so this was DCI Turner's idea. Has she forgiven me yet for sending her former fiancé back to London with his tail between his legs?'

'I think you'd be surprised how grateful she is to you, actually. She'd have come herself, but I thought you might feel more comfortable seeing me instead,' Callanach said, doing up his jacket and looking out at the pouring rain.

'Well, I am glad to see you, but I don't hold grudges. Tell Ava she owes me a drink, nothing more. I don't want to profit from a case like this. I'll call you as soon as I have something. I should know if I can crack their firewall in a few hours. Take care, Luc.'

He disappeared out of the door with the carefree smile of a twenty-something who was successful and in love. Luc envied him. There wasn't much success happening inside MIT. None at all, actually. As for being in love, he'd forgotten how that felt. Selina was amazing, and remarkably persistent in the face of a lack of response from him, but in relationship terms he was just going through the motions. It was only a matter of time before Selina figured that out.

★　★　★

Ava walked into Overbeck's office. Her superior officer glared at her. 'It's 11 p.m. Make it fast.'

'I want permission to follow up at the Leverhulme School,' Ava said. 'I backed off when you told me to, but we have no other leads and this is now a murder investigation.'

'Rationale?'

'One of Melanie Long's attackers called another a cretin. It's not common language these days. Also there's evidence suggesting that a photo was taken during the course of the attack, probably from a mobile phone. I think it was a trophy, or thrill-seeker behaviour. I want to find out who Leo Plunkett's closest friends are and question them. Nothing heavy-handed, but it would be irresponsible not to follow up the lead.'

'If I say no?' Overbeck asked.

'Would you say no if I was asking permission to speak with a few kids in the local state school?' Ava countered.

'Don't get smart with me and don't be childish. You know what's at stake,' Overbeck snapped.

'Your next promotion?'

'Is this what the moral high ground looks like, DCI Turner, because from where I'm standing you're grasping at pretty thin fucking straws. Take DS Lively with you. You are making enquiries of potential witnesses, not interviewing suspects. They are young people, and they must have an adult with them or you do not speak to them at all. Understood?'

'Of course,' Ava said, turning towards the door.

'Before you go, how are we doing on Kate Bailey? Any closer to finding her?'

'Not much,' Ava replied, softening her voice. Conflict at work was unsustainable when a life hung in the balance. 'We're doing what we can with the CCTV footage. The killer's not on our database, we know that. We're currently double-checking vehicles seen on camera in the area where Lorna was dropped off, and which were also in the city when Kate disappeared, but it's taking a lot of manpower and yielding too few results.'

'You know you have to find this girl in time, Turner. We can't have any more mutilated young women dumped on our streets.'

'And I'm sure Kate's parents would appreciate not burying their daughter, too,' Ava said through gritted teeth as she shut Overbeck's door behind her, striding towards the staircase to the lower floor. 'Salter!' she shouted, as she walked down the corridor past the incident room.

'I'm here,' Salter replied, poking her head out of the kitchen.

'You're coming with me to Leverhulme School first thing tomorrow morning. Meet me there at 9 a.m.'

'Sure,' Salter said.

'And tell DS Lively you'll be coming with me to question Leo Plunkett again. He's to remain here, coordinating the Kate Bailey search and answering to DI Callanach.'

Sod Superintendent Overbeck, Ava thought, using her lover to keep an eye on her. She would handle Leo Plunkett however she liked. The time for going easy had passed when Melanie Long hit the front of a bus and left a little boy without a mother.

'This is Callanach,' he muttered into his mobile, wondering why his arms were so slow to work, before realising he'd fallen asleep at his desk using his arms as a pillow.

'Hey, I should have let you sleep. You sound like you need it,' Ben Paulson said.

'No, I'm fine. What did you find?'

'Not a lot, but better than nothing. I got John White's profile back. It was cached in the data on Kate's laptop. She was obviously wary. I found a lot of pages that she'd looked through, so she did the best homework she could. Sadly, there wasn't a lot to find. The photo he used as his profile picture was a stock image he'd downloaded from the internet then just blurred it a bit. Easily done with any standard software these days. I used image recognition software and found the original picture in minutes. The email he used gave me an IP address that leads to an internet cafe. That's a bit more interesting. I was able to trace it pretty easily.'

'So the man we're looking for isn't some computer genius,' Callanach said.

'Not at all. He did enough not to have you walking straight to his front door, but it was the bare minimum.'

'All right. Which internet cafe?' Callanach asked.

'Coffee in the Cloud. It's in Livingston. Interesting that he didn't come into Edinburgh. He'd have had much more choice of internet venue in the city,' Ben said.

'No, it makes sense. We believe he lives to the west of the city. Making another trip just increases the possibility of his car getting picked up on CCTV. If he believed that erasing his SugarPa profile was going to be enough to prevent us tracing him, he might well have been less concerned about his choice of cafe.'

'Okay, well the downside of that particular establishment is that they still accept cash for user time. Most cafes now insist on card payment simply because if anyone uploads or downloads anything that's criminal in nature, the individual user can be traced. Avoids any sticky situations with the police.'

'What about his payment for membership of SugarPa? He must have used a card for that,' Callanach commented.

'Actually, it was an online direct payment facility, and here's where I'm going to be less helpful. It's Russian owned and run, same as the SugarPa servers. They process an international payments scheme, charging exorbitant fees to make international payments, but the guarantee is that provided you load up your account in advance sufficient to pay both your fees and whatever you want to purchase, they don't give out any information about you to anyone. And they have the sort of firewall that the CIA can only dream of.'

'I thought you said the killer wasn't that tech savvy?'

'He didn't need to be. Type "international online payments" into a search engine and the site comes up within the top three hits. It's a one-page form to fill in. You have an account within the hour. Couldn't be much easier.'

'Untraceable?' Callanach asked, although he already knew the answer.

'You got it. Want to buy a new passport, smuggle some women through a port under the radar, pay for weapons without a nasty trail of paperwork and import taxes, this is the website to use.'

'And they couldn't care less about European money laundering regulations,' Callanach said. 'At least we have the internet cafe. Perhaps someone there will remember him.'

'He accessed SugarPa through their system on at least three occasions. Once was to set up his email and make the international payment, the next to put up his SugarPa profile, and the third time he arranged the meeting with Kate. I'm emailing you the dates and times of those sessions now.'

'So did you manage to do anything about the SugarPa website? I know it was asking a lot. Ava is worried that the killer might have identified other profiles through which he could find more victims.'

'Why do you think it took me so long?' Ben laughed. 'Have a look at their new website. I strongly suspect they'll be avoiding too much publicity about it. Their members are going to get a nasty shock when they realise that all the data from the site is in the hands of someone so self-righteous.'

'You're a good man, Ben. Ava will want to thank you in person when this is over.'

'Tell her from me to string the bastard up, that's all the thanks I need. Only sorry I couldn't do more.'

'You've given us somewhere to start. That feels pretty good to me. Talk soon.' He hung up, quickly typing the SugarPa web address into his laptop. The sugar-coated prostitution club had been replaced with a site that advised women on their rights and legal remedies for abuse, sexual harassment and domestic violence, with a petition calling for organisations profiting from prostitution in all but name to be criminalised. Callanach allowed himself a small smile. A tiny fragment of good had been done in the midst of a dreadful and bloody waste of human life. It was a reminder to celebrate the small victories.

Alone in the dark, Kate felt exactly the same as she finally managed to wriggle one wrist free of its restraints. For the first time in days, she felt a rush of hope.

Chapter Twenty-Nine

Anthony McGowan, the Leverhulme School's headmaster, appeared frazzled when Ava and DC Salter were shown into his rooms at 9 a.m. His clock chimed prettily as they entered. He scowled at it in response.

'DCI Turner, I rather thought we'd concluded our part in your investigations on your last visit,' he said.

'So did I,' replied Ava. 'Then it occurred to me that as Leo Plunkett almost certainly never goes through the Meadows alone, and as we know from his key that he uses the path where one of the attacks took place, his friends might have witnessed something of use to us.'

McGowan raised sceptical eyebrows.

'Witnesses often have no idea what they've seen until we prompt them, sir,' Salter said. 'Especially young people who were probably distracted, talking about rugby or girls, or which universities they're applying to. We just want to see if there's anything we might have missed.'

'Exactly,' Ava continued. 'And I'm sure that given the sort of community ethics your school encourages, they'll be pleased to do their civic duty.' That was possibly overdoing it, Ava thought, but McGowan was the sort of man who would be unable to resist the call to moral arms.

'Well, all right then, but I have no choice other than to notify the parents of any child you wish to speak to. They will then have the choice of whether to attend themselves to accompany their child, or to allow a staff member to stand in for them.'

'Absolutely, we'd have insisted on that if you hadn't suggested it,' Salter said. Ava raised her eyebrows at the detective constable. Salter was such a natural police officer. It made it all the more unfair that fate had treated her so cruelly. Still, Ava had decided to do all she could to put that right.

'So to start us off, could you tell us the names of Leo Plunkett's closest friends, the young men he normally spends time with, especially if you've seen them entering or leaving the school grounds together,' Salter said, smiling as she poured a cup of tea from the tray the headmaster's assistant had left them, and handing it to McGowan before serving herself and Ava. He smiled graciously and took a sip before answering.

'That's the easy part. All the boys have been here for some years, so by the sixth form they have firm friendship groups established. Leo Plunkett is particularly close to Oliver Davenport and Noah Alby-Croft. Bright boys. Spirited and confident. I'll have my assistant contact their parents straight away. Naturally I'll need your assurance that this will not take long. I can't have parents paying for the boys to be in lessons while they are actually in conversation with the police, no matter how well-intentioned.'

'Ten minutes with each boy should suffice. I believe we'll know straight away if any of the boys has seen anything that might prove useful to our investigation,' Ava smiled.

'That sounds fine. Excuse me a moment. I'll just pop out

and get this underway.' He left the room, leaving them sipping their tea in front of a roaring applewood fire.

'You all right?' Salter asked Ava. 'You made a funny face when he was saying the boys' names.'

'Alby-Croft,' Ava said. 'I know the name, and it's unusual. I just can't place it. Probably a coincidence. Well done, by the way. You charmed him so completely that I forgot why we were really here.'

'We haven't told any lies,' Salter grinned. 'I'll just bet the boys are spirited and confident. How many times do you think he's used those euphemisms?'

'My headmistress once told my parents I was independently-minded with strong views on the world that defined my sense of natural justice,' Ava said.

'Meaning?' Salter asked.

'That when the school bully told a friend of mine she was too ugly to be allowed to fancy one particular boy, I shouldn't have hit her in the face with the raw chicken we were about to roast in our home economics class.'

Salter clapped a hand over her mouth to avoid spraying tea across the room. Ava joined in laughing with her. The memory was precious, as was the moment. A few seconds of feeling an emotion other than desperation was as good as a vacation. It buoyed her. She would do her job, find out what the boys knew and shift the stagnant investigation. Luc was on his way to Livingston with a squad to shut down the Coffee in the Cloud internet cafe until they had some information on the bastard who was holding Kate Bailey. Finally, the pace had shifted and there seemed to be progress.

'Right,' Anthony McGowan said, as he reappeared through the grand oak doorway. 'Oliver Davenport's mother will be here in a few minutes. Noah Alby-Croft's mother has asked that I accompany her son during the questioning. We're still attempting to make contact with Leo Plunkett's father, whom I gather you've met.'

'That's quite all right,' Salter said, setting her cup down on the tray and standing up. 'We can get started with Oliver. We don't want to keep you longer than necessary.'

The introductions were made quickly. Mrs Davenport had either dressed up for the occasion or she naturally spent every day in a Chanel suit, ready for whatever the world threw at her. The headmaster allowed them the use of his rooms, which had the added benefit of making everyone relax in front of the fire.

'Oliver, we just want to know if you might have seen anything strange in the Meadows. I believe you're friendly with Leo Plunkett,' Ava began.

'Uh huh,' was the reply.

'Were you with him when he dropped his locker key?' she continued.

'I'm not sure when he dropped it, so I don't know,' he said.

'Well, this would have been near the playground area. Do you take that route regularly?' Ava asked.

'Sometimes,' Oliver said, with a sideways glance at his mother.

Ava wrote a note on a piece of paper and handed it to Salter without a word. Oliver's eyes followed the progress of the note, and he watched Salter's face carefully as she read it. Salter gave a single nod to Ava.

'I should be in physics,' the boy said.

'A woman is dead, Oliver,' Ava said, noting the wobble of his throat. 'So I'm sure your tutor won't mind spending a few minutes covering the lesson with you.'

'Who's dead?' Mrs Davenport interrupted. 'I thought this was about an assault that happened in the park.'

'We believe that the same people who attacked the man in the park also injured a woman who ended up in the road and was hit by a bus. That lady died from her injuries,' Salter said. Mrs Davenport pressed a hand against her mouth. 'We're so sorry to have to talk about such awful things. I appreciate this is difficult. Of course, the people responsible are now wanted for murder, given that the traffic accident was a direct result of the assault.'

Oliver opened his mouth to say something then quickly closed it again. 'I don't think I saw anything that would help you,' he muttered.

'Have you ever noticed a group of homeless adults hanging around the park area? Or drug users, perhaps?' Salter asked.

Ava watched as he slid one foot on top of the other and pressed down. He was stressed. Everyone had a tell-tale sign.

'I've seen homeless people in the Meadows sometimes. I always feel sorry for them. It's not so bad in the summer, I suppose, but in the winter it must be dreadful. I wish they had somewhere to go,' Oliver said.

Mrs Davenport patted his arm, gazing lovingly at her boy's face. In another year or so he'd be a man, Ava thought, but now he was still sufficiently naive that he believed he could get away with delivering what was obviously a prepared speech.

'That's a kind thought, Oliver,' Salter said. 'I don't suppose you've ever come across any Spice users, have you?'

'What sort of spice?' Mrs Davenport asked.

'It's a drug. Users are occasionally referred to as zombies, because it makes them unaware of their surroundings,' Salter explained.

'We tell Oliver to stay away from drugs and the people associated with them. He's not that sort of boy,' Mrs Davenport assured them.

Her son's half eye-roll told a different story. He was embarrassed by his mother's protectiveness and sick of being lectured.

He also knew a lot more about drugs than she would be happy about.

Ava leaned forward to make eye contact with the teenager. 'Do you ever use the word cretin, Oliver?'

He blinked, coughed, acted confused. 'Um, no. I mean I've heard it. I know what it means. But I don't use it.'

He didn't ask the relevance of the question. Ava waited until he looked away from her.

'That's fine, no need to worry. What about Noah? Do you and Leo spend a lot of time with him?'

'Quite a bit,' Oliver said.

'We're very friendly with the Alby-Crofts,' Mrs Davenport said. 'We holiday with them occasionally. We're skiing with them in February, in fact.'

'Are you? How lovely,' Ava said. 'Gosh, I did promise Mr McGowan I wouldn't keep you from your lessons for more than ten minutes, and it's been that already. You're free to go, Oliver.'

He looked from Ava to Salter to the headmaster. 'That's it?' he asked.

'Were you expecting something more?' Salter responded

He shook his head and made for the door as his mother picked up her handbag and coat.

'Send Alby-Croft in, would you please, Oliver? He should be waiting outside,' the headmaster said.

'Sorry, one last thing,' Ava said. 'Do you, Leo and Noah ever stay round each other's houses, or are you too old for sleepovers?' The headmaster frowned at the question. 'Forgive me. I'm just curious about what teenagers get up to these days. Coming into a school, I suddenly feel horribly out of touch.'

'I can sympathise,' Mrs Davenport said. 'It all seemed so easy when he was little. We restrict sleepovers to weekends unless the boys have special plans. They all have a lot of studying to do for their end-of-year exams.'

'Come on, Mum,' Oliver moaned from the doorway, his knuckles white pebbles as he gripped the handle.

Salter screwed up the note Ava had sent her and tossed it into the fire. The words 'Read this then nod at me' went up in flames as Noah Alby-Croft drifted with lazy self-assurance into the study.

'Noah, these police officers would like to ask you a few questions to ascertain if you have any useful witness testimony about an assault,' the headmaster said. 'Would you like a cup of tea?' He motioned towards the tray.

'Let me pour you one, sir,' Noah said, picking up the pot and straining the tea before handing over the china cup and saucer to McGowan.

'Noah will be going to Oxford, no doubt about it.' The headmaster glowed. 'Studying mathematics and philosophy. One of our best students.'

'That's kind of you, headmaster, but we have a lot of talented students here. I'm sure I'm no brighter than any of the others,' Noah said, but the tilt of his chin and his straight back suggested otherwise. Noah was a young man who knew exactly where he was going, and he was on the fast track. 'DCI Turner, my father has spoken highly of you on many occasions. I think initially he was slightly surprised about your promotion given that you were suspended for a while, but he says you're beginning to prove yourself in your new post.'

Salter was unable to mask her surprise and Ava did little better. She had imagined taking the boy by surprise, breaking down whatever defences he'd prepared. This boy was an adult in all but years. He took a chair and raised one leg slowly to rest across his other knee, smiling broadly at the women before him.

'That's right,' Ava said. 'I thought I recognised the surname. Your father's on the Police Scotland board. A relatively new appointment. Were you expecting a visit from me then, given that you know so much about me?'

'As you know, Leo Plunkett and I are close friends. Isn't that why you're here? He mentioned that he'd had a visit from you and I discussed it with my father. I'm afraid that's the only reason I was discussing you, although if I'd known how attractive you were I might have asked to attend some of the police social functions my father always claims are so dull.'

'Noah,' the headmaster chided with a small smile. 'I'm not sure the detective chief inspector should be the subject of your charms. Perhaps save those for women more your own age.'

'You can't blame me for trying.' Noah raised an eyebrow at Ava. So that's how it was. His father discussed police matters with him. His headmaster thought he was Leverhulme's golden boy. And Noah thought he was cleverer than the lot of them. 'So, please, let me know how I can help you. At this school, the students take social responsibility very seriously. Ask me anything you like. Anything at all.' He flashed a row of perfect white teeth and settled himself comfortably into the armchair.

'Leo Plunkett lost his locker key. No doubt you were aware of that,' Ava began. 'Did you—'

'Yes, that's right,' Noah interrupted. 'I'm not sure where he lost it, and I doubt he was aware of it at the time. After all, if you knew you'd dropped something you'd stop and pick it up. Certainly at school when he needed to open his locker, he asked me if I'd picked it up by mistake. A few of us had a look around the corridor but couldn't find it. I've done it myself a few times. It's annoying but not a big deal. Did you find it somewhere?'

'In the Meadows,' Salter said.

'Ah, well that makes sense. We go through there regularly, and I have to say there's a fair amount of horsing around. I lose coins from my pockets all the time when one of the lads rugby

251

tackles me as a joke. Frankly, it's a wonder any of us ever finds our key where we think we left it.'

'Where were you two nights ago?' Ava asked. 'Late in the evening.'

'At home, I would imagine.'

'What time do you normally go to bed?'

'Why are you interested?' he countered.

'A woman was attacked on George Street. She ended up dead. Did you hear about it?'

'I must be getting my dates confused. This isn't the same day as the attack in the Meadows that you're here to ask me about.'

'No, that was some days earlier,' Ava said.

'And you think that because we use the Meadows as a route into the city, I might have noticed something there that might help your investigation.'

'That's right,' Ava said.

'Great, I'm here to help. The Meadows can get a little rough at times. There is a homeless problem in the city, as I'm sure you're aware. We are warned not to go through the park after dark and it's my policy to follow school regulations that affect my safety. I've witnessed the odd drunken brawl there. Occasionally you'll see someone looking furtive, an exchange of money. It doesn't take much imagination to see that it's a prime area for drug dealing.'

'Do you know much about that then? Drug dealing?' Salter asked.

'We've been fortunate to have been given a number of drug and alcohol awareness lectures at this school. This may look like a traditional educational establishment, but I find it very forward looking.' Noah smiled.

'Thank you, Noah,' Anthony McGowan muttered.

'I'm afraid that at the time of the attack in the Meadows, I don't recall seeing any incidents. Certainly, if I'd seen a violent attack, I'd have intervened immediately to offer my assistance.'

'Noah, that's a very unwise stance,' the headmaster said. 'You should leave the area and phone the police. We've been through this. There is no sense putting your own life at risk.'

'So, two nights ago. We were discussing where you were,' Ava said.

'Yes, in bed, if it was late at night. I'm afraid the rugby team and the need to study make late nights a rarity, unless I have a test the next day. That usually keeps me up all night,' he said, laughing.

'I'm sure with your grades you don't need to worry too much,' Ava responded. 'The attacker two nights ago used an unusual word. Cretin. Is that a phrase your friends use regularly?'

'I thought you said an unusual word. I must hear it ten times a day. At school, at my sports clubs, at social events. Honestly, when you're with intelligent people there is an admirable depth to their lexicon. If that's the only lead you have, DCI Turner, it's no wonder you're at a school asking for help.' He checked his watch. 'Sir, I have Mandarin now. I probably shouldn't miss it given that I have a mock exam next week. May I go?'

'I had a couple more questions about your whereabouts this week actually,' Ava said. 'Just five more minutes should do it.'

'Oh, forgive me, I thought I was here to answer questions about what I might have seen in the Meadows. If we've covered that subject, then I'm afraid I'll have to leave. It was lovely to meet you. Leo said I'd enjoy it.' He reached out a hand to shake Ava's. 'Goodbye, Ava. I'm sure we'll meet under more interesting circumstances soon.'

He nodded to the headmaster then left the room. Ava had the urge to scrub her hands.

'Shall I see if we've managed to contact Leo Plunkett's father?' McGowan asked.

'No need,' Ava said. 'I can see we're wasting your time. What a very smart group of boys you have here. So much more grown up than the seventeen-year-olds we usually deal with. Quite sophisticated, in fact.'

'Thank you for saying so,' the headmaster said. 'I'll leave you to find your way out then, if you don't mind. Noah's father is expecting a call from me. Good day.'

Salter waited until they were in the street before speaking her mind. 'Little shithead,' she growled. 'My God, it was like dealing with a politician.'

'Not quite,' Ava replied. 'Politicians know when to trade confidence for the appearance of shock. The delightful Mr Alby-Croft has yet to recognise the value of pretending to be taken unawares. He was happy to let us know how masterful he is by preparing for our questions, but he forgot that the price he was going to pay for that was an ongoing investigation.'

'But there's no evidence against any of them,' Salter said. 'A coincidental key in the park and the use of language that Noah very astutely assured us was commonplace.'

'There's evidence somewhere. A droplet of blood on shoes. A weapon. Text messages with arrangements to meet. Perhaps even a memento in the form of a photograph taken just before Melanie Long's life ended. If we look hard enough, there'll be a trail.'

'I don't doubt it. The question is, will we be allowed to look at all?' Salter replied.

Chapter Thirty

Coffee in the Cloud was busy. Through the glass frontage, a middle-aged woman could be seen serving food and drink while a slightly older male handled computer queries. Callanach leaned against his car, an unlit Gauloise in his mouth, and studied the set-up. The small industrial unit just off Howden South Road looked unloved, having fallen prey to an outlet retail park nearby where you could park for hours and fulfil every retail, food or indoor leisure fetish imaginable. There was a hairdressing salon above the cafe, a Chinese takeaway to its right and a couple of empty units advertised as for rent. The internet cafe seemed to be the only one thriving. Tripp got off his phone and exited the car.

'We'll have backup units here in a few minutes, sir,' he said.

'Good. Tell them to wait until I ask them to enter. We'll get information faster if we don't have to bleed it out of the hard drives with warrants.'

'There are more people in there than I'd have expected. I don't get it. Anyone can wander into a library these days and use a computer with wifi. Why would you pay for something you can get for free?' Tripp mused.

'Because there are certain websites you can't access from the library, and lots of cameras. Here there's nothing. You can access any website you want without the police tracing your home computer address. God only knows what secrets those computers are hiding, and from a commercial standpoint it's all perfectly legal.'

'So it's a magnet for anyone who wants to do dodgy stuff online but who doesn't have the technical skills to cover their tracks at home,' Tripp said.

'Exactly. Which means the owners will be wary. Let's keep this friendly as long as possible. No one who's using the place now leaves without giving a statement. Some of them may be regulars and might have been here when our man came in.' A string of marked police cars entered the car park and filled the available spaces. 'Right, let's go.'

The chatter evaporated into silence as Callanach and Tripp went in. There was a sudden reaching for coats and wallets, the scraping of chairs and logging off of computers.

'Please take your seats again,' Callanach announced. 'We're only here to make a quick enquiry about a previous customer.' No one retook their seat. Tripp did a quick head count. There were eight men and two women at screens, and all appeared deeply uncomfortable. 'No one is obliged to stay, but when you leave, you will each need to answer a few questions and provide a statement regarding dates and times you were here. We're asking for your help, nothing more.'

There was a clatter of furniture as a young man bolted for the fire exit. Callanach noted the computer he'd been using and made a mental note to have it seized. Shouts from the rear of the property indicated what Callanach and Tripp already knew. They'd posted officers there earlier to assist people who might think using the alternative door was a good idea.

'If this is a raid, where's the paperwork?' the man behind the counter asked.

'It's not a raid. We're simply after your assistance, on a voluntary basis. Of course, if anything happens while we're here that gives us reasonable cause to believe that a crime has been or is being committed, that would change things.' Callanach took the schedule of the killer's visits to the cafe out of his pocket. 'We need to know what you can tell us about a man who visited on three occasions. These are the dates and times.' He slid the paper over the counter.

'If you know when he was here, you must know who he is. Do you want to give me a name or show me a photo at least?' the man asked.

'That's what we're trying to find out,' Tripp said. 'Do you have CCTV here?'

'No. It's a bunch of relatively old computers and we take all the cash out of the premises each night. How do you know this man came here, if you don't know who he is?'

'Are you the owner?' Callanach enquired.

'Yes. Richie Pleasance. This is my wife. We run the place together,' he said. His wife, who had been furiously wiping the countertop and putting cups in the sink, did her best to smile.

'Good. So you know that if you own these computers and it's your internet connection, I can hold you liable for anything that's on them. Anything, for example, that your customers might have accidentally downloaded to the hard drive. Do you check them regularly to make sure there's nothing illegal on the machines?' Callanach asked.

'It's not like we can check them every night. That would be crazy. We're here ten hours a day as it is,' Richie moaned.

'And making a profit, by the looks of it,' Tripp said. 'This man is six foot one. We have a video that shows his build but we don't have a good shot of his face. If you can help us with any other details, that would be useful.' He held up a still from the shopping mall CCTV footage. The man peered at it, looking unimpressed.

Richie shrugged. 'I don't know. We have a lot of people come through here and we don't take names or check identification.'

'Are you able to find out how he paid you?' Callanach asked.

'It would have been cash. We don't have a debit or credit card machine. Gets too expensive,' Richie said.

'You run a cash-only business,' Callanach noted. 'When did you last get a tax inspection?'

Richie sighed, taking the hint, snatching the picture from Tripp's hand and waving it in his wife's direction. 'Do you remember him?' he asked her.

'Sort of. I don't really pay that much attention. Most of our customers are men. I reckon women have too much to do at home to bother spending all day staring at a screen. I sure as hell don't get to sit down very often,' she moaned.

'Don't bloody start. Do you remember him or not?' Richie snapped.

'Vaguely. He was wearing these really thick glasses, I think. Big black frames and coke-bottle lenses. Couldn't really see his eyes. Been in three times, you reckon? I only remember him twice, but then I'm sometimes out shopping. Both times I saw him, he used the same computer, sat over in that corner.' She pointed to the far side of the room, where the computer screen was facing away from both the serving area and the window. It made sense, keeping himself to himself and out of others' memories. 'Never ordered anything to eat or drink that I was aware of, tight bastard, just paid for his time on the computer then left.'

'We're going to have to take that computer with us,' Callanach said. 'This is an important investigation. You'll get it back when we've finished checking the data. Also, you'll both need to make statements confirming what you've told us today.'

'You can't just take our stuff. That's how we make our living. I'll want to be compensated,' Richie blustered.

'Or,' Callanach said, 'I could decide that I'm deeply concerned about the lack of accountability here and the likely use these computers are being put to, and take all of them.' Richie gritted his teeth and motioned towards the computer in the corner. 'Thank you for your cooperation.'

'You won't be in touch with the Revenue about us, then?' the wife muttered.

'If we had additional details about the man we're looking for, I'm sure we'd be too busy to speak with the tax office,' Tripp said. Callanach was surprised at the younger officer. It wasn't like his detective constable to be so manipulative.

'Well . . .' Richie's wife mumbled. 'There was his vehicle.'

'For Christ's sake, if it gets out that you're blabbing, no one'll ever want to use this place again,' Richie groaned.

'But on the plus side, you won't be in prison for abetting a murderer,' Tripp said softly.

Richie and his wife stared at one another.

'I noticed it because of the mud all over the number plate. You couldn't read it at all. He parked at the far end of the unit spaces, nearly where you exit onto the main road. I only saw his car at all because I was putting the signs out the first time he came. The second time, I know it sounds stupid, but I looked to see if he'd washed the mud off the licence plate yet. He still hadn't. I think I may have even said something to him about it.'

'How did he respond?' Callanach asked.

'He didn't. Just ignored me. Not unusual in here. Most people want to be left alone with the screen.'

'I bet they do,' Tripp commented. 'What colour was the vehicle?'

'Very dark, like a deep shade of grey, but old, you know, and tatty. The paintwork was patchy.'

'Make and model?' Callanach pushed.

'It was some sort of minivan. Can't help more than that.'

Tripp and Callanach left the squad to question the other customers and seize the computer in question. For the first time since this all began, Callanach was starting to believe they might actually be able to find Kate Bailey and spare her parents the news they were braced for.

Chapter Thirty-One

The incident room was completely silent. Ava walked in, threw down her coat and checked her watch.

'It's midday,' she began. 'Before midnight I want to know who that minivan belongs to and where it is being kept. We don't have a licence plate, but the description of the exterior is very specific. The minivan is dark – either grey or black, possibly a deep blue – and the paintwork is tatty. "Patchy", is how DI Callanach said the witness described it. We also have locations for where the driver has been and very good timings. I want CCTV rechecked for every other known location this man has been. At the shopping mall, near Kate's halls of residence to drop off the doll, when he dropped off both Zoey and Lorna before they died. Identify all routes in and out where there are cameras for the relevant periods. If we still can't make out the licence number, we should start to see a route pattern. Where is this man coming from? Where does he live? What is the camera furthest from the city where we can get a shot of the vehicle?'

'Are we going to notify the public, ma'am?' Salter asked.

'No. We have more to lose than to gain at this point. We

might still see the van on the road or parked up somewhere. The danger with publicity is that the murderer will realise we have the details and swap to a different vehicle, ditching this one. He might even kill Kate faster and run. I'm authorising a cross-agencies alert – all police forces, parking attendants, fire service, paramedics. I want CCTV controllers on the lookout at all times, calling in all vehicles that could match the description. Our best hope is that we catch this bastard while he's driving around. Any progress on the woman seen staring out of the shop window at the suspect as he met with Kate?'

'No clear facial picture. She followed the same route out of the shopping centre that Kate and the male took, but was keeping her head down. It looks as if she didn't want the man to see she was following them,' Lively said. 'The girl from the shop gave us a description so vague it could apply to half the middle-aged women in the city.' He flipped open a notebook. 'Female, Caucasian, in her forties or fifties, mousy looking, brown hair tied up in bun. Did not notice eye colour. Height between five three and five six. Average build.'

'That's it?' Ava asked.

'She was carrying a shopping bag. No description of that either,' Lively added. 'That's the problem when your witness is nineteen. They literally don't see anyone over the age of twenty-nine. It's as if you cease to exist. When I began questioning her, the girl looked confused. She actually said, "Well, she just looked like all women that age." Now, if the woman had been standing in the optician's next door or chemist to the other side, we might have got something close to an actual description.'

'Bollocks,' Ava said. 'Right, we can only work with what we've got. The vehicle's the priority. If anyone needs me, I'll be in Superintendent Overbeck's office.' She picked up her coat and began walking towards the door.

PC Biddlecombe approached before she could escape. 'Just

before you go and see the super, there's a lady in your office. She did give me her name and I checked her ID, but I can't remember it.'

'Okay,' Ava said, determined not to take her frustration out on a colleague. 'Do you at least remember what it's about?'

'She said it was personal, ma'am,' Biddlecombe said, looking pleased with herself.

Ava considered explaining just how unhelpful that was, then decided it wasn't worth the time it would take. Instead, she strode to her office to get rid of the untimely visitor, throwing the door open to find Natasha staring out of the window.

'I'm sorry. I know you've got better things to do than to update me, but I just had to get news. I can't work. I can't sleep. I feel like I'm going insane. It's like when you were taken, Ava. Every minute is agony. How did Kate's parents take it?' Natasha asked, turning round.

Ava's first thought was that her friend looked awful, followed by the realisation that she probably looked the same herself. The toll of sleepless nights, too much coffee and insufficient vitamins could not be hidden.

'God, Natasha, come here. I'd forgotten that you'd been through this before.' She stepped forward to take her friend in her arms. Natasha was always so strong and outspoken. It was heartbreaking to see her devastated. 'I know this is hard, and that you care about Kate, but there's nothing you can do now. There's nothing you could ever have done,' Ava said.

'That's not true,' Natasha cried, pulling out of Ava's arms. 'I knew her father was ill. I knew she was using the money she earned for the basics. She wasn't buying clothes or going out clubbing. She was living on end-of-day bargains from the supermarkets and helping her friends with their assignments in return for borrowing their books. So I could have done something. I could have just given her the money, Ava. I've got enough, more than enough, to support myself. I never want for anything. Your father and my parents are in the same situation. We're going to inherit money. I'm already sitting on savings I don't spend. I could have given her a cheque for a thousand pounds and I wouldn't have missed it for a second.'

'Natasha, you can't do this . . .'

'Why not? I let a young woman I knew had already been assaulted continue to let vile, abusive men screw her so she could earn what, an extra fifty quid, a hundred, even two hundred. What the hell is wrong with me that I sat there listening to the details of the shit she was living through and did absolutely nothing about it?' she screeched.

'With the benefit of hindsight, maybe. But you didn't know what was going to happen to her. You didn't know if the following week you'd have another ten, twenty, thirty students at your door with similar stories. And I doubt Kate would have taken the cash from you. Everything I know about her indicates that she's a proud, brave, resourceful young woman who just rolled up her sleeves and did what she felt was necessary. If you'd offered her money, there was a chance she'd never have returned to you for help. Your conscience is clear, Tasha. You were there for Kate when she needed you. You came to me before anyone else realised she was missing. There's nothing more you could have done.'

'It's not fair,' Natasha said, sinking down into Ava's armchair. 'I know that sounds stupid and childish, but it's just not fair. She's a nice girl. You'd like her. I think she reminded me a bit of you, your fighting spirit. She was faced with a challenge and she decided to meet it head-on, whatever the cost to her. I can't stand waiting for her body to be found. The worst thing is that I've found myself wishing it was over, as if it would be easier to bear if she was dead already.'

'I can understand that. I don't let myself imagine what she

might be going through. You mustn't think about that. We're doing all we can. There's even been a small measure of progress today. Kate's not dead yet. She may even still be physically unharmed. You just have to let us find her.'

'And I'm slowing you down,' Natasha sniffed, wiping her tears on the back of her hand. 'I'm so sorry. What an idiot I'm being, taking up more of your time.'

'Not at all,' Ava said. 'Given how much I love an opportunity to call you an idiot, I think you can take that at face value.' Natasha gave a weak smile. 'Go home. Try to eat. Sleep if you can, but otherwise distract yourself. And remember this. I can tell you from experience that when you're being held captive, as Kate is, what gets you through is the thought of the people who care about you, those who'll be worried sick, like you are. Kate knows she was due to see you and that she missed the appointment. She's probably thankful right now that you were running the help centre, otherwise there wouldn't have been an appointment for her to miss at all. She knows we're looking for her, Tasha, and that will keep her strong and hopeful. The rest is up to us.'

Natasha took a deep breath and stood up. 'I love you,' she said, hugging Ava hard. 'I don't know what put that rod of steel in your backbone but I'm glad it's there. When this is over, will you come and stay with me a while? It'll be like old times. I just need to be around you a bit more. Even if I have to put up with your cooking.'

'That sounds good,' Ava said. 'I think I could use a bit of TLC too.'

They said their goodbyes and Ava locked her office door for a few minutes. It was an amazing truth that kidnappings, rapes and murders generated almost as much guilt as they did paperwork. Parental guilt, spousal guilt, friends, colleagues, people who'd walked past a victim on the street and didn't recognise the fear in their eyes until the television reconstruction. It was endless. The rigours of real life were the cause. It would be impossible to get through the day if you over-analysed every situation, imagined the possible repercussions of every action or inaction. But guilt lay in the cracks and the corners like cobwebs and shadows, waiting to darken every thought with that most futile of questions – what could I have done differently?

Checking her hair in the mirror, Ava tried not to think about Natasha's distress. This was the job. You notified the parents, then you got back to work. You picked up the body, then you went back to work. You bore witness to the grief of others, then you went back to work. Anything less clinical, anything more emotional, and you couldn't do your job properly. She pulled herself together. It was time to get tough with Superintendent Overbeck.

Her phone rang as she was about to leave her office.

'It's me,' Jonty announced. 'Sorry to bother you. I've just had some lab results back. They were puzzling, so I asked for some clarification. Apologies that this is rather late in the day. There's a substance I noticed because it glistened under bright light. It wasn't terribly obvious, not like glitter or a man-made substance, so we sent it away for clarification. I have no idea what the relevance of this might be, but it turned out to be marble, of all things.'

'Marble,' Ava said. 'Was it found on Zoey or Lorna?'

'Neither. But it was found on both the dolls.'

'So the absence of it on the girls means that presumably it's not environmental to where they're being held and operated on,' Ava said.

'Precisely. It's present in very small amounts, too. Frankly, it was a miracle we found it at all.'

'Could you email the paperwork to the incident room, please,

Dr Spurr? I'm just off to deal with something else, but we need to start fitting that into the picture immediately. I'm obliged for your help.'

Overbeck had just stepped out of her office for a minute. Ava elected to wait rather than get caught up in anything else until she had sorted out what progress could be made on Melanie Long's murder. She stared at the end of Overbeck's desk where her boss and her detective sergeant had created such a memorable tableau, and hoped it had been polished since the event, fighting the urge to get a cloth and wipe the area herself. Overbeck's stilettos clicking along the corridor tiles persuaded her against it.

'Good, you're here. Didn't think you'd get my message quite that fast,' was Overbeck's opener.

Ava shook her head slightly. 'I didn't get a message.'

'To explain what you did this morning,' Overbeck raised both her eyebrows and her voice. It was an unpleasant combination.

'Yes, that's why I need to talk to you, ma'am. DC Salter and I went to the Leverhulme School to speak with Leo Plunkett's friends,' Ava said.

'I'm aware of that, Turner. I've just been talking to DS Lively who explained that he was given instructions to remain coordinating in the incident room while you were out, which is strange because I issued you with strict, and I thought crystal clear, instructions that he was to accompany you.'

'Hold on,' Ava said. 'You were just discussing it with Lively? Before you talked to me? I am his superior officer . . .'

'And I am yours, yet you still felt entirely free to disobey a direct command,' Overbeck said.

'I can conduct day to day investigations as I choose. You might be my superior but that does not involve you micro-managing every decision I take. It was my view that Salter would be a friendlier face when interviewing young people, particularly given Lively's attitude to people like the headmaster,' Ava shot back.

'Don't blame this on Lively's attitude. You took Salter because you're certain Lively's reporting back to me,' Overbeck said, throwing herself into the chair behind her desk.

'A theory you just proved accurate when you discussed it with him first. And by the way, Salter was incredibly helpful at the school. My instincts were correct. There is no doubt whatsoever in my mind that Leo Plunkett and his closest friends Oliver Davenport and Noah Alby-Croft are involved. I don't know if there are any others yet, but it's a good place to start. I want warrants to check their homes, their mobile phones and computers—'

'What?' Overbeck interrupted.

'Warrants,' Ava said. 'The paperwork has to be in order. The boys made no secret of the fact they had been warned by Plunkett that they might be questioned.'

'The names. Again.'

Ava paused. 'Davenport and Alby-Croft.'

Overbeck said nothing. An imaginary clock ticked away thirty seconds of silence inside Ava's head.

'Are you out of your tiny, fucking, deluded, bloody moronic mind?' Overbeck yelled. 'Alby-Croft?'

Ava sighed.

'Alby frigging Croft? Tell me you immediately realised your mistake and asked no more than if he'd happened to notice anything odd in the Meadows,' Overbeck said, gripping the edge of her desk as if she were drowning.

'Nope,' Ava replied. 'I asked him his whereabouts on the night Melanie Long was killed,' she continued matter-of factly. 'So go ahead – shout, swear, whatever – but I'm not going to go easy on a suspect just because his father's on the police board, and frankly, ma'am, I'm absolutely fucking disgusted that you think I should have.'

Overbeck laughed. It sounded like a metal chair leg scraping along concrete. 'Is that what you think is happening here? How long have you been a police officer, Turner?'

'Twelve years,' Ava said.

'You've made DCI in just over a decade. Good old fast track. You must be feeling pretty smug,' Overbeck said.

'Not really. I worked hard and—'

'Don't give me the goddamned hard work speech. I've been at this game twice as long as you, from back in the days where no one had heard the word equality, and the concept of positive discrimination just meant that we didn't have to use toilets with piss all over the seats. You went to the school to treat those boys as witnesses. You had no evidence to link them to the Melanie Long scene. Was Alby-Croft's father there?'

'No. He agreed the headmaster could sit in during the questioning,' Ava said.

'On the basis that he wasn't being questioned as a suspect, a premise you then undermined by pushing one step too far. You were supposed to assess them subtly and carefully. For the record, that means without effectively accusing them of involvement in a violent stream of attacks culminating in a murder!'

The last word was shouted loudly enough that Ava's eardrums registered the air movement. She told herself to stay calm. Responding to Overbeck by fighting fire with fire was a mistake. Getting back on point was the only option.

'I need a warrant,' Ava said. 'The boys were involved. Davenport was shaken when I explained that this is a murder case. And Alby-Croft was more than just cocky about it – he was enjoying the process. He had a prepared speech and—'

'Just stop,' Overbeck said. 'Stop this crap right now. There are no grounds for a warrant.'

'The key is enough to check Leo Plunkett's phone records. If we can show he was with the other two boys during any of the attacks—'

'Noah Alby-Croft's father will already have instructed a lawyer. The parents of the three boys will, by now, have been in conference with one another. We won't get near those boys again without their fingerprints being found in blood on Ms Long's body. Why the fuck can you never just toe the shitting line, Turner?'

'Toe the line?' Ava stepped closer to her desk. 'That's what you want? That's what you think the Major Investigations Team should do? A woman is dead. Her child has been left without a mother. She took a blade to the eyeball and spun into the path of a bus, but you want me to toe the line? The woman who doesn't have a conscience about bending over her desk for a quick shag with a more junior officer is lecturing me about rules? God, you're a joke.'

'Turner, I swear, if you don't apologise for that right now, I will have your job.'

'No, you won't,' Ava said. 'We're in the middle of a multiple murder and kidnapping situation, with an additional series of violent attacks that has also resulted in a murder. If you sack me now, you're as good as quitting yourself. When did you get so soft? Is that what your promotion did to you? Now you have to suck up to the big boys and go easy on their over-privileged offspring, even when the price is that they will literally get away with murder. You disgust me. I may have been in the job fewer years than you, but perhaps that means I can still remember what it's all about. Did I break the rules? You bet I fucking did. Is the case going to get solved any other way? You know the answer to that. Those boys think they can do whatever they like and Daddy will protect them. After this, you'll be responsible for that. When they feel entitled to hit their wives. When they couldn't give a damn about stealing from their employees' pension funds. When they decide that no means yes at some drunken party and they destroy a girl's life. You make them untouchable now and we're all complicit. We're all guilty. Can you live with that?'

'Get out of my office,' Overbeck said. 'I'm not going to tolerate this. You need to learn to take orders, and understand that the police service has a structure whereby you do what you're told, like it or not. You're going to regret speaking to me like that.'

'You know what, I actually don't think I am,' Ava said, leaving the door swinging as she left.

Chapter Thirty-Two

Kate

Kate was praying as the man entered. She hadn't been inside a church since childhood, yet the words came easily. She lowered her voice to a whisper but continued the Lord's Prayer. It felt wrong to break off in the middle. The words were the only comfort she'd been able to find in the dark and cold. If she thought about her parents and the suffering they would be enduring now, she knew she would lose the will to live.

'For thine is the kingdom, the power and the glory . . .'

'What are you saying?' the man asked.

Kate opened her eyes and stared at him. He spoke so rarely, only to give instructions to eat or move.

'It's the Lord's Prayer,' Kate whispered. Her throat was so dry that normal speech was a strain.

'You dare address the Lord God? A sinner like you? Having brought yourself so low, using your body as an instrument of the devil. How dare you utter his name!' he said, throwing her bowl of food across the room where it hit a dead plant and exploded.

Kate jolted, her heart thumping. She hadn't seen him angry before. Even when she had freed one of her wrists, and he had caught her in the process of releasing her other hand, he had only grunted with mild surprise, then shaken his head as if in wonder at how she'd managed it. She'd paid a high price for her resourcefulness. Finding the sharp edge under the rough wooden table with her fingertips, she'd rubbed and rubbed to fray the twine that bound her. The skin of her wrist had filled with splinters though she'd ignored the pain and continued. It was only pain. She could stand that if the prize was freedom. Only when she'd been discovered, he'd retied her twice as forcefully. The splinters had grown hot beneath the bindings, then the itching had begun. For the first few hours it was simply an annoyance, then her brain had fully understood what she'd done. The splinters, so many of them, were infected. How could they not have been with all the dirt and debris around? Now there was a gross, sticky wetness beneath the bindings as she shifted. The sores on her wrist were suppurating. By the time twenty-four hours had passed, a sickly smell of rot had begun to issue from her arm and a fever had flared. Untreated, it would kill her, although that was a better prospect than lying here slowly fading while the man did just enough to keep her alive.

She wondered if her father would outlive her. His lung disease was reaching a critical point. Her mother had been increasingly unwilling to discuss his prognosis or the frequency of the doctor's visits, and her father's voice as her mother held the phone to his ear was slurred more often than not these days. The painkillers were slowly removing him from the world, which was both terrifying and comforting. All Kate wished was that she had access to the same oblivion before the man finally tired of her, or decided to introduce her to her fate. Being quiet hadn't induced sympathy. Trying to engage the man in conversation had proved pointless. This was the first time she'd seen a shred of human emotion from him. Kate decided she preferred his anger to being ignored. At least his ire might reveal something useful about him.

'I have as much right to speak with God as anyone else,' Kate said. 'More than you, anyway. You're a monster. Look at what you're doing to me. Do you think there's a god in existence who would call this anything but deviancy?'

The man strode across, standing over her, breathing heavily through his nose, eyes wide. 'You are nothing but a whore. You were willing to sell your body to me for no more than a hot meal and a few pounds. The Bible calls you harlot. I call you slut. Sinners like you must be brought to God's holy justice. I only do his bidding.'

'Wasn't Mary Magdalene a prostitute? Even so, Jesus kept her within his closest circle,' Kate said.

'Jesus cast the demons out of her,' the man yelled. 'She was repentant. You are covered in sin. You stink of it. It crawls over your flesh like maggots.'

'You think I wanted to sleep with you?' Kate shrieked. 'You really believe that I was happy to degrade myself by playing along with the idea that I chose to be with you? I needed the money to help support my parents. My father is dying! You want repentance, here it is. I regret all of it. Every single second. I regret having to wash my mouth out after foul men who repulse me shoved their tongues in it. I had to tolerate hours of old married pigs describing the things they wanted to do to me. I wanted to take my own life after one man tied me up and made me call him daddy. There is nothing, not one thing, I don't hate about what I've done. Except that I've eased my parents' burden. And if I had to, I'd do it all again. For them.'

The man blinked, frowned, his face slackening and softening. He reached a trembling hand towards the bindings on her ankle, his thumb and forefinger working the knot slowly. Then he lifted his head.

'Such a fool. I remember now. I was told this would happen. The silver tongue is inside you. You speak the devil's lies. And look. Look at me, believing you, letting you worm into my soul. Pure souls are the most easily fooled, and as the Lord is my witness, you are the most sly snake I have ever known.' He fell to his knees, arms extended, palms towards the ceiling, head lolling back as if he were looking directly into God's eyes.

In his eyes shone a madness so ferocious that Kate wondered how stupid she had been not to have seen it the second she'd walked up to him. As he knelt there, muttering words she could barely make out, begging an unseen deity for guidance and strength, Kate indulged in a momentary fantasy.

She had been persuaded to go out with friends to watch the University team play rugby, and therefore had never met the ridiculously pseudonymed John White. In a parallel universe, the SugarPa website had crashed for several days, making it impossible for her to arrange any meetings that week, thereby avoiding a trap that would deprive her of her life. Then her favourite imagining – that she had spent her last pound after doing her weekly food shop on a lottery ticket, which had unbelievably, astoundingly, left her with a hundred thousand pounds. She was unwilling to fantasise about a figure greater than that. It seemed to be inviting divine retribution. She imagined logging off from SugarPa for the last time, taking the train back to see her parents in Durham and presenting them with the cheque that would make all their lives – or at least what was left of her father's – that little bit easier.

But none of those realities were hers. Kate had spent three previous dates seeing a man who promised hundreds of pounds for her company, and who had instead decided to buy her a bracelet. When she'd taken it back to the shop, all they were willing to do was offer her a voucher to spend there in the sum of eighty-five pounds. In the end, she'd taken the bracelet to a pawnshop who had given her sixty pounds in cash.

The money had gone directly into an envelope to her parents. It would buy her mother a few hours of overnight care, so she could actually sleep. The harsh reality of being a full-time carer was that you neglected your own health to such a degree that both parties inevitably ended up ill. Kate worried constantly, as much about her mother as her father. The problem was that sending sixty pounds had left her short of the money she needed for food. So, in spite of all she'd gone through, in spite of how much she hated the use to which she was putting her body, she had logged back on to the SugarPa site. The system had not crashed. In fact, there was a new user who was incredibly keen to meet her.

The red umbrella had seemed old-fashioned, and the idea of meeting in the shopping centre was a good sign. Better than being picked up on some street corner. They would have a chance to walk and talk, for Kate to get the measure of him, perhaps even chat over a coffee. They weren't all bad. Not that they were using the site to find a life partner or because they respected women, but it wasn't all desperation and fat bellies. Still, she'd been through enough bad experiences to be wary.

He had seemed normal. Not trying too hard, not looking her up and down, not creepy. Her one thought, as they'd walked out of the mall, was that he seemed lonely. He'd given her money to buy each of them a takeaway coffee from a small cafe, but waited outside, explaining that he didn't like too much noise. She'd complied. He claimed to have made a reservation for a meal at a nice pub just outside the city. At the time, she'd been hungry, and the thought of a decent three-course meal, maybe even a couple of glasses of wine, was welcome. His car was a bit of a mess, but he'd explained that his other vehicle was being serviced. Still she hadn't suspected anything. Even hindsight hadn't revealed any clues she should have picked up on. Perhaps he was a little too quiet. Perhaps the other men before him had been more curious about her.

They were driving into the small village where he'd said the pub was, and past a lovely looking country inn, before Kate got the feeling that things weren't going to plan. He had begun to sweat by then, and it was cold in the minivan. She wondered if he was nervous, but that was ridiculous. He hadn't seemed nervous when he'd met her. She clarified again which pub they were going to and he changed the name. The Queen's Head became the Queen's Arms, or the other way around. It was enough for warning bells to sound. Then there was the change of story. He had forgotten his wallet, he'd said. They would just have to visit his house quickly to fetch it. Only that wasn't right, because he'd handed her a five-pound note from his wallet to buy the coffee earlier.

Kate suggested that he drop her to the pub first so she could make sure they didn't lose their table, then he could join her when he came back. That was a waste of time, he replied. Faster for them to stick together. She told herself she was imagining danger, overreacting, a reflex from past ill treatment. The atmosphere inside the minivan wasn't helping. As they'd travelled, an odour had become apparent, perhaps with the increasing heat from the engine, but this she knew was no figment of her nervous mind. The top note was antiseptic, sharp and acidic, but a truer stench lay beneath – all copper, sulphur and rotting red meat.

She pretended illness, that old chestnut, and it didn't matter to her that he might realise she was lying. What mattered was how he reacted to the lie. What man would force her to continue a date knowing that she didn't want to be there?

'Well,' he said. 'We're nearly at my place now. Only another minute or so. I'll stop off and fetch my wallet anyway, then drive you back to the city.'

'But you already have your wallet,' she said. There. She was pleased that she'd been brave and direct about it. 'I saw it when you asked me to get you a coffee.' She waited. And waited. When he didn't respond, she wondered if she was misreading him. 'Did you hear me?' she asked. 'Um, you know what, just pull over. I'll find my own way back. No need to put you out.' He didn't look at her. Didn't respond. 'Stop the car,' Kate said. 'Right now.'

The man turned a corner into a private driveway. The gravel tracks went past a house and into woods behind, turning to dirt. Then they were driving across down-trodden grass and nettles. By then Kate was beyond scared. Something skittered through her veins like a many-legged insect, making her shiver, rendering her nauseous. She grabbed the door handle. They weren't going too fast. She wouldn't be badly hurt. It was time to jump and run. Wrenching the handle backwards, she prepared for the shock of the door flying open. The only result was three broken nails and a bruised wrist. She tried it again. And again.

'Won't open,' the man said. He applied the brakes and finally turned to look at her.

Kate didn't waste the opportunity, too aware that it suddenly felt like her last. She folded her right elbow in, drew it across her chest sharply to get some driving force behind it, then slammed it as hard as she could into the man's throat, making him choke and gasp. As he fought for breath, she pushed between the front seats into the rear of the minivan, trying the door on the left, then the door on the right. Finally, she pushed to the very back, throwing her body weight against the boot and fiddling around to find the lock release. The hiking boot caught her directly on the right temple. Kate had time to register the

278

blurring of her eyesight and a flash of blinding pain that ran from her forehead, down her neck and into her shoulder. When she regained consciousness, she had been tied to a long wooden table, wearing what felt like a hospital gown, with her ankles and wrists tied at each corner to the table legs. Since then, every minute had felt like a day, every day a lifetime.

The man had stopped mumbling his prayer now, Kate realised. He was standing again, staring down at her, and he was trembling.

'You're a bad girl, just like the others,' he said, spittle flying from his lips to glisten on his chin. Kate looked away. 'Say it. Admit you're a bad girl.'

Kate said nothing. It was insanity. Whatever she said would be twisted. He lifted his hand and took hold of her right ankle, squeezing hard. Kate bit down on her bottom lip, rather than give him the satisfaction of crying out. The prickly numbness of her right ankle became agony when it was touched. She had long since ceased to feel her toes.

'Such a bad girl. Worse than the others. You sinned through choice. You sinned through laziness.' He moved his hand slowly upwards, on the outside of her leg, reaching her knee.

'Don't touch me,' Kate said. 'Don't do that.'

He laughed. 'Isn't this what you get paid for? You let men touch you all the time. What's different about this?'

'Permission,' Kate said. 'I'm saying no.' Even to her it felt ridiculous. He would do what he wanted. Surviving it was more important than getting into an argument about consent, and still she couldn't seem to stop herself.

'Bad girl,' he said, breathing heavily. 'God sent me to collect you to his side. He wants me to teach you a lesson. Fire with fire. Like with like.'

'Get the fuck off me,' Kate yelled, as he lifted the hem of the white gown she was wearing, revealing her nakedness

279

beneath. When he spread the cold cream on her stomach, then slid his hand beneath to do the same to her back, he kept her gown in place and his eyes closed. His touch was brief, impersonal. This was different. The threat – his intention – was absolutely clear.

'You must understand the wickedness of your harlotry,' he panted, staring between her legs, pulling frantically at his own belt.

'You fucking bastard,' Kate shouted. 'Help! Somebody help me!' She had screamed before and no one had heard her. She didn't believe anyone would come now either. But it was better than lying there, waiting to be raped. 'I'm being attacked! Police. Call the police!'

He let his trousers fall to his ankles, kicking off his shoes and pushing his underwear downwards, a condom in his hand. Kate's cheeks were wet, and she felt a moment of self-loathing for allowing her distress to betray her and hand him the victory.

'No,' she sobbed. 'No. No.'

Condom on, he began to climb onto the table, his hands all over her thighs. At least part of her was numb. It was the tiniest consolation. Her abdomen and back were sensation-free from the regular applications of cream, increasingly more frequent and in larger amounts in the last day. He began to lower himself down. Kate turned her face away, wondering how long it would take and if, when he had finished, he would also be finished with her completely.

The door flew open. 'Sam! What the hell are you doing to that girl?' a woman yelled. 'Get off her! Get off her right now.' Kate stared, caught in confusion. She hadn't dreamed that anyone would hear her cries.

'Help me,' she shouted. 'Please, please, please . . .'

The woman ran at the man, grabbing a shovel from a corner of the hut as she came, hitting him with it around the shoulders.

He fell off the table, sideways. Kate heard the crack of his knees and elbows hitting the hard ground, praying he had hurt himself badly enough that he would be slow to get up.

'Untie me,' Kate yelled. 'My name's Kate. We have to get to the police.'

The woman had moved round to the side of the table where the man was still on the floor. He was groaning, face to the floor, writhing in the cold dirt. The woman abandoned the shovel and was thumping and slapping him with her bare hands.

'Defiling yourself. Did you think I wouldn't hear? Did you really believe I wouldn't find out? How dare you be so weak,' the woman ranted.

'What?' Kate muttered.

The woman stood up, taking a gentle hold of the hem of Kate's gown and pulling it back down to cover her again.

'Did the devil in you ask him to do that?' the woman asked. She tutted, shaking her head. 'I should have known. You're an experienced temptress. He could never have had the strength to fight the demon once it spoke through you. But it's over now. I can help you.'

'Who are you?' Kate asked. 'I need you to untie me. He's held me here for days . . .'

'Not as long as we wanted you for,' the woman said. 'But apparently there were a number of police cars at the internet cafe, which can only mean one thing. Your time with us has to come to an earlier end. My schedule of prayers has been shortened, but the Lord will understand. He works through us for your sake, and to set an example to other sinners.'

'Why would you do this?' Kate slurred, panic and adrenaline making the room spin above her.

'It's our calling,' the woman said. 'To save those girls who turn from God's grace, those girls who defy him, those girls who break his laws and indulge in sin. We had one such girl ourselves, consumed by demons. We swore then to send her back to God, and to save other such lost souls.'

'I'm not lost,' Kate said. 'I was trying to help my parents, you have to understand, I never wanted—'

'Excuses come not from God.' The woman laid a hand on Kate's forehead. 'You will be reborn. You will be baptised again in God's purity and love.'

'What are you talking about?' Kate whispered.

The woman walked to the far end of the shed, where she opened a wooden box and unrolled a leather tool belt. Her dark hair, starting to grey, was pinned in a neat bun on her head. She had soft features and a voice that could have been grand-motherly but for the craziness of her words, and a slim frame with neat clothes.

A glint of light came as she held up her hand.

'Gag her,' the woman ordered. The man finally got himself up out of the dirt, taking a rag from his pocket and stuffing it into Kate's mouth.

The woman walked closer, pulling up Kate's gown once more to reveal her stomach. She placed a bag of bandages on the table beneath Kate's legs.

'You'll be unconscious in no time,' she said. 'The pain will cleanse your soul and the merciful Father will see to it that you do not suffer any more than you deserve.'

Kate tried to scream, but gagged on the cloth. The woman put something onto her abdomen, some flexible material, like a stiff cloth, before holding the scalpel to the light.

'The rebirth of the sinner, in the name of our sweet Jesus. Suffer the little children . . .'

Kate's eyes widened. She began to scream again as the woman lowered the blade, the man watching by her side. They prayed together as the woman cut her.

Chapter Thirty-Three

Callanach stared out of the window from the penthouse apartment on Western Harbour Drive. Selina had insisted on cooking him a meal when she'd found out how long it had been since he'd eaten anything but sandwiches and take-out. Her flat had stunning sea views, as well as a glimpse of the Royal Yacht *Britannia* that countless tourists would have paid good money for. To the north of Leith, the docks had seen a facelift, which left the area too expensive for local families while expanding the upper reach of the city to house businesses and savvy commuters. As much as he enjoyed being able to lose himself in the push and pull of the angry autumn tide, he could only afford an hour away from his desk. He'd already stopped at his flat to grab a change of clothes, and now had just about enough time to shower before he had to get back to his squad. They were still sifting through hours of CCTV footage and chasing up reports of possible vehicles that matched the description from the owner of the internet cafe.

His mobile rang just as he was stripping to get into the shower. 'Sir, a woman's been found, believed to be Kate Bailey. She's still alive. Address is 94 Ocean Drive,' Tripp said.

Callanach shouted the address to Selina. 'It's just down there,' she replied. 'You'd be able to see it if Ocean Terminal wasn't in the way.'

He sprinted, using the stairs rather than waiting for the lifts, throwing himself into his car, tyres squealing as he pulled away. He was applying the brakes again a minute later, abandoning his car between an ambulance and a marked police car, sirens closing in from every side. Leaving his car door hanging open, he ran, diving under the first stretch of crime scene tape and thrusting his ID into the hands of the officer who tried to stop him.

Paramedics were unloading a stretcher next to a limp heap on the ground, as one of them applied pressure to wounds that were never going to stop bleeding.

'Out of my way,' Callanach shouted. 'Move.'

'We're treating her. You can't speak to her until she's stable,' a paramedic said.

Callanach ignored them, landing heavily on the ground at the girl's head and lifting her gently until she was cradled in his lap. 'Kate,' he said softly. Her eyes flickered. 'Kate, you're safe. We're taking you to a hospital.'

The girl groaned. Her fingers danced in the air, grasping nothing. Callanach slid his hand into hers. 'Dirty,' she said. 'Cold.'

The paramedics continued their work, adding an additional blanket then sliding an intravenous drip into her arm and securing it with tape, even as her head lolled back in Callanach's arms.

'I spoke to your mother,' Callanach said, as Kate's breathing turned from shallow to rasping. Her eyes opened, darting left and right before finding his. 'She's so proud of you, Kate. Of what you've done to help your father.' Kate's mouth opened and closed but no sound would come. So much blood was spilled on the pavement around her that Callanach couldn't look at it. He kept his eyes fixed on hers. 'Is there anything you can tell me, Kate? We want to find the man who did this to you.'

Kate muttered incomprehensibly.

'You have to leave her alone,' the paramedic ordered. 'We need to get her on the stretcher.'

'Can she make it?' Tripp's voice sounded above Callanach's head.

'No,' the other paramedic said quietly.

'Then let him ask. It's the most we can do for her now,' Tripp responded with calm authority.

'W . . .' Kate's mouth scrunched together with the effort of making the letter.

'Again Kate,' Callanach said, stroking her hair and smiling into her eyes. 'Tell me about the man.'

'Wom . . .' Kate managed. 'Wom . . .'

'Kate, we need a name. Did you hear his name at all? Or initials? Do you know the place where you were being held?' Callanach persisted.

She coughed, her body shaking brutally in his arms. Her head was hot in spite of the freezing night and her lack of clothing. As she drew breath to speak, her lungs emitted a bubbling sound. The paramedics' eyes met and they shook their heads.

'Don't worry,' Callanach told her, stroking her hair and her cheek.

'Sam,' Kate said, a stream of blood accompanying the word as she forced it from her mouth.

She faded. There was no drama to it. The baby-strength grip she'd had on Callanach's fingers melted away. Her head became a dead weight in his arms. The rolling of her eyes heavenwards marked her release from the terror and pain of the last few days. Callanach couldn't control his instinct to

285

hold her tight, whatever damage he was doing to the scene and the forensics. He wrapped her butchered body in his and held her while the paramedics declared what they already knew. Kate Bailey was gone.

Ava arrived at the same time as Jonty Spurr. They walked to Callanach together, quietly, as if the road between the terminal building and a high-rise office block was a church rather than converted dockland. SOCOs worked around them respectfully, photographing the girl in Callanach's arms, preserving the evidence on the ground, preparing a body bag. Callanach stayed where he was, knowing his clothes would have to be taken, waiting for the reality of what he'd done to hit him. Fifty yards down the street, a girl was sobbing. The night sky flickered blue and red against an expanse of vertical glass. Kate Bailey lay softly in his arms.

'Luc,' Ava said. 'We're going to move her now, but we need to do some photography without you there, as she was when you found her. I'm going to help you up.' She extended a gloved hand as other officers supported Kate's corpse, lowering it carefully back to the ground as Callanach slid away. He stood up, then stepped onto the evidence mat that had been placed beside him to capture any debris or trace materials that might have been transferred to his clothes or shoes. Ava waited patiently without talking as his outer clothes were processed, his hands were swabbed and he pulled on a set of white overalls.

Jonty knelt by Kate's body, lifting the hospital gown away to inspect her injuries, taking her temperature and looking carefully at one of her wrists.

'What is it?' Ava asked, as Callanach finished with the forensics team.

'Her wrist is dreadfully infected. These lines, like tiny veins, show that the infection has reached all the way up to the armpit.

'I'll have to look under the microscope, as the inflammation and pus are masking the original wound, but I'd say this is the work of an infected cut or graze, and I can see debris left in the wound.'

'I'm sorry,' Callanach murmured to Ava.

'What for?' she asked, taking hold of his arm and leading him away from the body to the shelter of the side of an office block.

'Barging into a crime scene. Making things harder than they already are. It was unprofessional,' he said.

'Kate was still alive when you got here,' Ava replied. 'Of course you ignored the crime scene and did what needed to be done for her. Who's to say any of it would have made any difference.'

'She died in my arms,' Callanach said. 'And she knew she was dying. All I could do was tell her how proud her parents are of her.'

Ava stepped close to him, gripping his arm tightly. 'Kate Bailey died looking into the eyes of a man who was protecting her. She wasn't terrified, or distressed. She wasn't alone. You did what any good police officer would have done. You cared for the person before caring about the crime scene. I've already got CCTV teams looking for the van at all the key city inter-sections. Did she say anything to you that might help us?'

'She was almost incomprehensible, but she said what sounded like the word "womb" a couple of times, also "dirty" and "cold". At the very end, when I asked her for a name, Kate said "Sam". That was all I got.'

'It's a good start. What about a timeline? Do we know when she was found?' Ava asked.

'There was a girl crying when I arrived. A civilian.' Callanach looked around. 'Over there, the other side of the roundabout.' He pointed. They crossed the road together, towards the front of the cruise terminal building, which housed a variety of shops and restaurants.

The young woman was distraught. Two officers were with her and a blanket had been draped over her shoulders to ward off the inevitable shock. She was perched on a concrete bollard, her face a patchwork of pale skin and streaked mascara.

Ava knelt in front of her and introduced herself.

'I'm Erin Hendry,' the young woman responded. 'Is she . . .'

'Dead. I'm afraid so. Was it you who called the police?'

'Yes. I stayed late at work on a conference call with a couple of different time zones. I was walking to my car when I heard someone groaning. I came round the corner from the front entrance of the office and she was lying on the pavement. To start with I thought it was some sort of stupid, late Halloween prank, you know? Then I saw all the blood all over the road.' She sobbed, her eyes wandering up the street to where Kate's body, currently in the process of being moved, had been.

'Where do you work, Erin?' Ava asked.

She pointed to the nearest office block, several floors up. 'I'm a public relations manager for VisitScotland.'

Ava sighed. The irony would have been laughable had the tragedy not been so horrific.

'Did you see a vehicle at all?' Callanach asked.

'No. The area was deserted. There's rarely anyone on this road late at night.'

'So he knew the chances of being spotted were low,' Callanach commented. 'Erin, are you familiar with the history of this area?'

'Sure,' she said, looking surprised. 'It's always been docklands. Industrial, mostly. A war port at times. It dates back to medieval times.'

'Is there anything about this place that might link it to prostitution?' Ava asked.

Erin blinked hard, looking confused, then concentrating. 'All docks have a history of prostitution, I guess, but after the Second World War there was considered to be a need to clean up the area. Prostitution was a concern back then. The history of Leith docks is well documented.'

'That explains his choice of venue,' Ava said to Callanach. 'We'll make sure you get home safely, Erin. I'm sorry for what you witnessed.'

'Did you find what she dropped?' Erin asked.

'I'm not sure what you're talking about,' Callanach said. 'Did you hand it to a police officer?'

'No, it was near where she was lying. She opened her hand when I first ran over to her, only when I stood up to call for help she must have let it go. I didn't see it again. I'm so sorry. Was it important?' Erin asked, her eyes filling with fresh tears.

'Can you describe what you saw?' Callanach asked.

'It was covered in blood, but parts of it were green, I think, although the lighting isn't great at night. The end seemed to be some sort of spike,' she replied.

'It was definitely in her hand? It wasn't just on the road next to her?' Ava said.

'No, when I ran up to her she looked me in the eyes then opened her palm, as if she was showing it to me, only I was too scared about her injuries to pay any attention. I had to move away from her to get bars on my mobile and call for help,' Erin explained.

Callanach and Ava walked back across the roundabout and the few yards up the road. Now that Kate's body had been moved, the SOCOs were in the process of collecting evidence from the tarmac. There was nothing visible left on the ground.

'Hold on,' Callanach said, walking over to an officer and borrowing a torch. Leaning down, facing into the edge of the pavement where he'd sat with Kate in his arms, he directed the torch beam into the small semicircular drainage holes that punctuated the side of the concrete every half metre or so. 'There. Hold on.' He called over a forensics officer and requested an evidence bag. Using slim plastic tongs, he pulled out what looked like a piece of rubbish from within the small drain. 'What is it?' he asked, holding up a gore-covered green spike with a horizontal clip across the top.

Ava stepped closer to inspect it. 'Not what I would have expected. It's a plant marker. You put it into a pot after planting something like a herb, so you can remember what the seed or cutting was. She brought it to help us find him.' She took the evidence bag from Callanach's hand. 'Clever girl, even in all the pain and fear.'

'That won't be any comfort to her parents,' Luc said.

'It won't,' she said, 'but I'm going to find the bastard who did this to her, and I hope he fights or runs or does something that makes me entitled to grab the nearest sharp object and shove it through his neck, because no sentence any court will give him can make up for what he's done.'

'Nothing can,' Callanach said. 'Not even death. All we can do is find him and make absolutely sure he can't hurt anyone else.'

It was 2 a.m. before they left the scene. In fewer than six hours, the next victim was due to be taken.

Chapter Thirty-Four

'We have a possible name for the suspect. Kate Bailey said "Sam", so we're looking for the full version, Samuel, in vehicle licensing. Double-check with the DVLA for minivans registered to a male of that name in this area. We know that the vehicle left Leith travelling in a westerly direction. We last picked it up on Queensferry Road. It has not been identified getting onto any motorways so we're assuming he took minor roads to his final destination. Once again, the few sightings we have of the van indicate that the licence plates are still muddied and un-readable. The CCTV sightings are some fifteen minutes after Kate was found, which means she survived for a substantial period after being dropped off,' Ava said.

'So did the killer miscalculate or is he getting more daring?' DC Tripp asked.

'My gut feeling is that it was a miscalculation. I don't think he'd have left her if he'd known she was still able to communi-cate. It might be that she was unconscious when he dropped her off, and he wrongly assumed she would not regain consciousness, or that she was faking it. Given that she managed to smuggle the plant marker out, I strongly suspect that Kate was playing dead in order to survive long enough to provide information,' Ava finished.

'How did she do that? Surely the killer would have noticed if she'd had the plant marker in her hand,' Tripp said.

Ava glanced down at her notes, more to give herself a moment to think about how to phrase the answer than to refresh her mind of the facts. A decade could pass and that particular detail would be just as crisp in her mind.

'Dr Spurr found some disturbance to the wound packing in Kate's abdomen and some dirt inside the wound itself.' Ava frowned, trying to keep her voice even. 'We believe she might have shoved the plant marker into the wound beneath the packing while the killer was distracted, then continued to feign unconsciousness.'

'Brave kid,' Lively said, as the scene etched itself into the imagination of every person at the briefing.

'Indeed,' said Ava. 'Brave, but very much aware of what had happened to her and of what her assailant was intending to do next, I believe. So let's repay Kate's courage and quick thinking by finding the animal who butchered her before he kills again.'

'We're assuming he drove further this time, if he's coming into the city from the west, and yet Kate obviously coped with the journey better. Do we know why?' Salter asked.

'Dr Spurr says the cuts were shallower and that the wound packing was much more effective. This is a learning-curve killer, who is improving their surgical skills each time. Also, Kate was delivered back to us earlier than expected. We don't know why, but one theory is that our enquiries have been noticed,' Ava said. 'We got closer than he likes, and he panicked.'

'But not enough to just kill Kate and dump her body without attracting attention,' Lively chipped in.

'No, not enough for that. We know this killer is driven and

obsessive. We think he is operating under what he believes to be a biblical mandate. Kate suffered exactly the same wounds as Zoey and Lorna, so we can assume we are waiting to find another doll. Kate Bailey's identity will be revealed to the press later this morning, once her parents have been moved from their usual address to a friend's house. I will not allow them to be dragged into a media circus. If Mr and Mrs Bailey wish to release a statement, they will do so through the Police Scotland media team.'

'Was Kate raped, like Lorna?' Tripp asked quietly.

'She was not,' Ava said. 'No solid theory on that except that perhaps the killer kept better control of himself, or something about Lorna appealed in a different way than the other two women. There's no evidence of sexual assault at all, but given the wounds and circumstantial evidence, there is no doubt that this is all the work of the same person.'

'Ma'am,' PC Biddlecombe hissed from the doorway. Ava held a finger up to her. Whatever it was would have to wait until she was finished briefing the team. Biddlecombe had three fingernails jammed into her mouth and was chewing frantically.

'It's now 7.45 a.m. Later this morning DI Callanach and I will be attending the City Mortuary to go through the post-mortem findings and so—'

'Ma'am, please, I was told . . .' Biddlecombe muttered, jiggling on the spot.

'What is it, Constable?' Ava asked her.

'You're wanted,' Biddlecombe blurted. 'By Superintendent Overlord. Overbeck. Oh my God.' The whole room turned to stare at Biddlecombe's crimson face.

'Tell the detective superintendent that I'll be up in a minute,' Ava replied softly.

'Not here,' Biddlecombe said in the direction of the floor. 'Over at the Fettes Avenue offices. They're waiting for you right

293

now. The super said that DI Callanach was to take over from you with immediate effect.'

The incident room quietened to something worse than silence, closer to a vacuum.

Callanach stood up. 'Lively, allocate roles,' he said. 'I'll walk you to your car,' he told Ava.

She sighed, grabbing her bag and coat from a chair and striding from the room. 'I don't have time for Overbeck to throw a strop now,' she muttered as they took the stairs.

'What's it about?' Callanach asked.

'A row, yesterday, about my handling of the Melanie Long murder, and the super's failure to have any moral backbone,' Ava said. 'I should have known she'd do this. That woman really can't take criticism.'

'Just how much criticism did you aim at her?' Callanach asked.

'Oh, you know . . . some,' Ava said. 'I should be back within the hour. She's going to haul me over the coals, let me know who's boss. Threaten to demote me. I'm guessing she's organised a disciplinary board, by the book. Just don't get distracted. I need to keep Salter and a couple of other officers on the Long case. Her family deserves answers just as much as the other girls' do.'

'Meet me at the mortuary then?' Callanach asked. 'I can come with you, if it'll help. Back up your assessment of the case. It might be better to present a show of force from the squad.'

'Not necessary,' Ava said. 'This is a storm in a teacup. I'll eat some humble pie, get a bollocking, nothing I haven't had before. I need you here to keep the squad on track. See you shortly.'

She climbed into her car, cursing her big mouth. It had been obvious that Overbeck wasn't going to tolerate her much longer, especially given what she knew about DS Lively, and yet still

Ava had been unable to stop herself fighting back. Overbeck wanted her pound of flesh. So be it. All Ava wanted was to get on with the job.

Twenty minutes later she was being shown along a top-floor corridor by a civilian who looked nothing less than terrified. Detective Superintendent Overbeck had that effect on people. Pausing just long enough to turn her mobile to silent and run her fingers through out-of-control hair, she pushed the door handle down hard and walked into the conference room.

Six men and two women – Overbeck was one of them – sat around a conference table. The Police Scotland board had indeed been summoned. A secretary sat poised to take notes in a corner and breakfast had been delivered by caterers. This was no impromptu meeting then. It had been organised the night before, and yet no one had seen fit to advise Ava of it until twenty minutes earlier. She seethed beneath a calm facade. Overbeck meant business. This was no normal disciplinary meeting, that might get passed over as a blip in her record.

'Good morning,' Ava said with a smile, taking a seat at the end of the table where a single chair had been left for her and a glass half filled with ice water was already leaving a mark on the polished wooden surface.

'DCI Turner, thank you for joining us,' the chairman began. He glanced over to check the secretary was making notes, then cleared his throat and continued. 'Would you like coffee before we commence?'

'Actually, I have work to do, so let's get started,' Ava said.

'That's exactly why this meeting's been called.' His eyes darted around the table. 'We have become increasingly concerned with the lack of progress in the murders MIT is currently investigating. I gather a third body was found last night.'

'It was. The missing woman, Kate Bailey, was left in a near

dead state at Ocean Terminal. She died at the scene in the early hours of the morning,' Ava reported.

'Is it definitely the work of the same man who killed the other two girls?' the chair asked.

'Without a doubt,' Ava replied.

'The prognosis for his detainment?' the woman next to her butted in.

'He's killed three times in under three weeks. We have DNA from a hair in Zoey's case, so if we pick up the murderer we will be able to identify him with certainty, and link the other two deaths to him also. We also have a description of his vehicle. We believe he lives in the area to the west of the city. There is even video footage of him, although his face is obscured and his body shape is difficult to make out because of a large overcoat.'

'And yet,' another man said, lips curling, the mockery resonant in his voice, 'your squad has still been unable to apprehend him, in spite of the building amount of peripheral evidence. Perhaps, DCI Turner, that is because you have distracted yourself with a less high-profile case? One it might be easier to find scapegoats for?'

Ava looked directly to Overbeck, who stared out of the window.

'MIT is currently investigating two cases. The second involves two serious incidents of assault to severe injury with a third victim who was assaulted so badly, she ended up falling into the path of a bus. Melanie Long is dead, leaving a grieving partner and young son. I don't regard either of those cases as being more or less high profile than the other. The perpetrators of both are dangerous, and constitute an ongoing threat to the people of Edinburgh,' Ava said. Her voice was quiet enough that the board members were leaning forward to hear her words. Beneath the table, her hands were fists in her lap. If Overbeck thought she could get rid of her like this, she might as well go down fighting.

'I'm sure Mr Alby-Croft didn't mean to imply that one case was less important than the other, although I believe last night's victim was studying at the University here. We certainly don't want others to be put off regarding Edinburgh as a safe place to visit or study.' The chairperson attempted a smile.

'Am I supposed to allocate resources depending on the victim's IQ?' Ava asked. 'Or is it that the board believes the loss of a few drug users is not a particularly big deal? I can see your point. Eradicate both the homeless problem and the drug problem in one fell swoop. Why would you want me to solve that particular crime?'

'DCI Turner, you are overstepping,' Overbeck said.

'I'm drawing a conclusion from what I'm hearing. That's a different thing. I thought I was being paid for my analytical and investigative skills,' Ava said.

'It's pity, then, that you were unable to use them effectively enough to save Kate Bailey's life,' Mr Alby-Croft interjected.

Ava swung her gaze across the table to meet his. She wondered if he had approached Overbeck, or vice versa. Clearly it suited both their purposes to have her ousted as soon as possible. A war was raging inside her, between honesty and diplomacy, or perhaps between pride and acceptance. Her conscience ached from having let Kate down. Ava had spent an hour on the phone to Natasha overnight, breaking the news of the young woman's death. Natasha had been heartbroken, and all Ava could do was hang on the end of the line and listen to her tears and self-recrimination. But Natasha hadn't been tasked with saving Kate's life. That job had been Ava's, and she had failed.

'Did your concerns arise before or after I questioned your son in relation to the Melanie Long murder, Mr Alby-Croft?' Ava asked him.

'If you mean before or after you approached my son to see if he had any potentially useful witness information to provide, as that is what you told his headmaster, then the answer is afterwards. It simply alerted me to the fact that you seem to be wasting police time and resources rather than achieving results.'

Like father, like son. Smug, well prepared, devious. Everything Overbeck needed to help her get Ava dismissed.

'My squad is working to capacity investigating both sets of offences. We are using uniformed officers to conduct on-the-street enquiries and civilians are checking non-sensitive information such as CCTV. Your son, Mr Alby-Croft, might have proved a very important witness. My visit to Leverhulme School was far from a waste of time. In fact, I believe there might be a link between the students there and the perpetrators of the offences.'

'Do you have evidence to support that theory?' the chairman asked.

'Some. Not enough to charge anyone, but what we found could not be ignored,' Ava said.

'So you're telling the board that you have evidence in both cases and yet you still haven't been able to pursue either to a significant conclusion,' Alby-Croft said. 'Perhaps, DCI Turner, you are out of your depth. That is what the board has been convened to consider today. We appreciate you have risen through the ranks with considerable speed. Our concern is whether or not Police Scotland is now feeling the rather unfortunate effect of style over substance.'

'I would like to add . . .' Overbeck said.

'Just a minute,' Ava said, pushing her chair back from the table and standing up. 'I have something to say. Police work is not applying a mathematical theory to a set of known quantities. It requires psychology. It takes time. Yes, it's frustrating and slow, not to mention imperfect. More often than not, an investigation follows false leads before stumbling onto the path that takes us forward, but good police officers recognise the value of the false leads. We fill our time, rather than waiting for the answer to fall into our laps. Real life does not resemble an episode of a *CSI* television show. The answer isn't always in the forensics. The vast majority of serial murders are solved only when the killer makes a mistake. The problem is that until you can see the pattern clearly, you don't know what the mistakes are. My squad are dedicated and tireless. They are building up a picture of the man we're looking for – physically, emotionally, his actions and needs – and we will find him. Rest assured, I will also find those responsible for Melanie Long's death. I have not, at any stage, prioritised one investigation to the detriment of the other.'

'We believe we can help you with that,' the chair said. 'Having heard all you have to say, it seems to me that our discussions prior to this meeting are an appropriate way forward.'

Ava watched as Overbeck pulled her mobile from her handbag and began texting. She didn't even bother to look up as Ava's sentence was pronounced.

'As the Major Investigation Team is currently operating short of one detective inspector, we are redefining roles for the purpose of the investigations. Detective Superintendent Overbeck has kindly offered to step into the Melanie Long investigations with hour-by-hour practical and operational control of the squad. You, DCI Turner, are relieved of control of that investigation. We feel this will leave you freer to focus your efforts on the Kate Bailey enquiry.'

'You're taking all the assaults out of my hands?' Ava asked.

'We are,' the chair replied, taking a sip of his coffee and studying the bottom of his cup.

'May I ask whose idea that was?' Ava asked.

'It's the board's decision,' Alby-Croft said. 'Agreed unanimously.'

'It is not intended as a slight to you,' the chair said quickly.

'Merely to ensure that both cases are handled with the greatest possible efficacy.'

'And who is to be on Detective Superintendent Overbeck's squad?' Ava asked.

As one, all the heads at the table turned towards Overbeck, who folded her arms and directed her answer towards the chairman. 'DC Salter, DS Lively, a number of uniformed officers. I shouldn't like to take any more of DCI Turner's core squad members from her than that.'

'I bet,' Ava muttered.

Overbeck glared at her.

'Well, I'm glad we've reached an agreed resolution,' the chair said, as if they'd spent the previous minutes discussing who would organise the next Police Scotland social event. 'DCI Turner, we recognise how busy you are. Please don't let us keep you any longer, and feel free to come to us should you need our further guidance.'

Ava resisted the desire to reply but kept her thoughts on Kate Bailey, waiting for her on a cold metal tray at the mortuary.

'Thank you,' she said, picking up her bag from the floor and pulling her car keys from her pocket.

Chapter Thirty-Five

Caroline Ryan's chair sat empty at the 9 a.m. meeting, which had been scheduled four weeks previously. The architectural firm for which she worked had spent the best part of a year preparing plans, unpaid, to pitch for a massive contract regenerating an old industrial site, which city planners hoped would create jobs, attract shoppers and tourists and spread wealth. It wasn't merely an important day for Sky's the Limit Architects. It was make or break.

At 8.30 a.m. Caroline had officially been late for the pre-pitch meeting. At 8.35 a.m., texts to locate her were sent. The managing director had been nothing short of furious by 8.50 a.m., and personally called Caroline's mobile, which was switched off, then her home. Her fiancé, Jadyn Odoki, answered. By 9.05 a.m. he was on the telephone to the Police Scotland switchboard.

'She left here at seven thirty this morning,' he said, for the tenth time. 'It's now after nine o'clock. It's only a twenty-minute journey to her office, and that's if the traffic lights are against her. She wanted to get in early today.'

'Sir, I'm sorry. There's not much we can do. Miss Ryan has

only been missing for an hour and a half. I'm sure there's an explanation. Your girlfriend might just have gone for coffee and lost track of the time,' the switchboard operator replied.

'She's my fiancée, and this is the most important day of her career. If there was an explanation, she'd have phoned either the office or me,' Jadyn said.

'It sounds to me as if that might have been quite stressful. Maybe she just decided to go somewhere to clear her head, or made a different decision about going to the meeting. The best thing to do would be for you to wait at home for her. I'm sure—'

'Put me through to someone else,' Jadyn said.

'Sir, you'll be given the same advice that I've already—'

'Just put me through. Now,' he ordered.

'The phone lines are flooded, I'm afraid. We're coping with mass telephone contacts at the moment, with people offering information in relation to the murders of the two young women you might have seen in the papers. I do apologise, but there will be a delay. I should warn you that it's standard practice not to pursue a missing person case until an absence of twenty-four hours, unless you have reasonable cause to believe that a crime has been committed. Has anyone seen or told you anything that's given you that impression?'

'Put me through to someone else right now,' he repeated.

The civilian operator sighed and pressed the hold button, trying a couple of different extensions with no result. Reopening the line to Jadyn Odoki, she asked for his details and promised to get a police officer to call him straight back.

Caroline Ryan's office desk was immaculate. With the sort of mind that was all smooth lines and clean, crisp shapes, she couldn't bear mess or clutter. Her Mac sat centrally, keyboard and mouse tucked beneath the screen when she'd left the night before. A small metal pot held pens and pencils, and a 3D print out of the home she had designed for her and her future husband took pride of place in the far left-hand corner. In the centre of the desk sat a box, unmarked save for Caroline's name and the office address in capitals on the lid. There was no postage or courier details as the box had been left outside the office before security had arrived to open up that morning. The receptionist had given the parcel to one of Caroline's coworkers who had taken it up in the lift, and deposited it on Caroline's desk.

At 9.15 a.m., the Sky's the Limit secretary sat down at Caroline's desk to switch on her Mac in the hope that the missing architect was still logged into her emails, and that the content of one of them might indicate where she was and why she hadn't turned up. Not that it would matter for much longer, the secretary thought. Caroline's desk was likely to have been cleared out by the end of the day. You didn't simply fail to turn up for a meeting like this one, and think you'd still have a job to come back to.

The secretary pushed the box out of the way, noting a slightly odd smell coming from it and wondering initially if she was just imagining it. She began trawling through Caroline's multitude of emails – sent, received, even those in drafts. After ten minutes she moved the box further away, where the contents would be less bothersome. Whatever was inside that box was repulsive.

The emails were useless. Every email in or out over the last week related to that morning's meeting. More than that, although it hadn't been formalised, everyone knew that success with the pitch meant that Caroline would become a partner, and at just twenty-eight that was a really big deal. She stared at the box. Now that the heating was properly kicking in, the smell was getting worse. If someone had sent Caroline a food parcel, it needed to go in the fridge straight away. She picked it up and walked towards the kitchen. Then again, if it was already going off, putting it in the fridge was likely to contaminate everything else, and the caterers had left sandwich platters in the fridge in case the meeting ran on longer than expected.

She picked up a knife, checking the address on the box carefully. It didn't say that it was personal, and as it had been sent to the office rather than Caroline's home address, it was fair to assume it wouldn't embarrass Caroline if she opened it.

The conference room door opened and the managing director poked his head out, motioning that more coffee was required. The secretary put down the knife and busied herself with a new coffee filter instead. It was no good, if she didn't do something quickly the whole office would absolutely reek. Grabbing the knife again, she sank it into the gaffer tape that sealed the top, shoving her hand inside to free whatever the offending article was so that she could get it into a bin liner as quickly as possible. Her fingers slid through silky hair, and down onto something softer. It slipped through her fingers at first, then she got a firmer grasp and it came free from where it had been sticking to the base of the box. The scream she let out was loud enough to stop the pitch meeting mid-presentation, and to ensure it would not restart again that day.

Ava and Callanach met at Caroline's desk. The area had already been cleared of other staff members, and the central focus for the forensics team was the kitchen. They went in together to get a look at the skin doll and the box it had been delivered in. There was no doubt that it had come from Kate Bailey's body. The silky blonde hair was unmistakable. Only the lips were exaggerated, painted a bright red, more like a geisha's, then stitched over hard with thick black man-made fibre.

'What do we know about Caroline?' Ava asked Callanach.

'She's highly qualified. First-class degree from Cambridge. Was the shining young star of the firm. Alarm bells started ringing this morning when she failed to appear for a vital meeting. Apparently her fiancé had already called the police to report her missing, but it had only been a couple of hours so no one made the connection. A secretary found the doll as there was a smell coming from the box.'

'There still is,' Ava said. 'The others weren't this bad. I wonder what went wrong this time.'

'Hopefully Jonty can tell us that soon. He's waiting for us at the mortuary. The fiancé is on his way here. He has no idea where Caroline is and I instructed the officers bringing him not to talk to him about it. We need to know what it is about Caroline that attracted the killer to her. Nothing makes sense at the moment. Zoey, Lorna and Kate all had aspects of their life that made them targets.' Callanach stripped off the gloves he'd been wearing and stepped away from the kitchen area. Ava followed. 'So what happened this morning? Did Overbeck handle herself with her usual amount of tact and grace?'

'I'm off the Melanie Long investigation.' Ava smiled. 'Overbeck is heading it up directly. She's taking Lively and Salter. It's a demotion in all but name.'

'I don't understand. You were doing everything you could, and you had a lead. All that was required was to get the authority to follow up,' Callanach said.

'Yes, well, when the father of a suspect is on the police board, and the detective superintendent is more concerned with keeping in his good books than solving a murder, things don't go according to plan. For now, I'm still here. Possibly not for much longer though. You'd best be nice to me while you've still got me,' she grinned.

Callanach gritted his teeth. 'Ava, you've got to do something. There must be a complaints system, or a review—'

'There is. It would be handled by the same people who just decided I wasn't capable of running two investigations at once.'

'Ma'am, Caroline Ryan's fiancé has arrived,' a uniformed officer said from the doorway.

Ava and Luc walked out to meet him. Jadyn Odoki was shaking, but not from shock. That much was clear when he looked utterly disgusted as Callanach held out his hand to him.

'I called at 9 a.m. I was told someone would call me straight back. The next call I got was to tell me they were concerned about Caro's safety and that something had been found. What the fuck good is a police force who puts you on hold when you call to say someone is missing?' Jadyn said.

'You're right,' Ava said immediately. 'If I could turn back the clock, I would, but here's what we know now. Miss Ryan didn't enter the office this morning. Her car has been located in the public car park just down the street – where she usually parks, according to colleagues. The vehicle is undamaged and locked, so she wasn't involved in a traffic accident. Whatever happened to your fiancée took place between here and there.'

'So she might have been hit by another car, or taken ill. Did you call the hospitals?' he asked.

'Mr Odoki, a package addressed to Caroline was found on her desk this morning. It indicates that Caroline may be the victim of an abduction. We've found similar items when other young women have been taken. At present, we're working on the basis that Caroline has been put into another vehicle and driven out of the city, probably to a private address.'

'Jesus fucking Christ,' Jadyn said, swinging round to kick a door. Ava and Callanach let him have the moment. It was a fair reaction. 'How long's she been gone? What's going to happen to her?'

'We don't think it was a chance abduction. It seems likely the man knew where Caroline usually parks and was waiting for her. The positive news is that we know what vehicle he uses and we're in the process of tracing the CCTV for all the routes out of this area to see if we can narrow down his address.'

'What are you not telling me?' Jadyn asked. 'If you know so much about him, what is it he wants from her? Is he going to ask for money? Whatever it is, I'll pay, I'll find a way. He's done this before, right? When's he going to contact us?'

'It's not that kind of kidnapping, I'm afraid. He doesn't want money. The other young women he's taken have survived a few days, a week at most. He leaves their bodies somewhere public, but so far they have all been too badly hurt to have survived.'

'The Babydoll Killer?' he shouted. 'That's who has her – that monster? How could you let this happen? You knew he was out there. You knew he was taking women . . .'

'Not women like Caroline,' Callanach said quietly. 'That's what we need to understand. With the other three victims, we could see the pattern. It was horrible but it made sense. We could understand what the killer thought he was achieving. Caroline seems different. We're going to have to ask you some difficult questions, I'm afraid. The best thing you can do for her is to get angry later, ask all the questions you have after we've finished, but help us now. Can you do that, Mr Odoki?'

There were a few seconds where he stood completely still, breathing hard through his nose, looking as if he were considering either fighting or fleeing, but then his head came up and a new man emerged. 'Okay,' he said. 'What is it you need to know?'

'All the other girls had a troubled past, or were currently at a difficult stage of their life. This is no reflection on Caroline, but the best way to identify her abductor might be to understand how she was selected. Has Caroline ever had any problems involving drugs, violence, prostitution, criminal activity? Anything you can think of that's unusual?'

'Is this a joke?' he asked. They stood passively and waited. 'Fine, no, nothing like that. We met at Cambridge University, but she always wanted to come home to Scotland. She's never been in trouble, not once. She had sleepless nights if she missed a class, you know? She'd never have coped with doing anything seriously wrong, and she didn't need to. Her parents are well off. We're happy, settled. Six months ago we realised we'd saved enough money to buy a plot of land to build the house Caroline had always dreamed of, and I've got a place on an archaeological team. She doesn't drink alcohol let alone take drugs. Is this a case of mistaken identity? Do you think that perhaps he was after someone else and took Caro by mistake?'

Callanach looked at Ava. It was a scenario they would have to explore. Caroline Ryan would have to be hiding her secrets pretty well if her fiancé had no idea what could have attracted the killer to her. For now, the best they could do was hope that Jonty had more information for them courtesy of Kate Bailey's body, or that the latest doll would reveal something new. Given that Kate Bailey had been murdered earlier than expected, there was no knowing how long Caroline might survive.

Chapter Thirty-Six

'"Flee from sexual immorality. Every other sin a person commits is outside the body, but the sexually immoral person sins against his own body",' Jonty read from the miniature scroll of paper contained within the skin doll. 'Similar to the other two. Nothing unexpected given what you already knew about Kate.'

'From Corinthians,' Callanach said, checking the quote on his mobile. 'Doesn't take us any further forward.'

'Do you know what happened to Kate's wrist?' Ava asked Jonty.

'I'm pretty sure she rubbed her bindings against sharp wood to cut them. The skin below the infection was absolutely full of splinters. She must have been in agony,' Jonty told them.

'What about the new doll?' Callanach asked. 'The secretary from the architect's firm opened the box because of the smell. Did the killer do something differently this time?'

'Well, the inside of the skin hadn't been cleaned as thoroughly, so more flesh was still clinging to the skin. Must have been in more of a rush than on previous occasions. It's a difficult thing to work with, human skin. Normally there would be a drying process and some stretching.'

The two halves of the skin doll lay on a metal tray in front of them, identical in size and shape to those taken from Zoey and Lorna. 'He can't maintain this level of offending,' Callanach said. 'Even if he's as obsessed as he seems, he must appreciate that sooner or later he'll make a mistake. He's working to a fixed pattern. It's not realistic to think he'll never get caught.'

'Only this victim breaks the mould,' Ava said. 'Perhaps he's deliberately diversifying to make it harder for us to anticipate his next move. Jonty, I should have asked you this before, but I was in the middle of something when you called. You said there was marble residue found on both the other dolls. Do you have any more information about where that came from?'

'I don't,' he said. 'We swabbed both dolls completely after checking for fingerprints and trace evidence, then had a chemical breakdown performed to identify every substance. There was very little of it found, but it was common to both dolls, which is what struck us as odd.'

'Could you identify the type of marble so we can isolate the source?' Callanach asked.

'Not possible. There simply wasn't enough available to work with.'

'But the particles would sparkle under bright lights, surely? You might be able to identify them other than through a chemical sweep,' Callanach remarked.

'Quite possibly, although I'm not sure how that would help,' Jonty said, picking up the skin on a tray and moving it to an area below a high-powered light with a magnifying lens, then walking to the doors to turn off the main lights.

'Maybe the girls are lying on a marble countertop, in which case there would be more marble present on the skin of the rear of the doll than the front. It might help identify the place they're being held,' Callanach said.

'Worth a try,' Jonty said, walking back towards them through the semi-dark. He placed the rear skin below the light first of all as they crowded around to look. They inspected every square centimetre. Not a single reflection came off the skin's surface. They angled it in different directions and moved the light around in case any traces had caught within the tiny imperfections on the skin's surface. 'Nothing,' Jonty said. 'It might have been an anomaly with the first two dolls. Something caught on a tool from a different location perhaps.'

He exchanged the back skin segment for the front and slid it beneath the brilliant light. The glimmer was immediately visible. 'It's all on the face area,' Callanach said. 'Can we see it any more clearly?'

Jonty increased the magnification and they huddled to get a view. 'That's odd,' Ava said. 'It's literally in a pool on the forehead. I don't see how it could be there and nowhere else.'

'And it's dribbled into the front of the hairline, where the glue has been used. Assuming this represents something that the killer wanted to do to the victims, how and when do we pour a substance onto someone's head?' Jonty mused, tipping the skin from one side to another to allow the minute marble particles to shine on different angles of the skin.

They stepped away from the light. Ava rubbed her eyes as Jonty took out a camera to get close-up shots of the marble residue on the skin. 'I don't even want to say what I'm thinking out loud. This just keeps getting more and more twisted,' she muttered.

'That the dolls have been baptised? In the context of what the killer's trying to achieve, it makes sense. He takes the skin from a young woman he sees as a sinner, makes a new person – a baby – literally from their bodies, then cleanses or purifies the doll,' Callanach said.

'So they have access to a font. I'm guessing it's from an actual church or the ritual would be meaningless. The dolls wouldn't be purified of sin. Which makes me wonder what sort of religion would countenance using their facilities for such sick, bizarre activities,' Ava said.

'What about getting a profiler in?' Callanach asked. 'I'm not always keen on trying to draw up a psychological picture of an offender, but in this case it might just help.'

'Actually, I was thinking of someone more qualified to help us with the theological significance of what the killer is doing,' Ava said. 'Someone with theoretical knowledge and who can also offer an insight into local churches. I only hope she can bear to be in the same room as me again.'

The Reverend Jayne Magee smiled widely as she opened her front door to invite them into her home. The last time Callanach and Ava had been on that road, more than a year earlier, they were looking for a missing person who, it turned out, had been sedated, bundled into a large wheelie case and dragged down the road to the trunk of a car. As the victim of that abduction, Jayne Magee had done her best to save the lives of others whilst she herself had been imprisoned and fearing for her own life. Ava and she had spent many terrifying hours together, both hostages at the whim of a madman. Most of the other women he'd taken hadn't lived to tell the tale.

Jayne and Ava embraced gently, eyes closed, and Callanach wondered how badly the memories of their ordeal with Dr Reginald King still plagued them. Ava never talked about it. She always pretended it was part and parcel of the dangers of police work, but the truth was that no one signed up expecting to become the victim. Jayne Magee was well respected and much loved in Edinburgh's religious community, and it seemed her faith was unshaken, even having witnessed such evil first-hand. The human spirit was a remarkably resilient entity, Callanach thought, as they went to sit in Jayne's lounge and drink tea.

'I'm sorry to bother you,' Ava said. 'I hope you don't mind us reaching out to you for help after what you went through.'

'If I can help another person then I'm delighted,' Jayne said. 'Perhaps more so because of what we went through. You were there, too, Ava.'

'Not as long as you,' Ava said. 'I wasn't sure you'd even want to see me.'

'Actually, when you phoned, I was surprised at how uplifted I felt. I'm glad you've visited, but you look sad, and stressed. How can I assist?'

'You'll have heard on the news that three women were abducted, then left for dead a few days later. It's confidential, but another young woman has been taken. We need to understand the motivations of the man we believe is behind the offences. I thought you might be able to help,' Ava said, opening a folder and laying out a pile of documents on the coffee table between them.

'You believe this other girl's life is in danger right now?' Jayne asked.

'We do,' Ava said. 'And we don't know how long she has left. No more than six days, possibly less. He didn't wait a full week before killing the last one.'

Jayne sighed, blinking away tears before speaking again. 'I'll do whatever I can.'

'First, forgive me for bringing such atrocities to you. If I knew anyone better qualified, I'd have spared you it. The killer makes a doll from each woman's skin. Like a rag doll. What the media has not been told is that inside each doll is a line of scripture. Here.' Ava handed over a copy of each Bible quote for Jayne to read. 'Each girl had faced her own difficulties and the quote is relevant to their life – apparently it's why the killer regards them as steeped in sin. It now seems that these dolls are being baptised. There is marble residue left on the skin of their foreheads.'

'From a proper font then, you think. John, chapter three, verse five says, "Jesus answered, 'Truly, truly, I say to you, unless one is born of water and the Spirit, he cannot enter into the kingdom of God.'" It's pretty extreme stuff, although these are all well-known biblical quotes. Very brimstone though, all the wrath and punishment stuff. These days we try to focus on forgiveness and outreach rather than judgment.'

'What we don't know is why he chose the current victim,' Callanach said. 'Zoey had a history with her stepfather and had accused him of violence.'

'Respect thy father and mother . . .' Jayne said.

'Exactly. Then Lorna had a child out of wedlock, father unknown, with a history of drug misuse. Most recently Kate had been working, effectively, as a prostitute to help support her family and reduce her student debts.'

'And the young woman he has now?' Jayne asked.

'Caroline is an architect. Well qualified. No criminal record. Never known to social services. None of the lifestyle issues the other victims had. It makes no sense at all, and yet she was clearly targeted. The killer was waiting for her in the car park where she normally parks for work, and left the last doll in a box marked with her name. We've spoken to her fiancé, checked her online presence – which is virtually non-existent – and cross-referenced with every other government agency. We're coming up blank.'

'So the questions are, how is he locating and identifying his victims, how is he getting so much information about them and how does Caroline fit into the picture?' Jayne concluded.

'Yes. If we can answer any one of those questions, we stand a chance of finding him. At the moment, everything we have is evidence that will help convict him at trial, but which doesn't take us to his front door,' Ava said.

'Show me everything,' Jayne said. 'On all the victims.'

Ava spread the stack of documents out across the table, expanding to the floor, propping pictures, maps and statements against chair legs.

'So Caroline is older than the other three victims as well,' Jayne said.

'Yes, twenty-eight. Everything seems to have been going well in her life. She was hoping to make partner in her firm, and she and her fiancé had just bought a patch of land to build a house on. There's nothing in her life at all that suggests how she might have come to the killer's attention,' Callanach said, handing Jayne a photograph taken of Caroline and Jadyn.

Jayne looked at it, put it down on the floor, then picked it up again.

'When was this taken?' she asked quietly.

'At their engagement party,' Ava said. 'Her fiancé said this was the most recent photo of her. It went into a local newspaper when they announced they were getting married.'

Jayne frowned, shaking her head, then stood up and walked to a bookshelf. She took down a heavy textbook, running a fingertip down the index at the back and flicking through the pages, before flicking on a light to read the text. Ava and Callanach waited.

'This is very unusual interpretation of the Bible,' Jayne said. 'And not one I'm happy even discussing, but there are those – not accepted by any religion I could ally myself with – who profess such filth.'

'What is it?' Ava asked.

'Daniel chapter two, verse forty-three. "As you saw the iron mixed with soft clay, so they will mix with one another in marriage, but they will not hold together, just as iron does not mix with clay." Sometimes cited alongside that is Leviticus chapter nineteen, verse nineteen: "You shall keep my statutes. You shall not let your cattle breed with a different kind. You

315

shall not sow your field with two kinds of seed, nor shall you wear a garment of cloth made of two kinds of material."'

'I don't understand the relevance,' Callanach said.

'I've only come across it in certain extremist American churches – though to use the word church to describe them undermines everything about religion that is good. In reality, they are more like cults that exist for the purpose of excusing hatred and exclusion. Such groups operate outside the law and almost inevitably to the far-right extremes of politics. Yet there are one or two even in Scotland who share their vile beliefs. In the absence of anything else that might explain why Caroline Ryan has been abducted, I wonder if the man who has taken her objects to the colour of her fiancé's skin.'

'Because Jadyn Odoki is black? You think that could happen here, in Scotland? You think there's a religious sect who could actually act on such disgusting beliefs?' Ava asked.

'Religion gets a bad press for exactly such reasons. It's not unusual to have deviants misquote or misinterpret scripture to match their own beliefs. I've heard arguments from people who say that Mary was a teenager when she met Joseph, so why should sex with underage girls be condemned. History has produced innumerable holy wars based on the need to wipe out anyone not of their own religion. Plenty of prominent evangelists have overlooked serious crimes committed by their supporters in order to get their churches a stronger foothold in political circles. People will use scripture to excuse almost anything, twisting the words to match their own personal code. It's shocking, but no more so than committing murder in order, apparently, to free the victim of perceived sin,' Jayne said.

'We suspect the killer identified Caroline when this picture went in the paper,' Ava said. 'The article gave their full names, where they worked, everything he needed. How do we find him, Jayne? If there's a church or organisation in

Edinburgh that promotes such extreme hate, wouldn't we have heard about it by now?'

'The problem is that it never starts as a whole group or church at once. If you take a strict religious group that applies the Bible very literally, they attract members who think a certain way. They might hold very extreme views, but often keep them to themselves for fear of being rejected or misunderstood. Over time, that group will attract enough followers with strong views that the extremes become more mainstream – internally, at least. Then, as with certain groups who are well documented in other countries, there is more public interest. But at the start, when the seeds of extremism are being sown, who knows what's in one man's heart?'

'Murder, apparently,' Ava said. 'Jayne, thank you. I need to take this theory back to the squad so we can see where it takes us. You've been a huge help.'

'I'll pray for her,' Jayne said as they stood up.

Callanach looked at her sharply, then at Ava.

'What is it?' Ava asked him.

'Just a memory. Someone else said the same thing, right at the beginning of all this. I just can't recall who.'

Chapter Thirty-Seven

'We're looking for extremist groups that dress themselves up under the guise of religion, but that in reality practise racism and probably homophobia, very Old Testament, unrecognisable from the sort of churches and religious groups we're familiar with,' Ava said.

'You're talking about hate groups,' Tripp said. 'A cult, effectively.'

'Exactly. Caroline Ryan and Jadyn Odoki's photograph was put in the paper when they got engaged. Given how little she uses social media, we believe the press coverage may be when she was spotted and chosen as a target,' Ava explained.

'So does the murderer really believe in God but have a deranged view of the Bible, or is this whole thing just a front for extreme right-wing views?' a uniformed officer asked.

'We'll have to wait until we have the bastard in custody before we get an answer to that,' Ava said. 'What we're looking for is religious groups in the area who might attract fringe worshippers. Those who like their religion beyond mainstream parameters. They are likely to be careful about who they speak to. There are plenty of churches around who are selective about allowing new members into their congregations, and this group will be very cautious indeed, so don't expect to find what we're looking for on a public website.'

DS Lively put his head round the incident room door, scanning the crowd before beckoning Callanach into the corridor. Ava ignored them. Lively had chosen sides already. She had to let the Melanie Long investigation go. It wasn't as if she didn't have enough to keep her busy. When it was over, she'd make a decision about her future with Police Scotland. What was perfectly clear, however, was that she couldn't continue to work under Detective Superintendent Overbeck.

Callanach reappeared five minutes later and stood at the back of the room texting. Ava allocated tasks to different groups within the squad, then asked for a core team of officers to remain for an evidence review. As bodies filtered from the room, Ava pulled a group of chairs round in a semicircle to face the information board. The photographs, maps and victim information had grown too vast for its allocated space, spreading to the outer walls which were dappled with sticky tape, identifying possible exit routes from the city, the positions of CCTV cameras, and shots of each young woman in the location of her death. Next to each one was a picture of the doll made from her skin. It was a gruesome collage.

'Back to basics,' Ava said. 'We believe the killer lives to the west of Edinburgh, but within relatively easy driving distance of the city. There is a credible theory about how he chose Caroline Ryan, and it would have been easy to identify Kate Bailey through the SugarPa website by selecting Edinburgh in the geographical preferences. So the question is, how did he find Zoey and Lorna?'

'The earliest victim is the most likely to have a personal link to offender,' Callanach replied. 'Preliminary victims are rarely random selections, unless a physical search is being made for, say, a lone female in a specific geographical area at night. Even then, the offender has usually selected the particular area because it's well known to them.'

'So let's take another look at Zoey Cole in the context of what we now know about her murderer,' Ava said. 'Victim of domestic violence, living in a shelter. Limited social media use as she was keeping her location a secret. Query over Tyrone Leigh, boyfriend of the woman who runs the shelter.'

'The Myers had alibis that were backed up by multiple witnesses. Tyrone Leigh can't be linked to any of the victims who came after Zoey,' Tripp said. 'Lorna Shaw would have been a much more visible target. She had criminal convictions and was known to a variety of government agencies, as well as to the less charming personalities on Edinburgh's drug scene. It's not obvious how she might have come to the attention of a religious cult, but it could just have been word of mouth.'

'Perhaps a reformed drug user, talking about people from their past,' a uniformed officer suggested. 'A lot of the addicts we deal with have been helped by church groups. There's a substantial flow of unchecked information when users are trying to get drug-free. Addicts often have a very hazy recollection of the period.'

'Good,' Ava said. 'So one resource we can check is unofficial help for addicts, running support groups or charities, who might have attracted our killer. We should extend that to groups offering support for victims of domestic violence, to see if there's anyone we missed who might have been a cross-over factor between Zoey and Lorna. Tripp, you go with DI Callanach to make enquiries with the mother and baby unit about what external links they have. I'll go to the domestic violence shelter and see if any of the women there have had any contact with religious groups offering advice or support.' They stood up, gathering notebooks and coats on their way out of the door. 'Luc, a word,' she said, pulling him aside. 'Lively wanted to speak to you earlier. Is everything all right?'

'It was nothing important,' he said. 'He just wanted a phone number.'

'Okay, fine,' Ava said. 'Did he say anything at all about the Melanie Long investigation? I just feel so bad . . .'

'Ava,' Callanach interrupted. 'It's not your problem any more.'

'I very much doubt it's anyone's problem any more. It'll probably just get filed away as a dispute between drug dealers. That'll make for a quick and easy report to the board. No realistic prospect of a conviction. Investigation discontinued in the absence of further leads.'

'I know this is hard. Go to the shelter. See if you can find something more than Tripp and I did. I'll see you back here in a couple of hours, okay?'

'Ask how baby Tansy's doing for me, will you?' Ava said. 'I've been meaning to contact the mother and baby unit. I was hoping I'd have news for them by now.'

Twenty minutes later, Tripp and Callanach were dashing from the car into the unit through driving rain, soaking wet in just seconds. They stood in the corridor, shaking off their clothes and wiping their shoes on the mat.

'Detective Inspector,' said the unit manager, Arnold Jenkins, walking towards them and smiling gently. 'We hadn't expected to see you again. Do you have news?'

'Not exactly,' Callanach said, 'but we do have a few questions.' They walked to the manager's office and sat down. 'There's a quasi-religious element to this case. Not anything mainstream, perhaps not obvious to the outside world, but it seems the killer holds very strong, radical, even poisonous views.'

'Well, whoever could hurt a young woman like that is hardly

likely to be on the normal psychological spectrum,' Jenkins said. 'What do you need?'

'We're wondering if Lorna, or any of the other girls here at the same time as her, had been offered help or support by a church group, whether advice for recovering addicts, funding or guidance. Do you know of any groups that work with girls like Lorna in Edinburgh?'

'Many addiction support groups meet in church rooms, although to my knowledge religion is downplayed so as not to put attendees off. There are, of course, a variety of faith-based charities that offer free meals and hand out clothing during the colder months. Those may have an element of religious outreach, but none of it is the sort of thing you're describing. These are all well established, and extremely well intentioned. I don't believe they'd attract the sort of deviant responsible for murdering Lorna.'

'No offers of counselling, or specific church groups that have expressed a particular interest in the moral welfare of the mothers?' Tripp asked.

'We don't allow that sort of thing,' Jenkins said sternly. 'We apply two sets of principles here. The first is the law. Most of the women residing here have a court order that restricts where they can live and requires regular court reviews with reports on progress. We apply court orders to the letter. Beyond that, all medical advice is followed without question. If a baby is thought not to be thriving, or a mother fails to give a urine test or to take prescribed medication, we reference help immediately. What we do not tolerate, though, is judgment, so we ask staff to agree as part of their contract that no mention will be made of any religion or belief system inside this building. Whilst we respect the individual's right to follow whatever doctrine they choose, they may not bring it to work with them. It is absolutely vital that this is a judgment-free environment, where none of the women we are trying to help are subject to moral questioning.'

'It was here, though,' Callanach muttered to himself. Tripp and the manager stared at him. 'Sorry, you know when your mind makes a connection, but the pieces don't quite fit together. Someone told me a few hours ago that they would pray for one of the victims. It was a phrase I'd heard before, only I couldn't place where, but I'm sure it was here, from one of the nurses. Is that against your policy?'

'Normally, yes,' Jenkins said, 'but if they were talking to you about Lorna specifically, I can understand why someone might feel it was different. It's really the mothers we try to protect from issues of religion, unless they specifically request access to a particular church.'

'Do you mind if we have a look around again? Just to see if there's anything that strikes us as useful. We'll be careful not to disturb anyone,' Callanach asked.

'Of course,' Jenkins replied. 'You know your way by now.'

'And DCI Turner wanted to know how baby Tansy is getting on. Presumably she's been moved elsewhere by now.'

'The baby's in temporary foster care, but we're actively looking for an adoptive placement. I do hope the papers I sent to DCI Turner in that regard got to her safely.'

'Um, I'm sure they did,' Callanach said. 'We should go.' He motioned for Tripp to leave the office ahead of him, pulling the door shut behind them. He had no idea what papers the manager was talking about, but given how disillusioned Ava currently was with her job, he could understand why she might be looking for something else to give her purpose. A baby, though, might take her away from policing forever, and that would be a huge loss – to MIT, to Police Scotland and to the public she worked so hard to protect. And to him, after all they'd been through together.

323

'Sir,' Tripp said, 'you all right?'

'I'm fine,' he replied. 'Let's start in the staff room.' They walked through the unit together, checking the employee-only areas and staff facilities, but everyone was busy on shifts with the mothers and babies. 'It's no good. We can't go into the private rooms and interrupt them. I'll email Jenkins once we're back at the station and ask him to share the email with his staff, see if that jogs any memories. Maybe DCI Turner's had more luck.' They made their way to the exit, past the reception area where a board on the back wall showed the hierarchy of staff, with photographs and names.

'Hold on,' Callanach said, scanning the wall of faces. 'There, that's her. She's the nurse who said something about keeping Lorna in her prayers. Lydia McMahon.'

'We've got a photo of her in the incident room, I think. Not in uniform though, so I wouldn't have recognised her unless you'd pointed her out.' Tripp walked around the reception desk to get a better look. 'It must have got muddled in with another victim's file at some point. I'm sure it's not with Lorna's information.'

'Whose file is it in?' Callanach asked quietly.

'I'd have to look,' Tripp said, as Callanach got out his mobile and took a photo of the headshot. 'Excuse me,' he called to a passing staff member. 'Is Nurse McMahon working today?'

'No, she's off, but she's back in tomorrow. Would you like to leave her a message?' she replied.

'That's all right,' Callanach said. 'We can wait.'

Back in the incident room, Tripp was scanning the board to find the photo. 'I don't see it here,' he said. 'But I'm sure I've seen her somewhere. What other photos do we have that aren't pinned up?' He opened the large box files – one for each victim – and took out stacks of paper and photos. There were printouts of the contents from each woman's mobile phone – texts, photos and emails – as well as anything seized from their personal belongings that indicated boyfriends and upcoming plans. Flicking through increasingly fast, he began shaking his head. 'This isn't it,' he said. 'I'm trying to remember the context of the photo. It was taken outside. I just remember seeing her face, side on, and there was something in the background. Colourful. Like a line of washing or something.'

'Bunting?' Callanach asked. 'Could that have been it?'

'Yes, possibly, but I don't remember which of the victims . . .'

'Alibi photos,' Callanach said, reaching for a different filing cabinet and pulling out a brown folder. 'Zoey's mother and stepfather were at a community fete the day Zoey was taken. They produced endless witnesses to back up their story and confirm the timeline.' He spread forty or fifty photos out across the desk, checking each one then putting it in a pile. Tripp joined him. 'That's her,' Callanach said, holding up a photo. 'She looks different with her hair down. How did you remember this photo, Tripp? There are hundreds in the files.'

'Her nose is very slightly upturned at the end. I didn't notice when we saw her at the hospital. She must have been straight on to me when we spoke to her, but the reception photo is more in profile. I don't recall seeing her name on Zoey's stepfather's list of alibi witnesses though, or we'd have noticed her earlier. Shall I get a uniformed squad to find her and bring her in to the station?'

'No, let's go to her. I don't want to give her time to prepare for questions, and at this stage I'd rather keep it informal. As far as we know, right now, this is a coincidence. Let's see if she'll open up to us. I'm going to call DCI Turner to notify her. Call the mother and baby unit manager and ask him for Lydia McMahon's address. Let's see if this nurse can explain why she failed to mention that she knew the family of a different victim, when we were asking her about Lorna.'

Chapter Thirty-Eight

Lydia McMahon's hands could be seen before the remainder of her body, scrubbing the inside of her front room windows. She answered the door wearing yellow rubber gloves, looking confused but keeping a smile in place.

'DI Callanach, I wasn't expecting you. Is everything all right at the unit?'

'Yes, fine. DC Tripp and I have a few questions for you, though. Could we come in?' he asked.

'Certainly. Sorry about the mess. I was just cleaning. Would you like tea?'

'Please,' Tripp said. 'We can sit ourselves down.' They walked into the lounge as Lydia made for the kettle. Bowls of hot, soapy water, a vacuum cleaner and various sprays and polishes littered the living room floor. 'You're a few months early for spring cleaning,' he called to her, as they checked the room for signs that other people were resident.

'Oh, I know,' she said, coming back in to put coasters on the coffee table before their cups arrived. 'I have a bit of an obsession about cleaning. Probably why I'm still single.' She gave a shy laugh as she exited for the kitchen again.

Callanach silently pointed out the mantelpiece, where ten small ornaments sat sparkling, devoid of dust, each spaced a precise and equal distance from the next. Lydia came back with a tray bearing cups, saucers and a bowl of sugar cubes with tiny tongs balanced on top.

'Did you have more questions about Lorna?' she asked as she sat down and handed cups around.

'Just a couple,' Callanach said pleasantly. 'Were you aware whether or not Lorna had any particular religious inclination?'

'I shouldn't think so, given the life she lived,' Lydia said. 'Poor girl. I doubt her parents ever took her to a church in her life.'

'You told me you'd keep her in your prayers. Was that something you'd discussed with Lorna? Your own faith?'

She paused, her eyes flicking briefly to the side. The first sign of nerves, Callanach thought. She hadn't been expecting them, and she hadn't responded guiltily when they'd asked to speak with her, but now she was uncomfortable. 'We're not allowed to, actually. It's against unit rules. I try to keep my beliefs to myself. I didn't mean anything by it.'

'I wasn't suggesting you'd done anything wrong,' Callanach said. 'It's much the same in the police. You learn to keep your professional and private life separate.'

Lydia gave him a more relaxed smile, with a kindred-spirit nod. 'Exactly,' she said. 'But it's hard when you see so much suffering, and you know that while we take care of people's bodies, so much more could be done if we nourished their spirits, too. Are you a man of faith, Detective Inspector?'

'That depends on your definition of it,' he said. 'I remain open-minded. Tell us more about the church you attend. Is it local?'

'I'm new there, actually,' she said, stirring sugar into her tea. 'I attended a church in the city before, but I found they were more concerned with getting through the service and holding

328

charity functions than focusing on the needs of the soul. I think I was looking for something more personal.'

'So how did you find your new church?' Tripp asked.

'A friend of a friend attended there a few times when they moved to West Calder. I'd heard her talking about how she found it rather strict and oppressive, but a church is like a pair of gloves – it has to be the right fit for you. I enjoy the rigours of a disciplined religious community. I find it brings me closer to God. After all, rules are easy to live with if you just don't break them. I can't stand disorderliness.'

Callanach's eyes strayed back to the mantelpiece. It made sense for a woman suffering from OCD to seek out order in her spiritual life to match the order she needed from her physical surroundings. What was strange was how at odds her work was with the doctrine of the church she'd chosen.

'West Calder,' Tripp was saying. 'What's the name of the group?'

Lydia lowered her voice and leaned forward. 'Actually, we're discouraged from discussing the group with non-members. They're very distrustful, simply because others tend not to understand our beliefs. There's quite a process to become part of the congregation. I'm afraid religious persecution can be brutal and our members seek to lead quiet, holy lives, free of unwanted attention.'

'I'm sure,' Callanach said. 'Let me ask you about something different then. You attended a community fete a few weeks ago. We have a photo of you there.' He produced a copy of it and handed it to her. 'Can you tell us about it?'

She looked down at the photo, back up to Callanach, then to Tripp, her eyebrows drawing together. 'Where did you get this?'

'It was given to us in a batch of photos by a man called Christopher Myers. He and his wife Elsa were helping at the fete. Do you know them?' Callanach asked.

Lydia took a sip of her tea, a splash of it escaping with the wobble of her hand and marking the cream carpet. She gasped, staring at the brown liquid sinking into the spotless fibres.

'I have to get a cloth,' she said.

'Not yet,' Callanach told her. 'Do you know Christopher Myers?'

'It's going to mark the carpet,' Lydia said, the shake in her hands increasing. She deposited the cup and saucer back on the tray with a clatter.

'Did you know Christopher Myers' stepdaughter, Zoey?'

'I need to get a cloth,' Lydia whispered. 'Please.'

'Just as soon as you've answered the questions,' Callanach said.

Lydia looked at the spot on the carpet, rubbing her hands one over the other and breathing hard. 'We can't discuss other members of the group. It's one of the rules. He never talked about his stepdaughter at church meetings. When her name came out in the papers, I had no way of knowing. She has a different surname.'

'The name of your church group?' Callanach said, staring at the tea, which had now soaked into the pile.

'The Children of the Word,' Lydia shouted suddenly, bolting for the kitchen. Tripp was texting the information through to the incident room as she rushed back and dropped to her knees, furiously squirting carpet cleaner and rubbing the stain.

'We hire a chapel from an old private estate, Kirkbancroft. I think technically it was deconsecrated, but we're allowed to use it at weekends. You won't say it was me who told you? I don't want to be asked to leave.' Lydia sniffed.

'When did you realise that you were linked to two of the victims?' Tripp asked.

'I was never certain. People whispered things, of course, but I'm not in the circle as I'm so new. I'm allowed to attend services and celebrations, and to help with our group's community work, but I don't know much about the other members. We're not allowed to socialise except at agreed functions, to discourage distractions and cliques. All I knew was that Christopher and Elsa Myers hadn't been arrested. They were still at church every Sunday, so even when I thought it was a bit of a coincidence, it didn't seem to me that it was relevant.' She inspected the former tea stain closely, blowing on the damp spot on the carpet then peeling off her rubber gloves.

'So the link between you and the Myers family is purely coincidental,' Callanach said. 'I understand that. But we believe there may be a link between your church group and Lorna Shaw. At the moment you're the only person with connections to both. Can you explain that?'

'You can't believe that someone in my group hurt Lorna. We do unpaid work in the community. We raise money for homeless shelters and orphanages in third world countries. What you're suggesting is ridiculous. No one I know would hurt young women like that,' she said, gripping her knees where she knelt, rocking back and forward as she spoke.

'Lydia, did you talk to anyone at church about Lorna? About her history and her problems?' Callanach asked. Lydia leaned down over the now non-existent carpet stain, poking the strands with her finger to see if she could find any remnant of the drip of tea. 'Nurse McMahon, have you discussed Lorna with anyone at all outside the mother and baby unit?' he persisted.

'I'll get fired,' she whispered.

'Withholding information from us is much more serious than getting fired,' Callanach said. 'Have you ever been inside a prison? Even in women's prisons, the facilities are all shared. There are toilets in each cell, but you won't have access to cleaning materials. The shower blocks are used for all sorts of purposes other than actually washing. People secrete drugs in their body cavities, they do trades – usually sex for cigarettes – and the prison food is cooked and served by people you don't know who probably don't share your love of good hygiene.'

'Sir, I don't think . . .' Tripp muttered.

Lydia gagged, clutching her stomach, regaining control just before she was actually sick.

'I think it's only fair to let Nurse McMahon know just how serious this is,' Callanach said. 'How do you cope working as a nurse when you react this badly to the thought of spreading bacteria?'

'It's all right if I can clean it up,' she whispered. 'As long as I can scrub my hands with hot water. I didn't hurt Lorna Shaw. I'd never have done anything to hurt her. I prayed for her just like I said I would.'

'Who did you talk to?' Callanach asked again.

'I dedicated my sinner's prayer to her in church,' Lydia said, keeping her face low. 'Each week, we all talk about someone we've encountered who has broken God's laws. We discuss their transgressions, explain how the devil found his way into their heart and how we think they need to be saved. Then we pray for them, as a group. But we do it to save people, through God's love. We hold their names in our hearts and we ask God's forgiveness and for Him to intervene in their life.'

'I'm afraid someone other than God might have intervened on this occasion. We'll need the names of everyone in your church group. How many are there?' Callanach asked.

'Am I in trouble?' Lydia asked.

'You won't be, as long as you give us all the information we need. Is there anyone called Sam or Samuel in your group?' Tripp asked.

'Not that I've met or heard of,' she replied, shaking her head.

'Who's the group leader?' Callanach asked.

'We call him our shepherd. His name is Vince Ashton. He lives in West Calder, not far from the chapel. I can give you his address. It's on my mobile. I'll get it for you.'

'Tripp will go with you,' Callanach said, 'and we'll have officers remain with you for the rest of the day. You can't phone anyone from your church about this, Lydia. Whatever rules your group has, whatever duty to your shepherd, this comes first.' She flushed as Callanach spoke, and looked away from him out of the newly cleaned windows. 'In case I need to remind you, you don't want to end up in a prison cell with two or three other women, locked up for twenty hours a day, do you?'

'No,' she said, shaking her head in the direction of the pristine carpet.

'Good,' Callanach replied. 'We need that address quickly. Then we'll let you get back to your cleaning. One last thing.' He pulled a printout of a still taken from the shopping mall CCTV footage from his pocket. 'Do you recognise this man?'

Lydia looked closely, shrugged her shoulders. 'No, not at all,' she said. 'Should I?'

The road to West Calder was icy. Callanach messaged Ava as Tripp drove.

'You were tough on her,' Tripp said.

'Do you think so? You might feel differently if you'd been to Durham to speak with Kate Bailey's parents,' Callanach said.

'But Lydia McMahon is just a victim of her own good intentions. Was it necessary to use her own psychological condition against her?' Tripp asked quietly.

'Honestly? Yes. For expediency. If we'd had more time, I might have been gentler, but well intentioned or not, her indiscretion might well have made Lorna Shaw a target,' Callanach said.

'I think Nurse McMahon might spend the rest of her life coming to terms with that,' Tripp said. 'Isn't that punishment enough?'

'Lorna Shaw bled to death on a road outside a recycling centre having had two large sections of her skin cut away. If the people who let that happen spend the next few years with sleepless nights, then it seems a small price to pay. Good policing is about using whatever is available to you at the time to move an investigation forward. Would you grab a man by the neck and shove him against a wall if it meant you could save a life?' Callanach asked.

'If I believed it was necessary,' Tripp said.

'What I did to Nurse McMahon is exactly the same, only without the violence. Good and bad rarely come in conveniently labelled packages. Is Lydia a bad person? No, I don't think so. But was she judgmental, even with good intentions? Yes. Did she break the rules at work designed to protect those in her care, so she could share a judgment she had already made about someone else's life? Yes. Does her faith justify that sort of behaviour, irrespective of what happened to Lorna afterwards? I don't believe so. I haven't walked a mile in Lydia McMahon's shoes. I don't know what in her life has left her so insecure, so desperate for guidance from others, but I do know a lot about what Lorna went through, and I know that no one else had the right to brand her a sinner. Not at any stage of her life. I just can't get my head round any religion that believes it has the right to judge others.'

They drove on in silence until Callanach's mobile rang. He glanced at the screen and answered when he saw it was Ben Paulson, the hacker he'd used to break into the SugarPa site.

'Luc, I've got something you might be interested in.'

'I'm in the middle of something,' Callanach said. 'I'm going to text you the number of a colleague. He'll deal with it immediately, and thanks Ben. That's twice you've helped in the last week. I won't forget it.'

'You can tell DCI Turner that I'll accept payment for this last job. I am running a business here, after all. We can call it a buy one, get one free arrangement,' he joked.

'You'll have to bill me then,' Callanach said. 'Ava Turner has nothing to do with this, and that's the way I'd prefer to keep it.'

Chapter Thirty-Nine

Ava was waiting in the driveway for Christopher and Elsa Myers when they drove in from an after-work supermarket trip. She flashed her ID, forsaking any small talk.

'I need to get the freezer food inside,' Christopher said. 'It'll start to defrost otherwise.'

'Christopher, it's about Zoey,' Elsa said softly.

'This'll only take a minute,' he said. Ava watched him walk inside as she waited with Zoey's mother on the drive.

'Has your husband been supportive?' Ava asked. 'I can't imagine how you've coped with what Zoey went through.'

'Christopher thinks it's better not to dwell on it too much. He didn't give me all the details. I decided it was better not to know, and I avoid the television and news-papers,' Elsa said, waiting for her husband to reappear, wringing her hands.

'But you know there were other victims. Do you know there's another girl missing at the moment? We're afraid that if we don't find her soon, she'll be murdered too,' Ava said.

'Now, DCI Turner, I suppose you'd like to come in,' Christopher Myers said.

Ava nodded. 'After you, Mrs Myers,' she said, motioning for Elsa to move towards the door.

'That won't be necessary. My wife can put the dry goods away. Whatever it is you need to tell us can go through me. Elsa's been through more than enough,' Christopher said.

'I need to speak with you both, Mr Myers,' Ava replied. 'I need to ask questions rather than giving you information, so we can do this together or I'll speak with you and your wife separately, whichever you'd prefer.'

'Are we being accused of some wrongdoing again, Detective Turner, only we provided full alibi information and were told our lives would go back to normal,' Christopher said.

'Back to normal? Mrs Myers' daughter was murdered. Zoey's body has not yet been released for a funeral. The man who killed her has not yet been apprehended. Your life has gone back to normal, Mr Myers? I find that extremely disturbing,' Ava responded, taking a step closer to Christopher.

Elsa Myers stepped between the two of them, putting a delicate hand on her husband's forearm. 'That's okay. We'll talk to you together. I'm strong enough for that. Won't you come in?'

They sat in the lounge, Ava choosing the central seat on the only sofa to keep the Myers from huddling up together. They took an armchair each, Elsa perching on the edge of hers, hands folded in her lap, Christopher throwing himself backwards in the cushions and folding his legs.

'The community fete you were at when Zoey was taken, can you explain who organised that?'

'It was a fundraiser, to send money to an orphanage in Nairobi,' Christopher Myers said. 'It's an annual event. This year we raised more than two thousand pounds.'

'That's admirable, but I asked who organised it,' Ava said, looking at Elsa instead.

'It's a church event,' Elsa replied. 'We always help. Sometimes we run the barbecue, or maybe the bouncy castle. This year I baked for the cake stall too, and I helped set up the sweet stand.'

'Which church organised it?' Ava asked.

'Forgive me, but I think I'm right in saying that your questions should be relevant. Would you like to explain where this is going?' Christopher asked.

'Of course,' Ava said calmly. 'We have reason to believe that Zoey's killer has a link to a religious group. It came to our attention that you are members of a church, and we realised in checking your alibi that we didn't know very much about the event itself.'

'Why would you think our church has anything to do with what happened to Zoey?' Elsa asked.

'There are religious overtones to the crime itself. In addition, the second victim also knew someone who was present at the community fete. It's the only link between the victims that we've identified so far, so we're following it up.'

'Our church is very private,' Christopher said. 'Its members value their privacy. As has forever been the case, being outwardly religious can lead to all sorts of persecution. I can assure you, our church has nothing whatsoever to do with what happened to Zoey.'

'You can't be sure of that,' Elsa Myers whispered.

Christopher's eyes widened briefly, and he sat forward. 'This is upsetting you, Elsa. I knew it would. DCI Turner, I'm going to have to ask you to leave.'

'Did either of you ask for prayers to be said for Zoey?' Ava asked. 'Did you tell the rest of your group that she had sinned? Or did you feel that Zoey telling people you'd been violent to her, was worthy of punishment?'

'If you don't leave immediately, I will take matters into my own hands. You are no longer welcome in my home and I regard you as a trespasser,' Christopher said.

'You'll take matters into your own hands how, Mr Myers? The same way you did with Zoey?'

'Christopher, please don't,' Elsa whispered.

'Elsa, get upstairs to the bedroom,' he growled.

'I still have questions for Mrs Myers,' Ava said. 'Do I really need to call a backup unit, Mr Myers? I'm just trying to solve the question of who murdered your stepdaughter.'

'Our church group is the Children of the Word. We've worshipped there for a number of years. They're good people. I don't believe any of them would be involved in hurting my daughter,' Elsa said.

Christopher glared at her, but Elsa was looking Ava straight in the eyes.

'Did you ever believe you would end up living with a man who hit your daughter, and that you'd do absolutely nothing to protect her?' Ava asked.

'You little bitch.' Christopher rammed forward, raising a hand in the air. Elsa jumped backwards, closing her hands over her face, as Ava stepped into Christopher's chest, making the move she knew he would least expect. She brought her elbow up – hard – into the soft skin beneath his chin, then levelled her arm out to a horizontal position and pinned him against the wall with her forearm crushing his Adam's apple.

'That was a mistake,' Ava said. 'I advise you not to attempt to assault me again.'

'I'm going to have you fired,' he gurgled, his breath a strangulated whisper.

'Did you talk about Zoey at church? Did you tell the group her name and accuse her of sinning?'

'Fuck you,' Christopher Myers said.

'Mr Myers, you are under arrest for attempted assault of a

police officer. I require you to cease resisting, turn around and allow yourself to be handcuffed. Failure to do so will mean that additional charges will be brought against you.'

'Please don't,' Elsa cried. 'You'll make it worse . . .'

'Who knew about the conflict between you and Zoey within your church?' Ava asked.

'Everyone!' Elsa shouted. 'We prayed for her regularly. We prayed that she'd come home. We prayed that she would find God.'

'We prayed that the little cunt would stop spreading filth and lies and learn her place,' Christopher said.

Ava stepped away from him. 'Filth and lies? Is that what you told your church group? And you, Mrs Myers, did you stand by and let your husband accuse your daughter of being a sinner? Or did you call him out for the untruths he was telling to the people gathered supposedly in the sight of God?'

Elsa began to cry, one hand over her mouth, sobbing louder as she sank to the floor. 'I'm so sorry. I'm so sorry. I want to know who killed her. I want to know what happened. It's all my fault, like everything else that happened to her.'

'No,' Ava said, 'it's not your fault, Mrs Myers. No one chooses this. I need you to look at a photo for me and tell me if you recognise this man.' She pulled out the same CCTV image Callanach had shown to Lydia McMahon. Elsa looked hard at it, peering closer, then shook her head. 'No . . . I wish I did . . . I would help you. Truly. But I've never seen that man before in my life.'

Ava sighed. 'All right,' she said. 'I believe you. Mr Myers?' Christopher Myers looked at the photo, frowned and shrugged his shoulders. 'Fine,' Ava said. 'Mrs Myers, this is down to you. I can arrest your husband and have him removed from your home, or you can carry on leading the same life you have for the last decade or more. I won't force change upon you. It doesn't work like that.'

'You need to leave now,' Christopher Myers said grimly. 'I told you right at the start, this was nothing to do with us.'

'But it was!' Elsa Myers screeched. 'All those things you said about Zoey, the number of times you claimed she was touched by the devil, that you'd been a father above reproach. You stood there in our church and you made all those people feel sorry for you. You said . . . you said Zoey needed to be taught a lesson. How can this possibly not be our fault?'

'Don't you dare speak against me,' Christopher said. 'I've provided you with a home, with food, put clothes on your back. I've been your family when your children deserted you—'

'Because you beat them! They left because you hit them and belittled them, you called them names and you punished them endlessly. You drove them away from me!' she screamed.

'Mrs Myers?' Ava asked.

'Take him away,' she sobbed. 'I'll give you a statement. Violence to Zoey and to me . . . whatever you need. Just get him out of this house. I never want to see him again.' She turned to the wall, wailing into the flowery wallpaper.

Ava looked at her husband. 'Christopher Myers, I am arresting you on suspicion of assault. You do not have to say anything. But, it may harm your defence if you do not mention when questioned something which you later rely on in court. Anything you do say may be given in evidence.'

'This won't go to court,' he said, smirking. 'She'll change her mind. She's pathetic. And you'll be out of a job by tomorrow. I have a good lawyer and he knows people—'

'Mr Myers, spare me it,' Ava said quietly. 'As far as I'm concerned, this is my last week in the job anyway, and if the last thing I do is to get you out of this house, then it will be my lasting pleasure.' She turned him round and drew his wrists together, fastening them with handcuffs. 'We'll be out of here in just a few minutes, Mrs Myers. My officers will attend and I'm going to need you to give them a statement about everything that happened at your church group. I want a full list of names of other group members, with addresses where you know them. Do you understand?'

'Yes,' Elsa Myers whispered. 'Thank you. I might never have done this otherwise.'

Callanach and Tripp pulled up outside Vince Ashton's semi-detached house and watched Lydia's so-called shepherd guffawing at the television through the window of his front room. A yellow car was parked on the driveway and the road was quiet. West Calder was a relatively sleepy outlying town, that had insufficient to offer in terms of night-life for there to ever be any serious trouble. Until now. Caroline Ryan was still alive. Callanach was certain of it. Ava had just called to update them on the Christopher Myers situation. His wife, Elsa, had agreed to remain with uniformed officers to ensure that she had no contact with anyone from the church until every possible witness had been spoken to. The main problem was the length of the list of church members. If they had to go through each one individually, it would take days, and they couldn't afford to have any of them notifying the others. If the killer got spooked, the most likely course of action was that Caroline would be murdered immediately and her body dumped.

Two other cars pulled up. One parked across the street from Callanach and the other diverted down a side road. Those officers would be covering Vince Ashton's back door in case he decided he didn't want Callanach poking around inside the Children of the Word's business.

Callanach took a deep breath. This was their best chance at

finding Caroline Ryan alive. If the trail ran cold again this time, they would simply be waiting for another mutilated young woman to be left at the roadside. It didn't bear thinking about.

'Mr Ashton?' Tripp asked the balding fifty-something who appeared at the door. 'We're from Police Scotland's Major Investigation Team. Could we have a word?'

'Of course, come on in out of the cold,' Vince Ashton said. 'Make yourselves comfortable, gentlemen. Can I fetch you tea or coffee? I think I have hot chocolate if that's your thing.'

'No, thank you,' Tripp said. 'Is there anyone else at home?'

'I'm afraid not. It's just me. I've been alone for many years now. The Lord did not see fit to bless me with a second wife after my divorce.' He motioned towards a greying leather sofa.

'Mr Ashton . . .' Callanach began.

'Please, call me Vince.'

'We understand you're responsible for a church group called the Children of the Word. Is that correct?'

'I am the shepherd of that flock, yes, though I'm afraid saying that I am responsible for it may be promoting me too high.' Ashton smiled. 'Only God is responsible for the souls in our precious group.'

'Christopher and Elsa Myers have been members of your congregation for some years, is that correct?' Callanach asked.

'I don't deal in names, I'm afraid. Part of our rules is that we protect our privacy. It takes a long time to gain one another's confidence. You have to rise through each circle of the group in order to get to know one another better.'

'I've heard about the rules, Mr Ashton, but this is a criminal investigation and you providing names is non-negotiable,' Callanach snapped. 'Did you know that Christopher Myers' stepdaughter, Zoey, was the victim of a murder? Her body was found on Torduff Road three weeks ago.'

'It pained me a great deal,' Ashton said. 'We had prayed

for the girl many times. Alas, God's grace cannot enter where there is no willingness to allow him in. I spoke with Christopher and Elsa about their loss. Of course, their daughter had been a stranger to them for some time prior to the tragedy.'

'And did you know that another of your group members – Lydia McMahon – worked in the mother and baby unit from which the second victim was selected? She also died at a roadside, a week after Zoey. Both young women were mutilated. They bled to death. There is an indication that their perceived sinful behaviour had made them suitable targets for the killer,' Callanach said.

'Goodness me, what a terrible job you have. It never struck me until today, the sort of world the police are mired in. Are you weary of it? I'm not sure I could tolerate such a bleak existence. As a church member, I spend my time looking for the good in people.'

'What about Lydia McMahon? How long has she been a member of your flock?' Tripp asked.

'She's only just out of the probationary period, so to speak. We assess people, to find out how committed and disciplined they are. A group like ours doesn't work properly unless every member turns up each week without fail, including attending all our community activities. There are Bible study classes also. Too many religions allow their congregation to simply pay lip service to their beliefs once a week for an hour. We are more demanding, but then there is greater fulfilment.'

'DC Tripp asked you about Lydia McMahon,' Callanach interrupted.

'Quite so. She's been with us a few months. Nice woman. Intent upon bettering herself. Is she implicated in the case you're investigating?'

'She asked your church group to pray for a young woman

called Lorna Shaw, sharing details of her past life using drugs and falling in with desperate people. Lorna turned out to be the second victim. So you see, both girls were mentioned in your church and, it appears, labelled as sinners. Thereafter both girls ended up dead.'

'Forgive me, but I was under the impression that there were other victims. Are those women also linked to the activities of my flock?' Ashton asked, lifting his chin and folding his hands in his lap.

'We haven't found a connection yet, but that doesn't mean there isn't one,' Callanach said. 'More importantly, whoever the killer is, he quoted Bible scripture, so he appears to be someone with heavy religious leanings.'

'It seems to me that what we have here is a very unfortunate, very sad coincidence. The tragedy suffered by one of our own families is bad enough, but for your case to be linked to another of our worshippers, albeit in a rather obscure manner, is distressing. Do either of you have any particular beliefs? If so, I think this would be an opportune moment to seek comfort from our Lord.' Ashton bowed his head.

'I'm more concerned with the earthly safety of a young woman than with the need to seek comfort from a deity right now,' Callanach said. 'Do you recognise this man?' Once again, Callanach presented the printout.

'I do not,' Ashton said. 'Perhaps you are mistaken that the responsible party is a member of our group.'

'How many members of your group are non-Caucasian?' Tripp asked as Callanach slid the photograph back in his pocket.

'I beg your pardon?' Ashton asked.

'I'm just curious about the sociological makeup of your worshippers. Are there any racial minorities in your congregation?' Tripp continued.

'We're a relatively small group, so I wouldn't expect our

members to constitute a full cross-section of society,' Ashton said. 'Frankly, this is rather offensive.'

'Why? You've not been accused of anything. It's a simple question,' Callanach said.

'One I choose not to answer, thank you very much. There is an unpleasant implication behind it,' Ashton replied.

'Not at all, but perhaps you can help us with this passage. I believe it's from Daniel, chapter two, verse forty-three. "As you saw the iron mixed with soft clay, so they will mix with one another in marriage, but they will not hold together, just as iron does not mix with clay." I'm not sure I understand the context. What does the passage refer to?' Callanach asked.

'There are a variety of interpretations, like most biblical passages. That verse may reference people marrying from different religions, for example.'

'Do you discourage your flock from marrying outsiders?' Tripp asked.

'Plenty of religions, Constable, feel it is better if their followers marry others of the same belief system. We are not alone in that,' Ashton said, colour rising in his cheeks.

'And how do you feel about your followers marrying people of a different culture or race? Is that an issue?' Callanach asked.

'I'm not lowering myself to respond to that. We are a Christian body. You plainly do not understand what that means.'

'But it is one possible interpretation of the passage from Daniel, isn't it? Other less mainstream churches have adopted it in the past as an excuse to denounce interracial marriage,' Callanach said.

'I've done my best to help you, officers. I'm afraid, though, your questions have become unacceptable. If you require further information, it will have to be submitted in writing to my solicitor. Now if you'll excuse me, it's getting late.' He stood up.

Callanach remained seated in the armchair. 'Sit down, Mr

Ashton. At the moment, your church group, or your flock, however you think of it, is a key factor in this investigation. I have a few more questions, and I'm not done yet. You hire your chapel from a private estate. Does it have a font?'

'Yes, of course.' Ashton frowned. 'It's a sixteenth-century building, originally. We use it on Saturdays for Bible study and on Sundays for services.'

'Does the font have water in it all the time?' Tripp asked.

'Occasionally. We can't leave the water sitting for too long. It's a health hazard.'

'Are there any other buildings on the estate that you have access to? A garage, for example?' Tripp asked.

'None at all. What use would we make of it?' Ashton looked bemused.

'Any number of things,' Callanach muttered. 'We need to visit the chapel. Tripp, have a forensics team meet us there, and make sure someone from the incident room has notified the landowner in advance. Mr Ashton, I assume you have a key?'

'I can arrange to pick it up from the estate owner,' he replied.

It was 10.24 p.m.

Chapter Forty

'Okay. You go straight to the chapel. I've just finished making my statement regarding Christopher Myers, and I'm liaising with the officers with Elsa who are preparing a list of the other church members. Did Vince Ashton appear to be telling the truth when he said he didn't recognise the man in the photograph?' Ava asked.

'I think so,' Callanach replied. 'What about Elsa Myers?'

'Same goes for her. I didn't see any sign that she was lying and I don't think her husband was either. He was almost smug when he realised he didn't recognise the man in the photo.'

'I hope this isn't another false lead. How can the killer know what's being discussed in the church group if he's not a part of it?' Callanach asked.

'I don't know, but at the moment this is all we have to go on. Keep in touch overnight. See what forensics can get from the scene. I'll update the officers in the incident room. Tomorrow morning we'll have to start going through the members of the congregation one by one, and given the number of names on the list, that's going to take a couple of days, even if we send out multiple teams.' There was a knock at her door. 'Luc, I'm wanted. Let's speak later.'

Pax Graham appeared, his hair long around his face, wearing jeans and a rugby shirt.

'Are you off duty or undercover?' she asked.

'I was at home. Someone put this under my door,' he said. 'I thought you should see it.'

Ava took the sheet of paper from his hands. It was a schedule. Dates, times, phone numbers and a series of text messages. At the bottom of the page were notes.

'All text messages were deleted upon either sending or receipt, but were still within the retrievable time limit,' Ava read. 'OD is Oliver Davenport . . . DS Graham, I shouldn't be reading this. The police board has removed me from the investigation. You'll have to take it to Superintendent Overbeck.'

'I can't,' he said, smiling. 'There's absolutely no chance this information was obtained legally. If I take it to the super, it's going to raise questions I don't have answers to. At best it'll be ignored. At worst, there'll be an investigation into how it was acquired.'

'Damn it,' Ava muttered, reading on down the page. 'NAC is Noah Alby-Croft. EP is Elizabeth Prestwick. I haven't come across her before. So Oliver texted Elizabeth saying he needed to talk. She said she was busy. He texted back saying it was urgent and that he needed help. She asks what's wrong. He said "we did something" and "I'm scared". Hold on, is this the same date as . . .?'

'It's the same date as the third assault, when Melanie Long died. Time-wise, the texts would have been sent about an hour later,' DS Graham said.

'After Oliver Davenport got home,' Ava said. 'Elizabeth asks for more details, he says he can't talk about it on the mobile. It's pretty clear from these texts that this girl has no idea what he's referring to. She can't have been involved.' Ava continued skimming down the page. 'They agree to meet early the next day, before school. Is Elizabeth his girlfriend, do you think?'

'No kisses or anything suggesting more than just a very close friendship. Either way, they meet, then the texts stop. The other interesting one is from Noah Alby-Croft during the afternoon of the Melanie Long murder. They're having a normal text chat, then Alby-Croft instructs Davenport to swap to a chat app instead, one where the comments are erased within a minute. You can't retrieve those messages.'

Ava handed the paper back to the detective sergeant. 'How did you get this?'

'Some kind person slid it under my door. Must have been a police officer, or they couldn't have got my home address, given how careful I am during undercover ops. I keep myself to myself. No one knows what I do for a living.'

'And you brought it to me because?'

'I can't involve Lively or Salter even though I know they're handling the case. It'll implicate them in what is obviously improperly obtained material. You, on the other hand . . .'

'I'm already off the case, quite possibly soon to be off the force, so I don't matter. Is that it?'

'I was going to say that the impression I got was of a woman who cares more about getting the right result than doing things by the book. I thought you'd want me to protect your squad, too. DS Lively spoke highly of you. We need to speak with the girl. If she has information and we can get her to give a statement, then we'll have grounds for a warrant. It'll be easy to establish that we simply went to talk to a known associate of Oliver Davenport's. No one would ever need know that an illegal communications hack was undertaken. I can't do it without you, though. The girl's not going to open up to someone who looks like me.'

Ava stared at him, not certain she agreed. At seventeen, she was pretty sure she'd have been bowled over by Pax Graham. The rugby player physique, massive shoulders, long hair and chiselled highland jaw were the thing of bedroom posters. More of a problem was likely to be Elizabeth Prestwick's parents. If DS Graham turned up alone at night to speak with their daughter, they'd have either their lawyer or Superintendent Overbeck on the phone in minutes, and that would be the end of any possible break in the case.

'All right,' she said. 'We'll go. I can spare an hour, but I'll need to keep my phone on. We're in the middle of checking out the church we believe the skin doll killer is linked to. We'll ask Elizabeth's parents if we can record the interview. She's under eighteen. It'll have to be by the book.'

They travelled together, with Graham driving and Ava huddled into the passenger seat. Edinburgh's streets were quiet and frost had left a sparkling sheen everywhere. The Christmas decorations hadn't yet put in an appearance, and the nights were bitterly cold. Even the year-round roadworks didn't seem to be causing much of a problem, with the tourists all tucked up in their hotels. A few stragglers were out and about. The homeless were nowhere to be seen, either scared into hiding by the stream of attacks or seeking smaller, warmer places than shop doorways. Ava stared out of the window, wondering if this would be the straw that broke the camel's back and ended with her being fired. The board's decision had been unequivocal. There was no wiggle room for Ava to claim she hadn't understood. Yet here she was, pursuing one last lead. There was little doubt in her mind as to where the information had come from. Only one person she knew could have accessed Oliver Davenport's phone so quickly, and with complete disregard for legal constraints. Callanach's friend Ben Paulson had helped them before. No doubt his allegiance with Luc had meant that he'd been happy to help again.

'What would you do if you weren't a police officer?' Ava asked DS Graham.

'There was a time I'd have joined the military. If I had to choose something else now, I'd probably opt for charity work abroad. But undercover ops has meant that I've no ties here, save for the country herself. When I'm not working I travel whenever I can, driving north, camping. I'm not sure I could stay away more than a few months at a time. What about you?'

'No idea,' Ava said. 'Policing is all I've ever really been interested in. I don't care about commerce and I certainly couldn't ever swap to corporate security or private investigation. Farming maybe? Something where I could escape.'

'Is it really that bad?' Graham asked. 'You don't think Police Scotland would be stupid enough to let one of their best officers go.'

'I'm pretty sure they're thinking about me more as one of their greatest liabilities at the moment,' Ava said. 'Here we go. Greenhill Gardens. Nice houses. Here's hoping Elizabeth Prestwick is a little less prepared for our visit than the boys were.'

The Georgian house was symmetrically fronted with long rectangular windows and an impressive door. The grounds were gravelled, with manicured hedges, and three sports cars adorned the driveway. The doorbell issued a soft, welcoming tone and a swish of footsteps approached from within. Ava and Pax Graham had their ID badges out and ready for inspection.

'It's quite late,' Mrs Prestwick said quietly, but with a smile. 'Are you absolutely sure it can't wait?'

'I'm afraid not,' Ava said. 'It's a serious investigation, and while we're certain Elizabeth wasn't involved, she may inadvertently have been made party to some important information. I appreciate your concern as a parent. You can remain with your daughter at all times and we'll record the interview so that a record is kept.'

'All right. My husband will need to sit in as well. Do take a seat in the lounge while I fetch Lizzie.'

Ava and Graham looked around. The interior of the house was all reds and golds, with silk curtains and huge vases, the floors warmed with enormous, richly coloured rugs.

'Bit of a change from the places I normally do my policing,' Graham smiled.

'Which do you prefer?' Ava asked.

'Honestly, I'm not sure,' he said, as a teenage girl arrived, tears already in her eyes.

'Elizabeth, what's wrong? I've told you there's nothing to worry about, darling. The officers just thought you might be able to help. You're not in any trouble,' Mrs Prestwick cooed, rubbing her daughter's arm.

Her father appeared in the doorway behind, scowling. 'Liz, you've been acting strangely for days, now we've police officers at the door. What on earth is going on with you?' he demanded.

Ava saw the opportunity and stepped in. 'Mr Prestwick, forgive the late-night invasion. I'm sorry to disturb your family. Elizabeth,' she said, sitting down in the chair closest to the girl and looking her straight in the eyes with a smile, 'I promise, you're not in any trouble. In fact, quite the opposite. We're here because I think you might be able to help a little boy whose mother has been taken from him. He's too young to feel anything but grief at the moment, but he's going to have to grow up not knowing his mum. I can see from how much your own mum loves you, that it would be an awful thought to have a parent taken away from you, especially in such violent circumstances.'

'Violence? For God's sake, Elizabeth, what is all this about?' her father said, raising his voice.

Ava took hold of Elizabeth's hand and gave it a squeeze. 'I

think you may know something about it. Friends often talk to one another about the things in their life that scare them. It's not fair, though. They can't keep a secret themselves, and yet they expect you to be able to. Especially a secret this big and this dangerous. The best thing you can do is share it with me, like one of your friends might have done with you. Perhaps someone needed to talk and get it out of their system. If that's the case, then you've done nothing wrong except keep a confidence that you should never have been burdened with. It's not fair. I guarantee, if you've had no part in it, that you will be in no trouble at all. You might save further victims from being assaulted – even killed.'

Elizabeth looked at her mother, then her father, her eyes full of tears, hands shaking. She nodded.

'Do I have to?' Elizabeth asked, very quietly.

Ava looked at Pax, his phone in hand, recording the conversation. 'No,' she replied. 'You don't have to tell us anything at all. We're asking for a voluntary witness statement to assess if you know some details that might help us. We're only here because we believe you're friends with Oliver Davenport. The truth is that you can ask us to leave, right now, and we will. You don't have to do or say anything at all.'

'How old is the boy?' Mr Prestwick asked.

'Davenport?' Pax Graham queried.

'Not him. I know all about Oliver and his Leverhulme cronies. I meant the boy who lost his mother,' Mr Prestwick growled.

'Still a toddler,' Graham replied. 'Young enough to miss her. Not old enough to get his head round the fact that he won't ever see her again.'

'Answer the questions, Elizabeth,' her father said. 'All of them, as fully as you can. The police might be too polite to push, but I'm not.'

Elizabeth addressed the rug beneath her feet as she picked at nail varnish that was just starting to chip. 'I don't think Oliver wanted to be involved. He only told me about it after the third time. I saw the other attacks on the news, but I didn't realise then that Oli was there.'

'Can you explain what you're talking about more precisely?' Ava prompted.

'Those drug users who were . . .' She paused, more tears dampening her cheeks. 'Cut,' she finished.

'Do you know the names of anyone else involved?' Ava asked.

'Leo and Noah. They've all been best friends for years, only lately they started doing stupid dares. It just got out of hand. Oliver didn't want to get bullied by the other two and excluded from the other stuff they did together, so he went along with it. Then afterwards, Oli said he needed someone to talk to. He was really upset, you know? Couldn't sleep, couldn't stop thinking about it. After he explained what had happened, I said I didn't want to know. It scared me. Oliver's terrified, too, I know he is, but he just does whatever Noah tells him.'

'Did you know we'd already spoken to the boys?' Ava asked.

Elizabeth nodded. 'Oliver left a note to warn me. He said I had to delete any texts from him. I said I'd already done that. Then Noah came round . . .'

'Round here? To see you?' Graham asked.

'Yes. Once you found the key, they got worried. Oliver admitted to Noah that he'd spoken to me. Noah was really mad. He said . . . he said that if I spoke to anyone about what I knew, he'd tell everyone that we'd done things.' She turned to her mother, grabbing her hand and pushing her face into her shoulder. 'I didn't. I never let him touch me. I just didn't know how to tell you what was happening.'

'Oh, Lizzie, you poor thing. You should have spoken to me

straight away. I know Oliver's your friend, but you shouldn't have had to deal with this.'

They clung together on the sofa, with Elizabeth's father fuming behind them. 'I'm sorry,' Ava told him gently.

'You're sorry? What the hell for? You just saved my daughter from spending the next several years with this on her conscience. Thank God you found out she knew something. I'm going to kill the little bastard who involved her in this,' Mr Prestwick said.

'Actually, if you'd just give a formal statement, and agree to Elizabeth doing the same, we'll make sure the boys are dealt with properly,' Graham said. 'You can trust that we'll do our jobs, sir.'

'Do your jobs? Do you know who Noah Alby-Croft's father is? This case'll never see a courtroom. That man will have no scruples at all about using his influence to protect his son.'

'That's what started it all off in the first place,' Elizabeth said quietly.

'I'm sorry, Elizabeth. Started what off?' Ava asked.

'What they did. Hurting people. Noah Alby-Croft's dad is desperate for him to go to Oxford. Noah went down and spent a weekend there, looked around one of the colleges, met some of the older students. There's this club, apparently, but you only get to join it if you can show you're exceptional. You know, if you can operate beyond society's normal rules, or that they don't apply to you. Oli said Noah was determined to impress them. They're supposed to be some elite class. It all sounds awful. Anyway, Noah had to have witnesses. He roped Oli and Leo in.'

'This is about joining a club?' Graham asked. 'What exactly did Noah think he was going to get out of it that made slashing someone's face worthwhile?'

'Everything money can't buy,' Elizabeth's father said.

'Invitations to the right parties, weekends on yachts, the inner circles of the people who can make or break careers. Oxford's notorious for it. Just when you think that sort of stupidity's had its day, it rears its ugly head one more time.'

'I think Noah just wanted his dad to be proud of him. Get into the right university, have the right friends. His dad's a bit . . .'

'Pushy?' Ava offered.

'Yes. Pushy,' Elizabeth said.

'The third incident,' Ava said, 'the one Oliver told you about. Which of the three boys used the knife on that occasion?'

'Oliver said it was Leo,' she replied, finally breaking down with the weight of it all, sobbing on her mother's shoulder.

'Okay, so that's where we'll start,' Ava said to Graham. 'With Elizabeth's statement, we can arrest Leo Plunkett, then we'll be entitled to follow up with a house search and to access his mobile communications. Once Leo Plunkett is in interview, we can pursue Oliver, and it sounds as if he'll tell us what happened, given his need to talk it through with Elizabeth. Bring Noah in last. Before we go, Elizabeth, can you give us a list of other boys at Leverhulme School who know you're good friends with Oliver? That will help tie up any loose ends.'

'Sure,' the girl said, pulling herself together as her mother fussed over her. It was amazing, the difference confession could make. A changed young woman emerged as the fear and guilt slipped off her shoulders. Ava doubted the same would be true for Noah Alby-Croft and Leo Plunkett. Oliver Davenport, apparently, had rather more of a conscience. Elizabeth's mother handed the girl a pen and paper to draft the list.

'Walk me to the door?' Ava asked DS Graham. 'Find any of the names on the list. You don't need to visit. Just make a phone call and get confirmation from one of Oliver's friends that Oli is close with Elizabeth. This can look like a simple following up of known associates, kind of a lucky strike. No need to justify how we found Elizabeth after that.'

'Got it,' Graham said. 'You're sure Elizabeth wasn't involved?'

'The timing of the texts, and her reaction, makes it pretty clear she just got dragged into it unwillingly at the end. Keep her name low profile for as long as possible. You know what teenagers are like. She'll be on the receiving end of some nasty bullying when it gets out that she talked to us.'

'I'll look after her. Why don't you take my car? I'll get a squad vehicle out to pick me up and have Leo Plunkett in custody tonight.' Ava nodded and stepped out of the front door. 'You were amazing, by the way. It was the right thing to do, to tell the girl she was under no obligation to talk. Most people would have pushed her at that point.'

Ava smiled. 'Maybe I was just past caring,' she said.

'That's a lie, ma'am, and we both know it.'

'Doesn't really matter. I was never here, unless for any reason we have to produce that tape, and I don't think that'll be an issue once Elizabeth makes a formal statement.' Ava began to walk away, the gravel beneath her feet crunching softly in the pitch dark.

'I'm not prepared to take the credit for this,' he said, following her into the driveway and reaching for her arm in the dark. 'And I'm not prepared to see another officer bullied by bureaucrats, not even one of my superiors.'

'That's kind of you, DS Graham, but you can leave this to me. I don't need a protector,' Ava said.

'I know you don't,' Graham said softly. 'But a thing can be given without it being asked for, can't it, ma'am?'

Chapter Forty-One
Caroline

Her swollen eyes stung. Caroline had begun crying as soon as she'd woken up and realised she was trapped, and had barely stopped since then. He'd been parked in a red estate car next to her usual spot and she'd seen him grabbing at his chest and gasping for air as soon as she'd pulled up. Even with the pressure she was under, there was no chance she would leave someone ill in his car without helping, and so, like the good Samaritan she had been brought up to be, she had tried every door in the car until she'd found one that was unlocked. The front passenger seat, thankfully – or so she had thought at the time – allowed her access, and she talked gently to the hyperventilating male as she felt his pulse. It was only when she tried to get out again to retrieve her mobile from her handbag, which was still in her own car, that she realised there was a locking mechanism preventing the door from being opened from the inside. When she'd attempted to lean over the man to open the driver's door, he'd hit her in the temple so hard that she'd been rendered unconscious immediately. Her wake-up call had been a bottle of smelling salts waved beneath her nose, then she was marched, still staggering from the blow, to an outbuilding where she had fought uselessly as he tied her to a table.

Caroline had kept her eyes shut tight each time the man had come in to see to her needs or to rub thick, cold cream on her stomach and back. If she didn't look at him, if she didn't make eye contact with him or annoy him, if she couldn't identify him to the police, then perhaps he would let her live. Her terror was overwhelming. It brought waves of nausea every time she thought about what was going to happen to her. Her back ached from the lack of movement. Her wrists and ankles were sore and chafed. It was too cold. She'd been dressed in some sort of white gown with a couple of tatty, old blankets thrown over her, but she was still freezing. The roof above her had leaked during a rainstorm and her legs were wet where the drips had seeped through the blanket.

Making herself focus on the world outside, she wondered what had happened in the pitch meeting at work. Had they panicked when she didn't arrive? Had they realised she was missing quickly enough to trace her mobile phone? Not that she had any idea where it was now. Presumably the man had left it in her car. Or perhaps he had used her keys to take her handbag but had destroyed the SIM card. Jadyn would be in pieces by now, she thought, the tears beginning again. They'd had a celebration planned for the evening, so certain was she of making junior partner. A stack of wedding magazines was waiting on her bedside table. She hadn't allowed herself to look through them while she was still working to get the pitch perfect, but that evening she'd intended to light candles around a hot bubble bath and indulge herself with ideas for dresses, guest favours, locations and caterers. Her bridesmaids, she'd already decided, would wear the palest shade of green silk, with simple sleeveless dresses and tiny delicate rosebud tiaras, a minimalistic replica of the one she had already found for herself.

It wasn't fair to work so hard and to lose so much, to be left so scared and alone. It wasn't fair when she'd never hurt anyone in her life. Nor that she was going to die so young. She knew she was going to die. It was ridiculous to carry on pretending that the man holding her captive wasn't the same man who had killed the other girls, not least because there was still hair trapped in splinters on the table, and blood drips where her right wrist was now bound up. To start with, she had refused to be so defeatist as to admit where she was and whose company she was in, but now defeat seemed a more comfortable companion than hope. Hope was the boyfriend who didn't turn up to take you on the date you'd been waiting for all week, when you'd bought a new dress and had your hair done especially. Hope hurt.

Then there was a sense of just deserts, born of guilt. Those stories in the papers about the other girls had taken only seconds from her day. Front-page news, not that she'd bothered reading it. It hadn't applied to her – that was what she'd thought. The media had implied that a certain type of young woman was being taken – troubled, off the rails, the sort Caroline definitely wasn't. They had taken risks, she'd assumed, been careless with their lives. Reaching the fingers of her right hand down to the table leg, she could feel the old blood crumble away. They hadn't died here, she'd followed enough of the story to know that, but perhaps they'd wanted to. In her ivory tower of self-righteousness she'd assumed she didn't fit any victim profile. How wrong she'd been. And how very, very stupid. She'd climbed into a car with a strange man. At the time it had seemed heroic. Now she could see so much more clearly that it had simply been dumb.

Dumb, dumb, dumb. And she would pay for it with her own blood.

Perhaps the cold would finish her off instead. That was the

preferable outcome: to fall into a deep sleep, never to wake up, without knowing torture, pain or mutilation.

It was the middle of the night or thereabouts. Certainly there was no light in the sky, and the man hadn't troubled her for several hours now. Her breath made white clouds in the air and her tears left freezing trails on her cheeks. The toenails she had carefully painted a shade of teal had long since lost all sensation. Perhaps that was best. The numbness of her stomach and back were a match for her extremities. She sang to herself as she tried not to think about what the Babydoll Killer, as the papers had dubbed him, was going to do to her.

Caroline closed her eyes and began to sing the opening lines to her mother's favourite song, 'Daydream Believer' by The Monkees. Strange how at the worst of times it was childhood melodies that stuck in your mind. She forced the words out through unwilling lips, blue from the cold and clumsy with fear.

He made dolls from his victims' skin. The thought sliced through her pathetic attempt to distract herself. Caroline had heard a secretary at work whisper the details to a colleague. She'd ignored it, focused on her work.

She struggled to recall the next line of the song. Something about sleep in your eyes? But the next line was on the tip of her tongue before she could stop it. Suddenly the only image in her mind was a razor blade. Not the right song at all. Perhaps that was why it had sprung to mind. There really was no such thing as free choice after all.

He cut the skin from their bodies and drew their faces on the dolls. The press had been ruthless in their descriptions, colouring the reporting with saddened tones, but really, this was the stuff of editorial room fantasies. Caroline had refused to engage in conversation about it. The gruesomeness didn't bear discussion, and she had too much else on her mind. Besides, it wasn't relevant to her. She had a building to design and a wedding dress to pick out. Once they were married, she and Jadyn would oversee the building of their own home on the most perfect plot of land. It was on a hillside. She had studied Austrian mechanisms for stabilising buildings on steep land, and knew exactly how she wanted it built. The frontage would largely be glass. It would be expensive, and she would need to be clever about insulation, but using largely reclaimed materials meant that she could offset their carbon footprint.

He was going to cut her, too. That was why he was rubbing the cream into her belly and back. She would end up nothing more than a small rag doll, made from her own flesh. A miniature of herself, just like the scale model of the perfect house-to-be that sat on her desk at work.

The man had insisted on talking to her in spite of her closed eyes and tightly shut lips. When he entered the room, she didn't even like breathing the same air as him. He whispered insults as he rubbed her stomach, and eventually she'd had to ask. How could she not? If she had to die, it seemed ridiculous not to at least demand an explanation. In the end, only a single word from her had been necessary to kick-start his diatribe of hate.

'Why?' Caroline had asked, trembling as she spoke, terrified she might set off some unstoppable train of violence.

'Dirty,' he'd replied, bringing his head close over her face. Even with her eyes shut, she'd known how close he was to her. She could feel the heat of his skin, smell meat on his breath, feel the spittle landing on her forehead as he'd spoken. 'Dirty girl. Letting the infidel touch her. You like that? You enjoy having a man like him touch you? Filthy, bad girl. Tainted, Rachel says.'

Who was the infidel? That was what she'd wanted to ask. Why did he think she was dirty? She was anything but. The man she was engaged to was her first and only lover. While other friends had skipped from one partner to another through their twenties, she had stayed loyal and faithful. Was she here because she'd been mistaken for someone else? She wanted to know and yet couldn't bring herself to say the words out loud. She didn't want him to speak to her again. Didn't want to feel his breath blowing into her nose again. But she did want to know who Rachel was. It wasn't someone she knew. Her mother had a friend called Rachel when Caroline was little, but she'd passed away years ago. Was Rachel a name the man called himself – a second identity that crawled out when he was looking for affirmation or a scapegoat? She imagined herself screaming at him, demanding answers, not caring whether she lived or died. She imagined letting her rage explode at him, demanding he cut her loose, even headbutting him as he leaned over her, but she knew she would say and do nothing. Nothing except keep her eyes shut, her head turned to the side, the tears dribbling down her frigid cheek to splash on the grubby wood beneath.

For now, though, she remained alone. Caroline could open her eyes and stare at the greenish glass ceiling. He didn't come to her in the darkness. Small mercy. She didn't think she could take being trapped with him while it was dark. The spiders were bad enough, but even the largest of them couldn't raise the nausea that his touch did.

'Zoey,' she said aloud. Finally, she had managed to dredge one of the dead girls' names up from her memory. 'That's it. Zoey.' It was like finding a sliver of forgiveness. At least she could put a name to some of the cells on the table, share a moment. 'I'm sorry, Zoey. I should have read your story. I should have learned about you, and grieved for you. I hope you weren't as scared as me,' she said, letting her tears come for the hundredth time, knowing they were in good company with others shed there before. 'I hope you didn't feel it when he cut you,' she sobbed. 'I wish I could have met you, and told you that I know how it feels. I wish we could have been here together and held one another's hands. I'm so sorry. I'm so, so sorry.' She cried out into the dark. Death was a slowly creeping monster, and the terror was almost unbearable. If she'd had a gun, she would have aimed it at her own head. Poison, a fall, hanging – none of it seemed anything other than a blissful release compared to the atrocities she knew were coming. 'Can you hear me?' she asked the air. 'Zoey, is part of you still here? I need you. I need someone to hold me. I wish I'd been here to hold you.'

The sobs trailed off into hopeless sniffles. The tears ran out. She was arid. Nothing left. He would come in the morning, and next time she would ask him to just end it for her. Quickly. Perhaps if she begged, he would make it faster, painless. If she screamed at him, perhaps she could send him into a rage that would end with a rock smashed over her head. And perhaps, in spite of whatever she did or didn't do, there would be a doll after all. A tiny Caroline doll, with bright eyes and shiny hair, who would smile forever and ever and ever. Eventually, she slept

Chapter Forty-Two

'What's the time?' Ava asked Callanach, perching next to him on an ancient pew at the rear of the chapel.

He glanced at his watch. 'Five forty-five,' he said, 'and we've got virtually nothing. The font had water in it, and the stone has been confirmed by the owner of the estate as marble. If you take a vial of the water and hold up a torch to it, you can see some of the flecks shining, like on the dolls.'

'We've found nothing else on the estate,' Ava said. 'The owners let a squad go through every room of the manor, including the loft and cellar. They couldn't have been more helpful.'

'So why is this place being let out at weekends?' Callanach asked.

'They're atheists, and even if they weren't, the days when they could expect a vicar or priest to come to their chapel and hold a service for a handful of people have long since passed. They maintain the building because of their love of history, they said, but they don't feel it has any religious relevance to them. They seemed genuinely pleased that it was being used by a church group. Horrified, obviously, when I told them what we suspected, but they had no idea that anything other than mainstream Christianity was being practised here.'

'Yeah, well, Tripp says this group has a very strict new member test. It's more like one of those off-the-wall American sub-cults. There are a few odd comments online about it. Someone reporting they didn't like the way the group handled apparent insider infractions, and wanted to leave. Didn't go down too well.'

'Really? Can we trace who left the comment, see if we can get some more details?' Ava asked.

'Not easily. It was an old chat group, now closed, with a thread that hadn't been active for more than a year. All pseudonyms. Tracing it certainly won't help in the timeframe we have available.'

'Speaking of tracing,' Ava said quietly, 'thank you. I appreciate what you did in the Melanie Long case. I may have sealed my own fate as far as my job is concerned, but it was the right thing to do. Tell Ben how much I appreciate it, will you?'

'How did you know?' Callanach asked. 'I asked Ben not to involve you.'

'Detective Sergeant Graham brought me the text messages Ben got from the mobiles. They led us to a witness who wasn't physically involved, but who is prepared to give a statement about what she knows. By now we should have at least two of the boys in custody, and Pax will be executing search warrants that should also give us Noah Alby-Croft. Not that it's my case any more, but at least I can walk away knowing justice was done.'

'DS Graham?' Callanach asked. 'I asked Ben to send whatever he found to Lively.'

'Lively?'

'Ma'am, sir,' Tripp called to them. 'Could you come and have a look at this?'

They followed him through into a tiny space – no more than a large closet – set into one wall of the chapel. Previously, looking at the old wrought-iron hook on the wall, it would have provided an area for the priest to have prepared and hung his garments. Now, there was a noticeboard, a small safe and a bin. Tripp, gloved and suited, pointed to the bin.

'There were a few notices in there – times and dates for Bible study, plans for community events and a church-cleaning roster.' He held up a crumpled piece of paper. There were six names on it. 'These people all have access to the church at any time.'

'But the estate owners said there's only one key for the main door and that it's handed to their housekeeper on a Sunday evening and collected again the following Saturday morning,' Ava said.

'That's right,' Tripp said. 'But there's a second door.' He walked to a large tapestry and pulled it back, revealing a newer door with a modern lock. 'The estate had loaned them this key previously, but the current arrangement is that the key to this door isn't given out at all. I've spoken with the good shepherd Mr Ashton. He confirms that the people on the cleaning roster actually do have copies of that key – made, he says, in case the main exit was not accessible in a fire.'

'They all have keys?' Ava asked.

'That's right. There are currently six church group key-holders with permanent access to this building. Vince Ashton didn't tell us about it at first because he was aware he was in breach of his agreement with the estate owners and didn't want them to revoke his rental.'

'Right,' Ava said. 'Get addresses. Hopefully Mr Ashton will help us with those given that he withheld other useful information. Have the incident room find out if any of the properties has a dark-coloured minivan registered to them.'

She scanned the list. 'No Sam or Samuel on the list, though. Three men and three women. We'll start with the men. Callanach, you take Matthew Yeats. I'll start at Jacob Lesser's house. Tripp, take another team and search Paul Moseley's. Make sure no phone calls are made unless they express a desire to call their lawyer, and then I want numbers verified before those calls are made. Police officers must dial for them. Uniformed officers are to remain in each house with every person on the list until they are all cleared of involvement. Let's go.'

Forty-five minutes later, three front doors were knocked at the same time. At each house, officers stood guard at the back doors. Garages, loft spaces and a basement were searched. Children were lifted from their beds, bemused and crying. Ava's presence was met with a hard silence. Tripp was greeted with warm helpfulness. Callanach was called a variety of names that suggested the homeowner was no lover of the immigrant population. But no evidence was found to suggest that any of the girls had been known to any of the householders. No dark minivan was found. Tripp called Callanach, who called Ava.

'Nothing,' Callanach reported. 'They're all expressing genuine shock at the suggestion the perpetrator could be anything to do with their group. I think you'd probably call it righteous indignation, but it seems real.'

'Fine. We'll have to check the women on the list anyway,' Ava said.

'Tripp was told by Vince Ashton that Violet Parks is in her seventies and was hospitalised last week with flu. The incident room has since verified that information with the hospital and we sent a uniformed squad to her address. It's a flat in supported housing. She lives alone. No access to outbuildings and no living relatives, apparently.'

'That's one less to check on then. It's six fifty now. Send Tripp and a full backup unit to whoever's next on the list and we'll take the last. Text me the address, I'll meet you there,' Ava said.

Ava pulled her car up at the side of the road. She could see Callanach inside his own vehicle, poring over a map. She bolted from her car, coat over her head to avoid the drenching rain.

'Where the hell is this house? I've lived in Edinburgh most of my life and I swear I've never felt this lost before,' she said.

'The directions said that it was on an unnamed road off the A71, south of Livingston and west of Kirknewton. The postcode doesn't seem to be helping,' Callanach said.

'This is definitely not the sort of woman who gets a lot of mail-order deliveries,' Ava said.

'She must get some post, though, right? I'll get the incident room to speak with the postal service. Perhaps they'll be able to guide us there.' Callanach phoned through as Ava got Vince Ashton on the line.

'No joy,' Callanach said eventually, after the incident room had called him back. 'Post for this address goes to a PO box in Livingston.'

'And Vince Ashton has never been to this address,' Ava said, 'although apparently Rachel Jerome has been a church member for some years. He says she's a widow whose husband died before she moved to this area.'

'So she lives alone, as far as we know, is extremely religious and doesn't want the convenience of having her post brought to her door. Why do I already get the impression she might be less than chatty when we turn up? She's got to be here somewhere. Leave your car here and we'll go in mine. You look, I'll drive. This bloody rain isn't helping.'

They set off again, peering between the trees that rendered one side of the road in complete shadow, checking the ground for tyre tracks and bemoaning the dull grey skies.

'Do you think Caroline's still alive?' Callanach asked as they searched for signs of life.

'If she is, and her captor is anything to do with this church, she won't be for much longer. It's ten to seven now. I can't gag everyone whose houses we've searched today for more than a couple of hours, given that we've nothing to charge them with. By lunchtime, every single member of the Children of the Word will know what's happened. Honestly, if Caroline is still alive, I very much doubt she will be by the end of the day.'

Chapter Forty-Three

The man shook Caroline awake. She stared at him through the groggy haze of exhaustion and dehydration, incomprehension followed by a gasp of panic and a desperate attempt to sit up. She cried out, the bindings on her ankles and wrists having produced sores and swelling.

'Stay still,' he muttered, as he slid his hand beneath the blankets and her gown to smear more cream across her abdomen.

'Water,' she croaked, closing her eyes again and looking away.

'In a minute,' he snapped, 'if you make it easy for me to touch your back.'

All thought of rebellion was dormant. Caroline wanted only two things. The first was a drink to quench the throbbing ache in her throat. The second was to survive unhurt for just a little longer. Just another day. She used her fading strength to arch her back, shuddering as his hands slid across the tops of her buttocks and upwards along her spine. When he was done, he lifted a cup with a straw to the side of her mouth and let her sip.

'We're going to pray this morning,' he said.

Caroline frowned, shaking her head. 'What . . . what did you say?' she whispered.

'Going to pray. You need to repent, to be saved.' He set the cup on a bench and smoothed down Caroline's blankets.

'Why would we pray? You're going to kill me,' she said, wide-eyed, her policy of avoiding eye contact suddenly ridiculously outdated. She was going to die. Not looking at the man who would kill her wasn't going to change that.

'Not me,' he muttered, wiping his hands on a rag then dropping it on the floor. 'I never killed anyone.'

'Samson, what did I tell you about talking to them?' a woman asked sharply from the doorway.

Caroline stared at her. She was younger than the man by a few years. Her hair looked recently cut and styled. Where his was showing substantial amounts of grey, hers was a deep brunette, pixie short, neat and well defined. Her face was angular but not harsh, and her eyes shone. In her right hand she held a heavy book, the pages edged with gold. Holding it aloft, she smiled at Caroline.

'As Luke taught us, Jesus said, "It is not the healthy who need a doctor, but the sick. I have not come to call the righteous, but sinners, to repentance." I want only to save you, Caroline. You have transgressed. Allowing yourself to be touched by a man of a different race, of different skin. Are you not ashamed?'

Caroline's heart froze in her chest. Blood rushed to her cheeks, the first warmth she'd felt in hours. Clenching her fists and her jaws, she screeched.

'Fuck you! Fuck your filthy, racist, disgusting, pathetic, diseased minds. You stand before me with a Bible and spew this hatred? How dare you? If you're going to kill me, you'd better get on with it, because I'm not going to let you have one single second of peace.' She glared at Rachel then opened her mouth and began to scream, letting the sound fade and die before taking another breath and starting again.

'No one can hear you. Our closest neighbour is a mile away.

But go ahead and lose your voice. The Lord guides us all. Eventually his light will touch you, too, whether you choose to feel it or not,' Rachel cooed.

'You're monsters. Psychopaths. You're worse than other psychopaths, because you do this pretending to be Christians.'

'I'm going back to the house.' Rachel smiled to Samson. 'Don't touch this demon again today. And remove her blankets. We'll see if she feels more like receiving God's grace when she's a little colder.'

'Go to hell,' Caroline shouted.

'Spoken like a true follower of Satan,' Rachel said, making the sign of the cross in the air as she left.

Caroline stared at the man. 'So you just do everything she says? You let her control you? What sort of man are you? That crazy bitch is the one who killed the other girls, isn't she?' There was no answer. 'Isn't she?'

'Sometimes I do things she doesn't like,' Samson said. 'I try not to let her find out. When she finds out, I have to pray a lot and punish myself. It hurts.'

Caroline stared at him.

'You want me to show you the things I do that she doesn't like? You might like them. I'd enjoy showing you.' He grinned.

'No. That's okay,' Caroline muttered, the look on his face raising a tide of nausea in her stomach. 'I don't want to see.'

'Maybe you should. Maybe then you'd learn to be a good girl,' he whispered, leaning over her again.

Caroline turned her head away and closed her eyes. 'I'll be a good girl right now,' she said. 'I'll be quiet. Please, just leave me alone.'

'Not yet,' the man said. 'I have things I need to do.'

It was 7.12 a.m.

Chapter Forty-Four

'Down there,' Ava said. 'There's a light through the trees. Let's check it out.'

Callanach swung his car hard left into woodland, down a small dirt track, well hidden by the stormy night's leaf fall.

The house was small and neat, with well-groomed, low hedges along the front. A red estate car sat outside the garage. Light shone from one upstairs window and from one downstairs room, although the curtains were still drawn in both. The deep blue front door was recently painted, and the brickwork looked meticulously maintained.

'Hardly the sort of chaos we expect from a serial killer,' Callanach said as he turned off the engine.

They climbed out, looking for signs of life around them. It was completely silent. The birds had not yet begun to stir and the foxes were already back in their dens. The surrounding trees shielded the house from the road thanks to a bend in the access-way. It was picturesque and idyllic, if you had decided to forsake the commerciality and hustle of modern life without resorting to a distant island.

Ava rang the doorbell, which chimed in a distant room. No

one came. She checked her watch. 'It's only quarter past seven. I guess Ms Jerome might still be asleep. Shall we go round the back?'

'One more try,' Callanach said, stepping forward and knocking hard instead.

The door opened seconds later. A primly dressed woman, complete with apron, smiled at them, looking surprised but delighted by their appearance.

'Yes,' she said. 'Can I help you? Are you lost? I don't get many visitors out here.'

'Ms Rachel Jerome?' Ava asked her.

'That's me,' the woman said, a slight frown wrinkling her forehead, conflicting with the smile that remained fixed on her face.

'I'm DCI Turner and this is DI Callanach. May we come in for a moment?'

'Of course. Come inside, it's miserable out there. Has something happened? I think this is the first time in my life I've had the police at my door.'

'We understand you're on the cleaning rota for the Children of the Word church group. Is that right?' Ava asked.

'It is indeed. Come and sit yourselves down in the lounge. I'm afraid I haven't started my baking yet today – my bread doesn't go into the oven until 8 a.m. – so I've little to offer you. A hot drink might warm you up.'

'No, thank you. And we'll stay standing. This won't take long. There'll be other officers here shortly, too. I'm afraid we suspect a member of the church group in the deaths of three young women and for the kidnapping of another. We're talking to anyone who had a key to the chapel during the period in which the crimes were committed.'

Rachel Jerome put her hand to her throat. 'Oh my goodness, that's awful,' she said, tears welling in her eyes. 'Why would you think such a thing?'

'A number of circumstances indicated a church group member. Do you mind if we conduct a search of your home, Ms Jerome?' Callanach asked.

'Be my guest, please,' she said. 'You're welcome to go wherever you need.'

'Thank you,' Ava said, walking past her into the hallway, opening cupboard doors as she went, feeling around the back of the walls for hidden doorways. She went towards the kitchen at the rear of the property as Callanach took the stairs.

It was pristine. A series of baking tins hung on one wall and a variety of copper pans swung above the stove. The sink was free of debris and the floor shone. Ava opened a door to find an orderly pantry full of tins and dried foods, enough that shopping could be avoided for several weeks, if not months, should the necessity arise. Flicking though the drawers, she found that each had been assigned a single task – for cooking spoons, tea towels, knives. Not a speck of dust nor a crumb marred any surface or lurked in any corner.

'Next to godliness,' Ava muttered to herself as Luc appeared from the hallway.

'Where's Ms Jerome?' he asked.

'Lounge,' Ava said, following as he turned and disappeared.

'Rachel,' he said. She set down the book she was reading and inclined her head at him. 'There are three bedrooms. I assume the main one is yours. There's also what looks like a girl's room. Whose is that?'

'My daughter's,' she said quietly. 'Verity left to live in Australia with her boyfriend several years ago. I miss her a great deal. That's why I keep her room as it was. Sentimental, I know, but . . .'

'And the other bedroom? I found a man's clothes in the wardrobe and a second toothbrush in the bathroom. Are you married?'

'That would be my brother's room. He came to live with

me years ago. He's not much of a cook, you see. If I'd left him to his own devices Lord knows what would have become of him.'

'His name, Ms Jerome?' Ava asked.

'Is there a problem, because I really don't think he would—'

'His name?' Callanach repeated.

'Samson,' she said brightly. 'He's not part of my church group though, so I don't think he can be the man you're searching for.'

'Samson. Not Samuel,' Ava muttered quietly, raising her eyebrows at Callanach.

'Does he drive a car?' Callanach asked, striding towards the front window and looking out into the garden.

'Yes, of course. Living out here, you couldn't get by without driving. He's driven since he was—'

'Make and colour?' Ava demanded.

'Um, a dark old thing, quite big. I'm no good with makes and models, I'm afraid,' Rachel said apologetically.

'A minivan?' Callanach prompted.

'I guess you could describe it like that. He's had it for ages. I keep telling him it's a death trap.'

'Where is he now, Ms Jerome?' Ava asked, moving into the corridor to get a view through the rest of the house.

'Probably walking in the woods. It's what he does most mornings. He's a terribly early riser and he tries not to disturb me by banging around in the kitchen. I usually cook him breakfast when I get up.'

'Where's his car?' Callanach asked, peering down the driveway.

'He keeps it further down the track past the back of the house. I don't like that messy old thing sitting on the drive. I'm rather a keen housekeeper, as you can see.'

'Would you take us to the car, Ms Jerome?' Ava said.

'Would you not like to wait until the other officers get here,

378

only there'll be no one to open the door, is what I'm thinking,' she replied.

'They'll find us,' Ava said. 'We need to speak with your brother urgently. Let's go.' She stepped back to usher Rachel into the hallway.

They left the kitchen via the back door and stepped into the garden. The side gate took them onto a grass driveway. Closer inspection showed that a vehicle had driven through recently, although the majority of the grass had sprung back up.

'Gosh, it's been raining cats and dogs out here, I hadn't realised how soft the ground had become,' Rachel babbled.

'Would you mind being quiet please?' Callanach asked. 'I'd like to be able to listen.'

'Oh, yes, sorry. I hadn't thought about it,' she replied sweetly.

The trees' cover was absolute, the daylight not powerful enough to light the natural tunnel. Ava took a torch from her pocket to check to each side as they walked.

'It's a long way through the woods. Why would he park his van all the way back here?' Ava asked Rachel as they walked.

'He has greenhouses,' Rachel explained. 'He often goes to buy compost, tools or plants so it makes more sense to drive it to the door than carry it, I suppose. To be honest, I don't come out here. The kitchen is my domain. I leave him to freeze in the outdoors on his own. I think he likes the quiet, too. It's hard living in the same house as someone else and being under their feet all day. This way, we have something to talk to one another about in the evenings.'

The scream pierced the canopy, sending birds up in its wake and startling small rodents in the undergrowth.

'Go straight back to your house and stay indoors,' Ava ordered Rachel. 'When the other officers arrive, direct them towards the greenhouses.'

They began to sprint along the pathway. Ava threw her torch down as the greenhouses came into view.

'I'll go to the back,' Callanach said.

'Don't bother. There'll only be one entrance. We'll have to go in together,' Ava said, slowing down as she caught sight of a faint green glow behind one set of moss-obscured glass panes. They crouched, running low towards the noises. A man's voice rumbled deep as a higher one pleaded and cried. Ava grabbed a garden fork that was resting against the greenhouse, as Callanach picked up a brick from a pile of debris on the ground. 'On three,' Ava said, counting slowly in time with the seconds on her watch. They burst through the door at 7.23 a.m.

Chapter Forty-Five

'Police!' Ava shouted. 'Step away from the girl.'

The man swivelled his head. In his right hand he held a pair of secateurs, blades gleaming and open, like a small but lethal metal mouth, ready to snip.

'She's not a girl. She's the beast, the mother of lies . . .'

'Move away right now,' Ava said, moving left to make room for Callanach to get further into the greenhouse next to her.

It stank. A full pot of urine was darkening on the floor next to the exit. The stench of sweat and blood filled the air. Caroline lay frozen, trembling, trying desperately to speak, her eyes rolling wildly from Samson to Ava and back. Her feet and hands were blue from their bindings and the crusts of the cuts beneath were visible under the green garden twine with which she'd been bound. Dead tomato plants shielded the views out into the garden, and the rear panes had been boarded up. The table Caroline was laid out on was vast, an old kitchen table from a hundred years ago, reclaimed for the most hideous of purposes.

'Caroline,' Callanach said. 'It's all right. We're here to help you.'

'She must repent,' Samson said. 'Without repentance, her soul will burn in hell.'

'But you baptised the dolls and purified their souls, isn't that right?' Ava asked gently. 'If you care that much, why hurt the women?'

'The dolls were still pure. Newly born. Their lives had to be dedicated to God before being sent out into the world to deliver his word,' Samson droned, looking from Ava to Callanach and back again.

'Where did you baptise them, Samson?' Callanach asked, drawing the man's gaze to allow Ava to move further forward.

'In the font at the chapel,' he said. 'I took Rachel's key off the hook in the kitchen. I don't go to the services. Too many people. I can't hear God's voice with other people around me.' He swung back around to face Ava, dropping the secateurs and grabbing a large garden spade instead, turning it over in his hands so that the side of the metal scoop was facing the ground. Raising it above his head, he began to mutter a prayer.

'Samson,' Ava said. 'Put that down. You don't want to hurt Caroline. You haven't hurt her so far. There's no point making it worse now.'

Callanach took two steps forward, edging along the opposite side of the table from Samson, towards Caroline's head.

'Stop there,' Samson shouted at him, swinging the spade over Caroline's body and angling its blade two feet above her neck.

'Samson,' Ava said. 'Whatever you did to the other girls, we can talk about it. Do the right thing now. If you show mercy now, it will help. It'll show that you're capable of change. If you put down the spade and let my colleague untie Caroline, you and I can stay in here and talk this thing through.'

'I had no choice,' he said. 'There were orders, instructions. The girls were bad. All of them. I had to be the instrument. Or I'd have been damned too.'

'You have a choice now,' Ava said, lowering the fork she'd had pointed at him and placing it gently on the floor. 'You have my word we'll look after you. We'll get you the help you need. Sometimes people hear things, Samson, voices in their head that make them confused. It may be that none of this was your fault. I want you to tell me all about it. Just give me a little time. All you need to do is put down that spade.'

'Can't disobey,' he muttered, staring at Caroline's face as he raised the spade up another foot and took a deep breath. 'Not allowed to disobey . . .'

As he began to slice the blade of the spade through the air, Callanach lobbed the brick across the table towards Samson's head. It struck him squarely in his right eye, spinning him clockwise. There was a wet crunch as the spade missed the target of Caroline's neck, landing a foot higher and smashing into the top of her skull. Samson flew backwards, clutching his face and howling. Ava bent down and grabbed the garden fork, already launching herself towards Samson. Thrusting it hard into his shoulder, she forced him to the floor, one of the fork's tines piercing his flesh and driving right through to bone. She followed up with her body weight until he was on his back, blood spraying from his face and pooling across his shoulder, with Ava above him leaning on the handle.

'Is she alive?' she shouted to Callanach, who had his fingers on Caroline's neck, feeling for a pulse.

'Possibly just unconscious,' he said. 'She's so cold. If there's a pulse, it's too weak for me to find.'

'We've got to free her,' Ava said. 'Get her wrapped up.'

She pulled the fork from Samson's shoulder with a liquid sucking sound, ignored his injuries and hauled him over, snapping handcuffs onto his wrists behind his back and leaving him face down, crying and bleeding into the dirt. Picking up the secateurs, Ava snipped the bindings on Caroline's wrists and ankles.

Rachel Jerome burst through the door as they were covering Caroline in the tatty blankets and their own warm coats.

'Samson?' Rachel yelled. 'Oh my Lord, Samson! What have you done? What have you done?'

'Ms Jerome, I need you to get out of here right now,' Callanach said. 'I want you to call an ambulance and tell them there's a serious head injury. An air ambulance would be best. Go.' Rachel stood in the doorway sobbing, arms wrapped around herself.

'You do the right thing, now, Samson. Do you hear me? Put your faith in the Lord.'

'I'm so sorry,' he sobbed from the ground.

'Go!' Ava shouted at her.

Rachel fled.

At 7.44 a.m., backup police units arrived, wrapped Caroline in a silver thermal blanket and waited for the paramedic helicopter to land on the road, which had been closed for half a mile in each direction. Soon after that, the medics took over, declaring the injured woman alive but unconscious and unresponsive. Samson Jerome was handcuffed in spite of his injuries and taken to a police car for secure transfer to the hospital.

By the time the white-clad forensics army arrived to process the scene, the places was awash with police cordoning off the greenhouses, seizing all the contents from Samson's bedroom, and wrapping the dark-coloured minivan as best they could before loading it onto a vehicle for transfer to the lab. Ava asked to speak with Rachel Jerome who had been sitting with officers in the kitchen. The older woman appeared in a raincoat and wellington boots, her hair wrapped in a headscarf, handkerchief tucked in her hand.

'Ms Jerome, I need to have your car checked over by our forensics unit. I can take it anyway, but I'd rather have your consent.'

'Of course, whatever you need. I had no idea . . .' She broke down, sniffling into the handkerchief. 'Samson didn't borrow it very often. Only when the battery in his minivan was playing up. He said it didn't drive well in the rain.'

'I see. When did Samson last borrow it?'

'Two or three days ago. Is that when . . .' Rachel motioned towards the greenhouse. 'Did he use my car to take that poor girl?'

'I'm afraid that's a possibility,' said Ava. 'Could you show me where you keep the key to the chapel?'

Rachel nodded, and they followed her up the garden path and into the kitchen. The chapel key, neatly labelled, was hanging on a neat row of hooks next to the back door, along with others for the garage and house. Ava transferred it carefully into an evidence bag, handing it to an officer for proper labelling and logging.

'I feel responsible,' Rachel said, clutching her stomach. 'I should have known. He spent so many hours there. I just kept on with my church groups and my reading. If only I'd paid more attention. If there's anything I can do, anything at all . . . I want to help.'

'We'll need to interview you, Ms Jerome, just to make sure we have all the relevant information. Officers will take you to the station. Thank you for your cooperation,' Ava said quietly, calling another officer over to escort Rachel to a police car.

Ava and Callanach trudged back towards the greenhouse silently.

'I should have thrown the brick sooner,' he said.

'And I should have killed him with the garden fork while I had the opportunity,' Ava replied. 'The difference is, you saved Caroline Ryan's life.'

'I'm not convinced she'll make it as far as the hospital,' Callanach said.

'If she lives, at least she'll have the comfort of knowing that the man who abducted her will spend the rest of his life in prison, quite possibly with only one eye and a right arm that he'll never be able to use properly again.'

'What about Rachel? She won't be able to go back to the house until all the forensics have been completed. That could be a couple of weeks,' Callanach said.

'Perhaps the good shepherd Vince Ashton will let her stay at his place,' Ava said. 'She'll need to be seen by a doctor before interview. One of the uniformed officers said she vomited when the air ambulance arrived.'

'How much do you think she knew?' Callanach asked.

'I have no idea, but there's no evidence to suggest that she was involved. She wouldn't be the first person to find they were living with a serial killer without a clue. Makes you think, doesn't it? You look at your partner and see someone inoffensive – boring, even. Perhaps a bit quiet or moody. You don't look at them and wonder if they're spending their days stashing young women in the greenhouse. So many couples get complacent over the years. I wonder, if we really knew what the people we live with are capable of, if we wouldn't all choose to simply lock the door and exist with only the television for company, and delivery food.'

'Have you really lost faith in mankind to that extent?' he asked.

'Some days,' Ava said. 'Perhaps I have.'

'Well then, there's something I need to tell you about Detective Superintendent Overbeck that might change your mind. Turns out she did her best to defend you before you were called to the disciplinary board committee.'

'Who told you that?' Ava asked.

'Lively.'

'That figures, but I'm afraid he's not the most reliable source of information.'

'There's more. It was Overbeck – via Lively – who asked me to instruct Ben Paulson about the mobile data in the slashing case. She even paid him out of her own pocket. No question about it.'

'Are you sure? Only she's an easier woman to hate than to like. If you're even one per cent unsure about this . . .'

'I'm not, I'm afraid. It's not that I disagree with your assessment of Overbeck's qualities. I just thought you should know the truth.'

'Which would mean that I owe her an apology. Damn,' Ava said, pulling the sleeves of her jumper over her hands.

'And that is something I would absolutely love to see,' Callanach smiled, as they walked back through the tunnel of trees.

Chapter Forty-Six

'Ms Jerome, you understand that this interview is being recorded, but you are not under arrest. You may ask to stop at any time and you're not obliged to answer any of my questions, although it will assist us if you do. Given that we found your brother with Caroline, we will need to carry out substantial forensic investigations on not only the greenhouse, but also inside your home. You will need to find somewhere else to stay while that happens,' Ava said, casting a glance in the direction of the uniformed officer next to her who was taking notes.

Rachel Jerome sat opposite them, coat hugged tightly around her, a box of tissues in front of her. The puffy redness of her eyes and her hunched stance were evidence that her brother's arrest had started to sink in. There was always a time delay. Arresting a loved one for a serious crime had its own set of emotional stages, much like grief, Ava had found. Shock, disbelief, anger, horror, then the inevitable soul searching.

'Before you start, may I ask . . . How did Samson do it? Kill them, I mean,' Rachel asked.

'You haven't heard?' Ava replied.

'I don't have a television. I suppose I live a simple life. Old fashioned these days, I know. I find even listening to the news on the radio too distressing most of the time.'

'There were surgical wounds,' Ava said. 'Each girl suffered massive trauma and blood loss.' Rachel pressed the back of her right hand against her mouth, trembling, eyes closed. 'Ms Jerome, I know this is difficult but I need to press on. Can I confirm that you've been seen by a medic and that you feel well enough to speak with us now?'

Rachel nodded, sniffing a couple of times before sitting more upright in her chair and pushing the crumpled tissues she'd been clasping into her pocket. 'I'm fine, thank you. You must have a lot of questions. I'll answer what I can.'

'I appreciate that. Have you travelled with your brother in his vehicle into Edinburgh or the surrounding areas at any time in the last few weeks?'

'Not at all. I really don't like the van. It's terribly creaky. Doesn't feel altogether safe,' she replied.

'Has anyone other than you or your brother been in your house in the last few weeks?' Ava continued.

'No one at all. We live rather a long way from civilisation. Samson and I used to come and go independently of one another. He never gave away a thing. You'd think there'd have been some sort of change, something obvious . . . Did I miss something? If I missed something, perhaps I could have saved those poor girls . . . I'm so sorry. It's just awful. I can't believe it.' Rachel plucked more tissues from the box and blew her nose, leaning forward as her breath hitched.

'We're just trying to establish the facts and a timeline, Ms Jerome. No one's suggesting this is your fault. When did you last visit the greenhouse?'

'Perhaps six months ago, possibly more. Gardening's not my thing. I dislike the mud, and having dirt under my nails. Samson has green fingers though. He grows all our vegetables, and a little fruit if it's a warm summer. Where is he now? Has he told you why he did it? That's what I don't understand. He's never been a violent man. Not once. It defies logic.'

'Your brother made a series of voluntary statements to the officers who transported him to the hospital. Perhaps unsurprisingly, given the fact that we found him with Caroline, he has admitted abducting and killing each of the girls. For the record, he was advised that he shouldn't be confessing anything until he had legal advice. Apparently he insisted,' Ava said.

'Perhaps God was intervening, in an effort to save his soul. It's the first step to salvation,' Rachel said.

Ava resisted the urge to raise her eyebrows. Salvation for a serial killer who had tortured his victims and most likely raped one of them was a concept she found repugnant. Eternal damnation, yes. Working towards forgiveness? That really would have to be granted by an open-minded deity.

'He also said that you had no idea what he was doing. He was very clear about it,' Ava said, watching Rachel's face carefully as she delivered the news.

There was a remarkable blankness to her face, as if she hadn't heard what Ava had just said, or at least as if it hadn't sunk in. Any number of responses might have been forthcoming. Confusion at the suggestion that her involvement could ever have been contemplated. Outrage that anyone might have considered her involvement possible. Even fury that her brother had thought it necessary to make her innocence plain to the police. But there was nothing. Ava stared at her, conscious of the passing seconds and wondering if she needed to repeat the statement.

'Even with all the harm he's done, he still has space for truth in his heart,' Rachel said eventually. 'I'm grateful for that mercy. What will happen to him now?'

'Once he's been signed off by the doctor as fit to be interviewed,

I'll be cautioning and charging him,' Ava explained, shaking off the sense that Rachel's reactions were more staged than genuine. Shock made everyone behave abnormally.

'Can I see him?'

'I'm afraid not. Ms Jerome, there is one matter we don't yet understand. No one from the Children of the Word recognised your brother, and you said yourself he didn't attend services there.'

'That's right,' Rachel replied, frowning slightly, tipping her head to one side as if trying to properly comprehend where Ava was going with the line of questioning.

'But the first victims – Zoey and Lorna – both had links to your church group. Zoey was Christopher Myers' stepdaughter and Lorna was a patient of nurse Lydia McMahon. I am curious as to how your brother might have heard of those young women.'

There was a lengthy pause before Rachel let out a long sigh, her shoulders collapsing forward, head rolling towards her chest. Ava was about to reach forward and stop her before her forehead could hit the desk when suddenly Rachel bolted upright, howling and scratching at her own cheeks.

'God forgive me. It's my fault. It's my fault. They died because of me. Those poor little girls . . .'

Ava reached across the table, taking hold of Rachel's wrists. 'Ms Jerome, please stop, you're going to injure yourself.'

'But they died because I told him about them. If I'd only kept my mouth shut. I broke the rules because I had nothing else to talk about,' she sobbed. 'The church is my life. I bake and I read, but who wants to talk about that at the end of the day? It was all I had, the things I heard about other people's lives. I never thought, not for a second, that he would take it to heart . . . I should have died instead of them.' She began a low moaning, rocking back and forth, tears falling unchecked onto the desk.

Ava continued. 'What did you tell Samson about Zoey Cole, Ms Jerome?'

'Just her allegations against her stepfather. We prayed for the family regularly. The poor girl seemed determined to bring trouble to Christopher's door. Her mother didn't know what to do any more,' she cried.

'And Lorna?' Ava asked.

'Only what Lydia told the prayer group. That she was a lost soul who had brought a baby into the world without knowing who the father was. Personally, I blamed Lorna's parents. Children need guidance, boundaries . . .'

'Was your brother very religious, would you say?' Ava asked.

'Fiercely,' Rachel replied, curling her hands into fists. 'That's why I just can't understand this. We prayed together before every meal, and tried to live simply in God's image. What could have driven him to kill?'

'The notes he sent indicated that he felt the women were steeped in sin, for want of a better phrase. I'm not sure if he was punishing them or if he thought he was saving them,' Ava explained.

'Notes?' Rachel asked.

'A doll was made from each victim's skin. There was a Bible passage included inside each that seemed to be relevant to their background. Did he ever discuss any verses with you that he seemed especially interested in?'

Rachel shook her head, rising from her seat and letting her jacket fall onto her chair.

'Ms Jerome?' Ava said. 'Do you need something?'

Rachel Jerome sank to her knees on the floor. Ava wanted to tell her that of all the surfaces, the floor of a police interview room was not somewhere she would recommend kneeling down, but by then the woman had commenced praying. Crying and praying. Asking for forgiveness. Asking to be shown how to make amends for her brother's sins.

'Can you take it from here?' Ava asked the uniformed officer with her. It was clear that the useful part of the interview was over. It appeared Ms Jerome would only be speaking with God for a while.

Chapter Forty-Seven

Exiting Rachel Jerome's interview room, Ava walked two doors along to find DC Salter with a tearful Oliver Davenport and his lawyer. Through another window she could see Leo Plunkett rocking back in his chair, arms folded, being given heavily gesticulated advice by both his mother and two lawyers. The prosecution was far from a done deal. The first two victims might never be found to attend court, and if they did there was every chance they would be useless giving evidence. If that happened, then making the case stick that the Melanie Long killing was one in a chain might be difficult. So many hurdles to overcome, but MIT had done all it could. The legal system would take over now, and that always seemed a lottery.

'Excuse me please, madam,' a well-spoken English voice sounded from behind her.

Ava turned to see a bespectacled lawyer in a three-piece suit clutching a notebook, ushering in Noah Alby-Croft, who was handcuffed and being followed by the extraordinary bulk of Pax Graham. Behind them was Noah's father.

'All right, Ava.' Noah blew a kiss at her as he passed.

DS Graham put a hand against the boy's back, propelling

him forward into another interview suite, giving Ava a brief smile and nod. Alby-Croft senior paused next to Ava, leaning down to whisper in her ear. 'My son will walk out of here, and when he does, I'm going to see to it that your career is finished once and for all.'

'Oh, please, would you stop? Just forget the bullshit. Your son needs you. He's in a great deal of trouble. That has to be your priority. Has it occurred to you that if your parenting had been better earlier on, Noah wouldn't be here? Forget Oxford, forget whatever stupid club it was he wanted to join and think about what he really needs. Maybe take a few minutes to consider the sort of man you want your son to be. Perhaps that's also the sort of man you yourself should have aspired to be.'

She left the area and took the stairs, dropping her coat in her office before heading up to see Detective Superintendent Overbeck.

Lively was already in there. Of course he was. Ava would have laughed had she not been so exhausted.

'Ma'am,' Ava said. 'I gather the three boys will all be charged with the killing of Melanie Long.'

'Yes, we're confident that we can find blood residue on either shoes or clothing. A search of all their homes is being implemented. Also, we now have enough to get a warrant to check through their communications devices,' Overbeck said.

'Officially, this time.' Ava smiled.

'Yes, that French police officer didn't do a bad job, getting his hacker friend to find a way in. Well done with the girl, too. I spoke to DS Graham about how you handled it – off the record, of course. I would just like to say, that was beyond your remit given you'd been taken off the case.'

'You can stop now,' Ava said. 'I know it was you who got Lively to approach Callanach.'

'Frigging men, can't keep their mouths closed for a second. Did you spill it, Lively?'

'Not me. I told Detective Inspector Fancypants to keep it to himself.'

'How did you know Callanach was in contact with a hacker who would help?' Ava asked.

'I don't know what's more insulting. You thinking I'm stupid, or blind, or that I don't have a handle on absolutely everything that happens in my police station. Ben Paulson seems to be a valuable, if illegal, asset. You seem to have no scruples about abusing that friendship when it suits you so, why should I? It worked,' Overbeck said, raising her eyebrows and sticking her nose in the air.

'Daisy,' Ava said softly. 'I came to apologise.'

Overbeck scraped her chair back with a noise that would have been extreme even in a horror movie. Ava winced. The detective superintendent walked slowly, her heels clacking like a noisy clock's second hand as she moved around her desk to stand in front of Ava, putting one perfectly manicured finger-nail under Ava's chin to stare directly into her eyes.

'If you ever, ever, use my flowery fucking first name again, Detective Chief Inspector, I will not be responsible for using extreme violence against you, and I don't care about your expertise in the martial arts, or your tenacity, or your relative youth. I will destroy you.'

'Ay, she really doesn't like that,' Lively added with a laugh.

'Get your low-hanging scrotum out of my office, Lively. You're not a high enough pay grade to pronoun me,' Overbeck said, turning abruptly and opening a cupboard. She poured two glasses of whisky, the measure greater than Ava would have normally thought appropriate for lunchtime. She took it anyway.

There was only so much violence it was sensible to induce from a woman wearing six-inch stilettos with nails to match.

'As I was saying, I'm sorry. I assumed too much. I thought you were on Alby-Croft's side. I believed the disciplinary hearing was down to you because . . .' She trailed off.

'Because I'm screwing Lively, and you can't get it out of your head that I'm not going to punish you for what you saw?'

'I wasn't going to put it quite like that,' Ava said.

'Yes, well, however you were going to put it, just because I'm a bitch does not, contrary to popular opinion, mean I don't care about MIT's cases. Or my officers. You're not a bad DCI, Turner. A bit green, maybe. You need to knock off that dull crusader thing you've got going. Frankly, it's unhelpful. You want to be devious? Take my advice, it's best done with a smile rather than a statement of ball-breaking intent. You're like an overenthusiastic schoolgirl sometimes.'

'So, the fact that you had the hacked texts put under Pax Graham's door rather than pursue them yourself wasn't about making sure no resulting shit hit your personal fan, then?' Ava asked, sipping the whisky.

'Of course it fucking was. Lively delivered the texts to that somewhat impressive Hulk lookalike knowing he'd take them to you. I knew you wouldn't be able to resist following them up. My team stayed out of the questionable activity and you regained the moral high ground. Win, win, I'd say, or are you going to start moaning again?'

'No.' Ava shook her head. 'No more moaning. I underestimated you, ma'am. Both how manipulative you are and how good a police officer you are.'

'Same fucking thing, Turner. Same fucking thing. Now, update on this deviant wanker who's been carving up young women,' Overbeck said, slamming her empty glass onto the desk.

'He's in custody but hospitalised. DI Callanach and I found

it necessary to use substantial force to prevent an attempt on Caroline Ryan's life. He'll live to stand trial, though.'

'And Miss Ryan? What shape's she in?'

'We had confirmation half an hour ago that she's in a coma. Samson Jerome struck her a serious blow to her upper skull with a spade. It was aimed at her neck. Callanach saved her life, for what it's worth. He's a dab hand at brick lobbing. We won't know more until the hospital have had time to perform full scans. Her fiancé is with her. Other than severe dehydration and some damage to her wrists and ankles, she's otherwise unharmed,' Ava reported.

'Unharmed? She'll be traumatised for life if she ever comes round. Get the paperwork in order. I want that bastard to go down until all trace of him has been eaten by worms in his coffin. No screw-ups.'

'Got it,' Ava said. 'Before I go . . . About Lively. Are you two—'

'Really? None of your goddamned business. But the man needs to go on a diet if he's not going to keel over next time he exerts himself. From now on, I want all cakes and biscuits banned from the incident room.'

'Uh, I'm not sure I can implement that, given the . . .'

'God, you're tedious. It was a joke, Turner. You really do need to get a life.'

'Okay, I'll do that,' Ava said, feeling hijacked. 'Thank you, ma'am.'

'No problem. I'll be taking full credit for the Spice slashing cases, just so you know. Next time, don't piss off a Police Scotland board member.'

Ava smiled as she walked out. It was easier to leave when Overbeck was behaving like her normal self.

Callanach was waiting for her at the hospital. They spent a few minutes talking to Jadyn Odoki, who was sitting patiently with

Caroline, hoping desperately that his beloved future wife could somehow hear him. A section of her skull had been removed in surgery to relieve the pressure on her brain, and she looked ghostlike among the white sheets, bandaged and tubed. The doctors would only shake their heads when asked for a prognosis. It was too early to tell. Her life hung in the balance. Even if she did regain consciousness, which was by no means certain, she might never function as she had before. If only they'd handled the situation differently, Ava thought, stroking Caroline's hand before they left.

'I hate the words "if only",' she said to Callanach as they walked the corridors to where Samson Jerome was under constant guard, handcuffed to the railings of his bed.

'I'm pretty sure Caroline Ryan was thinking "If only some police officers would burst through the door right now" just before we did,' he replied.

'Not you as well. I think I've had enough words of wisdom this afternoon,' Ava said. 'Apparently Mr Jerome has been stitched and had his eye seen to, and the doctors say he's fit to be cautioned and charged. You ready?'

A siren sounded in the hall. Footsteps thundered around the squeal of a cart being sped along the corridor. Ava and Callanach backed themselves against the wall as a medical team rushed through, barging the double doors to Samson's room open, shouting instructions and information to one another as they stripped off Samson's gown and applied resuscitation pads to his chest.

'No,' Ava cried, watching the scene through the wire noughts and crosses of the glass on the door.

Flatline.

An increased charge.

'Excuse me, I need you to move. You can't be here now,' a nurse said.

'I'm in charge of that prisoner,' Ava said. 'What happened?'

'He's not a prisoner here, he's a patient, now if you could just . . .'

'He butchered three women and a fourth is in your hospital in a coma. So what the fuck just happened?' Ava demanded.

The nurse reddened and sighed. 'He pulled the needle from his arm.'

'He was handcuffed. How is that possible?' Callanach asked.

'It seems he used his mouth, then deliberately swallowed both the metal and surrounding plastic. He'll have been bleeding internally. It looks as if his heart just decided there wasn't enough pressure left to continue pumping,' she said.

'Nope. Can't get him back,' a doctor said from Samson's bedside.

'One last try,' someone replied. 'Stand back.' They applied the paddles again, charging, sending an electric shock through his chest. Nothing. There was silence. 'It's no good. I'm calling it.'

'No,' Ava yelled, turning her face into the wall and punching hard. 'It's too easy. How fucking dare he kill himself. It's not fucking fair!'

Time of death was 6.15 p.m.

Chapter Forty-Eight

Five weeks later, in mid December, with Edinburgh decked out in a foot of snow and crowded with shoppers, Ava got the call that Caroline Ryan had woken up. She was pulled out of a meeting with the procurator fiscal, who was still trying to explain to her why Oliver Davenport, Leo Plunkett and Noah Alby-Croft could be prosecuted for a single charge of assault to severe injury but not for Melanie Long's murder. Technicality upon technicality, all wrapped in sparkly jargon, and tied up with a bow of reasons why not. Against that backdrop, hearing that a young woman who until recently had a bright future ahead of her might still live to fulfil her potential was the best gift imaginable.

'She's awake,' Ava grinned, poking her head around Callanach's door. 'Let's go. I'm driving.' They made it to the hospital in record time, in spite of the weather, with Ava unable to contain her excitement. 'You know what? This whole autumn has been a disaster from start to finish. We haven't caught a break on either case. No one is going to really pay for what they did. At least, if nothing else, Caroline is going to be conscious for Christmas Day and she can start the New Year planning her wedding and healing. What are you doing for the festive season? Do you and Selina have anything fun planned?'

'She's going back to Spain to see her family. She's invited me, but . . .'

'But what? It's got to be warmer than here and you're due time off in lieu of all the overtime. You'd be crazy not to go. I, on the other hand, am going to let Natasha feed me until I'm sick. I'm going to buy myself a ton of gorgeous presents and I've decided to get a cleaner. New Year's treat.'

They walked from the car park into the hospital and made for the lifts.

'Finally. You think the cleaner will even be able to find the floor in your house?' Callanach smiled.

'Don't be so rude. Natasha invited you, too. I'll tell her you'll be drinking sangria and watching the sun go down on some romantic beach. She'll like that. Here we go. Jadyn's expecting us. I said we'd go very gently today, just a couple of questions, see how much she remembers. And I think I'll tell her that Samson's dead. If nothing else, it'll reassure her that she really is safe now.'

Caroline stared at them blankly as they walked in. Her hair, shaved from the surgery, had begun to grow back in spiky patches. Thin when they'd found her, she seemed emaciated now.

'Caroline,' Ava said, sitting down next to her and touching her hand briefly. 'Do you remember us?'

She nodded, looking from Callanach to Ava then back again.

'You stopped him from killing me,' she whispered slowly, her voice grating in her throat.

'They say her voice will recover. It's just lack of use,' Jadyn explained.

'You were very brave,' Callanach said walking closer. 'It takes a lot of strength to survive what you went through.'

'Thank God you came,' Caroline said, attempting a smile before closing her eyes for a few seconds. 'Sorry, I get tired and things are fuzzy.'

'Of course, but it'll get better,' Ava said. 'We'll wait until you're feeling stronger before we ask too many questions. There's no rush. The main thing is that no one can hurt you now. The man who abducted you is dead.'

Caroline stared. 'You're sure?'

'He committed suicide. We were there. We saw his body. You have nothing to worry about any more. We just wanted you to know that you're safe.'

'And her,' Caroline said, eyes closed, head sinking deep into the pillow. 'She's in prison?'

'Her?' Callanach asked.

'The woman. Her name was . . . it's unclear . . . began with R.'

'Rachel?' Ava said, glancing at Callanach. 'You met his sister?'

Caroline opened her eyes again, her lips trembling. 'Met her? She did it. All of it. Wanted to pray. She told me . . . told me . . .'

'Don't upset yourself,' Jadyn said. 'You need to stop. She's getting distressed. We can't risk her blood pressure going up. Please, you should leave now.'

'No,' Caroline said. 'Wait.' She breathed deeply, gathering strength. 'She told me to repent. It was her who cut those other girls. All her. He was just . . . carrying out orders. Where is she now?'

'You don't need to worry about that, Caroline,' Callanach said. 'We're keeping policemen outside your door. You can rest without worrying.'

Ava stood up, fighting to keep her face neutral against the

rage and pressure building inside her. 'Caroline, you've done really well. We'll come back in a day or so. Take care.'

Jadyn frowned at them, looking to the door, where no policemen stood.

'They'll be here in ten minutes,' Callanach whispered to him. 'Stay with her until then.'

They managed to walk normally until they were beyond Caroline's door. Then they ran.

Callanach called in instructions to get units over to Vince Ashton's address and hold Rachel Jerome until they could get there. They'd only been in the car five minutes before word came that Rachel could not be found.

'Mr Ashton said Rachel Jerome left his house a week ago. He hasn't heard from her since. Apparently she said the police had agreed that she could go back to her house,' a uniformed officer reported by phone.

'Search Mr Ashton's property and the chapel,' Ava said. 'Check nearby roads for her car, too. We'll go to her home and see if she's there.'

'Is the forensics team still working at the Jerome property?' Callanach asked.

'Not actively, but we've kept it closed off in case the lab results come back and suggest that more work needs to be done. Given that we thought we'd stopped having to build a case when Samson killed himself, the forensics became less of a priority,' Ava replied. 'But we missed something. We must have done.'

'The woman in the shopping mall,' Callanach said. 'It didn't make any sense at the time, so we disregarded it as irrelevant, but the estimated age matches Rachel Jerome's.'

'Not the description, though.' Even as she said it, she realised how easily they'd been fooled. Rachel Jerome's well-trimmed pixie cut and brown hair had seemed a million miles away from the woman with the greying bun who had stood in the dress shop and spied on Samson as he'd met up with Kate Bailey. 'She even gave Samson the order to kill himself. Do you remember what she shouted when she walked into the greenhouse? "Do the right thing, put your faith in the Lord." With Samson dead and no trial, the investigation would grind to a halt, making it far less likely she would be implicated. She was in charge the whole time, and she outsmarted us.'

'That's what he meant when he said there were orders, instructions. I assumed he'd been told what to do by some imaginary voice in his head. He really was just an instrument – only he was Rachel's,' Callanach said. 'That's why he was so keen to exonerate her on his way to the hospital. He confessed to everything to allow her to go free.'

They drove back to the Jeromes', both of them knowing the boat they wanted to catch had already left the harbour. Pulling up at the deserted property, it seemed pointless even going inside.

'I have to know for sure,' Ava said. 'Why don't you double-check the greenhouse? Just make sure she hasn't parked her car out of sight there. I'll take a look inside.'

Callanach walked away as Ava took a brick to the front door glass and hooked her hand around to unlock it, vaguely thinking, as she had so many times before, that no one should have glass near their door locks. Stepping into the house, she saw it differently now.

The obsessive neatness was not quaint country cottage style, but the rigour of fanaticism. The sweet bewilderment of Rachel as she'd talked about her brother, as if there was nothing in the world to hide, had been an act of cunning so sophisticated that everyone involved had fallen for it. Rachel was the churchgoer, so she had sent her brother out to do the dirty work. She had it all figured out from the start. If the police put two and two together, she would never be identified as the culprit. Her brother's greenhouse, her brother's car. A willing and unquestioning accomplice who would do whatever he was told. Not a scrap of evidence inside the house and an uncanny ability to appear devastated while she was being interviewed. Ava felt sick.

She took the stairs, walking quietly into the nearest bedroom, which had belonged to Samson Jerome. Every item, as well as his bedding, had been removed. Turning her attention instead to Rachel's room, she began to pull drawers open. These, too, were orderly to the point of obsession. Socks were in pairs. Pens had lids on. Blouses had been ironed before being hung in the wardrobe. The bedding was plain rather than flowery or patterned. It was comfortable enough, but bland. Exactly what Ava had seen before, but this time it told a story of a woman who either craved or prided herself on self-discipline through denial.

On the top shelf of the wardrobe, at the back in a box, was the photo album Ava had been searching for. Every home had one – at least every home belonging to the pre-internet generations. This was the original social media; showing the family photos to relatives once a year when they came over at Christmas or after a summer holiday.

Rachel Jerome had looked remarkably similar at twenty as she had at thirty, forty and fifty. A bun was pinned at the back of her head, the dark hair streaked through with grey. The image of the woman in the dress shop.

Callanach joined her on the floor of the bedroom, flicking through the cardboard pages, covered with sheets of sticky plastic.

'Rachel Jerome wasn't just clever, she was brilliant,' Ava said.

'She knew in the dress shop that the staff would look straight through a middle-aged woman. They wouldn't be bothered to strike up conversation or try to sell her their skimpy dresses. She chose a place where she might be seen, but not remembered. I think she was there to make sure her brother didn't screw up and scare Kate Bailey off straight away. I wonder how recently she had her hair coloured and restyled. She must have had a sense that we were getting closer.'

'Kate Bailey.' Callanach sighed. 'She told me. As she was dying, I told her I wanted to find the man who'd hurt her. I asked her to tell me anything that might help. I heard her reply as womb. I assumed, too easily, that it was to do with where he'd cut her, but now I wonder if she wasn't just saying half a word.'

'Woman,' Ava said. 'She was trying to tell you it wasn't the man who had mutilated her. You couldn't have known. This is hindsight policing. We should both know better.'

'I still don't get why. That's the missing piece of the puzzle. What made them kill together? Homicide conspiracies are so rare.'

'There are no wedding photos here,' Ava said. 'Not around the house or in the album.'

'She's supposed to be a widower, right? And the daughter . . .'

'Come on,' Ava said. 'Let's check out her bedroom. What did Rachel say? Something about how Verity had gone off to live in Australia with her boyfriend years ago.'

They opened Verity's bedroom door and peered in. This bed was more ornate, with white-painted ironwork and pale violet linen on the bed. The matching bedroom furniture, slightly childish, was covered in only the thinnest veil of dust. This room had been kept clean, cherished. It had not been allowed to grow up with its previous inhabitant.

'It's like a shrine,' Callanach said.

Ava stood in the middle of the room, looking around at the pink curtains and the tidy desk, just the right size for homework or drawing. There were still books on the bookcase and teddies on a shelf above the bed. It wasn't unknown for girls to keep their childhood toys, Ava thought, but perhaps only the most well-loved one or two. And then, there at the back . . .

She stood on tiptoes to look past the fluffy sheep and floppy bear, then stepped up onto the bed and reached over to the back of the shelf.

In her hand as she stepped back down was a rag doll. Homemade, with drawn-on lips, red wool hair and a pretty dress. Ava lifted the fabric to get a closer look at the body. It had been cut from two pieces of fabric, front and back, with neat little stitches all around the edge. The doll had been crafted with love.

'It's the same size as the skin dolls,' Callanach said. 'Even the head's the same shape.'

'Made from the same pattern,' Ava said. 'She was remaking her daughter's toy over and over again.'

'Or perhaps replacing her daughter,' Callanach said. 'Which means, I think, that she's not in Australia. The girls all had to repent. They were sinful.'

'It started with Zoey disrespecting her parents, accusing her stepfather of violence. After that, they couldn't stop taking the girls. Perhaps none of them repented properly.'

'Or perhaps there were a number of different sins they needed the victims to pay for . . .' Ava said. 'Call the station. I want an all-ports alert across the UK. She might have driven to an airport or ferry port by now, but we have to try. Circulate both photos – the one with the bun and with the new haircut. And get the cadaver dogs out here, with diggers.

Verity didn't go to Australia. That's why this room has been left untouched. The poor girl needs to be found. I may have messed up every other aspect of this case, but I can do this right.'

Chapter Forty-Nine

Verity

'I'm leaving and you're not going to stop me,' Verity said.

'I'm your mother, and I most certainly can stop you. What'll you do for money? Where will you live?' Rachel demanded, blocking the hallway to the front door.

'I don't care where I end up. I won't live in this house with him any more. I told you what he was doing to me, and what did you do? You prayed with him,' Verity said, crying again.

'Your uncle needs God's help. I saw to it that he punished himself. But we are family, Verity. You can't run away from it, from us. God won't let you,' Rachel insisted.

'It's not God!' she yelled. 'It's you. I don't want to live here any more. I don't have to. I'm over sixteen. I can go wherever I want with whoever I want. I'll get a job.'

'What do you mean, with whoever you want?'

Silence.

'What . . . did . . . you . . . mean?' Rachel hissed, taking hold of Verity's shoulder and forcing her thumbnail into the top curve of flesh.

Verity howled. 'You're hurting me!'

'Is there a boyfriend? Is that what this is about? Have you been dirtying yourself, you little whore?'

'I didn't dirty myself! Your brother did that, always pawing me when you're not here, staring at me, coming into my room when I'm undressing. Why shouldn't I have a boyfriend? You don't care what Samson does to me, so why can't I do what I want?'

The slap was hard, although not entirely unexpected. If Verity had time to rationalise it, she might have realised she wanted her mother to hit her. It would make the final act of leaving all the easier. Her face stung and her mother was panting hard, looking pained, as if she had sustained the blow rather than dealing it.

'Who is he? If you're so proud of him, why not do the decent thing and bring him here to meet me?'

Verity took three small, silent steps towards her mother. 'You really want to know? I didn't introduce him to you because you'd have hated him. You'd have taken one look at him and passed judgment. That's what you do.'

'So what's the problem then? Tattoos? A skinhead haircut? You might as well tell me now,' Rachel snarled.

'He's black, Mum. Just let it sink in for a moment. After all those years of listening to you and Uncle Samson spouting your racist comments, I'm going out with someone you hate, for no reason other than your own pathetic small-mindedness and prejudice. We're going away. We're going somewhere you'll never find us, and I'm never coming back.'

'I don't think you are. I don't think you're going anywhere at all. You'll go upstairs to your room, right now, and you'll stay there. You can eat in your room and when I think you've learned your lesson we'll pray together for God's forgiveness,' Rachel said, pointing her daughter towards the stairs.

'No. That's the last order you'll ever give me. You don't love

411

me. If you did, you'd have protected me better and put my needs before Bible study and prayers and your pride. I've hated you for so long now, I'd almost forgotten how it felt to love. Then I met Ade. He's a good, decent man and he'll look after me. I'm going, and you're not going to stop me,' Verity said, taking a step to her mother's side and reaching for the door handle.

'I don't think so, madam,' Rachel said, gripping her forearm hard and pulling her away from the door.

'Fine. I'll go out the back. You can't keep me here. I'm done with you.' Verity turned round, picking up her backpack and walking down the hallway towards the kitchen and the exit to freedom.

'Don't you dare,' Rachel hissed from behind her. 'You ungrateful little bitch. I'll see you in hell before I let you leave this house.'

'Whatever you say, Mum,' Verity replied, smiling as she glanced around to take a last look at her mother's face.

The bottle caught her on her right ear. Elderflower cordial, Verity had time to notice. The crazy old cow is actually going to hit me with the elderflower cordial, she thought. That blow sent her to the floor. She raised her hands enough to lessen the effect of the next blow, but by then her mother was standing over her, blowing hot air from her nose like a bull, shrieking a high, thin noise, the whites of her eyes bloody with the tension in her body.

'God will forgive me,' she paused to say, before smashing the end of the bottle on a countertop. 'He's the only one who matters.'

She brought the piercing shards down into her daughter's neck and watched the flowing of the blessed red river that would wash away Verity's sins. And as she watched, she prayed.

Chapter Fifty

They found Verity's body a week before Christmas Eve, buried beneath the greenhouse where Samson Jerome had held his sister's victims. Jonty Spurr attended, and treated the girl's body with sweet tenderness. No missing person report had ever been filed. A future had simply been wiped out in a flurry of blows to her skull and neck. Ava stood at the unofficial graveside and issued silent apologies for not having brought Rachel Jerome to justice. One day I will, Ava promised Verity. Whatever it takes, I'll find her and make her pay for what she did to you, and to Zoey, Lorna and Kate.

There was no news from the ports, no sightings, no leads. Rachel's bank account had been emptied soon after she'd been interviewed, and her passport hadn't been found at the house. It was easy enough for a middle-aged woman to travel the UK in relative anonymity. Harder to cross an international border unnoticed. The only lead they had was a list of other quasi-religious groups who supported the extremist views Rachel held, found on an old calendar. Ava was following them up, one by one, but the level of secrecy under which they operated within foreign jurisdictions made progress painstakingly slow.

She could do slow, Ava told herself. Rachel had gone to ground but she couldn't hide forever. Interpol had been alerted. Sooner or later, she would reveal herself again. The monster always showed its face eventually.

Jonty Spurr phoned on 23 December.

'DCI Turner,' he said. 'I thought you should know. Verity's DNA profile showed that Samson was her father and Rachel her mother. The sickness in that family goes back a long way. Decomposition was quite extensive, but I'd estimate she was buried four or five years ago. She'll be laid to rest properly now, somewhere quiet. There was no extended family traced so it'll be a state funeral.'

'Keep it light on the religion, would you, Jonty? I have a feeling the last thing Verity Jerome would want to hear is more scripture.'

'I hear you, and I'll leave instructions. I'm back off to Aberdeen tomorrow. Dr Ailsa Lambert will be back from leave, so I'm not needed any more. I can't say it's been a pleasure to work with you, not on this case, but I hope we meet again under happier circumstances.'

'Thank you, Dr Spurr,' Ava said. 'Have a good Christmas. I know Luc will miss you.'

Callanach walked in as they said their goodbyes.

'You all right?' he asked.

'The perfect end to a perfect case,' she said, pinching the bridge of her nose. 'What's up?'

'Christie Salter asked to see us both together,' he said. 'I'm not sure what it's about.'

'I think I do,' Ava said, as DC Salter knocked the door and entered.

'Ma'am, Sir,' Salter began. 'I'm sorry to do this. I know I said I was ready to come back to work, and it's been good

414

being with the squad – in lots of ways it was what I needed – but I know now that I was just running away from losing the baby and from how my life has changed. I've come to hand in my notice.'

'Good for you,' Ava said gently. Salter looked surprised. 'But not your notice. It's too soon for that. Take more time. Your place here stays open as long as you need. I have something else for you to think about. I was waiting for the right time to give this to you, and you chose the moment yourself.'

Ava reached into her desk and pulled out a large brown envelope with DC Salter's name in bold print on the front.

'I hope you'll forgive me for what I did,' Ava said. 'I think you'd be about the best mother Tansy Shaw could want. It's not a done deal, but you're a match in terms of culture, race and geography. You know her background. You tick all the boxes. It's up to you to apply, but they are looking for a forever family for her. I made some preliminary enquiries and they're waiting for your application, should you feel this is right for you.'

'Ma'am,' Salter said. 'That's . . .' She ran a hand down the set of documents in her hand, smiling through the tears. 'They'll consider me?'

'They will. In fact, you're everything they're looking for. No pressure. It's a big commitment, but you were ready to become a parent a while ago.'

'I can do it for Lorna,' Salter said. 'Make sure her daughter grows up with a mother and father who'll love her and protect her.'

'And there's still a job here for you. Women get to do both, these days. Don't forget us, Christie. You're a brilliant police officer.'

'Thank you,' Salter whispered, standing up. 'You're the most amazing boss. Everyone thinks so. Even Lively, and I never thought he'd put up with having a woman above him.'

'You have no idea,' Ava said. 'Go home, Christie. Spend more time with your husband. And have a wonderful Christmas.'

Callanach watched Salter go before he spoke.

'That was an extraordinary thing to have done, in the middle of the horrors of the last few weeks,' he said.

'It made sense, both for the baby and for Salter,' Ava said. 'Pure pragmatism, before you start polishing me up a halo.'

'I'm actually rather relieved. I have a confession to make. I might have overheard you asking about adoption at the mother and baby unit, and it's possible I'd assumed you were referring to . . .'

'Myself?' She laughed. 'I don't think I have the expletives to express how ridiculous that is.'

'Really? I think you'd make a great mother. Police Scotland hasn't exactly been kind to you recently. No one would blame you for wanting a break.'

'A break is the last thing I want. I have a month of paper-work to catch up on, and then I'm going to make bloody sure Rachel Jerome is found.'

'She could be anywhere by now, Ava. Every police force in the world has been alerted. No one's going to want to deal with the diplomatic nightmare of letting a wanted serial killer across their border, but Rachel's good at hiding. It could be years before we get a lead. You did all you could and you know the deal. File it for now and solve the next case. The ones that got away will drive you crazy. You need some time off after the stress of running two investigations concurrently.'

'Frankly, never having another day of leave would be a small price to pay if I could put her in handcuffs,' Ava said. 'But I know you're right. I'm not giving up hope though. Rachel has a taste for killing, but what will trip her up eventually is the fact that she believes she's entitled to kill. She's obsessed. You can't put out that sort of fire.'

'Will you settle for just one day of leave?' Callanach asked. 'Natasha has invited me for lunch on Christmas Day after all. I've agreed.'

'What happened to Spain with Selina?' Ava asked.

'Sunshine and relaxation? Are you kidding? That sounds awful. You'll be at Natasha's too, right? Then I thought we could watch an old black and white movie at mine in the evening. Or, at least, you can watch it while I pretend to be interested and hold your popcorn. My Christmas present to you.'

'Sounds about as good a Christmas as I could imagine,' Ava said.

'It's a date?' Callanach grinned.

'Not exactly, but I'll be there,' she replied.

It should have been quiet and sombre with just the three of them after so much of terror and grief, so they made it the opposite. They laughed and joked, and were rude to one another as only good friends can be. Natasha cooked a Victorian-style feast, with goose and beef and a ton of vegetables, and more mince pies than an army could have consumed. They hugged and kissed her goodbye at eight in the evening. She was off to see other friends, and Callanach and Ava made for Luc's apartment, where *It's a Wonderful Life* and *The Shop Around the Corner* awaited on DVD, with mulled wine, popcorn and an unopened bottle of Glenlivet.

Ava kicked off her shoes and settled herself on the couch as Callanach heated the popcorn. He returned to the lounge to find a small, silver parcel with red ribbon where he'd been planning to sit. Handing Ava a glass of steaming mulled wine, he stared at it.

'What's that?' he asked.

'Um, is that a trick question?' Ava smiled.

'We all agreed – you, me and Natasha – no presents.' He picked it up and planted himself on the sofa, shaking the box.

'Just open it, you idiot,' Ava said. He unwrapped it, ripping open the box, to find a bottle opener with a ceramic tartan handle. 'Wind it,' she grinned.

He turned the corkscrew as strains of 'Ding Dong Merrily On High' played on the bagpipes issued from a minute concealed speaker.

Ava began laughing, clutching her sides, struggling not to spill her drink. 'It's the single most Scottish yet Christmassy thing I could find. You love it, don't you? Come on, admit it.'

'How soon until the batteries run out?' He raised his eyebrows.

'That's what's great. It works on movement, so when you wind the corkscrew you generate the energy!'

'So . . . never.' He whistled. 'Wow, that's clever.'

'I know, you can't thank me enough. I've been waiting all day to see the panic on your face. It was absolutely worth it. There's something to be said for delayed gratification. Now come on, where's my movie? You promised me black and white and some proper old-fashioned acting.'

'This first,' he said, pulling another package from beneath the sofa. This one was longer and thinner, wrapped in gold paper with a floppy white bow. He threw it to her end of the couch.

'You cheated too!'

'Did you think it was only you the rules didn't apply to? Come on, open it up.'

Ava ripped the paper, peeping inside at soft brown leather and sheepskin. 'Gloves,' she breathed, smelling them and rubbing them against her face. 'They're so soft. I love them! But what's this for?' She held up a white wire that attached to each glove.

'You put the pin into each glove at the wrist, then put the wire into your car charger. They'll be hot by the time you arrive at an outdoor crime scene. No more cold hands. You've been moaning at me for the last year that you can never find your gloves. Problem solved.'

'Problem solved,' she said quietly, throwing herself forward and kissing him on the cheek. 'Thank you. That was so thoughtful. Now I feel kind of bad about the musical corkscrew.'

'Don't,' he said. 'I'm going to bring it every time I come to your place.'

'Selina will hate it. She's so sophisticated. I have no idea how some women turn out like that and other women turn out like . . . like me.' She laughed. 'You must be missing her.'

'Actually, this has turned out to be one of the best Christmases I can remember. And what was I supposed to do? I couldn't wait around forever for you to ask me out.' He winked at her and picked up the remote.

'Me, ask you out? Oh, hold on, that would be because of your startling good looks, natural charm and washboard stomach,' she said, grabbing the bowl of popcorn from the floor and balancing it on her lap.

'Are you saying you don't find those things attractive or is there something wrong with me that counteracts all of the above?' He pressed a button and film titles flared on the screen.

'As much as I'd like to list all the things that are wrong with you, I'd prefer to watch the film before it gets to New Year's Eve. Also, I don't want to dent your ego too much because I'm going to need a popcorn refill soon and it would be rude to insult my host.'

'That's fine, you just keep making excuses,' he said. 'I know how you really feel about me.'

'Open the Glenlivet and I'll love you forever,' she laughed. They started the film, legs up on the coffee table, blanket across the top of them, sipping whisky and talking through the action.

When the knock roused them, they were both asleep, with Ava's head on Callanach's shoulder as he leaned on a cushion. The film, long since finished, was frozen on the credits.

'Luc.' Ava shook him. 'You'd better get it. There's someone at your door.'

He ran a hand through his hair, pulling his arm gently from behind Ava's neck as he got himself fully awake.

He opened the door to reveal a uniformed officer looking nervous. 'Come in,' he said. 'What's going on?'

'Sorry, sir, only you weren't answering your phone and we couldn't find DCI Turner. Oh . . .' he said, as his eyes turned to Ava on the couch.

'What's happening, Constable?'

'Sorry to disturb your Christmas night, ma'am, only there's an incident happening over at Braidburn Valley Park. Superintendent Overbeck said she was sure you wouldn't mind taking command.'

'Ah, this is the Superintendent's decision, is it? All right, Constable, I'll be down in a minute.' He disappeared, looking grateful not to have been on the receiving end of any verbal abuse. Ava stretched, then reached for her coat.

'I'm coming with you,' Luc said.

'No need,' Ava told him. 'It's probably nothing serious. Just Overbeck getting her own back.'

'Getting her own back for what?' Luc asked, pulling on his own coat in spite of Ava's protests.

'Just a misunderstanding,' Ava smiled, taking her gloves from their wrapping. 'Looks like I'll be needing these sooner than I'd thought. Happy Christmas, Luc.'

Loved *Perfect Silence*? Then why not get back to where it all started with book one of the DI Callanach series?

On a remote Highland mountain, the body of Elaine Buxton is burning. All that will be left to identify the respected lawyer are her teeth and a fragment of clothing. Meanwhile, in the concealed back room of a house in Edinburgh, the real Elaine Buxton screams into the darkness . . .

Welcome to Edinburgh.
Murder capital of Europe.

There will
be blood...

Perfect
Prey

A DI CALLANACH THRILLER

HELEN FIELDS

A dark and twisted serial killer thriller that fans of M. J. Arlidge and Karin Slaughter won't be able to put down.

Available in all good bookshops now.

**The worst dangers are the
ones we can't see . . .**

DI Callanach is back in this stunning third novel from
the bestselling Helen Fields.

Available in all good bookshops now.